Mazurka
for
Two
Dead
Men

Camilo José Cela

Mazurka
for
Two
Dead
Men

Translated by Patricia Haugaard

A New Directions Book

This present edition has been translated with the help of the General Administration of Books and Libraries of the Cultural Ministry of Spain.

Manufactured in the United States of America.
New Directions Books are printed on acid-free paper.
First published clothbound by New Directions in 1992.
Published simultaneously in Canada by Penguin Books Canada Limited.

Library of Congress Cataloging-in-Publication Data
Cela, Camilo José, 1916–
     [Mazurca para dos muertos. English]
     Mazurka for two dead men / Camilo José Cela ; translated by
Patricia Haugaard.
         p.   cm.
     Translation of : Mazurca para dos muertos.
     ISBN 0–8112–1222–x (acid-free paper)
     I. Title.
PQ6605.E44M3313 1992
863' .64—dc20   92–12618
                                                                    CIP

New Directions Books are published for James Laughlin
by New Directions Publishing Corporation
80 Eighth Avenue, New York 10011

. . . our thoughts they were palsied and sere,
Our memories were treacherous and sere.

—Edgar Allan Poe, *Ulalume*

It Rains Gently and Unceasingly, It rains listlessly but with infinite patience, as it has always rained upon this earth which is the same color as the sky—somewhere between soft green and soft ashen grey, and the line of the mountain has been blotted out for a long time now.

"For hours?"

"No. For years. The line of the mountain was blotted out when Lázaro Codesal died, apparently the Good Lord didn't want it to be seen ever again."

Lázaro Codesal died at the Tizzi-Azza post in Morocco: killed by a Moor from the Tafersit tribe, chances are. Lázaro Codesal knew his stuff when it came to getting girls pregnant, he had a taste for it too, and had reddish hair and blue eyes. Lázaro Codesal died young, he can't have been as much as twenty-two, but what good did it do him to be able to play the field better than anyone for fifteen miles around or more? Lázaro Codesal was treacherously killed by a Moor, killed while jacking off beneath a fig tree, everybody knows that the shade of a fig tree is a fine place to sin in peace and quiet. If Lázaro Codesal hadn't had his back turned, nobody—neither a

Moor nor an Asturian, neither a Portuguese nor a Leonese—
nobody could have killed Lázaro Codesal face on. The line of
the mountain disappeared when Lázaro Codesal was killed and
it has never been seen since.

It has been raining both steadily and monotonously since
the Feast of St. Ramón Nonato, maybe even before, and today
is the Feast of St. Macario, who brings luck to playing cards
and raffle tickets. It has been slowly drizzling without letup for
nine months now upon the grass in the fields and on my
windowpane. It drizzles but it isn't cold, I mean not really
cold. If I could play the fiddle, I would spend the evenings
playing it, but I can't; if I could play the harmonica, I would
spend the evenings playing it, but I can't. What I can play are
the bagpipes but it's not the done thing to play the pipes indoors. Since I can play neither the fiddle nor the harmonica
and since the pipes shouldn't be played indoors, I spend the
evenings in bed, messing about with Benicia (later on I'll tell
you all about Benicia, the woman with nipples like chestnuts).
In the city you can go to the cinema to see Lily Pons, the
distinguished young soprano, playing the lead female role in *I
Dream Too Much*, so the papers say, but there's no cinema
around here.

The clear waters of the spring, which wash the bones as well
as the strangely cold livers of the dead, spurt forth in the cemetery; they call it the Miangueiro spring and that's where the
lepers wash their bodies in search of relief. The blackbird sings
in the very same cypress where the nightingale intones its
solitary lament by night. But there are hardly any lepers left
nowadays: it's not like the old times when the place was swarming with them, hooting like barn owls to give warning that the
monks from the mission were out after them to give them
absolution.

Every year the frogs wake up after the Feast of St. Joseph and their croaking announces that spring, with all its bad news and hard work, is on the way. Frogs are magical, half superstitious creatures: if you simmer five or six frogs' heads with tuberose blossom you get a potion that lifts the heart and soothes the virgin's sorrow. Frogs are difficult to train because when they are nearly trained you lose patience and flatten them with a wallop. Policarpo la Bagañeira is the best hand at training frogs in the whole country: frogs, blackbirds, weasels, foxes, everything. Policarpo trains everything—even lynxes (that was in the days when there were lynxes, of course): but what he never had much success with was the wild boar, which is a witless beast that neither listens nor reasons. Policarpo la Bagañeira, missing three fingers from one hand, lives in the village of Cela do Camparrón and sometimes goes down to the main road to watch the Santiago omnibus pass by, there are always two or three priests on it nibbling dried figs. Policarpo lost his index, middle, and ring fingers when he was bitten by a horse, but with his little finger and thumb he gets by fairly well.

"I can play neither the bagpipes nor the accordion, but what difference does that make?"

In Sprat's brothel in Orense there is a blind accordion player—he must be dead by now. Ah, yes, now I remember: he died in the spring of 1945, just a week after Hitler. He used to play dances and marches to keep the clients entertained—I'm talking about in the old days; his name was Gaudencio Beira and he had been a seminary student, they threw him out of the seminary when he lost his sight, just before he went totally blind.

"Was he a good hand at the pipes?"

"He surely was, a great hand at them, too! Truth to tell, he was a real artist, all clarity and style. He played with great depth and feeling."

In the whorehouse where he earned his living, Gaudencio would play a fairly wide repertoire of tunes but there is one mazurka, *Ma Petite Marianne,* that he played only twice: in November 1936 when Lionheart was killed, and in January 1940 when Moucho was killed. He never would play it again.

"No, no, I know what I'm doing, I know only too well. That mazurka is part soured and no good will come of meddling with it."

Benicia is Gaudencio Beira's niece and distant cousin to the Gamuzos—and there are nine of them, also to Policarpo la Bagañeira and the late Lázaro Codesal. We are all more or less related hereabouts, except for the Carroupos, and there's not one of them but has a pockmark like pigskin on their foreheads.

It rains upon the waters of the River Arnego which glide past, turning the watermills and scaring consumptives, while Catuxa Bainte, the half-wit from Martiñá, runs about Esbarrado hill in her birthday suit, with her tits drenched and her hair trailing about her waist.

"Keep away, you bad bitch! You are in a state of mortal sin and will yet burn in the furnace of hell!"

It rains upon the waters of the River Bermún which spurts along, whistling kyries and licking at the roots of oak trees while Fabián Minguela, or Moucho, rather, that spectre of death, sharpens his knife upon the whetstone.

"Keep away, you heathen! You will yet be called to account for your deeds in the next world!"

The Casandulfe Raimundo believes that Fabián Minguela sauntered through this life with the nine signs of the bastard upon him.

"And what are they?"

"Be patient. You'll find out soon enough."

The oldest of the Gamuzos is called Baldomero, well, that's what he was called for he is dead now: Baldomero Marvís Ventela, or Fernández according to some, but that's neither here nor there for he was known as Lionheart because he was very headstrong and feared no one, either living or dead. In 1933 on the Feast of the Apostle in Tecedeiras, which lies on the road from La Gudiña to Lalín, just before the Corredoira dolmen, Lionheart stripped a couple of Civil Guards of their guns, tied their hands behind their backs, and marched them to the barracks where he handed them over, rifles and all. In the barracks they told him that they were going to give him a thrashing, but they didn't and they threw the two guards out for being such simpletons and layabouts, they say. They were not from hereabouts so, as nobody knew where they were from, they went off and nothing more was heard of them. Lionheart has a scandalous tattoo on his arm of a red and blue snake coiled about the body of a naked woman.

Lionheart was born in 1906, at the time of King Alfonso XIII's wedding, and at the age of twenty he married Loliña Moscoso Rodríguez, a woman with such a temper that only a sound beating would keep her in her place. Loliña died in a senseless way—trampled by a panic-stricken ox that crushed her against the stable door. Loliña was already a widow when she was killed, she had been a widow for some four or five years. Lionheart had no sisters, only brothers. The parents of the nine Gamuzos—Baldomero Marvís Casares, Tripe-Butcher, and Teresa Ventela (or Fernández) Valduide, Wanton—died in 1920 in the famous train crash in Albares station. More than a hundred people were killed just as they were coming out, nearly suffocated, from the Lazo tunnel, which is like a bottomless tomb that can never be filled. Around about the area it was said that many were buried alive in order to save on the funeral expenses, but that may not be true.

The second of the Gamuzos is Tanis, they call him Demon for he is very quick to get up to mischief. Tanis is married to Rosa Roucón, who is the daughter of a customs official from Orense. Rosa is partial to a drop of anisette liqueur and she sleeps the whole day long. Not that she's a bad sort, I have to admit, but she overdoes it a bit with the anisette.

Tanis farms the land and raises cattle, just like two of his brothers and his cousin Policarpo la Bagañeira, trainer of birds, frogs, and beasts of the mountain. They are herdsmen for the sheer love of it and great at rounding up horses on the mountain, clipping and branding them in the pen amid clouds of dust, whinnies of rage and fear, and dripping sweat. Tanis is a great arm wrestler and always wins wagers against outsiders.

"Cough up the few *reales* you lost, stranger, and have a drink with us! We have no wish to make enemies hereabouts. And never forget what I'm about to tell you for it gives great comfort: May God live and the blackbird sing, for after winter comes the spring."

When the weather turns hot, and that's a while off yet, Demon likes to run after Catuxa Bainte, the half-wit from Martiñá, both of them in the nip, half snake and half wildcat, they head for Lucio Mouro's millpond to defile their flesh; well, defile, or so they say. It's not that Tanis takes advantage of her because she neither tries to run away nor tires of the sport, even clapping and cheering him on at every thrust and lunge. The half-wit from Martiñá can't swim so it's a laugh to see her floundering about as she throbs to the rhythm of their dance.

Benicia has nipples like sweet chestnuts, as everybody knows, just like chestnuts for St. John's Eve when they're ripe for the eating. Benicia has fire in her blood and neither tires nor wearies. Benicia has sparkling blue eyes and she's very lively in bed. Benicia was married once, maybe she still is, to a ninny of a Portuguese puppeteer who performed hereabouts and went as far afield as León at times, but then she ran away from her husband and came back home again.

Benicia's mother is the sister of Gaudencio, the blind accordion player in Sprat's brothel. Benicia Segade Beira is a blessing, with her powerful stride and her ready laugh. Her mother can read and write though Benicia can't: at times families get on a downward path and there is no stopping them until they hit the dust or maybe chance upon a crock of gold, but there's precious little of that around these days. Benicia's mother is called Ádega and she plays the accordion nearly as well as her brother; the *Fanfinette* polka she plays exquisitely.

"Now, I come from Vilar do Monte, between the Sarnoso crags and the Esbarrado Hill and I know the very milk on which each and every creature was reared. You, Don Camilo, come from a family of fighters and that, too, has its price to pay. Your grandfather clubbed Xan Amieiros, the miller from the River Pedriñas, to death and had to leave for fourteen years—he went off to Brazil, as you well know. Well, I'm from Vilar do Monte, beyond Silvaboa and Ricobelo, all up hill and down dale, but my old man—Cidrán Segade—was from Cazurraque at the foot of the Portelina crags, where they would have no truck with the people from Zamoiros and wouldn't as much as bid them time of day. Now I'm telling you this so that you know I'm a decent sort and not an outsider, for there's a lot of riffraff about these days. May God strike me down if we

7

mightn't even be relatives! Your grandfather went off to Brazil over a century ago, in the time of Queen Isabella II. Your grandfather had a scandalous love affair—you'll pardon me but that's what they say—with Manecha Amieiros, who was the sister of Xan and the other brother, whose name I forget, I think it was Fuco—that's right, he was called Fuco and he had only one eye, not that he had lost the other one, no, that's just the way he was born, with just one eye in the middle of his forehead. Your grandfather and Manecha Amieiros used to meet in a cave in the pine forest at las Bouzas, where they made a bed of dried hydrangeas and had a woodstove for frying sausages and for warmth. One night Manecha's two brothers, one armed with a machete and the other with an iron bar, lay in wait for your grandfather at the bend in the road at Claviliño. They meant to kill him, of course, but your grandfather charged at them with his horse and knocked them down. Fuco, the one-eyed brother dropped his iron bar and ran like a hare, but Xan stood up to your grandfather and they fought the bit out. Xan struck your grandfather a hefty blow on the ribs with the machete but Don Camilo, who wasn't much of a size but sure had guts, stood his ground and thrashed him with the brother's iron bar. They say that when they came to carry out the autopsy on the dead man, his lungs were a delight to behold: just nothing but water. He must have got a right good thrashing!"

The third of the Gamuzos is Roque; although he isn't a priest, for some reason or other he is known as the Cleric of Comesaña. The Cleric of Comesaña boasts an enormous penis, renowned throughout the whole area and talked about even beyond Ponferrada in the kingdom of León. The Cleric of Comesaña's penis may even be as glorious as the priest's in San Miguel de Buciños, which will, in due course, figure in this true story. When they want to astound travelers to the area, they do so by showing them the monastery at Oseira, the marks left by the devils on the Cargadoiro ridge (the cloven hoofprints are clear to be seen) and Roque's penis, which is said to be a blessing.

"Come on, Roque! Show this lady and gentleman from Madrid what you've got! It'll be worth a glass of *aguardiente** to you."

"Make it two."

"Alright then, two."

Then Roque undoes his fly and releases the said organ which dangles, like a hanged fox, almost to his knees. Although he should be used to it by now, Roque always fumbles a little at the critical moment.

"You must excuse him for being so clumsy, ma'am. It's just that he's still a bit shy . . ."

When Roque tells his wife—that's Chela Domínguez from los Avelaiños—to spread her legs, not a bit of it! she ties a serviette to him so that the whole kit and caboodle doesn't enter. She copes better that way.

"May St. Carallán** have mercy upon us and the Good Lord find us all confessed when the Last Trump sounds, Amen!"

Ádega knows full well what happened but she has been saving it up for some time now.

"You can't not tell . . . Not since we have the same blood coursing in our veins."

"No, sir, nor do I wish to remain silent. I've held my tongue for long enough. Will you have a drop more *aguardiente?*"

---

* A colorless liqueur distilled in Galicia. —Trans.
** Fictitious saint, patron of the male sexual organs. —C.J.C.

"I will. Thanks."

It does you good to watch the gentle litany of rain, to hear the patience of the drizzle falling upon the fields, upon the roof, and the panes of the bay window.

"My brother Secundino stole the papers from the courthouse in Carballiño, well, Xian Mosteirón, the clerk of the court, let him steal them—at one time he was a customs official and was known as Hopalong from Marañís—he did so because my brother, who wasn't one to count the pennies, gave him five *pesos* to squander on himself and another five to spend on charitable deeds—ten in total. Lionheart was killed by someone who is well and truly dead now, of course, you know that better than I do, and I don't say that for nothing. The men from Cazurraque are in a class of their own—that's why us women from Vilar do Monte, and elsewhere besides, get on so well with them, for when all's said and done, what a woman wants is someone that can churn the butter for her. Moucho is from farther afield, well, his father is, the family has been here for many years now, although they come from a long way away. I gather they're from la Maragateria in the kingdom of León, or so they say around here, but I wouldn't swear to it for I don't want to tell a lie. If you take my granddaughter Xila as a maid—she's already twelve years old but to the best of my knowledge she hasn't started messing around yet—I'll give you the papers as well as the boots of the dead man who killed Lionheart. They're not worth much, I know, but at least they're a souvenir. My brother Secundino used to keep his tobacco in them for it gave him a laugh: Father Silvio, the priest from Santa María de Carballeda—where your relation Fernández was from—even told him that if he didn't give the boots a holy burial he would burn in hell. But my brother paid not the slightest heed. Secundino wasn't one to fear hell for he believed that God was more of a friend to life and plenty than to death and starvation. Pour yourself more *aguardiente* for it's bitterly cold outside."

The first sign of a bastard is thin hair, and Fabián Minguela was noted for his thin, lank hair.

"What color was it?"

"That depends, it varied from day to day."

The fourth and fifth of the Gamuzos—Celestino and Ceferino—are twins and both of them entered the priesthood, they studied at the seminary in Orense and even managed to come out pure, or so it is said. Celestino is called Sprig and he's in the parish of San Miguel de Taboadela. Ceferino is known as Ferret and was in the parish of San Adrián de Zapeaus over in the Rairiz de Veiga area but now he's been moved to Santa María de Carballeda, in Piñor de Cea, where he took over from the late Father Silvio.

Yes, indeed; it does you good to watch the rain fall as ever; and it always rains, in winter and in summer, by day and by night, upon this earth and its wickedness, for the sake of men, women, and beasts.

Nobody would have dared tackle Baldomero Lionheart for he was as fierce as a wolf: his brother Tanis the Demon can lift a man off the ground with his little finger: their brother Roque, the Cleric of Comesaña, is a source of embarrassment: the twins, Celestino the Sprig and Ceferino the Ferret, celebrate Mass, as you already know, and together they play dominoes fairly well. Sprig is a hunter (rabbits and woodpigeon) and Ferret is an angler (perch, mullet, and, with a bit of luck, the odd trout). That still leaves four more of the Gamuzos.

Ádega is a cautious but generous woman, in her youth she must have been very hospitable and great fun, full of life and fond of a get-together.

"They say that the dead man who killed Lionheart also killed my old man and maybe a dozen others to boot. Apparently the bastard—if you'll pardon my French—grew trigger-happy: I can't say for sure, but when they killed the dead man I lighted a candle before the crucifix in the church of Santa María la Real in Oseira. Some deaths bring sorrow but there are also those that bring great joy, would you not agree? Other deaths—such as drownings and plague deaths—inspire fear, whereas some deaths would make you laugh—like the sight of a hanged man swaying in the breeze. When I was a slip of a girl in Bouza da Fondo there was a hanged man so stone dead that the youngsters were able to swing to and fro from his feet; when the Civil Guard arrived they sent the children packing for the judge was a very strait-laced man from Castile, a most pernickety type called Don León who, as I well remember, couldn't take a joke. But now all the old ways are disappearing and it's all thanks to this business of air travel."

The memory of Lázaro Codesal still lingers on. Ádega isn't the only one who knows these stories. One night when he was coming down la Cabreira (singing to let people know that he was out and about—Lázaro Codesal was always singing) a married man stopped him at the Chosco crossroads:

"I'm all alone and you, too, are out looking for a fight."

"Step aside there! I've no wish to pick a quarrel! I'm going about my own business!"

Events took a turn for the worse, the two men got involved in a scuffle, and soon the blows were flying in all directions. Lázaro Codesal gave his opponent a good hiding, put his hands behind his back, tied them to his prick, and sent him packing.

"Now go home and let your wife untie you! And in future don't seek to meddle with peaceable folk or you'll feel the consequences!"

At that time the line of the mountain could still be seen and if it hadn't been for that treacherous Moor, it would never have been blotted out. Fig trees don't thrive in these parts but, if I were rich, I would find a place where the fig trees grow strong and sturdy and I would buy a hundred fig trees in memory of Lázaro Codesal, the youngster who played the field better than anyone, and plant them so the birds could eat all the figs. It's a pity not to be rich so as to do so many things: see the world, give presents to women, buy fig trees . . . If you can't play the fiddle or the harmonica, then you spend the evenings in bed. Benicia is like an obedient sow, she never says no to anything. Benicia can neither read nor play the accordion but she is very young and she makes good blood puddings: she also knows how to give pleasure, in its place, and has big sweet nipples, as hard as chestnuts. Ádega picks up the story of the hanged men:

"The half-wit from Bidueiros, who was the bastard son of the priest in San Miguel de Buciños, did not hang himself but was hanged as a sort of trial run. The priest in San Miguel de Buciños is called Father Merexildo Agrexán Fenteira and is well-known for his proportions. May God forgive me, but when Father Merexildo has a hard on, it looks as though he has a pine tree beneath his cassock! 'Where are you off to with that, Father?' 'To see if the parish can cool my ardor, you bastard!' (or whore, if he is talking to a woman). You must excuse me! Look here, Don Camilo, I want to give you a bit of *chorizo** to taste, it's the very best and nourishing, too. The reason that my old man had such strength is that he used to down whole *chorizos* at one go; mark my words, the dead man who killed him could only have killed him the way you'd kill

* A spicy pork sausage. —Trans.

a fox. Cidrán surely can't have seen what was coming for, if he had, the dead man who killed him—and anyone else who was with him, for that matter—would still be running for his life."

"The priest in San Miguel de Buciños is always swarming with flies; maybe he tastes sweet."

"But don't they bother him?"

"Yes, but he puts up with them—not that he has much choice!"

Joker is the sixth of the Gamuzos, his name is Matías and he knows a little about fortunetelling and juggling. Matias was at one time a kennel boy in the parish of Santa María la Madre in Orense but later on he pulled his socks up and got himself a job in Carballiño, in the Repose Coffin Factory where he now earns a decent crust. Joker is a real live wire and dances with a great sense of rhythm; he has a fine singing voice and makes some small change on the side playing billiards. Joker is a great one for pranks, and witty, into the bargain. He tells stories about Otto and Fritz in a heavy German accent. Joker is a widower; Puriña, his widow, died of consumption (in the end the witches caught up with her and cast their spell upon her). She was the sister of Loliña Moscoso, the wife of the eldest brother. The daughters in that family weren't long for this world—they died even before their husbands had a chance to grow fed up with them.

"Did they leave an almighty muddle behind them?"

"No more than you'd expect."

Ádega fetches *chorizo* and more *aguardiente*. Ádega's *chorizo* and *aguardiente* are as fine as they come and nourishing, too.

"They tried it on with the half-wit from Bidueiros and with my old man, too, but in a different sort of way. There are always bad sorts knocking about but in those days—during the war years it was even worse. God will surely punish them for such things cannot be allowed to happen; many have already been called to account for their deeds and few died in the comfort of their own beds with the eldest son in attendance to close their eyes as God ordained. You see the end that the dead man that killed Lionheart and my old man met with. A terrible lot of bloodshed, and in the end he didn't even get beyond Meixo Eiros hill with his life! He who lives by the sword, dies by the sword. You know better than I do, though you needn't say so if you'd rather not, that the dead man who killed Lionheart and my old man was rounded up by your relative and he died in the das Bouzas do Gago spring, I need say no more. They call Rosalía Trasulfe the Crazy Goat because she is very brazen and always was. Rosalía Trasulfe undid her bodice, bared both breasts and told the dead man who was going about killing: 'Come on—suck!—I don't care! All I want is to go on living.' And now she says: 'The dead man sucked these breasts and explored other parts of my body, too, but I'm alive and kicking and, anyway, didn't I give myself a thorough scrubbing down afterwards? Indeed I washed my breasts and even my privates . . .' It's great to hear her say it!"

Each of the Gamuzos has a nickname. Julián Marvís Ventela, or Fernández—or Julián Gamuzo, rather, is called Wideawake because he is as quick as a flash of lightning and very witty, too. Wideawake has a watchmaker's shop in Chantada—well, his wife has. He went farther afield but did well for himself. Wideawake married a widowed watchmaker from Chantada: Pilar Moure Pernas, watchmaker—by a fluke. Pilar's first husband, Urbano Dapena Escairón, the owner of the watchmaker's shop, died of colic and their son Urbanito, who then inherited the business, died of anemia—he was always a sickly sort. That is the order of events and how Pilar came to inherit the shop. Wideawake and Pilar have five sons and three daughters, all of them hale and hearty and bright as buttons. It's unlikely that Wideawake will ever inherit the watchmaker's shop, that's for sure, not that it bothers him one bit, he is happy to be Watchmaker Consort and see that his children have a square meal and the chance to pursue their studies.

"The dead man who killed Lionheart and my old man—and maybe a dozen others to boot—sucked the breasts of Crazy Goat but the bastard is dead now though not buried, Don Camilo, for a woman (and one day I'll say who it is—hold your tongue, you, for I'm the one who's talking) stole his remains from the graveyard and did with them what shall never be known for I cannot bring myself to say it. In this world you've got to keep your feet on the ground, better ground than water. Crazy Goat has all her wits about her and she's still living— with her daughter Edelmira, I believe, who married a guard in Sarria. She is my age, or maybe a year or two older, and we were always close friends. From time to time somebody or other will feel the breasts of all us women—isn't that what we're for? and nobody can take the taste for it from us, the main thing is to have a good wash down afterwards: a lad in the hayloft, another in the stable, the priest in the sacristy, a peddler in the kitchen, the miller in his mill, a stranger on the mountain, and the husband whenever the fancy takes him . . . As I say, the main thing is to have a good wash down afterwards. When I was rearing my daughter Benicia and these were proper breasts—big and firm and full of milk—the serpent suckled at them but my old man split its head open with a hoe and killed it, now there are only dead men around here and the hungry wind soughing in the oak trees."

It rains down upon the Piñor crossroads and the Albarona

waterfall where the wolves keep watch as the oxcart from Roquiño goes by with its axle creaking to frighten them off. The slugs turn to water for the winter and sleep tucked away in the half-hidden roots of the sweet wild strawberries. Souls in purgatory also drink at the Miangueiro spring, like the lepers, and when they grow weary they wander with the holy company along the banks of the river. Benito Gamuzo is called Scorpion and he's as clumsy as a scorpion although he has no sting. Scorpion is a deaf-mute but smart enough; he's good at running errands and can plane wood, breed rabbits, and make blood puddings almost as well as Benicia. Scorpion is a bachelor and lives in Carballiño with his brother Matías. He works in the coffin factory, too, and earns enough to scrape by. Once a month Scorpion goes with prostitutes in the city and that leaves him short for the rest of the month. Another brother, Salustio, also lives with Joker and Scorpion. He is a simple soul and feeble, too. Between one thing and another he scrapes by and doesn't give them any trouble. Joker has no thought of marrying again for he doesn't know what would become of his brothers if he did.

"I'm just as well off as I am and they are my brothers."

The ninth and last Marvís is called Shrill because he is forever whining in that little cricket's voice of his, maybe he has a pain somewhere deep inside and isn't able to say so.

Ádega wants to see the sea before she dies.

"The worst is not dying but knowing that you are going to die, the worst is the mirth it gives folks who live on after you; I could content myself with living one day longer than the dead man and I've already lived a lot longer than that. The man who killed my old man is well and truly dead and I'm still alive and kicking, seeing others die off is what counts. What I want now is to see the sea before I die, it must be very beautiful. Crazy

Goat once told me that it is at least as big as the whole province of Orense—maybe even bigger. The man who killed Lionheart, and my old man as well, is dead now and that gives great comfort. You've got to stick close to the water and better water than air. Crazy Goat is a dab hand at training birds and small animals, she is as good at it as Policarpo la Bagañeira: owls, ravens (owls are slower to cotton on than ravens), toads, goats (they're very smart), pine-martens, bats, anything at all. Crazy Goat can also mesmerise hens, castrate snakes, and make foxes dance a merry jig—she rubs their asses with a hot pepper sliced in two, the best are the ones from her home town. What a laugh! Crazy Goat is far better than a whole lot of men put together! All us women have at some time or another got up to mischief with a dog—that's only normal, when you're young anything goes, or even with a half-wit if there's one handy and it's not too cold, or he starts to blubber; men go for a suckling nanny goat and hold her firmly by the horns for a more satisfying screw, it's all perfectly natural. Well, what the rest of us got up to with dogs, Crazy Goat did with wolves; nobody believes a word of it but it's true—I've seen it with my own two eyes. All wild animals obey Crazy Goat because she was conceived on the back of a galloping horse during the San Lourenciño storm which comes every year and kills a Castilian, a gypsy, a black, or a seminary student. It's a merciless, raging storm, full of bitterness. Crazy Goat plays a flute she has to warn the small defenseless animals that the storm is on its way: the mole beneath the ground, the centipede in the woods, the spider in the sweet pea, the snail in the turnip field, and others besides."

Policarpo la Bagañeira's surname is not Obenza but Portomourisco: his grandmother—a forceful, bossy woman—was surnamed Obenza.

The Carroupos have a pigskin pockmark on their foreheads,

they all have it, it's like a factory stamp, or a birthmark upon the damned. Moucho has Carroupo blood in his veins and is neither to be relied upon nor trusted. The Carroupos don't even know where they are from, they're certainly not from around here. They may have come from la Maragatería, beyond Porferrada, fleeing famine or the law, who can tell? Fabián Minguela—Moucho—is always sharpening and polishing a knife, one day it will get its own back on him. The Carroupos neither till the land nor raise livestock, the Carroupos are cobblers: that's what folks about these parts call shoemakers, tailors, apothecaries' assistants, barbers, clerks, and other jobs which require neither physical strength nor land. The second sign of the bastard is a jutting forehead. Have you noticed Fabián Minguela's? Well, something along those lines.

Moncho Requeixo Casbolado, who is known as Moncho Lazybones because he never wants to do a hand's turn save wandering about and watching the world go by, was in the war in Melilla* with Lázaro Codesal Grovas (maybe I didn't mention the second surname before) but he helped free the land from the Moors and lived to tell the tale, though with one leg less. Moncho Lazybones has been right around the world, he always served on Dutch ships: Guayaquil was the place he liked best.

"Believe it or not, life is not too bad with a wooden leg, provided it is properly adjusted, of course. Among the natives of New Titanic—an island in the Pacific which the English shelled and sank because the natives wanted to introduce the metric decimal system—a wooden leg was regarded as a sign of

* The easternmost city of Spanish Morocco where an uprising among army officers on July 17, 1936 signalled the start of the Spanish Civil War. —Trans.

distinction. They wanted to make me prime minister but I refused because I'd rather return to my native land."

Moncho Lazybones is cast in the mold of the old-style explorer: he's a liar, a womaniser, a storyteller, an idler, and as stubborn as a mule. According to Moncho Lazybones, he found a very rare tree, the *ombiel*, on Bastianiño beach whose leaves, overcome by sadness, tumble to the ground in fall, wrinkling softly like the flesh of a snail, and then turn into eyeless bats with a reddish skull painted on their wings. If the wind blows, it lifts them, breathes life into them, and sends them flying: if not, you have to leave them clinging to the ground until they wilt and die of starvation, because it's bad luck to kill them. But if they are left clinging to the ground no harm will come of it and the world continues upon its merry round.

Ádega is a close friend of Moncho Lazybones, at one time they were even sweethearts of a sort but it's years now since they have seen one another.

"Look here, Don Camilo, quit your teasing, at times I wonder if you do anything but tease! The best you can do is to hold out a while longer and die after folks who are dead and buried, after folks who are condemned to die, with death stamped in their eyes, upon their foreheads and in their hearts, folks that everybody wishes dead. Yes, indeed, that's God's law: he who lives by the sword, dies by the sword. Besides, there is no escape for all the doors in the world are barred against them. You've got to stick close to the air and better air than death. Folks grew sick and tired of those ashen creatures stalking about sowing death and when the hour of vengeance came— which comes when the Good Lord chooseth but come it must for each and every ashen creature, those who had mourned but were still alive planted a hazel tree to keep a reckoning and also to keep the wild boars happy. 'There are lots of hazel trees planted hereabouts!' said those ashen creatures to those for whom the hour of reckoning had not yet come, 'We're going to have to teach them a lesson.' 'No, sir,' would come the reply, 'those hazel trees mark the boundaries; they sprout of their own accord so that the wild boars have fresh hazelnuts to eat.'"

Ádega spoke these last words in a hoarse voice. Then she swallowed spittle and smiled.

"Pardon me. Shall I play the *Fanfinette* polka on the accordion for you? I'm getting long in the tooth now but you'll see I can still play it fairly well."

Ádega still played the accordion with great style and skill.

"You play very well."

"Not at all. Ever since my old man was killed I can find no peace inside my head and there's not a soul can play the accordion, or anything else for that matter, in a state like that, I've no heart in it, I play like a pianola . . . Do you mind if I cry a bit? I won't be long."

Ádega shed two or three tears.

"When they killed the dead man that killed my old man I thought I would breathe more easily but that isn't so. Before I hated and now I despise; that is sapping away my strength. Before I held my tongue but now I talk, maybe more than I ought. This business of the accordion is like drinking water at the fountain: some days you are thirsty and other days you aren't. Despising is the only thing I think I can do well. It was a tremendous effort at the start but now I can despise as well as anybody. I swear. It's important to know that a body's head may ache even though it doesn't really hurt. I'm from this land and nobody will throw me out of here; when I die, I'll become part of the earth that feeds the gorse. I'll turn into the golden flower on the gorse bushes, and in the meantime, well, here we are."

Ádega fell silent then poured two glasses of *aguardiente,* one for herself and one for me.

"Your good health."

Behind Miss Ramona's house the garden stretches down to the river with its reeds and bracken, its pool, its barbel, and its suicides: but three suicides in eleven years are not so very much. This is not a great spot for suicides: the odd homeless old man, a young girl in despair, the occasional married woman eaten up with boredom and remorse, but nobody knows if Miss Ramona's mother drowned by accident or design.

"You and I are cousins of the Casandulfe Raimundo, you on your mother's side and I on my father's. You and I are relations of relations and maybe, if you scratch a bit below the surface, you'll find we are related. Hereabouts we are all more or less related, except for the Carroupos that is, who appeared out of the blue and are now getting ahead like a house on fire."

Miss Ramona looks about thirty, perhaps a little older, she has a haughty, capricious manner, maybe a little distant, shy and mysterious at the same time. Miss Ramona has big black eyes like Compostela jet and a sallow complexion, maybe she's half Mexican, the Casandulfes had a grandmother—or was it a great-grandmother?—who was Mexican. Miss Ramona had three suitors but for the sake of her dignity she remained unmarried. Miss Ramona writes poems, plays sonatas on the piano, and lives with two old crocks of manservants and two old crones of maids she inherited from her father, Don Brégimo Faramiñás Jocín, who was a spiritualist and fond of playing the banjo and died a major in the Service Corps. Miss

Ramona's servants are four calamities, indeed four fiascos, but she cannot throw them out of the house to starve and die in destitution.

"No; stay here until they carry you out feet first in a wooden box. Chances are you won't last long."

"Thank you, Miss. May God reward you for your charity!"

Miss Ramona also inherited a somber black Packard from her father and an elegant white Isotta-Fraschini but she never takes them out of the coach-house, Miss Ramona can drive, she's the only woman hereabouts to have a driving license but, even so, she never takes them out of the coach-house.

"They guzzle too much gasoline. Let them rust!"

In Miss Ramona's parlor there hang two portraits by Fernando Alvarez de Sotomayor:* one of her dressed in local costume and one of her mother wearing a Spanish mantilla.

"There's a strong family likeness, don't you think?"

"I don't know. I never got to meet your mother."

"Well, never mind, all paintings look very much alike."

The Casandulfe Raimundo is the son of Salvadora, my mother's youngest sister, who is a good-looking woman with an education behind her. When Raimundo goes to visit our cousin Miss Ramona he always takes her a present of a white camellia.

"Here, Mona, so you can see that I love you and never forget you."

"I'm so grateful, Raimundo, you shouldn't have bothered."

Miss Ramona has a Pomeranian, an Angora cat, and a huge colorful macaw, a green parrot, a marmoset monkey, a tortoise, and two swans that glide on the garden pond, they sometimes venture as far as the river but they always come back.

---

* Galician artist (1875–1960) best known for his portraits and studies of manners, also director of the Prado Museum. —Trans.

Miss Ramona is very fond of animals, the only ones she doesn't like are those that are of some use: cows, pigs and chickens, except horses, of course. Miss Ramona has a bay horse that could be as much as twenty years old.

"Horses are like men: handsome and vacant, though some are noble in their feelings."

Except for the parrot, all Miss Ramona's animals have names: the dog is called Wilde and he sleeps with her; the cat, King; the macaw, Rabecho; the monkey, Jeremiah; the tortoise, Xaropa; the horse, Caruso; and the two swans, Romulus and Remus. The cat is neutered because one night, when the flesh would out, he left home and didn't return until the following morning: scruffy, sad, and wounded. Miss Ramona's response was firm:

"Poor little mite! This must not happen again—have him neutered!"

So, of course, they had him neutered and he never escaped again, indeed why would he? The macaw is red, white, and blue, just like the French flag, with a few green and yellow feathers. The macaw lives on a perch, where he is fastened with an ample chain; always weary but dignified and with a look of bored resignation, the macaw hops up and down, unhooks himself and climbs half-heartedly up to his perch. The monkey masturbates and coughs; the tortoise spends its life sleeping and the swans sail elegantly up and down in their boredom. In Miss Ramona's house, the only animal not down in the dumps is the horse.

"Don't poke fun at me, Raimundo! Being alone is not the worst. I've been alone all my life and for years now I've grown accustomed it . . . the worst of it is that I spend my days with my mind blank or drifting away in the clouds, as if I were losing my reason. With every day that passes we are all a little farther apart, a little wearier—even of ourselves. Don't you think I should go and live in Madrid?"

It rains in a steady downpour upon the sinners of God's earth and the land takes on the mild, gentle color of the sky as yet unbroken by the wing of the bird. Since I can play neither the fiddle nor the harmonica and, since I can't find the key of the harmonium where I keep my stamp collection, I spend the evenings in bed with Benicia, reading poems and listening to tangos. Benicia was in Orense the other day and she brought me back a present of a coffeepot, it's very handy and makes the cups in batches of two: one for me and one for her.

"Do you want more coffee?"

"Alright."

Benicia is a happy, hearty sinner and has big dark nipples that are hard and sweet. Benicia has blue eyes and she's surly and forceful in bed. She knows a thing or two about rolling in the hay and she screws skilfully but tyrannically. Benicia can neither read nor write but she laughs with great assurance.

"Shall we dance a tango?"

"No. I'm cold. Come here."

Benicia is always warm even when it's cold. Benicia is like a heater and a pleasure machine rolled into one. I'm glad that she can play neither the fiddle nor the harmonica.

"Give me a kiss."

"Alright."

"Pour me a glass of *aguardiente*."

"Alright."

"Fry me a sausage."

"Alright."

Benicia is like an obedient sow, she never says no to anything.

"Stay with me tonight."

"I can't. Ferret Gamuzo, the priest from San Adrián—well, now he's in Santa María de Carballeda—is coming over to see me. He comes over the first Tuesday of every month."

"Go on!"

Lázaro Codesal was killed by a Moor in the shade of a fig tree, treacherously shot with a flintlock at a time when he should have been farthest from such a sudden death. When death entered Lázaro Codesal through one ear, he had in his mind the figure of Ádega, spreadeagled naked as she sunned herself on a steep bank; we were all young once, I suppose. At the Miangueiro spring, where the lepers wash their sores nowadays, the fig tree is still growing from which they cut branches to whittle into lances so that the Figueiroas* could rescue from the Moors the seven maidens held in the tower of the Bosom Brothel. Nowadays there's not a soul left who can recall that story. Marraca, the wood-seller from the Francelos plain, mentioned by a friend of Ádega's in a book he wrote, had twelve daughters: not one of them reached the age of twelve a virgin and they all earned their living by their sex. Elvirita from Doña Rosa's cafe in Orense met one of them, Carlota, in Pelona's brothel. The clear water of the Miangueiro spring is not fit to drink, not even the birds drink it for it washes over the bones, the lungs, the miseries of the dead and brings nothing but grief.

Blind Gaudencio is well set up and never tires of playing the accordion.

"A two-step, Gaudencio!"

"Whatever you wish, sir."

Blind Gaudencio lives in the same place as he works, he sleeps on a straw mattress in a closet beneath the stairs in

* Los Figueiroas Romanones—family of Spanish aristocrats and landowners. —Trans.

Sprat's brothel, so he saves on lodgings: Gaudencio's den is warm and cosy. There's no light, of course, but he doesn't need one: blind men don't care a hoot whether they have light or not.

"You mean they can't tell the difference?"

"I don't know. I don't think so."

In the early morning when he stops playing at about five or half past five, Gaudencio goes to Mass in the Mercy Convent in Misery Street, then he goes to bed until midday. When he died, the prostitutes bought him a wreath of flowers and had several Masses said for his soul; they couldn't attend the funeral for the police wouldn't let them.

"Your grandfather went off to Brazil for several years when he killed Xan Amieiros and reduced Fuco to a pulp, but he gave Manecha fifty thousand *reales* of the ready stuff—that was a fortune in those days—and another whack in shares in the M.Z.A. Railroad Company, as well as a letter of introduction to Don Modesto Fernández y González the author of *Our Grandparents' Farm*, who signed himself Camilo de Cela and also wrote articles in *The Spanish and American Enlightenment* and in *Spanish Correspondence*. Manecha went off to Madrid and opened the Orense Inn on San Marcos Street; as she was willing, clean, and not afraid of hard work, she was able to save and make a go of it and wound up marrying a civil servant from the Parliament, Don León Roca Ibáñez, to whom she bore eight daughters, all of whom married well, and two sons, one who became a surveyor and the other a court prosecutor. A grandson of Don León and Manecha's, the son (by a second marriage) of their fourth daughter Marujita, went as far as undersecretary under the Republic and died in Barquisimeto, Venezuela in 1949. He was a member of parliament for the leftwing Republican Party and when he was alive and kicking was called Don Claro Comesaña Roca. Manecha was a handsome, shapely woman and her children and grandchildren, though perhaps not quite as good-looking as she, also had great presence. A daughter of the Undersecretary, thus Manecha's great-granddaughter, Haydée Comesaña Bethencourt, was selected Miss Barquisimeto back in the '50's."

There are fools with luck and fools with no luck, so it has been since the world began and so it will always be. Roquiño Borrén, a fool with no luck, was kept shut up inside a trunk for almost five years so that he couldn't be a nuisance to anyone: when they took him out he looked like a pale hairy spider.

"What difference does it make to him? Can't you see that he's a simpleton?"

"I'm sure I don't know, ma'am . . . maybe he would have liked to stretch his legs a bit and take a breath of fresh air."

"Well, let him! I'm not stopping him!"

Roquiño Borrén's mother thinks that simpletons neither feel nor suffer.

"They are half-wits, after all . . ."

In the old times you could take them out to *romerías** but nowadays there's so much deprivation that folks don't even want to lay eyes upon them any more. Folks keep themselves amused with other things nowadays, gossiping in low voices and recounting their sorrows—again in low voices, for there's no need to raise your voice about these parts. In the sacristan's vineyard there hangs a garland of strangled varmints, looking like grappling hooks, decomposing in the rain and stinking of rotting flesh. When nobody is looking, Catuxa Bainte, the

* Popular festivals of a religious nature rather like a fair or carnival. — Trans.

half-wit from Martiñá, sneaks up to the sacristan's vineyard to bare her bosom to the dead wild beasts.

"Here! Take a look at this! Everything is doomed in the end! St. Jude Thaddeus, glorious apostle, turn my sorrows into joy! Here, take a look at this! The rain will wipe out everything in the end. St. Jude Thaddeus up in heaven, bring me solace for my sorrows! The wind will wipe out everything in the end!"

The sacristan usually sends the half-wit from Martiñá packing with a shower of stones.

"Clear off, bloody half-wit! Go and show your tits to the devil and leave decent folks in peace!"

The half-wit covers her breasts and laughs aloud, then she runs off down the path, shrouded by the rain, laughing and glancing back over her shoulder every two or three paces.

Catuxa Bainte is an outspoken half-wit, not one of those bloody gaping ninnies: she lives hand to mouth and doesn't exert herself unduly, it would be hard to die of starvation hereabouts. Sometimes she coughs and spits spots of blood but she picks up every year close to midsummer when the skies clear. Catuxa Bainte must be about twenty or twenty-two years of age and what she enjoys better than anything is floundering about in the nip in Lucio Mouro's millpond.

The priest from San Miguel de Buciños goes about swarming with flies: there are always at least a thousand flies buzzing around him for apparently his flesh tastes sweet. One day when the priest in San Miguel de Buciños went to Orense to have his photo taken, he had to sit in the dark for half an hour so that the flies would settle down and go to sleep.

"But why didn't they douse him with fly-killer?"

"I don't know. Maybe they don't use it."

The priest in San Miguel de Buciños lives with a crippled old house-keeper who reeks of moth-balls and tipples coffee liqueur nearly every day.

"Dolores!"

"Yes, Father Merexildo?"

"This bread is stale—you eat it!"

"Yes, Father."

Years ago Dolores developed a boil—or maybe it was a malignant tumor—on her arm and, in order to avoid further complications, the doctor sent her to hospital to have her arm amputated so, naturally enough, it was amputated.

"With one arm less you can manage fine: folks are mighty grumblers, clearly she's not used to working."

The priest in San Miguel de Buciños is as big as an ox and belches like a lion.

"Us proper men have no need to go about making pretenses and putting on airs and graces—leave that to clowns and wimps."

"Yes, Father, leave that to clowns and wimps."

The priest in San Miguel de Buciños likes to eat and drink heartily.

"I fast for the whole of Lent as the Holy Church commands—so why don't they mention that?"

"That's just what you would wonder, Father: why don't they mention that?"

The priest in San Miguel de Buciños is also fond of other things that there is no need to mention, the flesh is weak and let him who is without sin cast the first stone.

"There are a lot of shameless gossipmongers around here."

"Yes, Father, they let their tongues run away with them, they talk a lot of nonsense and tell a pack of lies."

They say that Father Merexildo Agrexán, the priest in San

Miguel de Buciños, has some fifteen children, all born on the wrong side of the blanket.

"Is he to blame if women won't let him alone?"

Women run after the priest of San Miguel de Bucinas like bitches in heat; they tattle to each other about his proportions and give him no rest either by day or by night.

"Pardon me, Father, but why do you put up with them?"

"Why shouldn't I put up with them? Poor creatures, when all they want is a little comfort!"

The upper story of Policarpo's house in the village of Cela do Camparrón caved in when his father died, it tumbled down from the weight of people that were gathered there. God have mercy upon us! No one was killed but there were many broken bones and fractured skulls, many a soul was bruised and battered. Apparently the beams gave way, then the floor split in two and we all ended up covered with manure in the stable. The deceased had to be put back into his coffin because the poor man had shot out when he was sent flying through the air.

"You can't put him outside—he'll get wet! Can't you see he'll get wet? Set him up against the wall!"

In the hullaballoo that followed, three of Policarpo's trained weasels that could dance like clockwork to the sound of the tambourine escaped.

"They were first-class little beasts, I'll never find their like again!"

Policarpo's father died at the age of ninety after a drinking binge, the old fellow was fond of wine and it can't have done him that much harm when he lived so long. Nowadays young folks can't hold as much as they used to in the old times when men really did work and quaffed wine and smoked like fiends yet they could still tackle a wild boar and flay it with one stroke of the knife.

"Lord, what times they were!"

"Do you really believe they were better?"

Policarpo's father had squandered a fortune living as he pleased. When he was alive, Policarpo's father was called Benigno Portomourisco Turbisquedo and he was born into this world in a family of means that was later to wind up without two cents to rub together but that's another story. Don Benigno was full of notions and saw plots against him everywhere. Don Benigno always believed that woman was the most treacherous of all females, serpents included. Don Benigno married Dorotea Expósito, known as la Bagañeira, a pretty, languid, and rather mysterious young maid who worked in his mother's house. By her he had one son—Policarpo, the last of them—who was not stillborn. All the rest—as many as eleven of them—were either stillborn or miscarried. Dorotea was a woman of great beauty and in his jealousy Don Benigno could see only affairs and lewd indulgences on the side.

"That's what I get for being such a gullible hick! Why should I go saving fallen women like her? That woman is as great a slut as her mother before her—who ran off and was never heard of again. There are certain things that are best not known for they only cause deep hurt."

Don Benigno was as jealous as a Japanese—as a result of his mere suspicions—for he was never able to discover what he had imagined. He led Dorotea a life of misery; for twelve years he kept her shut up in a room on bread and water until Policarpo was born when, wearied of the wretchedness of her existence, she took her own life by slitting her wrists with a shard of broken glass. What a fright! What a turn things took then! Caring for and watching over Dorotea there was a freckled ex-seminary student with a stammer by the name of Luisiño Bocelo, Parrulo, whom Don Benigno had apprised of his duties where he took him into his service and castrated him with a sickle so as to avoid evil thoughts and disloyal deeds. At the start the youngster was up in arms but, when he saw he had no choice in the matter, he decided it wasn't so important after all and resigned himself to the situation.

"Better that way. He who removes the occasion of sin also removes the temptation: anyway, he was well fed and looked after in that house."

Don Benigno would not have his wife buried on consecrated ground and Ceferino Ferret, the priest in Santa María de Carballeda, had to intervene to avoid a public scandal. In Tunis they even held a funeral Mass for Princess Lella Jenaina, the wife of Achmed Pasha.

"That's neither here nor there."

Ceferino Ferret, or Ferret Gamuzo as he really was, would go every first and third Tuesday of the month to visit Benicia; he would arrive by night and be off before daybreak in order to keep up appearances, nobody should mind anybody else's business, much less so if the other party is a priest: priests are human too and there's nothing the matter with a man who needs a woman from time to time. Benicia is fiery and feisty in bed.

"Oh! Father Ceferino, such delight you give me! Press harder, harder! I'm almost there! Oh! Oh!"

Benicia always shows proper respect for the priest and never forgets to call him Father.

"Come here, Father, and let me wash your prick! You're great at screwing, Father, and you grow younger by the day!"

"Nonsense, woman!"

When it's the time of year for tithes and first fruits—well, nowadays there are no tithes or first fruits—so when the parishioners give him some gift or other, a couple of chickens, some eggs, sausages, a basket of apples, or when he catches the odd fish, he always takes something to Benicia.

"We all have to eat and the Good Lord does not look kindly upon avarice which, as we all know, is one of the mortal sins. Anyway, the produce of Spain is for the Spaniards."

Benicia is grateful by nature.

"Do you want to squeeze my breasts?"

"No. Keep that for later."

Moncho Requeixo—Moncho Lazybones, rather—Lázaro Codesal's fellow soldier in the Melilla campaign always speaks with great aplomb:

"In times past families showed greater respect and consideration to one another. My cousin Georgina, whom you know well, killed off her first husband with a potion brewed from St. James' wort, or buttercups, and kept her second at bay, purging him every Saturday with *olivillas*,* which have nothing to do with olives, as you might think, but are something quite different. Hand me over the wooden leg, please, it's in the hallstand, for I feel like a smoke. Thanks. My cousin Ádela, who is also sister to Georgina, spends her life munching herbal remedies and the seeds of wild rue, which doesn't grow hereabouts. I brought her back a tin of it years ago and now she grows it in flowerpots; the leaves of the *ombiel* hang like empty sacs, or rather empty balls, they're quite mysterious. The mother of my cousins, well, that's my aunt Micaela, who was my mother's sister, used to jack me off every evening in the corner of the hearth, while my grandfather was telling the story of the Cavite disaster. As I say, in the past families were closer-knit and more considerate to one another."

* Cneorum Tricoccon: a flowering shrub with small berries, widespread in Mediterranean countries. —Trans.

In the Cáticas archipelago, where the now disappeared island of New Titanic was situated, Moncho Lazybones discovered a bird shaped like a peony rose with fur instead of feathers, bright green fur, which the natives called the Little Jesus Cured, he never found out why, and used them to send messages to their lovers, never to wives or sweethearts mind you, just to lovers. Moncho Lazybones brought a pair of these little birds back home, but they died on the way, the journey across the Red Sea was too much for them.

Half-wit girls are better at canoodling than half-wit boys for their minds don't wander. Catuxa Bainte is a half-wit, as you know, otherwise she wouldn't be known as the half-wit from Martiñá, but once the prick is in the right place she writhes about to great effect.

"How do you know?"

"What business is that of yours?"

It rains mercilessly, perhaps it rains mercifully, upon all that is left of the world, between the blotted-out line of the mountain and here; beyond that we neither know, nor do we care, what happens. It drizzles upon this earth and falls on the ear like the sound of growing flesh, or a budding flower, and through the air flits a soul in distress, seeking shelter in some heart or other. You go to bed with a woman and when a son, or maybe a daughter, is born—only to run off on you fifteen years down the line with some tramp from León—the rain still falls upon the mountain as if nothing had happened. We are right in the thick of things, the beginning is right in the thick of things, and nobody knows what the end has in store. Two dogs have just been mating in the rain and now they wait, one looking east and the other west, for their bodies to return to normal.

"Look, if only you were shackled, like Wilde!"

"Don't be such a smart-ass, Mona."

As a tidbit after the earth moved, Miss Ramona took a square of chocolate.

"Bless you, Raimundo, you have made me so happy!"

Miss Ramona remained pensive for a few moments, then she laughed.

"It's as if your member had four gears, just like a car!"

"Don't be so fresh, Mona!"

Miss Ramona, her hair loose and breasts bare, though drooping slightly, glanced at her cousin Raimundo, sitting in the rocking chair rolling himself a cigarette.

"Don't be such an ass! Naked women can say whatever they please; nothing said between the sheets really counts. I'll shut up once I get dressed!"

Marcos Albite Muradás is missing both legs and he lives in an orange-painted crate with four wheels; the bow bears a five-pointed green star with his initials—M.A.M.—outlined in gold thumbtacks. Marcos Albite was bitten in the legs by a rabid fox, afterwards he was left paralysed, then they turned gangrenous and eventually had to be amputated—all in that order. Marcos Albite looks thoroughly fed up, boredom and misfortune are enough to weary anyone. Marcos Albite has a dull, droning voice and when he speaks he sounds like a cracked tambourine.

"Listen, I was off my rocker for nine years, during those nine years I lost my memory, my understanding, my will as well as my freedom. In those nine years my mother, my wife and my son died, one after the other; after that my legs were amputated. My mother hanged herself in the loft, my wife was killed by a freight train, and my son died of the croup, with a little money and good fortune he might have been saved . . . I didn't know anything about it for when you're nuts they don't bother to explain anything to you, they're just nuts and that's that."

The axle of the oxcart is God's bagpipes, screeching along the cart track scaring witches and souls in purgatory, the axle of the oxcart is the heart of both the world and loneliness. I took six cheroots from the factory in Coruña to Marcos Albite.

"They're highly aromatic, as you'll see, and a hell of a good smoke."

"Many thanks. It's the best present I've ever had."

Marcos Albite is skilled at carving wood, he turns out some very showy virgins and saints.

"Shall I make you a St. Camilo to keep as a souvenir?"

"Okay."

"Listen, did St. Camilo have a beard?"

"I really couldn't say."

During Lent there are always fewer clients in Sprat's brothel. As a mark of respect, Gaudencio doesn't play the accordion during Lent.

"It doesn't take a lot to be respectful and, as I say myself, there is no need to give offense to God."

In Orense it's often bitterly cold during Lent, at times it even snows, and a damp mist rises like vaseline from the River Miño. Gaudencio is fond of Anunciación Sabadelle's voice, it's most melodious, he also likes to fondle her bouncing breasts and springy hips. What a treat!

"Tonight, if there's nobody here to sleep, wait for me—I'll come to you!"

Anunciación Sabadelle was born in Lalín, she ran away from home to travel the world but she didn't get too far; now she doesn't dare go back for her father would bust her face. Anunciación is clean and affectionate. When she gets up to leave the kitchen, the overseer says to her:

"Where are you off to?"

"I'm off to milk Gaudencio, my heart bleeds for the poor soul. It's as quiet as a tomb here tonight, quiet and boring . . ."

"Off you go, then! I'll let you know if anyone calls."

Gaudencio gives himself a thorough wash down and sits down to wait on the rickety old bed, smoking a fag by the light of a candle he cannot see. Afterwards, when his spare, lustful writing are over, he always thanks her.

"Thanks a lot, Anuncia, God bless you!"

At half past five in the morning Gaudencio attends Mass in the Mercy Convent but his compassionate concubine prefers not to accompany him.

"No; off you go on your own, I'm cold. You'll find me here when you get back; don't be too long and take care!"

It could be that Anunciación is fond of Gaudencio, stranger things have been known to happen.

Many years back, during the Republic and shortly before Lionheart disarmed the pair of Civil Guards, the Gamuzos and me—the three eldest of them and some friends—went up to the corral in the Xurés mountain beyond Limia, on the border with Portugal; we went for a change of air and to stretch our legs a bit, as well as to help out some Marvís relations who lived hand-to-mouth from smuggling with the Portuguese, in Briñidelo, in the parish of San Pelayo de Arauxo, in Lovios, or Fondevila, rather.

"We neither clip nor brand like the folks from Sabucedo in the province of Pontevedra, but we're worth our salt, too."

On that sortie Policarpo Portomourisco Expósito, la Bagañeira's son, was to lose three of his fingers; a stroke of bad luck can throw everything into a spin but it won't stop the world in its tracks, either. Moncho Lazybones already had his wooden leg, a device which, if well made and properly adjusted, is scarcely noticeable. Tanis Gamuzo, the Demon, was always strong, very strong indeed. With one blow of his fist to the poll or the croup, Tanis could floor a horse, apparently by cutting off the flow of blood. His brother Roquiño, the Cleric of Comesaña used to win wagers by showing off you-know-what, and so long as the dough was up front on the table, all this without turning a hair and if you don't believe me, I'll eat my hat. At that time Brégimo Faramiñás was already a cadet in the Service Corps and respectfully addressed as "Don": Don Brégimo Faramiñás Jocín, a banjo concert performer, looked like a black Yankee, his interest in spirits developed at a later stage. Nor was Blind Gaudencio yet blind, he was still in the seminary, nor had Marcos Albite had his legs amputated, nor had he been in the nut-house, and Cidrán Segade, that handsome lad who was later to leave Ádega a widow, was still alive and kicking and just newly wed.

"Was there anybody else?"

"Who else would there be?"

Baldomero Gamuzo, Lionheart, would preside over gatherings stripped to the waist so that his tattoo was clearly visible: the woman signifies fortune and the serpent represents will power, that's quite clear, the serpent entwined about the woman, or rather, the will subjected to fortune and mankind triumphant in this life.

"Are we all here?"

"Why shouldn't we all be here?"

Cobblers don't ride horseback. We wouldn't let Fabián Minguela, Moucho, come up to the corral; all the Carroupos have a pigskin pockmark in the middle of their foreheads, that fellow would do to stop a bullet, though not for going up the mountain after the horses and swaggering about as if he were

39

one of us. Anyhow, the Carroupos are not from hereabouts, it's charity enough that we don't flush them out of the place with sticks and stones. And if they create bad blood, well, let them create what they like, for the world takes many a turn and the last word has yet to be spoken. The third sign of the bastard is a pallid face. Like the dead? Yes, or just like Fabián Minguela's.

"We have three days' journey up to Xurés along a route which we all know, but three days won't kill a body."

At the bottom of the Antela lagoon, entombed beneath the waters, lies the sleeping city of Antioch, paying the price for the centuries on centuries of its heinous sins. A master may not indulge his flesh with the flesh of his goatherd, though afterwards he strangles him with his belt, for this is forbidden by the law of God, nor may a wolf mount a doe, nor a woman crown with flowers another naked, pregnant, or leprous woman. Pealing the bells on midsummer's night, the dead of Antioch seek forgiveness, but to no avail, nor will they ever succeed for they are damned for the whole of eternity. Whoever crosses the Antela lagoon loses his memory, I don't know whether it's going from here to there, or on the way back from there to here; and when he went in search of the Holy Grail, King Arthur's soldiers were turned into mosquitoes; the Antela lagoon is swarming with mosquitoes, with frogs and water snakes as well.

"But isn't that way over yonder?"

"Yes, but the going is easier along this route."

The journey to Briñidelo was easy and fun and accomplished without any event of great moment; in Mourillones, on the second day of our walk, Moncho Lazybones had an altercation in an inn, it wasn't exactly a major conflict but Tanis the Demon was called in to mediate and everything was set to rights.

"There are folks who only enjoy creating trouble and there's nothing for it but to let them cool their heels a bit."

The Xurés corral is not much of a place but it's cosy and nice and quiet. Only us family go up to the corral for it's not worth taking anyone up there. The province of Orense has fewer wild horses than the rest of Galicia; there are some in the Quinxo mountains and in the Aircraft Beacon mountains over by Pontevedra. The Marvís relations were delighted to see us and produced a fine, carefully distilled *aguardiente*. The Xurés horses have whiskers, all wild horses have whiskers and are willful and fiery tempered. In the Xurés mountain they call the corral a corral, that's the clearing where the beasts are penned, as well as the rounding up, penning, clipping and branding in the stud; in other parts they call the work clipping, clipping the beasts. The Briñidelo Marvises are Segundo, Evaristo and Camilo, the three sons of Roque, Tripe-Butcher's younger brother, who married a local girl and wound up getting a separation; Roque had no wish to return to Piñor and now he has shacked up with a Portuguese woman in Esperelo, in the parish of San Fiz de Galez, in Entrimo which is not too far off. Roque gets on well with his sons and every year for the Feast of St. Rose he sends his wife a couple of chickens with the Portuguese woman. We handed over the running of the corral to Lionheart.

"You're better at giving orders, we'll follow you and do what you tell us."

"Fair enough."

The following morning, before daybreak, we herdsmen went up the mountain—in other parts they call us stockmen but to each his own—all cleaned up and well rested; our horses too had been fed, watered, and well rested in the warmth of the stable. The secret is to round up the horses quietly and patiently so that the beasts don't take fright and scatter; at the start you have to go and seek out the animals, talking to them softly and soothing them little by little. Whoa, boy! Easy does it, my fellow! Gently there! Later on, when day breaks, you can always drive them on with shouts and sticks once the beasts are filing along the track leading to the corral.

Twelve or thirteen men on horseback, in the half-light of dawn, riding after maybe a hundred wild beasts blind with terror, now that's something to leave your heart in your mouth.

"Cut them off over here!"

"Get them moving down there!"

"Watch out or they'll turn on you!"

But Policarpo was too late to watch out and the stallion turned upon him and with one bite snapped off the fingers on one hand, leaving him only two. Policarpo bound the wound tightly with his handkerchief, put what remained of his hand in his pocket and gritted his teeth; a split second of bad luck can throw everything into a spin but the sun continues on its round all the same. Policarpo dropped back and returned to Briñidelo where the Marvises' mother brewed him a remedy from an old recipe; figwort leaves, fresh cow dung, women's urine, spiders' webs, soil and sugar, all well licked over by a dog.

Once the herd is in the corral, it's best not to water them for a day or two but wait for them to settle down. Later on the mares in foal and those newly foaled are separated out or parted from their offspring, sickly horses or those with blemishes are turned loose, the wolves will make short work of them (nowadays they are sent to the abattoir), then they topple, clip, and brand those that are worth keeping. With three or four lusty young men and a little courage, Lionheart, his brother Tanis, Cidrán and Camilo—the youngest of the Marvís cousins—it's not a hard task, so long as you keep your wits about you. Sitting on a stone wall that was already green with age, Don Brégimo Faramiñás played the banjo while Gaudencio—torn between astonishment and envy—watched the cuts and capers of his companions, and Moncho Lazybones, on horseback in the midst of the herd, drove the horses on with his top quality wooden leg. The Cleric of Comesaña, Marcos Albite, Segundo, and Evaristo Marvís, and I watched about us, tended the fire, drank wine from the skin while we waited for the time to pass and the clipping to begin.

"Where's Policarpo?"

"He went back to Briñidelo, apparently he got hurt."

The clipping is carried out any old how, nobody takes too many pains over their work, the main thing is to get the job over and done with as soon as possible. Each animal yields its pound of mane, long clean mane cut in bunches and worth as much as the carcass of a steer. The Cleric of Comesaña stared at me.

"Around here we're all Guxindes, well, maybe not all of us, some of us more than others; we all have gaps between our teeth, that's how it is in our family, we're all over seven feet tall and weigh upwards of a hundred and twenty-five pounds. Our stock is still strong and sturdy! Glory be!"

Marcos Albite is in the habit of chewing Portuguese tobacco.

"The spittle is the worst for it spoils it, but chewing tobacco is healthier than smoking and doesn't burn out the lungs."

The colts are branded with a red-hot iron, like cattle, the mark of the Marvís family from Briñidelo is the L of the mother's surname, Rosa Loureses, and a nick on each ear. Sickly or wounded beasts, I mean the ones that will be devoured by the wolves or perish from hunger or cold—and every year there's over a thousand of them—aren't even branded, what would be the point? The sturdy little dwarf chestnut ponies, although there's the odd black or dappled one among them, that stand no more than twelve hands high, cannot be penned up because by midday in captivity they will have sickened and be pining away. When he's tired, Cidrán Segade has a fine singing voice, apparently exercise is good for the folds of the bellows and the vocal chords as well.

When Robín Lebozán finished writing the above, he read it aloud and then stood up.

"I think I've earned a coffee and a glass of brandy. Anyway, tonight I have to visit Rosicler, I have to take her chocolates to fatten her up a bit."

Rosicler is a nurse, she's great at giving injections, she's forever giving Miss Ramona iron, liver, and calcium injections so as to pick up her strength. Miss Ramona takes Deschiens wine for anemia, debility, and fatigue as well as Fitikal capsules, an intensive tonic. Rosicler has more knacks than one, or so they say, but she's very discreet about it all for around here there's no need to shout your business from the rooftops. At times, when no one is looking, Rosicler and Miss Ramona dance together and gently and fondly caress one another; Wilde, the dog, lets himself be stroked, too, he's both affectionate and obedient.

"Don't go, Rosicler! Stay a while longer!"

"But isn't your cousin Raimundo coming tonight?"

"What difference does that make? Raimundo is well able for both of us!"

"That's for sure . . . nor would it be the first time he laid us both!"

"Shut up, Rosicler! Don't be such a slut!"

"I'll be whatever I want, Mona. And, what's more, I don't like you calling me a slut, just like that in cold blood."

"I'm sorry."

Rosicler dined with Miss Ramona and stayed at her house until late.

"Are you going to leave now so late?"

"Yes; today I'm due to be unfaithful to you with Robín."

"You're not just trying to teach me a lesson, are you?"

"No."

Rosicler's father was taken out to be shot in the city of Orense during the Civil War, he was killed by the lawyer Don Jesús Manzanedo who became quite renowned for making widows, truth to tell, it wouldn't cross anybody's mind to name their daughter Rosicler, he who plays with fire gets his fingers burnt; girls should be named after virgins or saints, not given secular names of dubious taste: Rosicler, Dawn, Aurora . . . well, Aurora's alright, but Atmosphere, Venus, how ridiculous can you get! Rosicler's father was a cashier in a bank and the poor man paid with his life the price on his wretched head.

"Do you believe, Doña Arsenia, that things are really as he said?"

Lázaro Codesal was killed by misfortune as well as by his trusting nature; those Moors are not to be trusted for they're cunning in thought and deed. Nobody knows the name of the Moor who killed Lázaro Codesal while he was jacking off in the shade of a fig tree, with the image of Ádega, naked, in his thoughts, but that hardly matters. Lázaro Codesal was a dab hand at firing stones from a slingshot; he had a deadly aim.

"Bet you couldn't hit that pigeon on the telegraph pole!"

"You do?"

Lázaro Codesal would raise his slingshot and wham! the pigeon on the telegraph pole shot through the air in smithereens.

"Bet you couldn't hit that black cat!"

"You do?"

Lázaro Codesal would swing his slingshot and wham! the black cat shot off shitting sparks with its head split open.

"You don't think it could be the Devil?"

"I don't think so, the Devil hasn't been about here much of late."

The line of the mountain was blotted out when Lázaro Codesal was killed, since that misfortunate day it has never been seen again, as far as I can see, it might have been carried many leagues off, maybe even beyond the Canda and Padornelo gaps on the road to Sanabria. That married man who crossed Lázaro Codesal's path at the Chosco crossroads certainly didn't keep his distance! My God, what a thrashing he got for his pains! Cuckolds have no call to be forward but should conduct themselves in a cautious, prudent, God-fearing manner, it's no easy matter to be a cuckold with dignity and grace.

"I'm going my own way; step aside there! I've no wish to pick a quarrel."

But the other fellow wouldn't step aside so, of course, he got a drubbing and was sent packing, trussed up and blushing like a bride. Moncho Requeixo was with Lázaro Codesal in the Melilla war but he returned alive, lamed but alive and kicking.

"I don't know what became of my leg, I suppose they just chucked it out; I think that when a body has their leg cut off it should be returned to them, well packed down in coarse salt, to take home as a memento."

Moncho Lazybones' two carrier birds, male and female, died on him on the way across the Red Sea; the Little Jesus Cured is a delicate, dreamy little fowl that is only good for carrying *billets doux* and the moment you take it away from its homeland it catches cold and dies of a broken heart. Blind Gaudencio came back from Mass numb with cold.

"It's freezing out there, Anuncia, to my mind this is the end of the world."

"Not at all, man, come here and climb into bed and wait 'til I fetch you a nice hot coffee!"

It has been raining down without respite for either earth or sky for over two hundred days and nights now and the Xeixo vixen, which is already old, arthritic, and weary of life, or so they say, coughs listlessly at the entrance to her lair. If I knew how to play the psaltery—as they did in the old times, but there are no psalteries nowadays—I would spend the evenings playing the psaltery, but I can't. If I could play the banjo, like Don Brégimo Faramiñás, I would while away the hours playing the banjo, that would be company at least, but I can't. What I can play are the bagpipes but the bagpipes should be played outdoors, at the foot of an oak tree, while the lads hoot and cheer and the lasses wait with bated breath for night, with its sweet, swooning complicities, to fall. Since I can play neither the psaltery nor the banjo, and since the bagpipes shouldn't be played indoors, I spend the evenings in bed messing about with whoever I can, or at times alone; but what I can't manage is to bend right over and reach down with my mouth, I can nearly manage it, though not quite, but maybe nobody can, I must enquire. Benicia is very cheerful and never wearies but that, too, can become tiresome. Benicia makes great blood puddings and she has nipples like chestnuts, it's a laugh to see her making blood puddings with her breasts bare.

"Benicia."

"What?"

"Reach me the paper and give me a glass of wine."

"Alright."

The frogs in the Antela lagoon are even more ancient than all the other frogs in Galicia, León, Asturias, Portugal, and Castile; such historic, illustrious frogs are only to be found now in the Rivers Var and Touloulore in Provence, in Lake Balatón in Hungary and in the loughs in the counties of Tipperary and Waterford in Ireland. Our Lord Jesus Christ sprang from the dove and his mother, the Blessed Virgin, came forth from the virginal trumpet of the lily. From a frog called Liorta in the Antela lagoon nine different but related families are descended, they are: the Marvises, the Celas, the Segades, the Faramiñás, the Albites, the Beiras, the Portomouriscos, the Requeixos, and the Lebozáns; this side of the family is known as the Guxindes, there's a strong family likeness and altogether they're a powerful bunch.

It warms the heart to watch Benicia pouring wine stark naked while the rain beats down upon this earth and its fretful, aggrieved, unfettered souls.

"Pour wine over your tits."

"I don't feel like it."

According to the Benedictine monk Arnaldo Wion in his work *Lignum Vitae*, Venice 1595, St. Malachy, Bishop of Armagh in Ireland, laid it out fair and square to the Sisters of Clare in his account of the popes that, God willing, the end shall come to pass in the year 2053 with the second coming of Christ: "The Antela lagoon shall be drained by man and instead of water calamity and sickness shall smite them. And when the water be dried up, man shall delve into the bottom of the lagoon in search of minerals and from that moment hence, in place of the land, starvation and death shall smite them."

We Guxindes enjoy squabbling at *romerías*, what harm is there in that?, also dancing in cloisters and graveyards, cheek to cheek when the opportunity arises. I can play neither the fiddle, the harmonica, the psaltery, nor the banjo, I can play only the bagpipes and that's no good. Gaudencio played the accordion in Sprat's brothel; he played waltzes and two-steps, sometimes the odd tango to keep the clients entertained, but he wouldn't play that mazurka *Ma Petite Marianne*, he only played it in 1936 when Lionheart died and in 1940 when Fabián Minguela—Moucho Carroupo—died. He would never play it again.

"So he kept the clients entertained?"

"I believe so. Gaudencio was always a past master at scales."

His sister Ácega also plays the accordion but what she likes are polkas: *Fanfinette, Mon Amour,* and *Paris, Paris.*

"The dead man who killed my old man strayed from the straight and narrow and you saw yourself how he wound up. The dead man who killed my old man was not a Guxinde, Lord forgive me! he was an outsider and that's what we get for being charitable to tramps, when his father first came here begging alms for the love of God, if only we had well and truly clobbered him there and then, he would never have got to shed the blood of those that fed him; later on, when these matters have long since been forgotten, I won't forget. Let others do what they like! There's a lot of talk hereabouts so for that reason alone it's worth bearing these things in mind. You, Don Camilo, are descended from Guxindes, or rather, you are a Guxinde, and my old man, too, and that has its price to pay. But it also brings its own reward and sense of pride, men are men until after death and we women wait and watch and pass the tale on to our children. I'm going to tell you something that everybody knows, although you don't for you don't spend much time here, but I let it half slip already, d'you recall? I dug up the dead man who killed my old man; one night I went to the graveyard in Carballiño to rob the grave, I brought the remains home and threw them in with the swill for the pig that I later slaughtered and ate, the hams, the *chorizos*, the head, and so on 'til it was done. The Guxindes were delighted and held their tongues and the Carroupos were hopping mad but said nothing either, for they knew they would be the next in line if they did; that's God's law and I believe they wound up leaving the area: some have already gone to Switzerland, others to Germany; as far as I'm concerned they may all perish in the end of the world or be devoured by the gooks."

"Have you none of that Moucho-flavored pork left?"

"Not at all, how could I have any left now?"

The fourth sign of the bastard is a patchy beard, Fabián Minguela is a dapper little dandy. For at least four years Fabián Minguela, the dead man who went about sowing death all over, was bedding Rosalía Trasulfe, the Crazy Goat, just for the asking. The dead man who killed Lionheart as well as Ádega's old man, and maybe a dozen others to boot, was stroking Rosalía Trasulfe, the Crazy Goat's ass, squeezing her tits and stirring up fights from at least 1936 to 1940.

"And you'll sing dumb, too, for I can dispatch you to where I sent others, not one of them ever to return, as you well know!"

Three times Rosalía Trasulfe, the Crazy Goat, got pregnant by the dead man and on each occasion she went to the midwife Damiana Otarelo for an abortion and a parsley purge.

"For many years I've struggled to earn my crust, not as a whore mind you, so I don't want a bastard son by a bastard father."

Rosalía Trasulfe, the Crazy Goat, always says the same thing:

"He trampled all over me, that's for sure, he trampled me just as he wished, but I'm alive and kicking and I gave myself a thorough scrubbing down. Moucho was like the maggots that devour the dead, thriving only on the dead."

Marcos Albite's cart is like a fairground car, all it lacks is the music.

"I'm going to repaint it now, the little star is nearly worn away but the thumbtacks are still good; when I went nuts I didn't care about anything but now I like things to be nice and right as rain. Green paint is nice, I know, but when it dries out it doesn't look so good."

Marcos Albite has a good time in his cart, he gets a little fed up at times, for boredom would weary anyone, but he enjoys himself and there's many another who has a worse time of it.

"I'm going to make you a real humdinger of a St. Camilo, this St. Camilo will stop folks in their tracks."

We had to lug Policarpo la Bagañeira back from Briñidelo in a handcart for he was so heartsore from the business of his hand, that bite from the stallion really threw him out of sorts and he developed fever.

"A great deal?"

"Well, not so very much."

Rosa Loureses, the mother of the Marvises, wouldn't let him leave.

"He's the same flesh and blood as my own sons and he's not in the way here. He may take a turn for the worse up the mountain. You'll have to let him sleep for at least two days."

"Alright."

The folks from the corral, the Guxindes, rather, are scattered all over Briñidelo, Puxedo, and Cela. The Marvises and Policarpo, too, stayed with their cousins; Cidrán Segade and his brother-in-law Gaudencio, who was later to lose his sight, slept at the hearth of Urbano Randín—vermin hunter, smuggler, and as cross-eyed as they come.

"Don't catch his eye, Cidrán, don't you know cross-eyed folks can strike you senseless!"

Don Brégimo lodged with blind Pepiño Requiás who let him have his bed for a *peseta*. Marcos Albite and Moncho went off to the Laurentinas in Puxedo while Robín Lebozán and I headed on over to Cela to see my relations the Venceáses.

"Stay here both of you, the house is plenty big enough and it'll be company for us!"

The Venceáses lived with their mother, Dorinda, a hundred and three years of age and forever complaining of the cold, and with a maid who made the best coffee liqueur you could ask for.

"What's that woman's name?"

"We don't know, the poor creature is dumb so, of course, she couldn't tell us; she looks Portuguese but maybe she isn't from anywhere for she has no papers, she's been with us for donkey's years, over fifty years now, and she wouldn't harm a fly. In the village she's known as the Mute, not as a nickname but just because she is."

The Mute made a corker of a coffee liqueur, make a note of this if you wish: fill a pot with the following ingredients: a panful of top quality *aguardiente* distilled from grapes, two pounds of roasted coffee beans, four pounds of candy sugar, two handfuls of walnuts, shelled, of course, and broken into pieces to release the essence, and the rinds of two Seville oranges. For two weeks you stir it thoroughly with a hazel rod, a hundred clockwise turns at daybreak and another hundred counterclockwise at nightfall; after that you strain it through brown paper, bottle it, and lay it down for at least a year. Some folks store the liqueur in wide-necked jars sealed with wax and others don't strain it but let it mature in an oaken barrel, it's all a matter of taste. The Mute was delighted when Robín and I broached a bottle of her liqueur, clicking her tongue in excitement; when the Mute is happy, apparently she lets fly some long, rip-roaring farts.

Loliña Moscoso Rodríguez—that's the wife of Baldomero Gamuzo, well Baldomero Marvís Ventela or Fernández, Lionheart—keeps her five children as neat as pins, you'd swear she even polished them, while the children of Rosa Roucón— that's Tanis the Demon's wife—and there's five of them, too, run about bare-assed and snotty-nosed, but we're all as God made us and you don't buy anisette for nothing.

"Will you have a drop of anisette?"

"Is it time yet?"

Chelo Domínguez from los Avelaíños, that's the wife of Roque, representative of the blessed St. Carallan upon this earth, has a hard cross to bear through this vale of tears.

"Count your blessings, Chelo, better a feast than a famine."

"So they say "

Chelo Domínguez is a great cook, she bakes delicious pork pasties, joints of ham that she splits into three or four chunks and browns on the open coals before braising, her tripe—beef not lamb—and brains with cutlets are something to write home about.

"Do you think the Japanese are really so jealous?"

"Why do you ask?"

"For no reason at all, except that I've heard it said."

Don Benigno Portomourisco Turbisqueda went through life proclaiming he would live to be over a hundred but he died at ninety after drinking more wine than his body could hold.

"And you say that nobody ever saw him sozzled?"

"How could I say such a thing? Everybody saw Don Benigno half seas over and don't think he went out of his way to conceal it either!"

Don Benigno was as straight as a ramrod, although towards the end of his life he walked with a slight stoop.

"Coot!"

"Yes, Don Benigno?"

"Get into that vine there and don't come out 'til the sweat is dripping from your brow!"

"Yes, sir."

Luisiño Bocelo, Coot, was a gentle, obedient eunuch who was the butt of many jokes.

"Coot!"

"Yes, Don Benigno?"

"Drop your britches, I want to give you a wallop on the ass!"

"Yes, sir."

When Luisiño Bocelo, Coot, was in the seminary his companions used to wet his bed and afterwards he would feel the cold seep into his bones.

"Coot!"

"Yes, Don Benigno?"

"Did you take bread and water to the mistress?"

The second husband of Georgina, lame Moncho Lazybones' cousin, also wound up kicking the bucket.

"I've got to get the skids under me for I'm no spring chick any longer and in this neck of the woods you always need a man, although we may be widowed two or three times, we women should never be alone."

Moncho always speaks fondly of his aunt Micaela, Georgina's mother.

"She was always so good to me, when I was a lad she used to jack me off every night; in the past families were closer-knit."

Adela and Georgina are sisters but they don't take after one another, except maybe in their fondness for wine, tobacco, and their beds.

"What's the point of living after all?"

"Indeed you're right, girl, there's more to this life than passing on the genes."

Adela and Georgina love Miss Ramona to play tangos for them on the phonograph: *Peach Blossom*, *Shanty-town Tune*, and *Downhill*.

"How I'd love to be a man and dance the tango roughly!"

"What a thing to say, girl!"

One night last year Adela and Georgina danced tangos with Miss Ramona and Rosicler.

"Can I take off my blouse?"

"Do whatever you like."

My aunt Salvadora, that's the Casandulfe Raimundo's mother, lives alone in Madrid and doesn't want to hear tell of the village.

"Nor of her relations either?"

"Nor of her relations either."

On my mother's side of the family I still have four uncles and aunts: Aunt Salvadora and Uncle Cleto, both widowed, and Aunt Jesusa and Aunt Emilita, spinsters. Uncle Cleto whiles away the time playing percussion, his "jazz band," rather.

"How old is he?"

"I don't know, seventy-six or seventy-eight."

Aunt Jesusa and Aunt Emilita spend their time praying, gossiping and piddling, both of them are incontinent, you see. Aunt Jesusa and Aunt Emilita don't speak to Uncle Cleto, well, it's not so much that they don't speak to one another, they loathe and detest one another and make no bones about it.

"Men should be hanged! Cleto spends his day bashing that drum and cymbals just to annoy us. And he knows the migraines we suffer!"

My aunts and uncle live together in the same house, my two aunts downstairs, where it's damp, and my uncle upstairs, where it's drier. When he gets bored, Uncle Cleto throws up; he sticks his fingers down his throat and vomits his guts up wherever he happens to be, in a washbasin or behind the dresser, apparently he thoroughly enjoys throwing up. When Uncle Cleto was in Paris on his honeymoon, his wife fell ill and he left her in hospital with the excuse that sick people made him ill; he received notification of her death in a letter from the consul.

"Poor Lourdes wasn't long for this world, that's for sure, well, I did what I could for her, I left her in a good hospital with everything, even the funeral expenses, paid for; that was a stroke of bad luck."

My grandparents were well-heeled, they owned a tannery and a coffin factory, The Great Beyond, but my uncles and aunts squandered the inheritance so now they're stone broke and living hand-to-mouth.

"It's hard to say which is worse, hunger or filth; men plump for filth while we women opt for hunger, though maybe there's the odd slut that wouldn't."

The strangled vermin in the sacristan's vineyard grow more shrivelled and putrid by the day. The half-wit from

Martiñá bares her breasts to the dead fox as she munches hazelnuts.

"Clear off, you wretched half-wit! You bring more corruption than Sodom and Gomorrah! Cover up your miserable breasts and pray to the Lord Jesus Christ or we'll all be damned through your filthy fault!"

One day the sacristan caught Catuxa Bainte with a stone between the breasts and blood oozing from her mouth; the sacristan nearly died laughing.

"My God, got you nicely there! Just about mashed your lungs, too!"

Ducking from the raft in Lucio Mouro's millpond, Catuxa Bainte, the half-wit from Martiñá, is like a straying orphan lamb, angelic and untainted by original sin.

"Is the water cold?"

"No, sir, not really."

When a swarm of flies heaves into view you know that beneath them is the priest from San Miguel de Buciños, whose flesh must taste like honey.

"Dolores!"

"Yes, Father Merexildo?"

"This wine has turned sour, you drink it!"

"Yes, Father."

Dolores bends her elbow and is none too pernickety about what she drinks, almost anything will do. With one arm missing, Dolores loses her balance when she gets tipsy.

"There are days when everything goes askew, apparently there's a heavier load on one side than on the other!"

Father Merexildo is renowned for his bodily excesses and his rock-hard rigidity; had he not entered the priesthood, he could have made a living by displaying his natural endowments to the public at *romerías*.

"Roll up! Roll up! ladies and gentlemen! and view the organ of the Antichrist! the most enormous member, begging your pardon! throughout the whole of the Iberian peninsula. Don't shove! There's room for everybody, have no fear that the exhibit will shrivel with the passing of time!"

But, of course, there are certain things that priests cannot do out of consideration for the susceptibilities of others.

"Dolores!"

"Yes, Father Merexildo?"

"These apples are rotten, you eat them!"

"Yes, Father."

"If you ever serve me rotten apples again, I'll shove them up your ass!"

"Yes, sir."

Accompanied by Crown Prince Michael, King Carl of Romania visited Belgrade. Luisiño Bocelo, the eunuch servant belonging to Don Benigno, and Dolores, the crippled maid at the priest from San Miguel's farm, were two creatures singled out by the gnarled, sere, and shrivelled hand of wrath to be kicked around.

"Kicks aimed right in the pit of the stomach?"

"Just wherever they happen to land, that's neither here nor there."

I must make a note to ask my cousins in Corunna for more cheroots to give to Marcos Albite. I have to repay him for his carved St. Camilo, which, chances are, will be a work of art. When we went up to the Xurés corral, Marcos Albite and I addressed one another by the familiar *tú*, then the war came along and a great deal happened to mess things up so now sometimes we're close and others not; in the company of others we're more formal and use the polite form of address but on the whole I think I feel closer to him than he does to me. I must remember to ask my cousins in Corunna for more cheroots for him. Marcos Albite is a good sort and he must get fed up in that cart of his.

"You can hardly see the little star now, I must paint it again; green paint does very well, as everybody says, but it wears off just as soon as any other and then you have to touch it up again."

A record player is better than a phonograph, swankier and more up-to-date, a record player doesn't have a trumpet, the voice comes out through little slits in the side. Rosicler has some Argentinian relations who call the phonograph a gramophone, the gramophone is even older than the phonograph. The record player which the Casandulfe Raimundo gave our cousin is an Odeon Cadet model. For deep, soulful music, *Clair de Lune*, *Für Elise*, a Chopin polonaise, there's nothing to beat the piano, whereas for music for listening to while canoodling, when you let yourself be swept away, the record player is better for it is more mysterious and has more bite to it. For the *Candle Waltz*, which is somewhere in between, either the piano or the record player will do. The piano is small and made of lignum vitae with an ivory keyboard. Miss Ramona inherited it from her mother who played elegantly, even stylishly. One evening last winter, when they were both tired of dancing together, Miss Ramona said to Rosicler:

"Quit jacking off that monkey, it's all very well but it's bad luck for he's consumptive into the bargain!"

"Poor Jeremiah "

Miss Ramona's piano is a Cramer, Beale and Co. model adorned with two silver candlesticks; in the past folks lived better than they do nowadays.

"But people died younger, too."

"I'm not so sure of that."

Robín Lebozán used to take chocolates to Rosicler.

"Here, take these to keep your breasts firm and hard, firm breasts are what give me a hard-on."

"Shut up, you swine!"

Robín Lebozán lends Miss Ramona books of verse. When she wrote *On the Banks of the River Sar*, Rosalía de Castro* was already living in La Matanza opposite the west Depot and even closer to the River Ulla. *On the Banks of the River Sar* is written in Castilian whereas *New Broadsheets* is in the Galician tongue, though both are very beautiful and inspired. *On the Banks of the River Sar* was published shortly before her death, Rosalía de Castro croaked at an early age, she didn't even reach fifty. Robín Lebozán takes it for granted that Rosalía de Castro was not born into this world in Santiago de Compostela, as the books claim, but in the town of Padrón,** whence she was hastily removed to lessen the suffering of her mother, who had been brought into disrepute by a priest; if they had only known then that, with the passage of time, the infant girl was to become the province's greatest poet, maybe they wouldn't have acted so hastily and with so little foresight; why, they nearly let her die!

"Right asses they were!"

"Well, times were different then."

Robín Lebozán believes that Rosalía de Castro had a love affair with the poet Bécquer, but there's no proof. Bécquer was more or less the same age as Rosalía de Castro but he died even younger, in fact he hardly lived at all! Miss Ramona liked *Breezes from my land* by Curros,*** who was from Cela-

---

* Rosalía de Castro Murquía (1837–85), Galicia's best-known poet, wrote in both Galician and Castilian. —Trans.
** Birthplace of C.J.C. —Trans.
*** Manuel Curros Enriquéz (1851–1908), Galician poet/journalist. —Trans.

nova, on the road to Xurés, and was also Robín's great uncle.

"Maybe that's where you get your fondness for books from."

"Maybe!"

Sea Breeze by Don Ramón Cabanillas* is very good, too, He's from Cambados on the Arosa estuary, and he's hale and hearty, even though we're nearly halfway through the twentieth century; I'm delighted, for nowadays there are fewer and fewer poets around, these days there's nothing but footballers and army types. Rosicler, too, is fairly fond of poetry. The Casandulfe Raimundo hums *Sacred Heart* as he shaves.

"Don't you know anything else?"

"Why do you ask?"

"Never mind, forget it."

In Rauco's inn they serve excellent tripe, even better than their octopus. Raimundo and our cousin only spend the whole night together when they are travelling, at Easter they were in Lisbon; Raimundo always takes our cousin a white camellia when he goes to see her.

"Here, Mona, so you know I savor you and never forget you."

Raimundo gives Rosicler chocolates, each to their own. Fabián Minguela—Moucho—plays dominoes in Rauco's inn; the Carroupos are bad losers, the pockmark on their forehead flares up and they don't mince their words. Tripe-Butcher, the father of the Gamuzos, always held that a bad loser can't stick the course, or rather, a bad loser meets a sticky end, that's more like it: lying in the gutter with their head split open, or up the mountain where the Zacumeira wolf roams, or somewhere, with their guts spilling from their belly. Raimundo likes to go

---

* Ramón Cabanillas Enriquéz (1876–1959), Galician poet. —Trans.

up the mountain on horseback. Some mornings, if it isn't raining, he rides out with Miss Ramona; Caruso, our cousin's horse, is getting long in the tooth but he's still as sturdy as an ox.

"Do you think the Crazy Goat would dare mess about with the Zacumeira wolf?"

"Christ, what a thing to say!"

The outsider saw that Moucho Carroupo was out on his own. The fifth sign of the bastard is in the hands: they're limp, clammy, and cold. Fabián Minguela has hands that are sort of slimy.

"I don't like to raise my voice but if you don't cough up what you owe, I'll split your face."

The cat in Rauco's inn has no name but the landlady calls it pusscat and it understands. While Moucho coughs up the dough, the outsider strokes the cat and without even bothering to watch.

"Leave the money on the table, I'll fetch it if I feel like it."

Moucho had to swallow it for nobody came to his defense, nor, indeed, did he deserve them to. Fabián Minguela— Moucho—works sitting down like all the Carroupos, cobblers don't ride horseback nor do they farm the land. Moucho is a tailor and also fiddles about with bits of haberdashery, spools of thread, celluloid and metal buttons, cotton socks, hand-kerchieves, and other odds and ends. The Carroupos are not from hereabouts, God knows where they hail from.

"Leave the money where it can be clearly seen, leave the *pesos* and *pesetas* for all to see and then clear out! Bring out more wine, ma'am, if you don't mind, that is, for I have no wish to trouble anybody!"

On Sundays Moucho dresses his hair with Omega lotion and sports a bright green bow tie and crêpe handkerchief to match, which he fastens with a safety pin so that it can't be pinched.

"What a fop!"

"Of the first order!"

The sixth sign of the bastard is a furtive look about the eyes. Fabián Minguela would never look you in the eye. Miss Ramona's parakeet is as old as the hills, Miss Ramona's parakeet nibbles peanuts and recites the Holy Rosary; virgo potens, ora pro nobis, virgo clemens, ora pro nobis, virgo fidelis, ora pro nobis; there are too many virgins in that, it's like having the nuns in the whorehouse guiding the fallen women along the straight and narrow. Miss Ramona's four servants are as follows: Braulio Doade, 82 years of age, from Camposancos; Antonio Vegadecabo, 81 years of age, from Cenlle; Puriña Córrego, 84 years of age, from los Baños de Molgas, and Sabadela Soulecín, 79 years of age, from San Cristóbal de Cea. The parakeet is the oldest of the lot for nobody kicks the bucket over there: virgo prudentissima, ora pro nobis, virgo veneranda, ora pro nobis, virgo predicanda, ora pro nobis, there are even more virgins for you, it's like having the Jesuit nuns breaking in lustful young lads of good family. Miss Ramona's four servants are nearly blind and deaf as posts, some more so than others, of course, but all of them are bronchitic and arthritic; the truth of the matter is there's not one of them worth a tinker's damn but you can't chuck them out without further ado to be devoured by the wolves.

"I'm duty bound to them, I know; but what saddens me is to think that at some time or another each of these old biddies' hearts must have leapt with joy or love, way back before independence in the Colonies, of course. How absurd it seems! The parakeet was already well on in years when he arrived from Cuba, what beats me is how he adapted to the climate here."

Ádega carries on the tale of the dead men, someone has to keep track of the deaths relentlessly reaping the lives of men.

"The Bidueiros half-wit did not hang himself but was hanged, as a sort of experiment. They didn't mean him any harm they just sort of got carried away; sometimes the Devil sees to it that, through some slip or other, someone is accidentally hanged, it's all a matter of bad luck, the Bidueiros half-wit was hanged as a sort of experiment, they hanged him as a joke but he well and truly died, apparently they caught him unawares."

Roque Gamuzo is called the Cleric of Comesaña as a joke, it was also as a joke that they hanged the half-wit from Bidueiros and afterwards they had to bury him. The clerk of the court didn't know what to write on the form.

"What shall I put on the form?"

"Put whatever you like, it was a piece of bad luck, all his life the poor half-wit was dogged by bad luck and misfortune, some folks are born under a lucky star and others not, that's all."

Father Merexildo Agrexán, the priest in San Miguel de Buciños, said three Masses for his son the half-wit from Bidueiros without telling anyone the whys or the wherefores.

Chelo Domínguez bore her husband, Roque Gamuzo, six sons.

"Did any of them match up to their father's proportions?"

"Well now, there have been no complaints to date."

Chelo keeps her sons as neat as pins, she's very proud of them.

"Anyway, haven't I reason to be? Not many women have seven such manly men as Roque and the boys about the house; it would gladden your heart to see them!"

Aunt Lourdes, Uncle Cleto's wife, died in less than no time, she didn't last out the honeymoon. Aunt Lourdes died in Paris for she caught smallpox from the French, who are not overly fond of soap and water. But Ádega doesn't believe that's what carried her off in the end.

"That cannot be, for Miss Lourdes, God rest her soul! was born in a leap year and it's a well-known fact that nobody born in a leap year is smitten with smallpox."

"Is that a hard and fast rule?"

"As hard and fast as they come!"

When Uncle Cleto returned, having left Aunt Lourdes behind, my grandparents, who were still alive in those days, were deeply moved.

"Poor Lourdes! How distressed Cleto must be! The poor departed soul was useless, of course, but she might have hung on a while longer! Here at the factory we could have made her a coffin worthy of a daughter-in-law: a fine number 1 English casket in walnut with bronze fastenings. Poor Lourdes! How soon the Lord chose to call her home on high!"

Aunt Lourdes was buried in a common grave because Uncle Cleto had paid the funeral expenses but not for the grave itself, the French are very finicky when it comes to detail and the consul said it made no difference to him; dying in a foreign country is always a slap in the face for you're not used to their ways.

"Are the French Catholics?"

"Yes, I think so, well, they're Catholics in their own way; it's the English and the Germans that are Protestants."

"I see."

The Gamuzo twins, Celestino Sprig, the hunter, and Ceferino Ferret, the angler, are priests in San Miguel de Taboadela and Santa María de Carballeda near Piñor; before that Ferret was in San Adrián de Zapaeus, in Rairiz de Veiga, the hometown of that famous fighter Celso Masilde, Chapón, who was in Bailarín's Party until 1948 when they were all slain in an ambush. Of course, that Bailarín has nothing to do with Esteban Cortizas, the other Bailarín, fitter of fishing boat engines and head of the local Falangist Party in Mugardos, where he was shot by the Maquis in 1946. Chapón was also involved in the guerrilla campaign around about the Ordenes area with Benigno García Andrade, Foucellas, head of the Fourth Battalion, who was executed in Corunna in 1951. Ferret goes to visit Benicia on the first and third Tuesday of every month; a bit of order never goes amiss. Benicia is a lively lay but also very deferential, she always addresses Ferret, well, I mean Don Ceferino, as Father. When he takes leave of her she kisses his hand.

"Keep in good health, Father Ceferino. Did you enjoy that?"

"Yes, my dear, God bless you! I enjoyed it a great deal."

Priests are God's creatures, too, just like spiders, flowers, and young girls skipping out of school, and God forgives these transgressions.

"Harder! Harder, Father Ceferino! Don't stop now! Oh! Oh!"

Benicia has blue eyes and nipples like chestnuts, Benicia can neither read nor write but she goes through this life sensing everything by instinct: love and boredom, life and death, pleasure and pain, indeed everything. The Casandulfe Raimundo is even more skilled than Ferret in bed, well, he was at university and it shows; when he was a student in Santiago de Compostela he learnt a lot of tricks in the whorehouses there, a good start will set you up for life. Ferret is an angler and often takes the odd trout to Benicia.

"Here, when we've . . . , well, you know what I mean
. . . , you can fry one for me and another for yourself."

"Yes, Father, whatever you wish."

Sprig is a hunter and he slakes his thirst at other wells.

"Fina."

"Yes, Father Celestino?"

"I've brought you a rabbit for us to eat tomorrow night."

"It's that time of the month, Father."

"What difference does that make? You know that doesn't
bother me at all."

Fina is a widow, raven-haired and willowy; Fina is thirty or
thirty-two years of age and she's a fun-loving, lustful gal from
Pontevedra, she came here some time back and stayed put, she
is nicknamed the Pontevedra woman, also the Sea Cow,
though nobody quite knows why.

"Listen, what you say about her being lustful, is that not a
bit over the top?"

"Maybe."

They say Fina broke her husband's heart and drove him into
an early grave, but that's not true; cuckolds are as tough as
nails. Fina has always shown a strong predilection for the
cloth, she took to it like a duck to water and the moment she
saw a priest her eyes would light up.

"They're very manly men altogether and, since they haven't
a care in the world, they go at it great guns, what a treat it is to
do it with them!"

Fina is not so deferential to Father Celestino as Benicia to
Father Ceferino, she also calls him Father but sometimes, in
the heat of the moment, she slips up.

"You give me the hots, you bugger . . . ! Sorry, Father
Celestino, God forgive me! but you took my breath away."

Nobody could sing the song that grates in the axle of the ox-cart as it rumbles along the dirt track warning death to keep at bay, the wolf howls and the wild boar snorts but the brambles never take fright, you can tell they're tough mountain stock.

"Did you enjoy that?"

It drizzles down with faith, hope, and charity upon the fields of maize and rye, upon virtue and vice in partnership as well as upon solitary vice, upon the docile cow and the mountain fox, maybe it even drizzles down without faith, hope, and charity and nobody knows, maybe nobody pays any heed, it drizzles down steadfastly as the world continues upon its daily round: a man gets involved in racketeering, a woman rubs her privates with a dead rabbit, and a child dies of stomach cramps from eating greengage plums. Robín Lebozán gives chocolates to Rosicler who persists in jacking off Jeremiah the monkey, a little girl dies kicked by a horse, Archimedes said something about give me a fulcrum etc. It drizzles even-handedly, even monotonously upon this world, there's nothing left beyond the line of the mountain, the Good Lord wiped everything out when Lázaro Codesal was killed in the land of the Moor. Fina's late husband was called Antón Guntimil and he was always in ill health, he was delicate and sickly and even had a stutter, it was a tremendous effort for him to get the words out. Fina treated him unkindly and laughed at his weak points, in that respect she behaved badly.

"You're just like a simpleton, for your information: the Franciscan friar from the Missions has got a far bigger and firmer one than you, at least twice as big. He didn't know much, that's for sure, well nobody is born knowing everything, but at least he was able to learn."

Antón's blood boiled and he struck out at his wife and hit her

on the ribs; she struck him with a frying pan right in the middle
of his face.

"Have you had enough, you bloody cuckold?"

Fina stamped off shifting her ass as if to break wind and
slammed the door behind her. What a way to behave!

"Come and get me, if you want me!"

Miss Ramona's house is just outside the village of Mesós do
Reino, coming from Lalín it's on the left-hand side. Mesós do
Reino is a new hamlet. In the past this cluster of houses was
known as Mesós do Moire because when they built the N 527,
the Zamora-Santiago highway, the first folks to set up shop
were from the nearby region of Moire, also within the boundaries of Piñor, on the right-hand side going towards Castile.
The name Mesós do Reino—Inns of the Kingdom—came
later and has nothing at all to do with the Kingdom of Heaven,
the Kingdom of Galicia, nor even the Kingdom of Spain. The
name came about because the most influential shopkeeper in
the area was a man named José Blanco García, nicknamed
José the Kingdom. Miss Ramona's house isn't very old, it
couldn't be much more than two hundred years old but it
enshrines great mystery and nobility, as well as many's the tale
of passion, illness, and calamity. Miss Ramona's family is important, hereabouts at least, and in important families there is
always some mishap or other. Miss Ramona's mother drowned
in the River Asneiros, which is not so very deep, whether by
accident or design it was never known. Miss Ramona's garden,
with its bay trees and hydrangeas, slopes down to the river,
where you might easily slip and fall in; at times Romulus and
Remus, the two swans on the pond, glide as far as the river,
folks say they bring bad luck. Antón, Fina's husband, was
killed by a train in full view of everyone in Orense station.

"Why didn't he jump out of the way?"

"How would I know? The poor man never had his wits about him."

Fina was already roasting rabbits for Father Celestino while her husband was alive. Fina always did her best to please priests and be nice to them. My mother's house—well, now it belongs to my uncle and aunts—is in Albarona in the parish of San Xoan de Barrán. When Uncle Cleto can't sleep he plays the drums and swigs brandy, which he buys from the keg, nearly always on credit in the hope of better times to come, from Rauco's inn. When Aunt Jesusa and Aunt Emilita aren't praying they're tittle-tattling.

"And pissing?"

"Oh, something dreadful! They've been pissing to beat the band for well-nigh twenty years now."

I think Aunt Lourdes was lucky to be buried in Paris, though the truth is you never know; of course, my grandparents would have liked her to die in Galicia, in accordance with tradition.

"She was pretty useless, that was as plain as the nose on your face, but other pretty useless women manage to hold on a while longer. Did you ever see the like of the coffins the French use?! Little better than papier-mâché!"

Aunt Jesusa and Aunt Emilita won't break breath to their brother except to enquire if he has fulfilled his obligations.

"To hell with you both! I'll do just whatever takes my fancy!"

"Lord, what a way to behave!"

When Aunt Jesusa and Aunt Emilita cross his path they look the other way so Uncle Cleto whistles just to enrage them.

"Holy God! What have we done to deserve such a heavy cross to bear?"

My aunts and uncle wouldn't speak to one another, they got embroiled in a dispute about who was to occupy which plot in the cemetery and wound up grievously insulting one another, quietly, of course, but grievous insults all the same. When Uncle Cleto had goaded them into a passion, he would let go a rip-roaring fart—a huge, thundering, demonic fart—and Aunt Jesusa and Aunt Emilita would be vexed to the point of tears.

"A fart that thundered like the end of the world?"

"Something like that, more or less."

Uncle Cleto plays the drums quite well by ear, whistling and humming along, Uncle Cleto never fears loneliness for he keeps it at bay with his cymbals and drums. Aunt Jesusa and Aunt Emilita have cascarilla tea and buns in the afternoon, it doesn't cost much but tastes delicious. Fabián Minguela— Moucho—is barred from these homes: the aunts and uncle's, Miss Ramona's, Raimundo's, and all the Guxinde houses; although nothing untoward ever happened—and many things do happen—he's better kept out. Not because he's an outsider, why, the man who ordered him to place the *pesos* on the table when he lost the game of dominoes is even more of an outsider and nobody ever ordered him to shut up or threw him out; we've nothing against foreigners in these parts. The seventh sign of the bastard is a reedy little voice, Fabián Minguela has that squeaky sort of voice like the Brides of the Lamb of God who sing in the church choir. Despite his respectful title, Don Jesús Manzanedo was a well-known murderer; chances are he'll burn in hell for the whole of eternity and for centuries of centuries. Amen. Don Jesús died in his bed, indeed that's a fact, but with his body rotting and reeking of death, his children left the room for they couldn't bear the stench and used to soak their handkerchieves with eau de cologne, he also died racked with pain, in just as much pain as he had remorse in his soul. God metes out His punishment without recourse to stick or stone, and as for Moucho—he shouldn't have got involved—indeed not even his mortal remains endure, nor shall they be treated with respect.

"Is it cold out?"

"Not really. Many's the morning chillier than today."

Benicia is like a heater, she's good company and gives great delight, listen to what we're telling you: since we love you, we're glad you can play neither the fiddle not the harmonica, Benicia is like a mill that goes on and on and never stops.

"Will you hand me the paper?"

"What do you want it for?"

"For no reason at all, really, I've already read it."

Benicia is as gentle as a whelped she-wolf, she enjoys doing good.

"Will you move over in the bed?"

"Alright."

Benicia can hold her breath for over a minute and gulp for air afterwards, that's very unusual, she holds her breath while you mount her as if she were dead, dead bodies are cold but she's not, Benicia burns like fire; when she comes alive again all of a sudden and breathes as freely as anyone, she hots up and tears you to shreds, kissing the nape of your neck even your blessed soul, you have to watch your step.

"Close the shutters for me there, I want to sleep a bit."

When Miss Ramona was a girl they used to take her to bathe in the sea because she was a very bad color, they went to Cambados on the Arosa estuary, where her cousins the Méndez Cotabads lived, there were hordes of them and they were very nice and affectionate, there were nine of them always raising a hullaballoo, fishing for crabs, eating bread and honey. The two youngest—Mercedes and Beatriz—were twins, with long braids and glasses, proper little minxes they were, they used to run over the rooftops and not a soul said boo to them.

"Why would they? Those little girls wouldn't have fallen even if they had been pushed."

In Cambados there's at least three, maybe four, meters between high and low water and when the tide goes out the fishing boats lie in the mud, surrounded by live crabs, scavenging gulls, dead cats, and the odd dead hen. In Cambados they stayed right on the seashore, in the Pearl of Cuba Inn, run by the descendants of the Widow Domínguez; Doña Pilar, the landlady, served delicious food. In those years Miss Ramona was always called Mona, now she's only called that on occasion. Every morning at seven o'clock—there's no point in wasting time—they used to take Mona to La Toja because you can't bathe in Cambados, they used to take her across in the motor launch which is a lovely, exciting crossing, with the bow slicing through the waves and the wake trailing behind the stern, which always seemed so romantic, at times you would see dolphins; they used to return from La Toja on the four o'clock crossing. The best time for bathing is after the blessing of the waters for the Feast of the Virgin of Carmen, that's after July 16. They used to give Mona three batches of nine dips then let her rest for three days in between, as well as bathing she used to take Scott's emulsion, a tonic for the blood and nervous system. Before the bathing season, they would purge Mona for three days in a row with Carabaña water to cleanse her bowels so that the bathing would do her good, afterwards they would allow her a little bottle of soda water to take the taste away. The memory of those days still strikes terror in Miss Ramona's heart, being a child is even harder than being a woman.

"What I like best is when you go to bed with me, Raimundo . . . , and you haven't slept with me for over a week now, I used to get very bored as a child, I was always bored and now I'm well on the way to old age, I'm nearly an old woman now. Help yourself to more brandy and pour me a snifter, too. Why don't you take me to Lisbon again?"

The Casandulfe Raimundo could not for the life of him figure out how he got the dose of crab lice he had, the other day he went to Orense and spent a while in Sprat's brothel, that's true, but the girls there usually take good care of themselves. Raimundo said nothing to our cousin Ramona, it's hard to explain and, anyway, women are very put off by that sort of thing, it really turns them off. Raimundo doused himself with Crabesol, the most effective, rapid, and economical parasiticide, English Oyl is good, too, though everybody knows what it's for, it doesn't leave a stain, smells of lavender, and kills all types of parasites instantaneously without any nasty side effects and then there's Magic Oil which has the advantage of not leaving a stain and at the same time it has a pleasant smell; Raimundo chose Crabesol because it's manufactured locally.

"I'm concerned for at times I get sort of palpitations and my heart starts pounding."

"Could it be that you're smoking too much?"

"I've no idea. Maybe."

General Rogelio Caridad Pita, head of the XV Brigade, was shot in Corunna before the war began, later on we'll hear more about that; his son Paco came over from America in 1941, or maybe 1940, to make contact with the guerrillas but he was arrested by the authorities. The Briñidelo Marvises—Roque and his three sons Segundo, Evaristo, and Camilo—were in with Bermes' Party but luckily they got away and were able to return home safe and sound. Those relations from the Cela area, over by Padrenda, with the River Limia in between, are neither Galicians nor Portuguese, their dialect is more Portuguese than Galician, they neither speak nor understand Spanish, the border is not closely guarded and cattle smuggling thrives in those parts, the children from around about go to school in Paradela on the other side of the Portuguese border, my cousins the Briñidelo Marvises went as far afield as Asturias with Bermes' Party.

Things didn't work out too well for Marcos Albite, you can survive without legs but it's better to have them so you can get about from one place to another and kick things about a bit if you want. When he's in his little cart, Marcos Albite pisses into an old pepper tin, the half-wit from Martiñá rinses it out for him in the stream so that it doesn't get smelly, the half-wit from Martiñá has a heart of gold.

"Do you think this rain will last much longer?"

"That I couldn't say, ma'am; don't think that I wouldn't like the sun to come out too."

Plastered Pepiño works in the Repose, that's the same coffin factory as Matías Marvís, Joker, works in. Plastered Pepiño is an electrician's assistant and he wanders around with his mouth hanging open, he's either a simpleton or can't breathe properly through his nose. Pepiño Pousada Coires is known as Plastered because of the way he walks. Plastered Pepiño had meningitis as a child and is heeled over to one side for life as a result. Nowadays there's a lot of talk about the sexual question, about the sexual problem: that's the same as the sexual question, maybe it even springs from the sexual problem etc.

"Do you think so?"

"No, I don't. But you won't deny that there's a lot of talk about it."

Plastered Pepiño's problem is that he likes groping little boys, whereas others go for big, fat, buxom women. First he gives them sweets and then, once he has built up their trust, he fondles their bottoms, their thighs, and their little willies, he would have done well at one of those private schools, but the truth of the matter is that Pepiño's parents, seeing he was a sort of moron, never paid too much attention to him.

"He'll sort things out in his own way, you'll see; that sort of lad is governed by instinct, they're just like serpents."

"Really?"

"You bet! Even worse!"

Plastered Pepiño grew up left to his own devices and abandoned by the hand of God and, in due course, married like everyone else and produced two daughters, both of them feeble-minded, who died before the year was out. His wife (I can't remember her name for the life of me, it's on the tip of my tongue but it won't come to me) ran away with a travelling salesman, a native of Astorga, and she's still with him. When Plastered Pepiño's wife ran off and he recovered his freedom, a look of happiness lit up his face.

"To hell with it, life's great on your own!"

One black day Plastered Pepiño was caught messing about with little Simon the Lamb, a six-year-old deaf-mute, that he had almost strangled, so he was sent first to prison and later to the nut-house; after they caught him they whacked him and rained kicks and blows upon him, not that they meant him any real harm, of course, more as a way of passing the time. When his wife found out . . . , just a moment, her name was Concepción Estivelle Gresande, they used to call her Concha the Clam, she said she wanted nothing to do with it, that as far as she was concerned he could drop dead or shrivel up and die, for all she cared.

"I have nothing against him, I swear, he doesn't matter a

damn to me, but if he dropped dead tomorrow, believe me, I wouldn't lose any sleep over it."

After she ran off with the fellow from Astorga, Concha the Clam blossomed. What a difference!

"A change does a woman good!"

"Come on now! What about men?!"

Matías the Joker has things well sorted out and has no thought of remarrying.

"If I had children I would have to look out for them, but since I don't have any . . . Puriña was very good, although she was always delicate and telling tales of woe; the worst about women is not that they fall sick, they're always sick, and that's a fact, but the worst is when they tell you all about their illnesses and there's not a soul—not even the Blessed Lord himself—could put up with that sort of thing."

Matías the Joker is fond of dancing, playing cards, and conjuring tricks, he also plays snooker and dominoes, tells funny stories and drinks glasses of sweet anisette and he's fond of coconut cookies and coffee-flavored lozenges. Matías' two younger brothers live with him: Scorpion, who's a deaf-mute but smart enough and Shrill who's sickly in health and a touch simple-minded. Benito Scorpion goes with prostitutes once a month, but at least he works and earns his crust; Salustio Shrill hardly budges from the house and sits about sighing. Puriña was very beautiful, a languid beauty, not like her younger sister Loliña, Lionheart's wife, who was a wild, fierce beauty; hereabouts there are many women who are good-looking in either of these ways. Loliña was crushed up against the wall by an ox. Julián Wideawake was also known as Jules. The wife of Jules Marvís Ventela, or Fernández, the Chantada watchmaker, Pilar Moure Pernas, bleaches her hair, since she's on the plump side it's more noticeable and she wears a corset, she has to dust herself with talcum powder so that it doesn't stick to her skin which is always a bit clammy, of course, the corset has little holes in it. Pilar's first husband was very jealous and would neither let her bleach her hair nor don a corset.

"Definitely not, a decent woman should be herself, you start off by dyeing your hair and using a corset and you never know where it will lead to."

"But my sister Milagros uses one!"

"That's her husband's affair! I don't give a damn what your sister Milagros does, it's what you do that's my concern."

When Urbano Dapena, Pilar Moure's first husband, died of a blockage of the bowel, and passed on vomiting up blobs of his own faeces, his newly widowed wife breathed a sigh of relief; some demises bring great peace to families. Urbanito was at his father's deathbed, the poor little mite hid behind the curtains to get a better view and asked his mother:

"Mama, why was Papa shitting through his mouth?"

As soon as the law would allow, Pilar Moure married Wideawake.

"May I kiss your breasts, Pilar?"

"Do whatever you wish, my king, you know that I'm all yours, all that's left to do is to sort out the papers, but my breasts and my whole body belong to you."

"Good grief!"

Pilar dyed her hair blonde and purchased the corset even before the second marriage took place, there are some matters, some very intimate things, in which the legislator cannot get involved. Little Urbanito went up to heaven just about the time when his second stepbrother arrived—his mother and her new husband didn't waste any time. Urbanito died of anemia, his shoulderblade collapsed when he was very small and it did him no good at all when they fed him on rosemary blossom with corn bread and lice nurtured by his own mother.

"What wouldn't a mother do for her child!"

"Indeed!"

Pilar Moure gave birth easily and with no great effort.

"There's no call to create a scene, that's what we women are for, after all, bringing children into the world. It's no big deal."

Saintly Fernández was not a saint but a pious man. My relation the Saintly Fernández was born in Moire in the parish of Santa María de Carballeda, near Piñor, on the Feast of the Apostle in 1808, shortly after Carlos IV had renounced the Spanish crown. The Espasa encyclopedia claims he was born in Cea, in the province of León, but that's not true and the entry devoted to Don Modesto Fernández y González, the fellow that signed himself Camilo de Cela, makes him a native of Carballeda de Avia, which isn't right either; Carballeda de Avia is over by Ribadavia and miles away from here. Saintly Fernández was the son of my great-grandparents, Don Benito, a physician, and Doña María Benita, gentlewoman, who married on May 26, 1794, the year of the execution of Louis XVI of France. The Espasa encyclopedia is also mistaken when it calls him Brother Juan Santiago; he was Brother Juan Jacobo, which is more or less the same only different, his father named him thus in honor of Rousseau. My great-grandfather was a compiler of the encyclopedia and there were eight or ten letters from d'Alembert and three or four from Diderot lying about his house until my aunts Jesusa and Emilita burned them at the outbreak of the civil war because Father Santisteban, S.J., a real saint, told them they were both ungodly heretics and advised them to burn the letters the better to salve their consciences.

"The Evil Enemy resorts to umpteen wiles to incite us to sin and lead us astray from the path of righteousness."

"Yes, Father."

"What's more, as far as I can see, those letters were written in French. Rid yourselves of the occasion of sin!"

"Yes, Father."

Father Santisteban, S.J., took a pinch of snuff, sneezed three times (Bless you! Bless you! Bless you!), blew his nose loudly, savored the last sip of his cascarilla tea, folded his cassock with a knowing gesture, and adopted a solemn, senatorial and judicious air:

"Cast them into the flames!"

"Which flames, Father?"

"Any flames at all!"

"Yes, Father."

The distinguished Dominican friar from Santander, the Rev. Father Daniel Avellanosa, preacher and member of the Geographical Society, predicted that number 25,888 would, as indeed proved the case, be the winning number in the Christmas Lottery. When the Casandulfe Raimundo got rid of his dose of crabs, Miss Ramona sighed with relief.

"I thought you didn't love me, Raimundo, I thought you were no longer interested in me. You've been putting me through torment!"

"You silly goose. I had a lot of problems and worries, that's all."

"But couldn't you tell me?"

"No, they're not women's matters, you wouldn't even understand."

"Is it something to do with politics?"

"Look, let's drop this! All that matters is that we're together again."

Ádega knows the history of the Guxinde family inside out, some folks call them the Moranes, which is nearly the same thing.

"Your relation the Saintly Fernández was the brother of your great-grandmother Rose. Your relation the Saintly Fernández was martyred by the infidels in Damascus, they cast him down from the top of the bell tower and he took several hours to die. Your relation the Saintly Fernández died proclaiming the Catholic faith, the infidels told him: Forswear your faith, you Christian dog! and he replied: Not on your life! Mine is the true faith! Your relation the Saintly Fernández was always ready for the fray. Before he went off and was martyred, your relation the Saintly Fernández had several children, some say he had eleven, each time he came back to Spain he would leave some woman with child. So as to be able to recognize his children when needs be, he used to brand them just below the left nipple with a little iron signet ring he had. I remember one of them well, the youngest, Fortunato Ramón María Rey, whom your relation the Saintly Fernández dumped in the Santiago foundling home with as many *pesetas* as there are days in the year for someone to rear him. When his father was called on high, Fortunato was brought to Orense by a certain Señor Pedro from the Peares mountains, he took him off to a hamlet called Moura or Lourada, I can't remember which it was. The child left Santiago as Fortunato Ramón María Rey but he grew up with the name Ramón Iglesias, which lost him the inheritance of a million *reales* which his father the Saintly Fernández left to be handed over when he came of age; your relatives were always very slapdash when it came to inheritances, well, some more than others, of course.

Uncle Cleto is scrupulously clean and squeamish, all day

long he is wiping his hands with alcohol until his knuckles are in raw flesh.

"What trouble is it to maintain a few basic standards?"

"Indeed you're right."

Uncle Cleto always wears gloves, he even plays his jazz band with gloves on, he dusts the insides with antiseptic powder so they don't cling to his chafed knuckles.

"We live in the midst of a miasma so we have to defend ourselves against the infections preying upon us: cholera, leprosy, tetanus, gangrene, glanders, need I go on?"

Uncle Cleto empties his bowels in the open air facing into the wind (when he wants to spit he faces the other way) and wipes his ass with the tenderest leaves from the heart of a freshly cut lettuce.

"The precautions we take are but a drop in the ocean."

"Maybe."

Aunt Jesusa and Aunt Emilita recite the entire Rosary, the fifteen mysteries, until finally they bore themselves to sleep. Aunt Jesusa and Aunt Emilita bore themselves to tears, they're also half-dazed, mulling over how badly Uncle Cleto treats them is the only thing that livens them up a bit; well, what of it, to heck with him! He'll cook his own goose in the end!

Aunt Jesusa and Aunt Emilita speak in a reedy, Holy-Joe tone of voice, you'd think they were about to preach a hellfire sermon.

"Many's the account our poor brother will have to render to His Maker when the Day of Judgement comes!"

"Indeed, each and every one of us, without exception, will find ourselves at such a juncture."

"That's why it behooves us to prepare for death, Camilo, don't be too cocky! Just remember Fleta, who died all of a sudden without even a chance to confess!"

"Don't you worry your head about me, Auntie! I'm mindful of these matters."

The aunts never met Plastered Pepiño, they heard tell of him alright but they never met him. There are folks that go through life drawing attention to themselves, although they don't mean to, and others who pass unnoticed however hard they try. Concha the Clam grew prettier and livelier by the day, young women usually grow very lascivious in widowhood. In her wisdom, Mother Nature generally glosses over grief with fun and frolics so as to allow us get on with life. Concha the Clam plays the castanets like a gypsy.

"Where did you pick that up?"

"At home, it took a little patience; but playing the castanets is just like drawing breath, eventually you do it without even thinking."

Concha the Clam performs music-hall songs with great gusto in her fine singing voice. Concha the Clam was made for living, whereas Plastered Pepiño was made for dying, some things just never work out. Concha the Clam has a haughty, brazen look about her, maybe she's the daughter of some count or general, blood from a family which has long since been eating square meals will out. Concha the Clam sleeps stretched out, another sign of confidence.

"Have you noticed her silken hair and that swing of her hips as she walks? With a little training, Concha the Clam would have gone far, she could have run a guesthouse, been a hair-dresser, opened a haberdashery or something like that, but Concha the Clam can neither read nor write so she's stuck where she is."

"Have a bit of patience, girl!"

"That's just it: patience and health to keep on struggling."

Once upon a time when Concha the Clam was in faraway

places (Valladolid, Bilbao, Saragossa) she was a painter's model, she gave it up because she had the bitter cold to contend with while not even escaping the clutches of poverty, and it's not worth baring your tits for that.

"Anyway it'd make your blood boil the way they look at you as though you were a block of wood."

Aunt Jesusa had a sweetheart who was a pharmacist—well, he hadn't yet finished his degree, he still had two subjects left to do—Ricardo Vázquez Vilariño, who was killed in the war, he enlisted in the Galician Banners and was killed on New Year's Day 1938 in Teruel, at the same time as his commander, Barja de Quiroga. Aunt Emilita had a sweetheart, too; Celso Varelo Fernández, a building supervisor, who left her in the lurch to run off with an actress, but Aunt Emilita forgave him.

"She was a minx, a proper minx she was, in the clutches of a woman like that men are defenseless, Celso wasn't a bad soul at all, but that bitch bewitched him with her wiles and she nothing but old mutton dressed as lamb! Poor Celso!"

That's not true: Aunt Jesusa and Aunt Emilita never had sweethearts, both of them were left on the shelf at an early age. Robín Lebozán stood in front of the mirror and said with great composure:

"I'll always hold they had sweethearts, I'm a charitable sort and always will be, but Aunt Jesusa and Aunt Emilita were old enough to be the mothers of the student pharmacist and the building supervisor. I don't care if folks get it wrong, I merely wish to follow the dictates of my conscience."

Celestino Sprig or, rather, Father Celestino, the priest from San Miguel de Taboadela, has his little tiffs with Marica Rubeiras from los Tunos, a handsome young married woman from the village of Mingarabeiza, whose husband has borne the lot of a cuckold with precious little dignity. Father Celes-

tino is to be seen with Marica in the belfry, it's not a comfortable spot but quiet it certainly is.

"And airy, too?"

"Airy, too."

Santos Cófora, Piggy, sixty-two years of age and at least two
hundred and fifty pounds in weight, claimed that his wife,
Marica Rubeiras, who had not yet reached the age of twenty,
was true to her marriage vows.

"What utter nonsense!"

"Look, I don't know what to say to you, but to claim she isn't
playing around!"

Piggy didn't want to raise a rumpus, nor did he want Marica
to leave him, of course, but he had so much rage pent up
inside him that he didn't know which way to turn in order to
take his revenge.

"That damned priest will pay for this! As sure as there's a
God up in heaven, that priest will pay for this!"

The relations in Piñor were swept clean away by the broom
of time which never wearies of gathering souls. My uncle
Claudio Montenegro, a relative of the Virgin Mary, died an
old man just after the war; he was an odd sort who never got
flustered, raised his voice nor batted an eyelid at anything, not
even at eclipses or the sight of the aurora borealis, during the
war years the aurora borealis was seen. When he heard that
Piggy had gone off to Orense to catch a dose of crab lice to take
his revenge upon Father Sprig, he found it perfectly natural.

"Apparently this is a great year for crabs, the belfries are just
crawling with crab lice, God help us!"

My grandmother Teresa had two sisters, Manuela and Pepa,
and a brother, Manuel. Teresa Fernández, Pinoxa, who lived
with her blind father, was the daughter of Manuela and Claudio Otero, the String, he and his brother Manuel, a cutter,

were Pepa's sons. Uncle Claudio was the father of two unfortunate blind girls and Uncle Manolo was pissed as a coot most of the time; when he died it was discovered that he had nearly two hundred brand-new shirts still in their wrappers, his son Manolito, who owned a store in Montevideo, used to send them to him. Manuela Fernández was Manuel's daughter and she was always very fond of us for my grandmother had absolved her of some debt or other. Families are like rivers, never flagging and flowing on and on. Grandmother Teresa was the niece of the Saintly Fernández. Fortunato Ramón María Rey—later known as Ramón Iglesias—the illegitimate son of the Saintly Fernández, married Nicolasa Pérez and had seven children with her: Antonio, who married Josefa Barrera in Cuba, their son José Ramón lives in New York; Hortensia who married Julio Fuentes in Cuba, their children Delia, Maruja, and Francisco live in New York; Mercedes who first married Idelfonso Fernández and later José Uceda: by the first marriage she had a son, Julio, who now lives in Vigo and is married to Dolores Ramos (he has two children: Alfonso, married to Concepción—I can't remember her surname—who lives in Barcelona and Mercedes, married to Maximino Lago, who lives in Vigo) and by the second marriage she had another five children: Maruja, married to Justo Núñez and living in Orense (she has two sons: Justo and Jorge, who live in Madrid), Antonio, married to Aurora del Río, lives in Orense (he has two sons: José Luis, married to María Luisa Gonzalez, and Roberto, married to Elisa Camba), Matilde, married to Román Alonso (she has two sons: Carlos, married to Pilar Jiménez and Álvaro, a bachelor), José, a bachelor, who lives in Madrid and Ramón, married to Nieves Pereira, who lives in Corunna. The fourth grandson of the Saintly Fernández is César, married to Sara Carballo, both dead now, he had a son called César, who is the only one to bear the surname Rey, all the others are called Iglesias: César is married to Benigna. I can't remember her surname either, and he has two daughters: Lourdes and Raquel. Next comes Orentino, married to Luisa Novoa, he has two daughters: Carmen, married to Adolfo Chamorro, and Pilar, married to Francisco Sueiro. Then there's María, José Dorribo's widow, with five children: Angelines, married to José Rodriguez: Rafael, married to Aurora Pérez: Eulalia, who is single: Luisa, married to Serrafín Ferreiro and Sara, married to Arturo Casares. And finally there's Herminia, the baby of the family and Cáncido Valcárcel's widow, with four children: Antonio, married to Dolores do Campo, and María del Pilar, Matilde, and Antonio, all unmarried. Families are like the sea: they go on forever and have neither beginning nor end.

It drizzles down upon families, people, and animals, both wild and tame, upon men and women, parents and children, the healthy and the infirm, the dead and buried, the dead and the unburied, and upon travelers, too. It drizzles the way the blood courses in your veins. It drizzles the way gorse bushes and maize sprout, the way a man runs after a woman until he wears her down or kills her off from tedium, love, or desire. Maybe the drizzle is really God, keeping a close eye on men, but that's something nobody knows. Plastered Pepiño left the nut-house thanks to the good offices of a doctor, a lawyer, and a judge, it's a fact that young folks nowadays are greatly given to experiments and theories and that they relate behavior to hormones.

"And how exactly does that work?"

"I don't know: I'm only writing down what I was told."

The doctor, the lawyer, and the judge asked Plastered Pepiño if he would allow himself to be castrated (removing the gonads is to remove the danger) and he said yes, well, that he didn't mind. The doctors, the lawyers, and the judges use the word "sterilize."

"But did they not warn him about his metabolism and slow, painful decalcification of the bones?"

"Maybe they did, I really couldn't say."

Some folks die one way and some another, in war or in peacetime, in sickness, in an accident or slip up, there's no hard and fast rule nor is it permitted to choose, why, there isn't even a general rule. There are men who die heroically defending a blockhouse, unfurling a flag, and chanting patriotic slogans but there are also those whose hearts simply stop beating while they are masturbating with their minds full of fantasies; where I'm from there are no prickly pears, an ungodly plant proper to the land of the Moors: kaftans, figs, donkeys, lizards, goats, and dust, clouds of dust, it's hardly worth coming this far to die. The Moors from the Tafersit tribe are a sissy bunch, well, they really are pansies, it's all the same to them. Lázaro Codesal had blue eyes and hair as red as chili pepper. Lázaro Codesal was jerking off, letting fly, inside his head, as was his wont, with Ádega in the nip, what a godsend! there's nothing like being young for having it off with someone just from memory inside your head. It was a great pity that Lázaro Codesal died, some deaths bring more sorrow than others and there are also those that bring delight. The Carroupos have a patch of rough pockmarked skin on their forehead, like cattle scarred from chewing poisonous plants.

"Can you tell a poisonous plant?"

"Yes, sirree, from the smell, the color, and some from the sound, well, the sound they make when you flail them through the air."

Gorecho Tundas went up the mountain with a coffin on his back, a demijohn of gasoline, and a sackful of wood shavings.

"Where are you off to, Gorecho?"

"I'm going up the mountain to bury the Holy Ghost."

"Christ, what rubbish you talk!"

"Well, you'll soon see when night falls."

When night fell Gorecho sought out a snug spot, a bracken-filled cave still bearing the traces of a vixen's presence, he clambered into the coffin, covered himself up with the wood shavings, sprinkled gasoline over the top until he was well and truly drenched and then set it alight. He died writhing but did not open his mouth for apparently the Holy Ghost gave him strength. Concha the Clam came across him as she roamed the mountain setting rabbit snares.

"What did he look like?"

"Well, handsome you might even say, a bit charred but handsome."

The Gorecho Tundas incident was much talked about by all and sundry.

"Folks don't know what to do to draw attention to themselves!"

Man is a strange creature who does things back to front, a creature at odds with himself from the moment of birth. Do you fancy that slender woman going down to the river to wash? The one with the plait? You do? Well, marry her and you'll see what it is to have to put up with a shrew, women turn into shrews the minute they marry, well, soon after they marry, nobody knows why, maybe that's just the law of nature. Do you fancy that plump woman going to buy chili pepper at the shop, the one with the green scarf? You do? Well, kill her with a shotgun cartridge or flee for your life like a soul spirited off by the devil, or she'll cling to you like a limpet! Or like a crab louse? Like a crab louse, too, this is a great year for crab lice, was it not spiders? Not at all, woman, are you an idiot or what?

How would it be spiders, it was crab lice, of course! Do you fancy that dark-haired woman carrying a pitcher of milk on her head, the one in the flouncy skirt? You do? Well, run for your life for chances are she's a hotbed of scorpions, man is a strange creature who doesn't always play above board. Lázaro Codesal was treacherously killed without being given a chance, bumping off a lad who is peacefully jerking off beneath a fig tree is an unspeakable deed, no man should do a thing like that, war is war, indeed as we all know, but hitting a blind target or shooting in the back is a base deed. No corpse ever stank so foul as did Don Jesús Manzanédo, it was a just punishment from God, his children sprinkled him with eau de cologne to no effect.

"Are you going to Don Jesús' funeral?"

"I'm not, I think that it's best that his soul shouldn't be saved, he stank to high heaven of death."

Celso Varela, the building supervisor, has a vermouth every morning in La Bilbaína Café, sometimes he goes to the Superior Bar too. His relationship with Marujita petered out ages ago, although they say he later went back to her. On the terrace of the Bilbaína Café, a month or two before the outbreak of the civil war, two men were shot dead: at the funeral another two deaths took place and the authorities banned the Corpus Christi processions. Feeling ran high and folks were up in arms, shouting and fighting one another with sticks, even gunshots, too. Maruja Bodelón Alvarez, Marujita the Ponferrada lioness, was the actress who stole Celso Varela from Aunt Emilita, well, she wasn't really an actress, she just looked like one. Celso wanted to go back to Aunt Emilita but too much water had flowed under the bridge and it wasn't to be, things grow cold and when they fizzle out it's very hard to rekindle them.

"No, no; I'm staying with my sister Jesusa. I'm devoting my life to prayer and charitable deeds now."

"Fair enough, as you wish."

Baldomero Marvís, Lionheart rather, has a little star on his forehead; not everyone can see it, but it's there alright! The little star which Lionheart has on his forehead changes color depending: at times it's as red as rubies; then tawny like topaz; sometimes as green as emeralds, or white like diamonds and so on. When Lionheart's little star lights up, no matter what color, sometimes one color and then another, nobody knows, the best thing is to cross yourself and get out of his way. Lionheart calls the shots in the Gamuzo family, there's a whole host of them, and in the Guxinde family (or Moranes some folks call them) and there are even more of them. If it weren't such a topsy-turvy world, nobody would move through these mountains without Lionheart's permission, the line of the last mountain was blotted out when Lázaro Codesal was killed, but things run out of kilter and a starveling wretch from a family from outside went to snip the thread of Lionheart's life. The Devil took advantage of the day when Lionheart's little star failed to light up to kill him by treachery. In these mountains you cannot kill and get off scot free, hereabouts he who kills, must die, it may take a while but die he will. Loliña Moscoso, Baldomero Lionheart's wife, fanned the flames and kept the law of the mountain burning: he who does the deed, must pay the price. He didn't do the deed? Well, let him pay the price all the same! In this neck of the woods we see no need to absolve blood. Loliña Moscoso is a wild, fierce beauty and when she loses her temper she is even more beautiful. Lionheart must have been caught from behind and by night for not a soul would have dared face up to Lionheart for his looks were as fierce as a wolf. Lionheart was killed by a dead man that nobody cares to remember, some folks won't even utter his name so as, gradually, to forget him; the dead man who killed Lionheart also killed Ádega's old man and maybe a dozen others to boot, the dead man who killed Lionheart was rounded up by a relation of mine and he met his death like an old nag in the Bouzas do Gago spring. When the wolf attacks, the mares form a circle with their heads facing inwards the better to defend their foals, they lash out at the wolf and if they kick him good and hard they smash him to smithereens. An ousted stallion has no defense, nor does he have the strength to defend himself, the wolves pull him down, first they drag him down, then they devour him, what the wolf doesn't want goes to the fox and what the fox leaves goes to the crows, creatures resigned to their lot, some crows can whistle scales in tune, some years ago in Allariz, during the Primo de Rivera dictatorship, there lived a Republican who trained crows to whistle the Marseillaise, maybe he only did so to rile the priest, his name was Leoncio Coutelo and he was a brother of Blind Eulalio, tall and thin as a beanpole and spattered with pockmarks, who used to grope women at *romerías*, since he couldn't see he let himself be guided by the scent and he never set a foot wrong. Ricardo Vázquez Vilariño died in the war, a bullet pierced his heart (that's just an expression), that's what happens in wars. Through these mountains wandered the ripper Manuel Blanco Romasanta, the werewolf who tore a baker's dozen of people asunder. Felipiño the Stutterer, one-eyed and with six fingers on each hand, knew the story well.

The ripper used to mooch about with two men from Valencia, Don Jenaro and Don Antonio, who had a touch of the werewolf in their blood when they lost their wits; now this happened many years back, maybe a century ago or more, but hereabouts everybody knows the tale. The ripper savaged thirteen souls: nine men and four women. One night when the moon brought out the wolf in him, he killed Manueliña García, a woman by whom he had had a child, Rosendiño, which he killed too. He was taking Manueliña to Santander, which is miles away, on the Sea of Castile, where he was going to put her into service in the house of a priest, but at the spot known as Malladavella, in the Redondela woods, the urge came over him so he killed and half-devoured the both of them. Afterwards he fell quiet for a while, quiet yet faraway, until he was overcome again and he killed Benitiña García, who was Manueliña's sister, as well as her son Farruquiño, who was still a suckling babe and tasted of fish. He killed them in Corgo de Boy, beyond Arrúas, just before you come to Transirelos. The ripper wasn't much of a size, in fact he was smallish and had decaying teeth. The ripper killed others, too: Josefa García, Manueliña and Benitiña's sister—apparently he couldn't resist that blood—and she died on the road to Correchouso. Her son little José, too. And Toniña Rúa and her two daughters Peregrina and Marica, who were killed in Rebordechao. The ripper dearly loved Toniña, he was madly in love with her and used to show her what he'd got when their paths crossed up the mountain. He killed another four, too: Xila Millarados, who grazed pigs in Chaguazoso; Chucha Lombao Celmán, whom he attacked just coming in at As de Xarxes; Fuco Naveaus, a lad who hunted birds over by the Alvar meadow, and Benitoña Cardoeiros, a spent old woman.

Felipiño the Stutterer smiles gratefully every time someone buys him a couple of glasses of *aguardiente*.

"May the Good Lord reward you in the next world, Amen!"

Tanis Gamuzo breeds hunting mastiffs: Kaiser, Sultan, Moor, good, big, strong dogs that you can rely upon 'til the end of the world.

"With these beasts a man could go to the ends of the earth without a care in the world, when they have their spiked collars on, nothing—not even a lion—would stop these dogs."

Tanis Gamuzo's dogs have coats like silk (fleece is what sheep have) and they're white in color with brown spots on the face and the back of the neck. Tanis brought his dogs from León, in Galicia there are nice, smart go-getters of dogs— cattle dogs, mountain dogs, farm dogs, hunting dogs—but they're not such sturdy stock as the dogs from León, where apparently they're less inbred.

"How much do you want for a nine-week-old pup?"

"Nothing. I don't sell dogs but if you swear you'll treat it right, I'll make you a present of one."

Tanis Gamuzo is known as Demon because he figures things out so fast, he's just like a bicycle he moves so fast, doesn't matter whether it's good or bad. Rosa Roucón is Tanis Gamuzo's wife and she's partial to a drop of anisette, she spends the whole day tippling from a hip flask. Rosa Roucón's father is called Eleuterio the Britches and he's the most bloody-minded customs official there ever was in Orense, nobody remembers his like ever before.

"That man will meet a sticky end, mark my words, one of these days somebody will ram an iron bar through him without a moment's notice."

The country folk fear Britches and try to have as little as possible to do with him.

"There's not a decent bone in his body, the best thing is to pay up and get away as fast as possible."

Last year in Sprat's brothel Britches spat in Blind Gaudencio's face because he wouldn't play the mazurka *Ma Petite Marianne.*

"I play whatever I like, so you can spit at me or beat me, that's not hard to do for I'm blind, but what you can't do is make me play a tune if I don't want to, if I don't feel like it, I mean. That piece of music isn't for any Tom, Dick, or Harry and I'm the only one that knows when to play it and what it means."

Portuguese Marta refused to go to bed with Britches.

"I'd sooner starve! Why don't you spit in the face of your son-in-law, you bastard? Or are you afraid he'd give you a thrashing?"

Sprat turned Britches out into the street to avoid an unholy row.

"Go on, get out and cool your heels, you big baby—for that's all you are—you can come back when you've calmed down!"

Tanis Gamuzo is stronger than anyone, he gets a kick out of his own strength, as a lad he was the terror of *romerías*. If it weren't for the anisette he'd be contented with Rosa, his wife, a decent woman and a good sort but the anisette is a dreadful curse. Their children run about filthy and with their boots falling apart, there are five of them all running wild with nobody to look after them. Nor does Tanis the Demon take much notice of them, he's more wrapped up in messing about with Catuxa Bainte, the half-wit from Martiñá, both of them stark naked, in Lucio Mouro's millpond when the weather hots up and the flesh seeks wholesome refreshment and delight. The half-wit can't swim, one of these days she's going to drown as she let's herself be laid afloat in the shade of the ferns.

"That would be a laugh, don't you think?"

"Not at all, man! Poor Catuxa! What harm has she ever done you?"

Tanis Gamuzo, Demon, also likes to swing from the boughs of the oak trees, that's how he never catches the mange, twirling and brandishing his cudgel in the air, it's as hard as a rock and has his initials carved in it.

"Shall I split your nut in two like the pit of a peach?"

"Don't be stupid, Demon, don't play jokes like that!"

"Alright. Shall I puncture your loins like a car tire?"

"Shut up, you nitwit!"

Ádega's face was pale.

"Are you alright?"

"Yes, just let me fetch a drop of *aguardiente.*"

Ádega is no spring chicken but she still walks straight as an arrow.

"Let's see now. The dead man that killed my old man never found respite again, either in this world or in the next. Blood will choke blood and we've no call to absolve blood around here. The family of the dead man that killed my old man wasn't from hereabouts but, God knows, he had plenty of time to learn the ways of these parts. Hopalong from Marañís, the clerk of the Court in Carballiño, formerly a Civil Guard and later lamed in a fight with Pontevedra smugglers, let my brother Secundino steal the papers—that you already know for I told you plain and clear—showing where the family of the dead man that killed my old man—his father was from Foncebadón over by Astorga—hailed from. You, Don Camilo, are a Guxinde, well, a Morán—it makes no difference—and that has its price to pay, as I know full well, but it's also something which you should stand up for to the end. Some day I'll tell you how I stole the mortal remains of Moucho, God blast him! How the Carroupos were hopping mad! Will you have another glass of *aguardiente?*"

The eighth sign of the bastard is a measly, flaccid organ. In Sprat's brothel the whores used to laugh at Fabián Minguela's lollipop.

"Like a little cherub! Just like a little cherub!"

Moncho Requeixo, or Moncho Lazybones rather, is a dreamer, maybe he has a touch of the poet about him.

"If you want I'll draw figures of eight on the ground with my wooden leg, it's never beneath my dignity to please a lady."

Moncho Lazybones is like a nobleman fallen upon hard times, a courtier reduced in circumstance, and—Lord save us!—come down in the world.

"Before she was widowed by her first husband, the late Adolfito, my cousin Georgina was already having an affair with Carmelo Méndez, whom she later married, as soon as she could, that is. My cousins Georgina and Adela were always predisposed to sin, life is short and you have to live it to the full. The pair of Little Jesus Cured, male and female, died on me crossing the Red Sea, I think it was all for the best for my cousins would have fried and eaten them to annoy me, just to get my goat. My aunt Micaela, the mother of my cousins, you know, was also fond of stroking and very grateful to her I am, too. When I was little she used to let me slip a hand down her bodice and fondle her and also tickle her thighs, but she never took her knickers off, Aunt Micaela never let me take her knickers off, in that respect she was very superstitious. May I have another coffee? Thanks very much. My cousins sometimes dance the tango with Miss Ramona and Rosicler, the one that gives injections and my cousin Georgina, when she gets going, asks if she may undress. May I take this blouse off? Do what you like! May I take my bra off? Do what you like!

May I take my drawers off? Do what you like. Do you like me, Mona? Shut up, you slut, and lie down on the bed! Shall I switch off the light? No."

Moncho Lazybones puts on a falsetto voice when he does the dialogue between the women.

"What an odd bunch women are! Don't you think so?"

"That all depends."

In the cemetery lies the source of the spring of that miraculous water which cures dizzy spells without having to tear your clothes apart and burn them, it's better than holy water for it is blessed by God before it gushes forth from the earth, while it is still coursing through the conduits of the earth among stray moles, short-sighted earthworms, and evil intentions: it's called the Miangueiro spring and the water, if taken good and cold, yields relief to leprous sores, it neither dries them up nor heals them but simply yields relief.

"I think all women go straight to heaven."

"Well I don't. I think that over half of them are damned and wind up burning in hell: some for being whores, others for their greed, and others for being so loathsome, there are some loathsome creatures in this world: the French and the Moors for a start."

It rains upon the roof of Miss Ramona's house, around about as well, upon the windowpanes of the gallery, it rains upon the rhododendrons, the cypress and the myrtles in the garden which slopes down to the river, everything is sodden and the soil is waterlogged: three suicides in a little over ten years is not so very much: an old woman in greater pain than she can bear, a traveling salesman who gambled and lost all he had at cards (even then he was cheating), and a little lass whose breasts were just beginning to bud.

"You and I are relations, around here we're all related except for those weeds the Carroupos. I'll order chocolate, if you like. Why don't you stay for dinner?

When he was still alive, Don Brégimo, Miss Ramona's late father, was a great hand at playing foxtrots and charlestons on the banjo.

"My father was very good, I know, but he had a gift for it, I think he was half crazy, they can say what they like but I hold that tangos are far better for dancing to."

Zalacaín the Adventurer by Pío Baroja is a fine novel, there's a great deal of action and feeling in it. I can't remember who I lent it to now, that's what happens when you lend out books, you never get them back, Robín Lebozán returns books, but maybe I didn't lend it to anyone and it's lying at the back of some cupboard or other, this house has gone to the dogs and that's the truth

"Why don't you stay and have dinner with me? I've a bottle of apple brandy that they sent me from Asturias."

Nobody heeds the prudent onward march of the world spinning and turning as the drizzle falls with neither beginning nor end: a man denounces another man and later when he is found dead in the gutter or in the ditches of the cemetery there are few qualms of conscience: a woman closes her eyes and inserts a bottle of warm water wherever she feels like and nobody cares: a child falls down the stairs and is killed, all in the twinkling of an eye. Rosicler goes on monkeying around with the marmoset whose cough worsens by the day, it's a bee she has in her bonnet. All the Carroupos have an odious pockmark like pigskin on their foreheads, maybe they had a wild boar for a grandfather, who knows? Blind Gaudencio plays the mazurka *Ma Petite Marianne* when he wants, not when he's told to, it's one matter to be blind and quite another not to have the will to do something. Gaudencio's repertoire is varied, folks are full of notions and at times they don't realize what it is they're asking. Can't you see that mazurka is to be played only upon certain solemn occasions? That mazurka is like a sung Mass, it requires both a time and a place as well as a certain lavishness. The accordion is a sensitive instrument that suffers when something goes against the grain, folks have lost all respect, we seem to be heading for the end of the world. Policarpo Portomourisco Expósito, la Bagañeira, is missing three fingers from one hand, a stallion snapped them off in the Xurés mountains one day when he went up to the corral with his relations. Policarpo la Bagañeira lives in Cela do Camparrón, the upper floor of his house caved in at the time his father died and three trained weasels, obedient and able to dance, escaped on him. Policarpo la Bagañeira can manage them with just the little finger and the thumb of his right hand, a body can get used to anything. From time to time Policarpo goes up to the main road, on the Santiago omnibus there are always two or three priests nibbling hazelnuts and dried figs, they're a rough-looking bunch, unshaven and always chuckling mysteriously like conspirators, before the war priests who traveled by omnibus used to gobble *chorizos* and belch and let out thundering farts amid loud guffaws. Father Mariano Vilobal was the priest best-known for his ability to break wind either upwards or downwards, in the whole province there was no one could hold a candle to him. Father Mariano died just after the outbreak of war, he went up to the belfry to see to the bells, lost his footing and cracked the back of his neck off the tombstones in the atrium. When he was downing hearty meals, Father Mariano could belch and fart for a full six hours or more.

"Here's one for the heathens!"

"Will you stop it, Father Mariano, or you'll give yourself a hernia!"

"A hernia? Me? What sort of a sissy do you take me for? Here's another for the Protestants, right bastards that they are! Death to Luther!"

The best *chorizos* in the world (well, that's just a turn of phrase, maybe there are others just as good) are the ones Ádega makes.

"My old man had a good color because he used to eat whole *chorizos* at one go, he would snip the string off the end and devour them whole. Poor Cidrán. God rest his soul! how he loved my *chorizos*! At times he would tell me: they go straight down to my privates, Ádega, and isn't that all the better for you, my girl? The dead man that killed my old man never ate such good *chorizos*, the dead man that killed my old man was a starveling of an outsider.

Ádega makes *chorizo* with great care and skill, the main thing is to use a local pig reared as they do hereabouts, on maize and a thick swill of cabbage, potatoes, maize flour, stale bread, broad beans, and anything else you care to throw in; the pig also needs to be out of doors and get a bit of exercise up the mountain, rooting about in the soil for worms and bugs. It should be slaughtered with a soft iron blade, not steel, following time-honored custom, that is to say for the hell of it, with venomous delight and treachery, for nobody's to blame. The best filling is made from finely chopped loin, shoulder, and rib meat—taking care with the bone—plenty of paprika as well as all the chili pepper it will take, salt, crushed garlic, and just a touch of water but not too much; then you knead it carefully and let it stand for a whole day. The following morning you taste the filling raw and then fry it in the pan to get the flavor of it and add anything else it requires, it always needs a touch of something. On the third day you knead it again and on the fourth you fill it into the skins then, depending on the size you require, tie them up with a length of string. Then they are smoked for two or three weeks in the smokehouse until they are firm, stiffness and hardness are signs of a good cure, and then they're ready to eat: oak timber gives the best, most wholesome smoke. The ones you want to eat first are hung and then, after a good cleaning, are packed in lard.

"My old man was as strong as an ox for he used to down whole *chorizos*, he would cut off the string, sometimes he didn't even bother, toss back his head and swallow whole *chorizos* at one go. Time was when he could hold his breath and swallow five whole *chorizos* without them ever going down the wrong way."

It rains upon the waters of the streams beyond the plots of cultivated land of Catucha and Sualvariza while the ghost of a child who has just died flits through the air, cherubs to heaven! Children don't even know when they're dying, they die peacefully, old folks are the worst, what with the rumpus they raise and the expenses they incur, what with doctors, herbalists, priests, top quality coffins, mourning weeds, Masses to be said, if it's time for the will to be read now and then the rows break out . . . Marujita Bodelón, the Ponferrada woman who had an affair with Celso Varelo the building supervisor, Aunt Emilita's former sweetheart, isn't an actress though she looks like one, she also looks like a jeweller's sweetheart. Marujita dyes her hair blonde and uses eye shadow.

"Does she paint her lips in a Cupid's bow?"

"No, why?"

"Does she smoke in front of men?"

"She doesn't do that either."

Marujita is a fine-looking woman with a strong, masterful stride that shows her breeding. Marujita is on the buxom side, but men generally like big-breasted women, and she has long legs and a pert little ass, but what isn't nice about her is her voice, she squawks like a magpie. Marujita does smoke in front of men and she does paint her lips in a Cupid's bow. Michel, king of the lipsticks. Celso Varela spent sums of money he couldn't afford buying her trifles: a vermouth here, a box of chocolates there, a handbag, earrings, more and more, until he wound up stone broke and in debt to boot. Marujita responded with her favors and trimmed his nails and washed his hair, too.

"Bet you have a better time with me than with that frump?"

Ricardo Vázcuez Vilariño, Aunt Jesusa's sweetheart, was killed just when he was on the point of becoming a pharmacist, he had only two subjects left to do.

"They might have killed somebody else, mightn't they? I was very unlucky there."

"I don't know what to say to you, ma'am, seems to me your sweetheart was even more unlucky."

"Indeed you're right."

Gorecho Tundas wanders the fringes of the other world with a fishing rod on his shoulder.

"Where are you off to, Gorecho?"

"To Bethlehem in Judaea, to fish for the Christ child."

"Holy God! What utter claptrap!"

"Well, you'll soon see when day breaks."

It drizzles at daybreak, it drizzles down on Gorecho Tundas, sitting on a rock in the river, busy fishing trout, he looks more dead than alive.

"Are you dead Gorecho?"

"I am. I've been dead for over six hours now and nobody takes a blind bit of notice. They carried the Christ child off to Egypt on the back of a donkey for his own land didn't suit him."

Folks think that us Guxindes and Moranes are the same but we're not, folks get confused about this business of relationships, we are all descended from Adam and Eve (but not Ponferrada women, Aunt Emilita says, Ponferrada women are descended from the apes, thank you very much), not all Guxindes are Moranes but all us Moranes are Guxindes, it's as clear as mud but there you are. There are fewer Moranes than Guxindes, there could be more of us but there aren't. Us Moranes are the Portomouriscos, the Marvises, the Celas, and the Faramiñáses, the others are relations but not Moranes, it doesn't make a hair of difference and we're all hale and hearty. In the Great Beyond—my grandparents' coffin factory—there worked an Italian, nobody knows how he came to be here, he's dead now, and my cousins gummed up his ass with sealing wax then stitched it up with string and tied him to a tree near the village of Carballediña, beyond the Oseira monastery. I forget his name but what I do remember is the rage that came over him when they set him free, true enough there was no reason for him to put up with such annoying pranks. Poor Aunt Lourdes' skeleton cannot be gathered together until the Day of Judgement for she was thrown into a common grave in Paris. Uncle Cleto plays the jazz band by ear, he does so very well indeed, and every February 11, which is his late wife's Feast day, he blasts hell out of the world playing all his instruments at once: the drum, the bass drum, the kettledrums, the tambourine, the triangle, and the cymbals, maybe there are other instruments too: in memory of Don Jesús Manzanedo, that educated but wicked man who went about killing people, not even his children request music.

"Do you think that Crazy Goat would dare mess about with a ram?"

"Go on! What harm is there in it? Better than going to bed

with Fabián Minguela! Anyway, if she can swallow her pride, a woman can put up with a lot, indeed she can cope with anything."

The ninth sign of the bastard is avarice. Fabián Minguela is poor but he might be a rich man now the way he hoards his loot.

"What did he do with his earnings?"

"Nobody knows, maybe he didn't earn as much as they say."

Speaking of music, Don Brégimo Faramiñas Jocín was a good friend of Don Faustino Santalices Pérez, from Bande, he greatly admired his knowledge and his skill at singing ballads and playing the hurdy-gurdy.

"Now there's a distinguished art—not like that crummy banjo! If only I could play the instrument as well as my friend Faustino, I'd chuck the banjo out the window!"

What Don Brégimo most liked to hear was the ballad of Don Gaiferos.

"I don't know what the Middle Ages were like, thronging with beggardly monks, mangy noblemen, consumptive troubadors, and thieving pilgrims, all to-ing and fro-ing and unconfessed, that was donkeys' years back, but chances are it was better than the Modern Age, in spite of the radio, airplanes, and other inventions; the ballad of Don Sancho is very lovely too."

Doña Pura Garrote, Sprat, wraps herself in an embroidered silk shawl when storms break, the moment the first lightning flashes and the thunder starts to rumble, Sprat runs for her shawl, fear affects each of us in our own way, she crouches upon her bed—preferably a wooden bedstead to an iron one—covers up her head and her whole body and grits her teeth in the darkness, lying as still as a corpse, with her eyes closed as she tells the Litany of Our Lady in a whisper until the danger is over. She, who is always so careful of what belongs to her, could be robbed at such a moment and wouldn't even notice. Sprat's shawl is famous, when Doña Pura was young she had at least twenty studio photographs taken in the nude with only the shawl on: with one breast peeking out and a vase of flowers, with both breasts bared before a canvas painted with the Egyptian pyramids, stretched out upon a couch with her legs crossed, with her buttocks reflected in a mirror, with her smooth, statuesque back bared and the Eiffel Tower in the background, etc., she had them taken in the Méndez Studios, in Lamas de Carvajal Street and paid Méndez, the owner of the studio, in kind. Terrible how time flies! Sprat's shawl is cream-colored with a long fringe and at least three hundred chinamen, each with a little ivory face, embroidered in all the colors of the rainbow. Father Silverio, the canon, says they're celluloid but that's not true, they're ivory: some strolling about, others doing balancing acts, and others shading themselves from the sun with parasols and so on.

"How much is Sprat's shawl worth?"

"I don't know. I'd say a pretty penny: why, it might even be the finest silk shawl in the whole province of Orense."

Pepiño Pousada Coires came down with meningitis and never fully got over it, he didn't die, true enough, but it left him a bit touched in the upper story as well as with the stagger of a drunk man, they call him Plastered Pepiño because he looks plastered. Plastered Pepiño works in the Repose Coffin Factory, he's an electrician's assistant and he's also good at packing: they say that Plastered Pepiño is a bit of a pansy, well, that he's a queer, what he likes best is groping small boys, he would never leave Simon the Lamb in peace no matter where he went, it's not hard to take liberties with deaf-mutes, but no good will come of it. Plastered Pepiño had the bright idea of getting married and his wife, Concha the Clam, ran off on him in the end, the most natural and sensible thing to do. Plastered Pepiño left jail because he agreed to be castrated, full credit to science. Plastered Pepiño didn't improve with the operation: doctors, lawyers, and judges say sterilize, which has a more refined and subtle ring to it, and what's more, his bones and his head ached.

"Do your bones ache, Pepiño?"

"Yes, sir, a little."

"What about your head?"

"Yes, sir, my head too."

"Well, all you can do is lump it!"

"I see, sir."

They gave Plastered Pepiño hormones to see if it would improve him but it didn't, maybe they only gave them to him to experiment

"Wasn't he afraid?"

"Of course, he was terrified. The only way to get over his fear was to go up to a little boy and stroke his ass. When the Civil Guard caught him, he said to the sergeant at the police station: Little Simon showed me his willy for me to touch, I didn't want to touch it."

The braying of the oxcart as it rumbles along the track rings in your ears so you hear it even when it isn't there; the axle of the oxcart always evokes a response: if there's no other cart then the echo replies, if the echo is asleep then God replies with his fiddles. Benicia has nipples like chestnuts, hard and the very same color, Benicia is the niece of Gaudencio Beira, the blind accordion-player in Sprat's brothel.

"Gaudencia, I'll give you a *peseta* if you play a mazurka."

"Depends which one."

Benicia can neither read nor write, nor does she need

to. Benicia is cheerful and breathes life into things wherever she goes.

"Shall we arm wrestle? If you win, I'll let you suck my tits, but if you lose you have to let me pull your willy until you cry quits! Alright?"

"No."

Benicia is a delectable gadget, designed not only to take but to yield delight. As soon as she saves up a little money, Benicia buys a present for somebody or other: a coffeepot, a box of cigars, a belt—men need a lot of tender loving care.

"Shall we dance a tango?"

"No: I'm tired, get in here beside me for a while."

Benicia has a visit from Ceferino Gamuzo, Ferret, the priest from Santa María de Carballeda the first and third Tuesdays of every month, a bit of order never goes amiss.

"Oh, Father Ceferino! You give me greater pleasure each passing day! God forgive me! Don't be afraid to press harder!"

Benicia likes to cook in the nip.

"Doesn't she spatter the oil?"

"No, she's careful."

Benicia is a dab hand at frying trout as well as cabbage shoots stuffed with a little chopped pork loin, a bit of ham, a clove of garlic, parsley, onion, herbs, and an egg. It's a tasty morsel and good, wholesome food, too. Ferret the priest is an angler and he treats Benicia well, anglers are generally very well-mannered. Benicia has blue eyes and she's like a water mill, she never stops.

"Will you make room for me over on your side?"

"I will."

Benicia tells the tale that when he was in Barco de Valdeorras, Petín and Rubiana killing Saracens, St. Roldán came across two very beautiful Moorish women, just as he was scrambling up the Enciña de Lastra mountains, but he couldn't catch up with them even though he galloped after them on horseback, pelting along so fast that it left him winded: cast into despair at the flight of the two beauties, St. Roldán cursed them and turned them both into the White Boulders, those two dazzling white quartz rocks still standing on either side of the road.

"It was at the Boulders that the ghost of St. Roldán appeared to me and although I wanted to run away I couldn't, well, I didn't really want to run away for it was so nice and peaceful there. St. Roldán spoke in a strange way, I'd say he wasn't all there."

"Did St. Roldán address you in Castilian or in Galician?"

"I think he spoke to me in Latin but I understood every word he said, mind you."

Ádega, Benicia's mother, knows many tales and many mysteries of the country hereabouts, she also plays the accordion with great skill, the *Fanfinette* polka is what she plays better than anything.

"Your grandfather had some much talked of affairs which ended in blood. Manecha Amieiros was a fine woman, your grandfather knew what he was doing, very handsome with long legs and hair like silk, they say she was a delight to behold, your grandfather beat Xan Amieiros—Manecha's brother, and that's the least of it—to death, that happens at times when two men fight and there's nobody there to separate them in time, he killed him at the hairpin bend at Claviliño, but he treated Manecha well. The girl went off to the capital, opened an inn and did well for herself. Your grandfather then went off to Brazil for a few years, before leaving he asked his official sweetheart—the one who was later to become your grandmother—will you wait for me, Teresa? She said she would and then off he went overseas. He was over in South America for fourteen years and married upon his return, he hadn't written a single letter to his sweetheart in all those years, but a man's word is his bond. Shall I pour you a drop more *aguardiente?*"

The mother of Roquiño Borrén, the half-wit who spent five years shut up in a tin trunk painted ultramarine blue, gold, orange, and lettuce green, does not have a charitable nature. Roquiño Borrén's mother takes it for granted that half-wits are closer to clods of earth than to people or even animals.

"God made them that way for some reason or another, don't you think?"

When she scalds herself, spills oil, or nicks her finger when she's peeling potatoes, Roquiño Borrén's mother takes a swipe at her half-wit son to console herself.

"What are you gawping at, you half-wit? You worse than half-wit!"

Roquiño Borrén's mother is called Secundina and she's as cranky as a bag of cats.

"What a heavy cross the Good Lord gave me to bear when he sent me this half-wit for my sins! Watch out, Roquiño, for I'll make you pay for this, just you wait and see!"

Roquiño Borrén's mother smokes when there is nobody around to see, she smokes the butts that she gathers up in Rauco's inn. She's a friend of Remedios, the landlady; she launders for her, helps with slaughtering pigs, and runs errands, she smokes magnolia leaves, too. Secundina has a dog that eats the rotting butts and is always tipsy and half-crazy, the poor little beast catches it too when his mistress blows her top. They say that Roquiño turned out as he did because when his mother was suckling him she would suckle the serpent by night and the poor devil had to do without. Be that as it may, I maintain that he was born into this world a half-wit for you can generally tell from that look they have about them.

"You know what a silver coin is good for?"

"Yes, sir, it's good for wasp stings."

Eleuterio the Britches wears his hair cropped short like a scrubbing brush, his eyebrows meet in the middle and he has a low brow, truth to tell, he's a miserable looking wretch.

"Eleuterio, I heard Portuguese Marta wouldn't go to bed with you because you spat at Gaudencio."

"Whoever told you that is a son of a bitch, Don Servando, begging your pardon."

Don Servando won't allow bad language to be used in his presence.

"Get a grip on yourself, bloody Britches, or I'll beat the living daylights out of you!"

Eleuterio got a grip on himself because Don Servando was a deputy for the province. Eleuterio knew when to shut his trap.

"Eleuterio, run down to the newsstand and buy me a packet of cigarette papers."

"What type? Bamboo?"

"Preferably Indian Rose."

What Fina enjoys better than anything is to be mounted like a wild beast and for that sort of business there's nobody better than a middle-aged priest, neither young nor old. Celestino Sprig, the priest in San Miguel de Taboada, is a past master at taming women in bed. Anton Guntimil, Fina's late husband, the poor Stutterer killed by a freight train in Orense station, could never quite make it with his wife.

"The Franciscan friar from the Missions had a prick that was twice the size of yours, dimwit—for that's what you are, a dimwit."

Fina makes delicious rabbit stew, Celestino Gamuzo doesn't mind that she has her monthlies.

"That's neither here nor there, you know that I'm not fussy."

The French are Catholics but in their own way of course, not like us Spaniards. Aunt Lourdes got smitten with smallpox and then they chucked her into a common grave, after she died, of course, the French don't beat about the bush and are quick to look out for number one. Aunt Lourdes died on her honeymoon, from the marriage bed to the icy grave, it's like the title of a novel by Ponson du Terrail,* everyone dies at the time and place appointed, the French infected her with smallpox and Uncle Cleto had no choice in the matter but wound up a widower.

Manueliño Remeseiro Domínguez hatched out a crow's egg in his armpit, it's just a matter of keeping still so as not to crush the shell. Manueliño Remeseiro Domínguez is locked up in jail because he thrashed somebody to death, you wouldn't credit the free-for-alls that go on at *romerías*, indeed, just one taken up the wrong way is enough to trigger off disaster.

"And sow the seeds of calamity?"

"Precisely. And sow the seeds of calamity. Nobody knows what the designs of divine Providence are, for the ways of God are unknown to man."

A silence fell and then Don Claudio Dopico Labuñeiro asked:

"Listen, what you've just said, where did you get that from?"

---

* Ponson du Terrail (1829–71) French novelist and Vicomte de Bordeaux. His serialized novels—particularly *Las Hazañas de Rocambole* (*The Exploits of Rocambole*)—gained immense popularity in Spain. —Trans.

"What a thing to ask! What the hell does that matter to you?"

When the crow hatched from its shell, Manueliño Remeseiro Domínguez tended it carefully and now the creature is his constant companion.

"What's the crow's name?"

"Moncho, just like a cousin of mine that died of whooping cough. Do you like it?"

"Yes, it's a lovely name, but I don't know that it quite fits."

"Ah, go on! Why not?"

In the mornings Moncho slips through the bars of the window and swoops about.

"It's great to watch him flap his wings; he's like Old Nick himself, he's so smart."

In the evenings, just before sunset, Moncho returns to the cell, he never flies to the wrong one, and he perches on Manueliño's head or upon his shoulder.

"And he always comes back?"

"Indeed he does. I don't think he would know to go anywhere else and anyway he always brings me a present of something: a piece of glass, a shell, a chestnut . . ."

Manueliño is teaching Moncho to whistle, he already knows a few bars of *Ma Petite Marianne*, the mazurka that Blind Gaudencio plays only on certain fateful occasions.

"Will you play that mazurka, Gaudencio?"

"Shut up, you good-for-nothing!"

Moncho can also speak a few words, Manueliño would like him to greet folks, Good morning, Don Cristóbal, Good afternoon, Doña Rita, Good evening, Castora, have a good time! Mamerto Paixón, a fellow Manueliño knows, has a crow that can recite the districts of Orense in alphabetical order: Allariz,

Bande, Carballiño, Celanova, etc. It's easier to teach a crow to speak than to learn their language, crows can sense rain, sickness and, death, and they croak with seventy-odd different caws, one for each different thing they sense.

"What I'd like to do now is raise a goldfinch, they're fine songsters, but where would I get hold of a goldfinch's egg?"

Adrián Estévez, from Ferreiravella in the district of Foz, is a well-known diver, in the Foz estuary he came across a German submarine nestling upon the sea bed with all the dead crew still inside. Adrián Estévez is known as Shark because he's so daring and swims like a fish. Shark is a friend of Baldomero Lionheart's and wants him to accompany him to the Antela lagoon.

"In Sandiás I have a relative who knows as sure as shootin' where the city of Antioch lies, he's from around there so he should know. I'll go with you but I won't set foot in the water, the only stipulation I make is that you mustn't kill any frogs because they're cousins of mine. Laugh if you like, see if I care! but the frogs in the Antela lagoon are cousins of mine, I swear."

Baldomero Lionheart has a tattoo on his arm of a naked woman with a serpent coiled about her, the woman is good luck and the serpent represents the three faculties of the soul.

"I don't get you."

"Makes no difference."

Shark wants to dive in the Antela lagoon, dodging the blood stains of Decio the Galician's Romans and King Arthur's Welshmen, to steal the bells of Antioch.

"I know that there are three curses on them but it's well worth the trouble all the same, the bells of Antioch are worth a fortune."

One night when the nightingale was trilling, the owl hooting, and the stars twinkling high in the sky, Shark plunged into the water, stark naked, with the Caravaca cross painted in red ochre upon his chest.

"Will it not wash off?"

"I don't think so. This stuff is made to last."

Lionheart waited on the shore with a shotgun, there was nobody else with them. Shark would come up every minute or minute and a half for air, then he would dive down again.

"Are you alright?"

"For the time being, so long as the cold doesn't get to me!"

At the hundredth dive, Shark was overcome with the cold and had to give up.

"The bells are not so very deep down but they're quite firmly fastened, on the clapper of the biggest one there is a hanged wolf. What a sight! the fishes have almost devoured him already. Don't you tell anybody where we went!"

"Don't worry."

The Venceás family's mute and nameless maidservant was savaged to death by dogs, it was a stroke of bad luck. Judging from her appearance, the Venceás family's mute and nameless maidservant might have been Portuguese. Expertly, lovingly, she used to brew a coffee liqueur that nobody could hold a candle to. Dorinda, the mother of the Venceás family, was deeply moved by the death of her maidservant. At a hundred and three years of age she really needed someone to do the chores for her.

"Shall we head for Orense and go into Sprat's place to warm ourselves up?"

"Fair enough."

The Venceás family's mute and nameless maidservant, around about the time of Don Manuel García Prieto's administration—you know the fellow from La Maragatería?, not that he was really from La Maragatería, he came more from Astorga way, but it's more or less the same thing—had a child by a corporal from the Civil Guard who used to wear a corset and was called Doroteo.

"Where was he from?"

"I don't know. He claimed to be from around Celanova, or Ramiranes, but to my mind he was from Asturias and didn't want to let on, some folks are full of notions, you know."

Doroteo used to do physical exercises and would recite *The Pirate's Song* by Espronceda in a fine voice:

With ten cannons a side,
under full sail before an aft wind. . . .

Doroteo wasn't one for frequenting bars or *romerías* and, when he was on leave, he would stay in the barracks reading verses by Espronceda, Núñez de Arce, Campoamor, and Antonio Grilo. Corporal Doroteo also liked carnal dealings with women, as the saying goes, he had chosen the Venceás family's maid because she was discreet and wouldn't tattle, well, the reason she didn't tattle was because she was mute rather than discreet, not that it makes any difference. Doroteo's moustache, a magnificent big handlebar moustache, would catch the eye of many a woman. Well, the deaf-mute was crazy about him, head over heels in love—as the saying goes—with Doroteo and when he set her on his lap and groped about, she would break out in strange little grunts of pleasure and delight.

"Like a rat?"

"Not really, more like a sheep."

The son of Doroteo and the mute now has a taxi in Allariz and they get by well enough, his wife is a midwife and their three children are studying in Santiago: the daughter, pharmacy; one son, teacher training; and the other, medicine.

Manueliño Remeseiro Domínguez wasn't so fortunate and now he's deprived of his freedom, in this life some folks have better luck than others.

"When is he getting out?"

"That all depends."

In the Agrosantiño mountains there lurks a vixen which kills only tender young fryers, she doesn't like hens for apparently she finds them too old and tough.

"What an uppity miss of a vixen! In years gone by they were hardier and not so choosy!"

"Indeed, in years gone by."

Don Claudio Dopico Labuñeiro lodges in Doña Elvira's inn, and has an affair with her in secret, or so it is said. Don Claudio is also doing a line with Castora, the maid, who in turn bestows her favors upon Don Cristóbal.

"Bestows her favors?"

"Well, you know what I mean."

Besides reciting poetry, Corporal Doroteo plays the harp, waltzes are what he's best at. Manuel Blanco Romasanta, the ripper who turned into a wolf and savaged folks to death, was saved from garrotting by a Chinese doctor, who was neither a doctor nor Chinese, but an English hypnotist, his name was Mr. Phillips and he taught electrobiology in Algiers: the Chinese doctor wrote a letter to the Spanish Ministry of Justice, which caused a great stir, and when she learned of the advances of science, Queen Isabella II granted the prisoner a reprieve. Wolves respond badly to captivity so, after a year in captivity, Manuel Blanco Romasanta pined away and died for want of his freedom, there are folks who are very sensitive to being penned up and may even die as a result, it's the same with sparrows, too. In the parish of San Verísimo de Espiñeiros, in Allariz, a Mass was said for the soul of the werewolf every February 29th, that is each leap year, until the custom died out with the Civil War. The bell of San Verísimo de Espiñeiros is so noble and grateful that it peals out when the sun shines upon it, folks who don't know find it confusing.

"Uncle Cleto."

"What, Camilito?"

"Will you give me ten *reales?*"

"No."

"Six, then?"

"No."

The house where my aunts and uncle live is in Albarona, overgrown with ivy and sweet pea, it's a handsome, spacious house now going to rack and ruin.

"Do you remember the blackbird that used to steal food from the blind man from Senderiz? He was the worst blind man in the world and then God punished him by sending a bird to steal his food, shortly afterwards he starved to death."

Don Claudio Dopico Labuñeiro is a schoolteacher and it seems he is having an affair with Doña Elvira, the landlady, something to that effect has already been mentioned.

"Castora is a slut, I know, but she's thirty years younger than me, and that counts for a lot. I don't chuck her out so as to have a hold over you, will you love me forever?"

"Forever and ever, Elvira . . . forever and ever, as they say, but who knows!"

Doña Elvira and Don Claudio drop the "Don" only in bed, it pays to keep up appearances. It wasn't easy for Don Claudio to get to bed with Castora, Doña Elvira keeps a close eye on them both, but he was able to squeeze her breasts or stroke her ass when he bumped into her in the hallway.

"Easy on, Don Claudio! What are you up to? You'll get what you're after once Sunday comes."

Don Claudio and Castora meet on Sunday afternoons in an imports warehouse on the Rairo road. The owner, a friend of Don Claudio's gives him the key, they even have a divan and a washstand. Doña Elvira allows Don Cristóbal a freer rein for she's not in love with him.

"You certainly have all the luck, Don Cristóbal, when to go to bed with me all you have to do is push open the door!"

"Hold your tongue, woman, and don't be fresh! You mind your own business!"

Mamerto Paixón, Manueliño Domínguez's friend, wanted to be a footballer but he destroyed himself with an invention he made so he had to give the idea up.

"Did you never think of becoming a priest?"

"No, ma'am, never."

Moncho Lazybones is a ferocious liar, by and large men with limps are almighty fibbers, well, not all of them, of course, but as a rule of thumb.

"When her first husband—Adolfito—was alive, my cousin Georgina used to bathe in the altogether in Lucio Mouro's millpond, like Catuxa Bainte. There was a trout that would hover motionless staring at her breasts until my cousin left or whatever, my cousin always had fine-looking tits, but what's odd about it is that a trout should gawp at her like a Peeping Tom."

Adolfito Penouta Augalevada, alias the Buffoon, had been María Auxiliadora Porrás' sweetheart but she left him because he was going to die.

"That fellow's not long for this world, just mark my words, you have only to touch his hands."

Moncho Lazybones also saw a weasel and a hare, perched on a rock on the shore, delighting, even gloating, at the sight of his cousin's breasts.

"Animals have to be seen to be believed! Just look at the instincts they have!"

María Auxiliadora stoutly argued her case:

"That fellow's not long for this world, you have only to see how dull his skin is, you have only to touch his hands. Georgina is welcome to him! Let her be the one to wear widow's weeds! No dead man is going to get my virginity, I won't have it."

"But María Auxiliadora, are you a virgin?"

"Shut up, you idiot! What's bitten you?"

"Get a grip on yourself, María Auxiliadora, and don't raise your voice to me!"

Adolfito Buffoon married Georgina but he wasn't long for this world, it was God's will for him to last a while longer but he found being a cuckold hard to bear so he hanged himself from the bar in the wardrobe, some say his wife killed him off with a potion of herbs, who knows? When the judge opened the wardrobe door the dead body tumbled out on top of him and gave him an awful fright.

"My God, a bloody dead man! What a way to treat a judge!"

Carmelo Méndez accompanied Georgina throughout the formalities and when the judge wasn't looking he would slip a hand up her skirts.

"Cut it out, Méndez! We can play around once the deceased is dead and buried."

"As you wish, my love, you know that your wish is my command, I only want to please you."

Moncho Lazybones used to speak fondly of his cousins Georgina and Adela and their mother.

"She was just like a mother to me, Aunt Micaela was always so good to me, when I was small she gave me the adventures of

Dick Turpin and used to jack me off the moment we were on our own. My heart would leap when she asked me: Do you like that, you dirty little pig?"

There was a big turnout at Adolfito's funeral, folks were very fond of him since he was a nosey-parker. Folks at the funeral talked about the local football team and how attractive and tantalizing the widow was.

"But just look at her sister!"

"There's no call to make comparisons, they're different but both fine-looking women."

Moncho Lazybones was lamed on Moorish soil, he came back from Melilla with a wooden leg and splitting his sides with laughter.

"What are you laughing at, you wretch?"

"I'm laughing at how much worse it would have been if they'd given me a wooden soul!"

Knocking about for years and years in my family home there were three Carlist berets with gold tassels that belonged to Don Severino Losada, an uncle of my mother's who rose to the rank of colonel in the Carlist forces and went off to fight around Ordenes and Arzúa, on either side of the River Tambre, between the Dubra valley and Melide, just in the spot where at the end of the last civil war the guerrilla fighters Manuel Ponte and Benigno García Andrade got a gang together: certain landscapes lend themselves to the smell of gunpowder and the color of blood. Uncle Cleto used to sport Don Severino's three berets during carnival until they wound up bedraggled and motheaten; in my family it was normal for things to get motheaten; in my family weariness and neglect are cultivated as fine arts.

"Jesusa."

"Yes, Emilita?"

"Do you remember that silver rosary, blessed by Pope Leo XIII, which our dear mother brought us from Rome?"

"Goodness knows! I haven't seen it around for ages, chances are it's lost."

"More than likely."

By dint of excessive prayer, incessant gossiping, and frenzied piddling, Aunt Jesusa and Aunt Emilita have lost all hope, faith is their consolation and charity beyond their grasp. When Uncle Cleto feels bored to tears, he spends the day vomiting in his chamber pot or behind the bureau.

"What a relief that was!"

Uncle Cleto's dog is called Hornet and she eats what her master heaves up or gently regurgitates, for Uncle Cleto has various ways of throwing up. At times Hornet acts strange and staggers and lurches drunkenly about, apparently some days Uncle Cleto's vomit is too strong for her. Uncle Cleto is a great hand at jazz, all he needs is to be black, for this business of playing jazz, or the flute, the mandola or whatever, by ear, it's just as well to be a widower, for it lends a certain interest to the performance.

"I don't understand."

"Go on! Why do you have to understand? There are many things that cannot be understood, my friend, and one has no choice but put up with it."

"Now I get you."

The remains of the Saintly Fernández and his seven martyred companions (there's no need to list the names here, let their relations see to that) are interred in the Spanish convent in the Holy Land, in the Christian quarter of Bab Tuma in Damascus, nearly all the information given in the encyclopedia is erroneous but that's the least of it for he was only a minor saint, though he's the only one we have in our family. Father Santisteban, S.J., was a hick who took snuff and my aunts' cascarilla tea was nearly the death of him

"Another little cup Don Obdulio? It'll give you strength."

"Just to please you, my dear friends, just to please you . . ."

Father Santisteban, S.J., knew no pity.

"On the Day of Judgement we the righteous shall receive our just reward amidst great merriment and rejoicing while the damned shall be cast into the terrible flames where they shall burn for centuries in that unconsuming fire, will you pass me a cookie there, my dear Jesusa? God bless you! In the full knowledge of our righteousness we shall say unto them 'Did you not taste the pleasures of the wicked world and savor the delights of sinful flesh? Here you have your reward! Burn, you wretches, and suffer, whilst we reap the rewards of eternal bliss! Will you pour me a drop of tea, my dear Emilita? Bless you!'"

Father Santisteban, S.J., is not very distinguished for a Jesuit, he's like a Christian Brother, nor does he smell too sweet either, truth to tell, he reeks with the rankness of a billy goat.

"That's because he lives like a real saint and neglects his personal hygiene, he isn't caught up with such worldly cares."

"More than likely."

"Indeed so highly likely, my dear friend! for answer me this: what shall it profit a man to scent his mortal flesh and temporal garments with myrrh and musk, if he should lose his soul?"

"True enough!"

"Indeed so very true! Let us attend to the great task of saving the soul and set aside the pomp and vanities of this vile world!"

"Jesus Christ, our Lord, humble man and yet divine . . ."

In 1935 there were no accidents in S.P.A.L.—Spanish

Postal Air Lines—after six years of service during which they had traveled the equivalent of 126 times around the world. Mamerto Paixón invented a flying machine which he called the Swallow, it looked like a bat with pedals and fixed wings but he called it the Swallow.

"I named it so after the bird that's best at flying, it's a delight to watch them glide. Do you realize, Miss Jesusa, that very shortly—God willing—I shall be swooping through the air like a swallow? There'll be nothing to beat launching myself from the belfry of the church of San Juan de Barrán for a bit of a thrust."

"Don't do it, Mamerto, you might hurt yourself!"

"Not at all, Miss, you just wait and see."

After High Mass on Easter Sunday in the year 1935, Mamerto leant out of the belfry of San Juan, donned the wings of his flying machine and whoosh! leaped into the void, but instead of soaring upwards he plummetted down on to the ground of the churchyard. Crowds of people had turned out to watch, they had even come from as far off as Carballiño, from Chantada, and Lalín, from all over they'd come, and when Mamerto was about to be smashed into smithereens upon the ground there was a great commotion with everyone scurrying to and fro.

"Keep calm! Just keep calm!" exhorted Father Romualdo, the priest. "He's just been to confession and received the sacraments so he'll go straight up to heaven, put a stone under his head as a pillow and let him breathe his last in peace and in the grace of God. Prepared for death at this moment as he'll never be again!"

"No, Father! We'd better take him to Orense to see if they can do anything to save him at the hospital!"

"Do as you wish! But I wash my hands of all responsibility for such a rash decision!"

Father Romualdo spoke with great precision but the parishioners heard only the patter of his words. They wrapped Mamerto Paixón in a blanket and carted him off to Orense in Reboredo's taxi which came straight away; he was at death's door upon arrival, but an operation did the trick and within a few days he was on the mend.

"Is there anything left of the Swallow?"

"Precious little, why?"

"Nothing, I just want to get well so as to have another go, I think it was a fault in the transmission."

"Look, quit this tomfoolery! Count yourself lucky to be alive and don't go tempting Fate!"

Doña María Auxiliadora Mourence, Porrás' widow—the mother of the girl who wouldn't marry Adolfito because he wasn't long for this world—was a very hefty lady indeed with bunions and a waddle chronometrically synchronized with her various reflexes, features, and exhalations, for a bit of order never goes amiss, like this: two paces, five heartbeats, a pen slips from her grasp, a pause, a fit of coughing, a volley of farts, a twitch of her snout, a pause, half-suppressed wind, she heaves a heavy sigh, a single hiccup, a pause, and so forth all day long, tomorrow, next month, next year, God willing. The famous Losada file painlessly removes corns, callouses, and thickened toe nails as if by magic.

Below the River Miño, to the south that is, midway between Orense and Castrelo, between the Rábeda valley and the Ribeiro, are the Trelle earthworks where dead Moors dwell. Trelle is in the district of Toén, in the parish of Santa María dos Anxos. There are still plenty of Moors living in Galicia, it's

Camilo José Cela

just that you can't see them because they're dead and bewitched and wander below the earth. In the Trelle ruins there
lives the richest Moorish colony in the whole region, ruled by
the wizard Abd Alá el-Azziz ben Meruán, the Portuguese Vali,
Moorish governor of Monforte, who is one-eyed, red-haired,
and leprous but has the power to turn anything he pleases into
gold: a pebble, a beetle, a poppy, a slave, anything at all; the
Trelle ruins are littered with gold pebbles, beetles, poppies,
and slaves. Basilio Ribadelo, a muleteer from Sobrado do Bispo, used to cart wine to the Moors by night so that the Christians wouldn't see him, and in payment they gave him slabs of
slate that turned into gold on his way home, the Moors made
Basilio swear an oath that he would tell nobody on condition
that, if he didn't keep his word, the slabs would revert to their
former wretched state. Casilda Gorgulfe, his wife, was alarmed
at the sight of such riches.

"That comes from smuggling," she told her husband. "And
don't deny it; the Civil Guard will nab you and beat the living
daylights out of you, just wait and see!"

"Not at all, woman," replied Basilio. "I earned that money
by the honest sweat of my brow, but I can't tell you how."

But Casilda insisted and insisted and begged and threatened
and implored until finally, harried by her insults and whee-
dling, Basilio blurted out the truth.

"Don't breathe a word to a soul for if the Moors get wind of it
they won't pay me a single cent ever again."

But despite her better judgement, Casilda's tongue ran away
with her, the Moors got wind of it and, as a just punishment
meted out to Basilio, they never again opened the doors of the
earthworks to him. Basilio beat the living daylights out of his
wife but his good fortune had dried up forever and years later,

as fate would have it, he ended his days an impoverished carter.

"Will you pour me a brandy?"

"Of course."

Miss Ramona's robe is very elegant, revealing and very elegant.

"I'd like to be utterly stark naked but I feel the cold."

"Not at all, woman."

Miss Ramona believes that life is short and old age but a habit.

"A proper nuisance it is, too, Raimundo, mark my words. A woman is old at the age twenty-five, a man has a while longer ahead of him, a man can even go on to thirty or thirty-five years of age. Will you give me a kiss? I'm sort of depressed today, I don't know what's wrong with me . . . If you think I'm a slut, Raimundo, that's where you're wrong, the dog gives me at least as much pleasure as you do, the only difference is that I love you. Poor Wilde! You men are capricious creatures, and you are the most capricious of all but it's worth giving in to as many of your whims as I can, we women are more solitary than men, that's why there are more dykes than fairies, if I could be sure that I wouldn't feel the cold I would get into bed stark naked and I wouldn't get up for a whole month."

The Casandulfe Raimundo fell silent.

"Will you pour me more brandy?"

"Of course."

"Will you invite me to canned asparagus for supper?"

"I'm glad you ask, Raimundo."

Everybody says that Doña Rita Freire, the proprietress of the English Biscuit cookie factory, has be-nookied her second husband but there's not a word of truth in it. Nobody be-nookies

Don Rosendo Vilar Santeiro, he's very much his own master, even when it comes to be-nookification, what there is more truth in is that Doña Rita is bewitched, or be-dicked I should say, by Don Rosendo, and she will drain to the last drop whoever can go to bed with her twice a day. Doña Rita is a lioness always ready for a tumble, though at times she doesn't even get as far as the hay: anywhere will do.

Luisiño Bocelo, Don Benigno's eunuch servant, died in the war but he died of natural causes, first he went blind then he caught a dose of the flu and died. They used to call Luisiño Boeclo "Coot" but all in good fun, not from spite.

"Coot!"

"Yes, Don Benigno?"

"Hop about as long as you can!"

"Yes, sir."

Ádega knows the story of the mountain inside out.

"They got carried away with the half-wit from Bidueiros and the poor creature was killed like a common criminal, you can't fool about with the gallows for there's no going back, they hanged the Bidueiros half-wit without meaning to but they hanged him all the same, and what difference does it make to him whether they meant to hang him or not? His father, the priest from San Miguel de Buciños, did his duty by him: he said three Masses for him and buried him on consecrated ground.

They allow Eleuterio the Britches into Sprat's brothel but they won't let him breathe as much as a word.

"Either you mind your own business or you're out on your ear, but you needn't come here to talk the hind leg off a donkey."

Tanis Gamuzo, his son-in-law, won't even speak to him.

"My father-in-law is a turd, if it wasn't for Rosa's sake,

I would have bust his face two years ago, you can't trust his sort, give them an inch and they take a mile, as the saying goes."

Portuguese Marta would sooner go hungry than hit the hay with Britches.

"I'd sooner starve or die a beggar! Eleuterio is a bastard and he turns my stomach, he's revolting."

Doña Rita's first husband was a tall, stout, squashy storekeeper who did himself in with a shotgun, so fed up was he. When he was alive and kicking, Doña Rita's first husband was named Don Clemente, Fat-of-the-Land they used to call him, Don Clemente Bariz Carballo was from the village of Monteveloso in the parish of Santas Eufemia de Piornedo, in the district of Castrelo, over Riós way south of the Nofre crags, and he made a pretty penny from wolfram, though little good did it do him. Don Clemente gradually grew sick and tired of life—that's the worst—until one day he couldn't take it any longer so he loaded his shotgun with wolf slugs, settled himself comfortably in an armchair in the parlor, placed the barrel in his mouth, pulled the trigger, and shot his head off into smithereens, the biggest piece of which was the size of a greengage plum, his brains stuck to the lamp so they had to clean it down with disinfectant. Don Clemente and Doña Rita had seven children, they were still only tiny tots at the time; when she was widowed Doña Rita would have been about thirty-two or thirty-three years of age and she longed for a bit of rough and tumble, if the flesh yearns for a tussle it's like a parching thirst. Doña Rita found consolation from her spiritual adviser, Father Rosendo Vilar Santeiro, a priest, with whom she had been having an affair for many years.

"Why don't you give up the cloth, Rosendo, and we'll get properly married?"

"How could I get married when I am in holy orders? Do you not realize or what?"

"Go on! What a hoot! But you sure broke your vows of chastity with me, didn't you?"

Father Rosendo lost his cool.

"What has a piece of ass got to do with the Ember Days, for God's sake?"

Tanis Gamuzo's mastiffs—Lion, Sailor, and Tsar—are obedient and brave and loyal, with those dogs you could wander about with your eyes closed and neither the wild boar nor the wolf would set a foot near you. Tanis also breeds smart, frisky, mischievous sheepdogs, not above worrying beasts up the mountain given half a chance. Tanis knows a great deal about dogs, he takes good care of them, trains them, and makes a bit on the side from them.

"There are worse vices, don't you think?"

"Oh! Do I ever, son? Do I ever!"

In Rauco's inn the Casandulfe Raimundo and Robín Lebozán are arguing with a Castilian gentleman flashing visiting cards emblazoned with the Calatrava cross and his name embossed in heavy lettering: Toribio de Mogrovejo y de Bustillo del Oro.

"Was he an aristocrat?"

"So we all thought until a pair of Civil Guards led him off in handcuffs for swindling a tobacconist in Orense."

"For goodness sake!"

"As true as I'm here! His real name was Toribio Expósito, that name Toribio de Mogrovejo is the name of a saint, not his own name: St. Toribio de Mogrovejo, Archbishop of Lima, Peru, who zealously spread the faith and ecclesiastical doctrine throughout Latin America."

"Well I never!"

"I got the full story from the secretary, you see."

"Indeed."

"The name Bustillo del Oro he took from his home town in Zamora. It seems there were various suits filed against him in several courts."

"For different offenses?"

"More than likely."

To return to our story: Toribio de Mogrovejo, the Casandulfe Raimundo, and Robín Lebozán were embroiled in a lofty argument, the rest held their tongues not daring even to voice their opinion. The positions were as follows: Toribio de Mogrovejo believed both in God and in priests, he had the best developed argument, while the Casandulfe Raimundo believed in God (although preferring the term the Supreme Maker) but not in priests, that smacks of Free Masonry, and Robín Lebozán, apparently so as not to let the conversation flag, believed in priests though not in God.

"What a load of baloney!"

"Indeed."

The dispute was interrupted by the pair of Civil Guards, it was after one o'clock in the morning. Toribio de Mogrovejo blanched when the Civil Guard pounced on him with:

"Are you Toribio Expósito?"

"At your service."

"You are under arrest!"

Toribio offered no resistance, he let himself be handcuffed and disappeared off into the night along the main road with a Civil Guard on either side of him.

"It's cold."

"Walking will soon warm you up."

Doña Rita made up her mind that Father Rosendo should

not escape her clutches and she got her way, perseverance yields results. Doña Rita launched her attack upon the priest by means of his stomach (through his lust she already had him in the palm of her hand), his vanity, and avarice for Father Rosendo was greedy, lustful, and avaricious.

"Here, take this gold watch that belonged to my idiot of a late husband, you might as well have it since you're more of a man than he was."

"Thanks, I'll have the date on which you gave it to me engraved upon it."

One day Doña Rita made so bold as to say:

"I'm not going to beat about the bush. Goodness me! But if you ditch your habit and come and live with me, I'll give you a million *pesos*. It's up to you."

Father Rosendo said yes, of course he would, and that was that, he took the million *pesos* and went to live with the widow. The scandal that followed was monumental, but Father Rosendo merely smiled.

"The fuss will soon die down and in the meantime the money stays put. Rita and I are very happy, and as soon as I can sort my situation out, we'll get married. What more does the Good Lord ask than for his creatures to be happy?"

In the Santa Rosiña de Xericó graveyard the mandrake grows, both male and female, the attributes of which can be seen in the roots to which a dog is tethered. Any woman who touches the mandrake becomes with child, sometimes just to catch the whiff of it is enough, and the dog howls when it wants someone to sleep, to tell the truth: I confess to killing with an axe the traveler who decorated his hat with daisies and his beard with butterflies in myriad colors, I killed him because he cast me an evil glance and pulled a fast one on me at half past seven, it doesn't matter a whit to me if they hang me because I know that God will forgive my sins. I burned the dead man with camellia twigs so that he wouldn't harbor a grudge against me. The hangman raised the gallows in the Santa Rosiña graveyard, just above the tenderest mandrake shoots for the hanged man to nourish them with life-giving semen, with sustaining, strength-giving blood and the spittle to bind and tell the tale. Luisiño Coot had sensitive eyes and Don Benigno prescribed a cure of mandrake root beaten with oil and wine.

"And did it cure him?"

"No, sir, he went blind."

If the male organs are to be seen in the mandrake root, any man that passes by the plant will be loved by women until the end of his days, until he is loved to death and priests bury him out of charity. The Civil Guard conveyed Toribio de Mogrovejo y de Bustillo del Oro to Ponferrada by ordinary transport; they took nine days because it's quite far off, all uphill and down dale. If the female organs are to be seen in the roots of the mandrake, any woman that passes the plant shall be loved by a dapper dwarf with a shock of tousled hair called Mandrake, who feeds on nettles and semolina and speaks without opening his lips.

"Will you love me, beautiful woman?"

"Shut up, you slobberer! Drop dead!"

Before uprooting the mandrake from the earth you must draw around it three circles with a sword, while a whore sings psalms and a lay brother dances the cancan hoisting his habit to reveal his privates. It may also be uprooted by tethering a starving dog to it and making it tug without stopping for breath, when the plant shrieks out in pain, the dog dies of fright.

"Don't bury it, just leave it for the crows to eat."

Doña Rita held Don Rosendo captive by means of his palate

and his prick, or by his taste buds and the delicate bud of that other organ.

"Screw me, isn't that what I pay you for, you bugger! Don't you enjoy being well-fed and having your privates fondled? Well, then, put the children to bed and don't be long about it! Don't forget to give them your blessing!"

"Not to worry!"

Braulio Doade, one of Miss Ramona's servants (all four of them have one foot in the grave and are half-blind as well as half-deaf, bronchitic, and rheumatic, too) was out in the Philippines when they were still a Spanish colony, Braulio was always very natty and dressed to the nines.

"Do you remember General Camilo Polavieja's famous proclamation on the island of Mindinao in which he declared he would castrate every Moor that he caught with a weapon in his hand?"

"No, I don't remember that at all. Are you sure you're not making it up?"

When Braulio Doade died he was so wizened away that he weighed scarcely anything at all.

"Shall we have a Mass said for him, Miss?"

"Pshaw! I think an Our Father will be more than ample."

Pigs cannily root up mountain truffles and dogs tear up mandrake roots with their teeth, though it should be a black dog and die afterwards.

"Shall we turn men into porcupines and women into earthworms?"

The Devil sells his flying ointment at the fairs of the saints Dionís and Leonís at San Roguiño de Malta, if only Mamerto Paixón had known! It is peddled under license by a witch, maybe it's the devil himself in disguise, and until sun-up she sells it at half-price so that the poor may also reap its benefits.

"Fly like the birds of the air and the blessed souls in purgatory! Whoever wishes to fly can do so!"

The ointment—there's also a cream, which is thicker—is made from boiling a Moorish or an unbaptised child in a copper cauldron of rose water; when the water has reduced enough you mix the sediment with a widow's menstrual blood, ground bones from a hanged man, woman's urine, mandrake roots, and the three plants of Beelzebub: henbane, which helps you fly through the air and relieves toothache, headache, and earache; deadly nightshade, which women and actors use to paint their eyes; and thorn apple with its ghostly, infernal spines, which releases a flood of sweet dreams of death. At San Roquiño the elixir of long life is sold as well as badwives' syrup at one *real* a swallow.

"You want to blot out the horns of cuckoldry or that mole of adultery to fade from your skin?"

One day when Don Rosendo was too prompt to pull the trigger Doña Rita gave him such a drubbing that the workers from the English Biscuit Factory were forced to intervene, headed by the overseer, Casiano Real, who was always a most responsible person.

"Easy on, missus! for God's sake, or you'll kill him! If Don Rosendo isn't up to the job, then one of us will finish it off! Take it easy, ma'am, before we come to blows! And cover up your tits, begging your pardon! or you'll catch your death!"

In the Santa Rosiña de Xericó graveyard the Civil Guard Fausto Belinchón González, from Motilla del Palancar over Cuenca way, in la Mancha, and Uncle Cleto play checkers, unbelievable though it may be, but it happened for I saw it with my own two eyes.

"Meanness has a charm of its own, Camilito, the worst is not trampling the mandrake but hurtling and tumbling downhill, just look at Rita Freire, a young woman of means, yet she's begging along the road to death."

In a single night the wolves killed three cows and their calves on the St. Cristobo mountain and nobody knew that they were there. Armed with a shotgun, Tanis Gamuzo set out with his dogs to track them down and the following night he killed two wolves, one weighing about a hundred and fifty pounds, it wasn't the Zacumeira wolf but not far off it; the dog Kaiser was badly wounded and they had to destroy him with a knife, that's always a terrible pity. Tanis sent the pelts of both wolves, along with three others that he had, for tanning and then presented them to Anunciación Sabadelle, Sprat's tart.

"Here, take these and make a coverlet for Gaudencio, they're good and warm."

When my cousins from Corunna sent me the cheroots, I took them along to Marcos Albite.

"A promise is a promise."

"Thanks, I was a bit fed up with chewing Portuguese tobacco, all the good of it goes in the spittle, you'll give me bad habits."

Catuxa Bainte brought Marcos Albite a quart of wine from the inn.

"Today I'm as I want to be, there aren't many such days."

The man's voice changed.

"Forgive me for addressing you so familiarly in front of folks, well, not that Catuxa really counts."

It seemed to me an opportune moment.

"Better that we should use the *tú* form all the time—before the war we did, you're a Guxinde, too, indeed as much a Guxinde as I am."

"True enough, but I'm a poor Guxinde, a pretty useless Guxinde . . ."

Catuxa brought two glasses of wine, one for Marcos Albite and another for me, mine was as clean as a whistle and a delight to behold.

"Shall I rinse out your piddle can?"

"Do."

Marcos Albite patted his cheroots.

"You prefer them to the shorter ones?"

"I couldn't really say."

Something like a flash of hope shot through the sky, maybe it was a dove.

"I don't trust a single devil, before I was able to stand up for myself, but look at me now, trapped in this coffin on wheels!"

The oxcart sings as it rumbles along the track and its squeaking affrights the wolf and alerts the vixen, the world is like a sound box and the crust of the earth like the skin of the drum, just like the taut covering of the drum. Marcos Albite repainted the little star and polished up the tacks which showed his initials.

"I've nearly finished that saint for you, it's a real humdinger of a St. Camilo, just wait and see, I'll give it to you next week, all I have to do now is to sand it down a bit."

Feliciano Vilagabe San Martiño took his time about getting married; he was sweetheart to Angustias Zoñán Corvacín for twenty-three years and their marriage was shortlived, indeed it can't have lasted as much as an hour and a half. When the bride and groom came out of the church, she said to him:

"Shall we go to the graveyard with mamma for a moment to lay a bunch of flowers on my father's grave?"

And he replied:

"You two go. I'll wait here."

When Angustias returned, Feliciano had skipped off like a

spring breeze; Remedios, the landlady, stepped out of Rauco's inn and handed Angustias an envelope.

"Here! Feliciano left this for you."

In a fit of nerves Angustias tore the envelope open, and inside she found a scrap of paper with a message written in a rounded hand: Go to hell! She never heard from Feliciano again, it was as though the earth had swallowed him up, although somebody said they saw him in Madrid, working as a bus conductor.

"So what did Angustias do?"

"What could she do? First she waited—she was well used to waiting—she waited for four or five years, and then she became a nun, she didn't fit the bill for a whore, for that sort of thing you need to be of tender years, well, less of a wrinkled old bag."

The Vilagabes are very hoity-toity folks and always were. Truth to tell they were a pretty useless bunch but always very toffee-nosed and finicky, very proper and particular in their tastes and interests. Angustias, on the other hand, was a common conceited little swank full of airs and graces like holding her knife in a horrible way, cocking her little finger in the air when she lifted her cup, and saying "crocrettes" and "just an eensty-weensty bit."

"That's hard to take."

"Very hard, it's even worse than adultery; adultery happens in the best of families, and Angustias' family are nothing but riff-raff, the whole world is turned upside down these days."

"But why didn't he ditch her while they were still sweethearts?"

"How would I know? They say he was stringing her along for years."

"It would have been worse if he had been boring the pants off her for years."

"You're right there. Just look what might have been!"

Miss Ramona always held that Angustias was like a block of wood.

"She's just like a homemade bedside table hewn from rough mountain pine, if even that. Angustias was always very dim, some women don't even rank among the human race, and that's the truth. Angustias is a cow, just like a dun heifer."

Everybody gets by as best they can, Feliciano Vilagabe made his getaway, a hard thing to do just right for each case has its own peculiar characteristics.

"Do you remember Medardo Congos, the Pontevedra vet who had a dick the length of your finger and cheated at cards?"

"Why wouldn't I remember him?"

"Well, he did the very opposite: he didn't run away, his wife ran away on him and he threw a banquet for over a hundred people to celebrate, it cost him a pretty penny. I don't think my wife will dare come back after this, he told his friends. If you only knew what peace descended when she packed her bags and left!"

From his father, who was a lighthouse keeper, Medardo inherited a cage with a stuffed seagull inside.

"It's called Dulce Nombre, in memory of a sweetheart my good father had before he entered into marriage with my blessed mother, God rest their souls! Those were proper patriarchal ways not like nowadays, which are the very devil of a debauchery."

"Congos, get a grip on yourself!"

"Pardon me."

Teresita del Niño Jesús Minguez Gandarela, the runaway wife of the vet, wears her hair cropped short and smokes in front of men.

"Brazen hussy! And where did she run off to?"

"Not too far away, she went to Sarria with an unauthorized attorney who danced the tango and the foxtrot well, apparently she was fed up with the shortcomings of that husband of hers, to tell the truth there are women whose minds it wouldn't even cross."

The Casandulfe Raimundo and I watched our cousin Ramona strolling beneath the trees in the garden, dressed to the nines, all alone and so haughty under her umbrella, she had the little dog Wilde at her side. Raimundo and I watched her for some time without uttering a word, indeed why would we? Our cousin Ramona went as far as the river, fixed her gaze upon the current for some time, then walked slowly back towards the house. I went off and Raimundo pretended that he had just arrived.

"Here, your camellia as usual."

"Thanks a lot."

"Were you out for a stroll?"

"No, I just went down to the river to watch the water flow past, it's years ago today that my mother drowned."

"That's right!"

Our cousin Ramona smiled wistfully.

"How time passes, Raimundo! When my mother died I was just a little girl, I was thirteen years old and felt that the world was caving in on top of me, but the world never caves in on top of anyone."

"No."

"We all grow old and all our many airs and graces pass with the years."

"Indeed."

"And the bees in our bonnets, too."

"Those, too."

Our cousin Ramona was in a strange mood, to Raimundo she appeared very beautiful.

"Leave me alone, I just want to weep."

In Sarria when she moved in with Filemón Toucido Rozabales, an attorney whose affairs were in a mess, Teresita del Niño Jesús behaved in an exemplary fashion, apparently to pull the wool over the eyes of the folks in the area.

"We need to organize three societies: clothes for the poor, milk distribution centers, and the encouragement of late vocations."

"Yes, of course. And we'll ask His Holiness for His blessing so that we have everything, it's important to do things right from the word go."

"We could also found an organisation to lead fallen young women back to the straight and narrow from which they should never have strayed."

"Naturally. And another for the integration of gypsies within Spanish Christian society in order to cherish them to the bosom of our Holy Catholic religion."

Doña Asunción Trasparga de Méndez is known as Sweet Choniña because she's married to Méndez the candy-maker, Filomeno Méndez Vilamuín. Sweet Choniña shyly enquired:

"Will we have enough money to get by?"

"Aw, what a killjoy!"

When Teresita del Niño Jesús began to feel secure—little by little everybody gets to feel secure, it's the law of nature—she began to forget all about charitable institutions. To hell with the poor! this business of milk distribution is nothing but a curse! To hell with whoever thinks of joining the priesthood late in life! May the fallen young women have a ball, for life is short! I was just saying that when Teresita del Niño Jesús began to feel secure, she took to whoring like a duck to water. Toucido did his best to console her but with doubtful success.

"Just do whatever you want, Teresita, but don't go raising a rumpus or shouting it from the rooftops, I see no need to make a song and dance about fornication in front of everyone, causing scandal and preaching the dissolute life. Think it over and you'll see I'm right, I'm a modern man, as you well know, but patience has its limits, too."

"Of course! Forgive me once more, Filemón, my love! It's just that I can't help it, don't ever leave me alone! Will you take me dancing?"

Teresita del Niño Jesús likes to cut a dash in a wide-brimmed hat and twirl spinning tops.

"Is she not a bit long in the tooth for that?"

"Go on! Why not!"

Teresita del Niño Jesús gabbles faster than most.

"I'd like them to cut off both your legs as they did to Marcos Albite, my love, just to dandle you on my lap and put you out in the street to pee-pee with your little willy sticking out, so that all the world could see how much I love you and how well I take care of you, I would treat you like a little prince."

"Hush, woman! You're talking rubbish!"

"Not rubbish at all, my love! It's you I love dearly, not Congos!"

"That's all very well and thanks a lot. But why don't you take a little nap? You're rather overwrought."

Sweet Choniña is a hard worker and keeps an eye on the purse strings.

"Don't you like to have a fling?"

"Indeed I do! Doesn't everyone?!"

Sweet Choniña is having an affair with two employees in her husband's candy store, the pastry chef and the oven boy, proper respect should always be paid to rank and professional titles, both of them are cheerful and lively in their fornication but, since she is discreet, neither one suspects that her charms are not enjoyed exclusively by him but that she has a sleeping-partner.

"I'm all yours, my love! I couldn't love anyone else as much as I love you!"

Robín Lebozán sits down on the rocking chair and reads all the above aloud.

"I think I've earned myself a coffee and a brandy. If I come across any chocolates, though it's getting late now, I'll take them over to Rosicler to fatten her up a bit. Did you ever see the likes of this notion she's taken into her head about jacking off Mona's monkey! Not a devil alive can make head nor tail of women!"

Robín Lebozán is handsome—like father like son—in his home they've been enjoying three square meals a day for five generations now.

"You have to take things with a pinch of salt, folks will favor the hierarchy over truth, which is always relative."

Robín Lebozán rolls a cigarette.

"Each passing day there are more threads in this tobacco, still, what can we do?!"

Robín Lebozán looks out the window, the cornfields are sodden and a young lad is cycling up the track.

"Yes, indeed, Poe was right: our thoughts are palsied and sere, our memories treacherous, sere and rusted like old knives, apparently that's how it is, it must be in the nature of things."

Camilo José Cela

The première of Azorín's play *La Guerrilla* in the Benavente Theater in Madrid was a resounding success, premières are always resounding successes, what utter baloney!

"We live in our thoughts, memory is like the guide rope trailing behind a hot air balloon."

Ramona Faramiñás has a seven valve Telefunken radio that set her back a thousand *pesetas*, she doesn't listen to it a great deal but it's a good one, indeed the very best. Policarpo la Bagañeira can train anything you care to give him, well, not quite everything, he can't manage the wild boar, the wild boar has no savvy or understanding, nor does it want to, the wild boar might as well have cotton wool or pumice stone between its two ears. When things get out of kilter the best you can do is retreat into your shell and wait for them to settle down. Policarpo la Bagañeira is missing three fingers from his right hand, a stallion snapped them off once when he went up to the corral, two or three years back, maybe more, maybe even four or five years back. There are days when you think the sun is trying to come out then it clouds over again and everything is back to square one again. Robín Lebozán doesn't want to keep a diary for he doesn't want to admit that mankind is a hairy, gregarious beast, wearisome and devoted to miracles and happenings, the worst of all possible blows is losing your appetites, your strength, and even your wits, wild boars always trot along the same path, which is why you can lie in wait to polish them off with a knife. Policarpo has killed fourteen or fifteen of them now, an injured one got away on him once but he doesn't count it since he couldn't find it again, it's not the same thing at all when a trembling barber kicks the bucket as when a haughty cavalry general, bedecked with medals and decorations passes on. Robín Lebozán is well-read and has a good memory, he knows the *Episodios Nacionales** off by heart. Lázaro Codesal died an uneventful death, through no fault of his own, at the Tizzi-Azza post in Morocco, that's the worst about wars: straight away they begin to reek either of camphor or rankness, that's neither here nor there. Gaudencio Beira plays the accordion really well, indeed as well as he can. Gaudencio Beira is blind and has been playing the accordion for many years now in Pura Garrote's—Sprat's—whorehouse, younger clients call her Doña Pura. Benicia is the niece of blind Gaudencio and they say she has nipples like chestnuts, not that I would know. Catuxa Bainte, the half-wit from Martiñá, is like a gorse bush with its golden flowers, every corner of the world has its point of balance and its center of gravity and it's unwise to try to change it. Catuxa Bainte likes to wander up the mountain with her tits drenched, she does right. Getting on for two or three years ago, Baldomero Lionheart disarmed a couple of Civil Guards. Baldomero Lionheart has a tattoo on his arm of a naked woman with a serpent coiled about her body, it makes women sit up and take notice. Lionheart hasn't turned thirty yet but he's not far off it, his parents were killed in a train crash, they weren't squashed but suffocated. Tanis the Demon is even stronger than his brother Lionheart and anybody else, for that matter, Tanis the Demon can floor an ox with a single blow of his fist. Ádega is Benicia's mother, Ádega plays the accordion almost as well as her brother, the piece she plays best is the *Fanfinette* polka. Ádega's husband, I mean, Benicia's husband, is called Apóstol Braga Mendes and he may have gone back to Portugal for he hasn't shown his face about here and Ádega—I mean Benicia—doesn't know if she is still a

---

* By Benito Pérez Galdós (1843–1920). *Los Episodios Nacionales* is in three series, comprising twenty-six volumes. —Trans.

married woman or a widow, truth to tell it doesn't bother her one way or the other. King George V has just died, God rest his soul! and the Prince of Wales has succeeded him to the throne. Ádega is the memory of this land as far as the eye can see, after that it's the kingdom of León, the Portuguese border, foreign parts, and the land of Moors, the line of the mountain was blotted out a long time ago, nobody can remember where it was. For the first time our national football team has been defeated on home ground: Spain 4—Austria 5. Rudyard Kipling has died, too, many strange and startling things are afoot, it's as though the music of the spheres were out of tune.

"What did you say?"

"You heard me: it's as though the music of the spheres were out of tune, that's what Father Santisteban said last year in his sermon on the Crucifixion."

Ádega speaks good Castilian and she can cure beasts that have had the evil eye cast upon them: Jesus Christ my Lord, sir, healer of my pain, I can find nothing to my taste nor anything that tickles my fancy, Lord Christ, sir, all I need is bread and wine from your table. The divine doctor enters through the portals of pain, asking God for guidance, bringing healing and love, he sits down beside my bed and says: What ails thee, my sister? I'm riddled with sin, my body is like a leper's. Take, eat my bread, drink of my blood, thus, my sister, shalt thou be healed. Xan Amieiros failed to keep his distance and was beaten to death, seven well-aimed blows, one on each side and two right in the soul itself are enough to kill a man, it's just a matter of hitting the mark. Manecha was like a filly in her birthday suit and she never felt the cold. Her brother Fuco had only one eye but he could run like a hare, your grandfather went off to Brazil and had a photograph taken which said on the back: F. Villela, Photographo de A Casa Imperial do Brazil, 18 Rua do Cabugá 18, Pernambuco, he's a real dandy in the photo, with a moustache, a bow tie, and walking cane, reclining elegantly upon the back of a chair, his trousers are a bit creased, though, if your grandfather hadn't beaten the living daylights out of Xan Amieiros, maybe we'd still be racing around this stamping ground.

"More than likely. And Manecha Amieiros wouldn't have had a grandson an undersecretary."

"True enough."

Apóstol Braga was cured of epilepsy with four thieves' vinegar, containing garlic, devil's mustard, and resin. They call Roque Gamuzo the Cleric of Comesaña for no particular reason, for cleric he certainly is not, the fame of Roque Gamuzo's privates and his proportions runs before him, maybe even as far afield as Aragon or beyond, to Catalonia and the Mediterranean Sea. As a rule Ádega doesn't tell what happened though she knows full well, I'm certain she knows better than anybody, to my mind, some of the things she tells she heard from Robín Lebozán.

"Us Galicians could have sorted this out in less than a week but then you-know-who stuck their noses in and look what happened! Raimundo calls them adventurers, patriots, gamblers, martyrs, and Messiahs of China and Japan and you know how it all wound up: with the country awash in blood, with folks starving and up to their ears in shit and folks hardly daring to look out of their eyes, you've got to be able to look folks straight in the eye, without lowering your gaze or looking away, I mean without feeling any shame or fear that your most secret bad habits will be discovered, folks got the wrong end of the stick: it wasn't a matter of egging anyone on against anyone else but simply of throwing water upon the flames of ill intentions, you have to live and let live but that's what folks couldn't do, nor would they allow it. The office clerks weren't accomplices but maybe they were aiding and abetting, fear is never a good counsellor and knives and pistols always lurk in fearful pockets. You, Don Camilo, are descended from the cocks of the walk: brave fighting sorts, not the type to die in their beds, for they don't get the chance, but that makes no difference for every man has to die of something, here in the country they won't run to seed, don't you worry! Your grandfather and Manecha Amieiros used to meet in the das Bouzas pine forest, your grandfather knew how to live better than you do, though you're taller and better dressed, you even wear a silk tie and sport a gold watch but your grandfather lived better than you do, he was small but stocky and as fierce as a lion and he lived better than you or anybody else for that matter."

It's not often somebody has all the nine signs of the bastard, there's usually one or two of them missing.

"And Moucho has all of them?"

"Maybe."

Plunging into the river, Xila fishes for trout, catching them with her bare hands when they back into holes or under stones, it's against the law, of course, but that's neither here nor there. Xila is Ádega's granddaughter and she has a lively look about her and a graceful, springing step, twelve years of age and in good health, her grandmother claims she hasn't started messing about yet, maybe she has and maybe she hasn't. Priests should have children so as not to become lechers, also so as to hear confession from women without putting their foot in it, priests should help folks instead of alarming them, well, let them do as they like! Everyone is answerable to his own conscience! Celestino Sprig and Ceferino Ferret are priests and, what's more, they're full of the best intentions and inclinations. Celestino and Ceferino are twins, neither priests nor bullfighters grow moustaches, they're too full of respect.

"I was just a slip of a girl in Bouza da Fondo when they hanged a man so well and truly dead that the youngsters were able to swing from his feet, they were swinging to and fro for a whole day until Don León arrived and ordered the police to send them packing."

Ádega is the sister of blind Gaudencio, and aunt, or aunt once removed, to the Gamuzos and Lázaro Codesal, it was a terrible pity that Lázaro died for he was a resolute, fearless young man, if you don't believe me then ask that married man who crossed his path at the Chosco crossroads. The line of the mountains was blotted out by the Moors, so that they could tell the Christians: thus far come the fig trees and no further, that's the law of Mohammed and must be obeyed. There's no need to play any music, either by ear or from sheet music. Benicia is just like a bitch in heat and she can warble as well as a goldfinch, Benicia has small tits and large nipples. Benicia is well able to put up with the assaults of the priest from San Miguel de Buciños, who lives surrounded by flies, who wanders about swarming with flies, maybe he hatches them under his cassock.

"Push as hard as you like, Father Merexildo, sir, Yours Truly is a first class screw, so you go right ahead and have a good time."

Cidrán Segade, Ádega's old man, that's Benicia's father, must have been killed from behind for if they had looked into his face they wouldn't have killed him, they would never have dared.

"Do you believe that the ones that are going about killing look folks in the face?"

"It takes all sorts, that's what I say. When they're dead,

maybe, but then maybe not, and as for while they're still alive, that all depends."

Lucio Segade, Cidrán's brother, who had a whole troupe of sons used to say that you couldn't lift your eye off them for fear they'd leave the straight and narrow.

"Quit your joking! if the lads are rheumy-eyed and can't take the light, sweat too much, have trembling hands, or are never done scratching themselves, then you might as well ditch them down a gully, for what we need around here are folks of real flesh and blood and not mere shadows, if men were more manly there wouldn't be so many criminals about."

Puriña Moscoso, Matías—Joker—Gamuzo's wife, died of consumption, she was languid and skinny and faded away from consumption. Joker has no children but he looks after his brothers Benito, who is a deaf-mute, and Salustio, who is a bit simple. Joker is good at playing billiards, he could even put a show on.

"What about checkers?"

"Checkers, too, and cards and dominoes. Joker is good at playing everything."

Casimiro Bocamaos Vilariño and Trinidad Mazo Luxilde, his wife, fight like cat and dog, but they won't separate because of the children, neither of them wants to be lumbered with them. Casimiro is the sacristan in Santiago de Torcela and doubles up as gravedigger too, he keeps two heifers and a few pigs and pokes about a bit in a patch of land he has. Casimiro went half-way around the world then but then things weren't working out for him and he came back. Trinidad married young and had fifteen children, Trinidad has a screw loose, motherhood didn't agree with her apparently, the problem is that by the time she found out it was already too late. Trinidad would like to live away from the eyes of the world and die quietly and unannounced.

"If you'll stay with this horde of little ones, I'll go up the mountain on my own, I'm not scared."

"No, you were the one that had the children, the children are more yours than mine and it's already asking enough of me not to go off roaming the world and let you all go to hell."

At times Robín Lebozán ponders upon events.

"Killings are meant to give rise to disappointment and remorse, the less remorse there is the greater the disappointment, it's the old story, go back over history from the Roman Empire until our times, killings solve nothing but spoil a great deal for a long time to come, at times even stifling two generations or more and sowing the seeds of hatred wherever they pass."

Robín Lebozán wants Miss Ramona to read *Don Quixote*.

"Just let me be, I prefer verse, *Don Quixote* is as dull as could be."

"Not at all, woman."

"I prefer the verses of Rosalía de Castro and Bécquer."

"Do you know that Bécquer was born a hundred years ago this year?"

"No, I didn't know that."

In Rauco's inn the news arrives all jumbled up, a commercial traveler tells tall tales, the revolt of army generals and movements of troops in Morocco, the radio also broadcasts news which you can't make head nor tail of and they're forever playing military marches and bullfighters' *paso doble*, it's no easy matter to point out the boundary dividing us, I don't know what that is that's playing at the moment, that other piece was *The Volunteers*, nice, wasn't it? Joker earns a decent wage in the Repose Coffin Factory, he gives frequent thanks to God that he is able to earn an honest crust. Rosalía Trasulfe is called the Crazy Goat—she's very embittered but she has her head screwed on and always wears her heart on her sleeve.

"It's true that I went to bed with the dead man, but what of it! Just look at how he wound up, you know full well how he wound up, he who goes about doing evil deeds will be hunted down in the end! And hunt him down they will! Let Ádega speak out if she wants, she was always a good friend, a decent woman and a right good sort."

It's not a good thing if the rain stops all of a sudden, around here the rain hardly ever stops all of a sudden, it stops raining bit by bit, and folks hardly notice whether it is raining or not. Benito, or Scorpion, the deaf-mute, goes with prostitutes once a month and doesn't worry about the money, he spends whatever it takes, for isn't that what he works for. Benito Gamuzo is always as happy as a lark, things have worked out well for him, he's in good health and always has a *peseta* or two left over, you know Benito is happy when he grunts like a weasel and grins, it's an awful pity he can't talk for chances are he'd tell some very funny stories; unlike his brother, Salustio Shrill—the simple-minded one—who always looks as though his ears are paining him. After the war they took Ádega to see the sea, they took her to Vigo.

"What you see over there on the far side—is that America?"

"No, what you see over there is Cangas on the other side of the bay."

"For goodness sake!"

Ádega went to Samil beach but she didn't bathe, she's from inland, after all, and not used to bathing. The rules governing bathers are very strict: the bathing costume must be of a non-transparent material and cover up the body without fitting tightly, women's costumes must reach the knee or be full-length, comprising a blouse and skirt, they shall also wear drawers reaching to the knee, the neckline must be such that upon no occasion shall it separate from the body, the sleeves must be sufficiently tight so that no sudden movement will reveal the armpit, lying upon the sand is strictly forbidden, even when the body is clothed in a robe, sitting will, however, be permitted.

Crazy Goat also knows how to train birds and beasts, some animals are easier than others, that's always the way, her mother conceived on horseback during the San Lourenciño thunderstorm, all animals without exception obey girls conceived in that way, though not boys, they turn out run-of-the-mill, it all depends upon the skill involved. Fabián Minguela has a pigskin pockmark on his forehead, it looks as though he's wearing a patch, and he has lank hair and a jutting forehead, well then, it's more or less obvious that he's a bastard. The worst punishment that these characters have to bear is that, however much they try to hide it, you can still see them for what they are, all cobblers work sitting down, but thank God not all of them are Carroupos, there are some decent, respectable sorts among them.

"Where do they hail from?"

"That's something nobody knows."

Where Moncho Requeixo Casbolado—Moncho Lazybones, rather—likes better than anywhere else in the whole wide world is Guayaquil.

"It's even better than Amsterdam, different but better, believe you me! In Guayaquil I had a sweetheart who used to polish my wooden leg with wax rendered down with turpentine. She was called Marigold Cotocachi López and she was very pretty, on the buxom side but very pretty, I wonder what ever became of her, chances are she's dead by now, over there everybody kicks the bucket."

Once, many years back, the Méndez Cotabad twins, who were still only little girls at the time, didn't come home until after nine o'clock at night, both had broken their spectacles and both had pinnies stained with blackberry juice and their braids full of thistle prickles, their mother gave them a thorough scolding, bathed them, you've even got ants in your belly buttons! and sent them to bed without any supper.

"That'll teach you a lesson. Let's hope your father doesn't find out for he'd give you both a sound whipping."

Beatriz had said to Mercedes:

"Shall we go gathering blackberries and wild strawberries?"

And Mercedes replied:

"Let's!"

Then, quite simply, they lost their way and night descended upon them.

"Did you reprimand the twins?"

"Of course I did! I told them that you didn't know and I sent them to bed without any supper."

"Ah, at least give them a banana and a glass of milk!"

According to Moncho Lazybones, on Bastianiño beach he found some very rare clams with caramel-colored rock crystal shells, which cannot be eaten because they're highly poisonous, but if instead you coax them, they open up and out flies a tiny little witch who's hard to catch because she flies so fast and so high up, however, folks from the province of Lugo are able to catch them, though we folks from Orense are not so good at it, over in Lugo they dry them in the smokehouse and later on, when they grow to the size of women, put them into service. Ádega and Moncho Lazybones were once sweethearts of a sort but then it fizzled out.

"God will stop the blood of him who sheds blood, or put him to the sword so that he dies spewing blood. God does not pardon the criminal and although he may hide under the very stones, no matter where he hides he shall always be found, God does not forget, that's why he invented hell."

The Casandulfe Raimundo finds Fabián Minguela very stuck up.

"Don't be getting up to any dirty tricks, Fabián, we all know one another well around here and it's a very small world."

"I'll do what I like and it's no concern of yours."

"Fair enough."

Raimundo told our cousin Ramona that he was getting worried for things were not looking good.

"Baldomero Lionheart won't go into hiding, to my mind he's misguided, folks with a weapon in their hand will invariably blunder, the best thing would be to send him over to the Venceáses' house in Cela, but he won't go, I've reasoned with him but he won't go, you know that Cela is just on the Portuguese border."

Pomeranians have a hard time in their old age, they shed a great deal, Wilde the dog is well on in years. Raimundo gave our cousin Ramona a borzoi which answers to the name of Tsarevitch.

"Would a change of name not be advisable?"

"No, I don't think so, let's wait and see what happens."

King the cat is no youngster either. Since he's neutered he doesn't come in for much wear and tear so he's weathering the years well. Rabecho the macaw spends his day hopping up and down from his perch, there's no sheen from the colors of his feathers, apparently this light doesn't do him justice. The parakeet has no name, he used to be called Rocambole but suddenly his name was dropped, that's what happens! when the parakeet isn't feeling the cold he squawks: parakeet royal, parakeet royal, up Spain, down with Portugal! He's the sort of parakeet that repeats the same thing over and over again, he can also recite the Holy Rosary.

"I think women should have to go to war, that would be one way of putting an end to wars, women have their feet more firmly planted on the ground than men do, they've more common sense, they're smarter and more practical and very soon they'd see that wars are a terrible blunder where everything—reason, health, patience, savings—even life itself—is lost. In wars everybody loses out and nobody gains anything, not even the ones that win the war."

"You're very pessimistic."

"No, I'm just worried that's all."

"Shall I turn off the radio?"

"Yes, play a few records on the gramophone."

"Tangos?"

"No, waltzes."

The bat is a crafty, cunning little beast, bats venture where angels fear to tread, bats have one foot in the realm of earth, like devils out hunting for souls, and one foot in the realm of hell, like devils out ministering unto souls. At times bats may even harbor a vampire in their breast.

"Go on."

"Well, I will then. Sick people, prisoners, and even the dead never change. To hell with all your fads, your qualms of conscience, your repentance and remorse, your heart-felt grief! Death dangles in the darkness from the loftiest, mildewy, motheaten beams, it would send shivers down your spine to see death swaying like a hanged man above a grease stain shaped like the Iberian peninsula."

"Shall we dance?"

"Later on."

The wan faces roamed about sowing the seeds of death but, as God willed, they also began to die off and the ones who had mourned but were still alive—mankind is a creature that can endure a great deal—sowed a hazel tree for each wan corpse so that the wild boars would always have fresh hazelnuts. Jeremiah the monkey grows more consumptive and pampered by the day, but he's not entirely to blame, for Miss Ramona is incapable of defending him against Rosicler's pestering.

"If I've told you once I've told you a thousand times to quit jacking off that monkey, can't you see the poor creature is never done coughing?"

Xaropa the tortoise has been hidden away for months, until the warm weather comes, he won't appear, and Caruso the horse is wearing well, he's the only animal in the house that isn't pining away, Etelvino takes him out every morning to stretch his legs a bit and also currycombs him down. The moment the sun sets in the evening, Doña Gemma says to her husband:

"Give me a drop of anisette, Teodosio, for I just can't breathe. Stick your head in an oilcloth bag and if you can't breathe, well, so much the worse for you!"

Doña Gemma is neither nice nor big-hearted, indeed she's a filthy Holy Joe, the one thing makes up for the other, Doña Gemma had a tumultuous past but now she reads *Mothers' Joy, Meditations for the Christian Woman* by the Rev. Father Zaqueo Mantecón, P.P., Huelva, 1920. Doña Gemma suffers from an anal itch which she keeps at bay with sitz baths of camomile.

"For my part, I don't think the anisette agrees with you, Gemma, I'm sure it irritates your ass."

"Hold your tongue!"

"Well, do as you wish, you're the one suffering the itch. What a dreadful way to behave!"

In the baptismal font, Don Teodosio was christened Casiano but, later on, at the time of his confirmation, he changed his name. Doña Gemma and Don Teodosio live on San Cosme Square in Orense in the apartment where her parents died. The house is infested with cockroaches, it's like the jungle, and the lavatory has been clogged up for over ten years, what it needs is a good scrubbing down and sluicing out with a couple of bucketfuls of water. The gallery tiles are decorated with stripes, angles, and crosses, each tile has four stripes and four angles, and each angle is formed by two stripes, the continuation of which form three or more angles, one to the north (or south), another to the east, and another to the west. Don Teodosio does his utmost not to tread upon the stripes, angles, or crosses so, of course, he lurches along in a zig-zag pattern. When Don Teodosio goes to Sprat's brothel he heads straight for the kitchen.

"Is Visi in?"

"She's busy, Don Teodosio, though I don't think she'll be long for she's been with Don Ezekiel from the pawnshop for quite a while now. Shall I call Ferminita? Don Ezekiel can be a pain in the neck."

"No, I'd rather wait, thanks all the same."

"Certainly, sir, as you wish."

Gaudencio plays the accordion wistfully, the notes don't ring out as sharp as usual. Gaudencio has been downcast and preoccupied for some days now.

"Have folks gone off their rockers or what?"

"I don't know, but they sure don't seem to be in their right minds."

Doña Gemma hails from Villamarín, her parents had a factory, Vilela Soda Waters, that produced siphons and lemonade, and another one, The Sovereign, that manufactured bleach. They were doing well and living in comfort until Don Antonio, the head of the household, created the concentrated beef extract Excavation, and then the health inspectors closed down the factory for dogs and lizards were being used, and that was the ruination of him. Don Teodosio receives extra special treatment in Sprat's place.

"Shall I call Portuguese Marta for you so you can be warming up?"

"That's very good of you! You're so kind and thoughtful!"

"Not at all, Don Teodosio! All Yours Truly wants is to keep old friends happy!"

Visi is from Penapetada, in Puebla de Trives, but she speaks with a southern accent, she's not the most accomplished for the time being but she'll soon get the hang of it. Sprat has three very valuable collections: one of fans, one of stamps, and another of gold coins, bequeathed to her in his will by Don Perpetuo Carnero Llamazares, a storekeeper in the city of León, in the secret dealings of the brothel many a strange deed is let slip, it's a crying shame that story was never written, Sprat hasn't made her mind up what to do with her collections when she dies.

"If only I could come across some decent, trustworthy sort to name as my sole heir! I never had any children and my nephews and nieces will have nothing to do with me! So much the worse for them! I can't leave it to a gentleman friend, nor to the city fathers either, what a mess! I'll end up leaving it all to the girls, who will sell up and share out the loot. I'd like to be buried with the fans, the Manila shawl, and the gold coins, though not the stamps, but my grave would only be robbed."

"No doubt."

Folks are forever requesting Gaudencio to play two-steps, the gentlemen holler *¡ Viva España!* and request two-steps, no end of two-steps, while the women laugh, some heartily and others half-heartedly.

"Take off your bra."

"I don't want to."

Romulus and Remus, the swans on Miss Ramona's pond, go as far as the river in the mornings, sometimes they catch the odd fish and swallow it whole and start digesting it before it is even dead. If it stopped raining all of a sudden it would throw us all out of kilter. Don Jesús Manzanedo was also a good customer of Sprat's, when he started acting the lout in the early mornings Don Teodosio stopped speaking to him, it wasn't that he cut him off without a reply, no, gradually he just stopped greeting him, there's quite a difference.

"Did you get wind of anything, Pura? Have you heard what they're saying around about?"

"I'm both deaf and blind, Don Teodosio, I neither know nor want to know. As far as I can see, folks have gone stark crazy, there's no other explanation. God help us!"

Gaudencio's throat was parched.

"Will you bring me a lemonade?"

"I will."

Don Jesús Manzanedo is extremely meticulous, a bit of order never goes amiss, and he keeps a note of the deaths in a little book: giving the number according to his personal reckoning, as well as date, name and surname, profession, place, and any other details, though there were hardly ever any other details: Number 37, 21 Oct. '36: Inocencio Solleiros Nande, bank clerk, from Alto do Furriolo, died after receiving absolution. Inocencio Solleiro Nande was Rosicler's father, what a funny idea to name your child Rosicler!

"But, Doña Arsenia, do you think that's a good enough reason to dispatch a body to the next world?"

"Look. I say neither yea nor nay, it makes no difference to me, just leave me in peace, that's all I ask."

"Alright, alright."

Fabián Minguela is a rogue, Fabián Minguela isn't really small, just smallish, no Carroupo is ever big or strong, there are small ones and smallish ones but there are also some very motley rogues among them. Beside Don Jesús Manzanedo, Fabián Moucho is but a mouse, a mere apprentice. Don Jesús Manzanedo kills people from his high regard for order as well as for pleasure, some folks thrive on the sheer delight of pressing the trigger, whereas Fabián Minguela kills in order to suck up to someone, who we don't know, but someone is surely smirking, that's always the way, he kills from fear, too, nor do we know fear of what, but there must be something that frightens him, that's always the way, fear scuttles like a creepy crawly up the sewage pipe of terror. Benicia has blue eyes and is always willing. Cidrán Segade, Benicia's father, came from Cazurraque, below the Portelina crags, and he also died in the hullabaloo, as the world spins, men may die at the hands of those pulling the strings, but this won't happen so long as God remains in charge.

"Will you fry me a sausage?"

"I will."

The waters of the Miangueiro spring are poisoned, it's not the flesh they wither but the spirit, whoever drinks from the Miangueiro spring goes crazy and maybe even kills folks as he shits his britches from fear. It's chilly in the Mercy Church but Gaudencio doesn't mind. Gaudencio goes to Mass every morning when he finishes playing the accordion, then he sleeps until midday in his little cot under the stairs, there's no light but what does that matter? what would he need it for anyway? Blind men are easy to please, they have no choice in the matter.

"Do you know who the countess was who put a price on Benigno's head?"

"Indeed I do, but I don't want to say who it was. Anyway, it was a marchioness, not a countess for your information."

St. Andrew the Apostle was jealous of the Apostle St. James because he drew the crowds.

"Pilgrims come to Santiago de Compostela from all over the world, even from as far afield as Zipangu, Tartary, and Ethiopia while to Teixido they don't even come from around about, why they don't even come from Ferrol, Vivero, or from Ortigueira, just up the road, that's hardly fair for I'm an apostle too, just as much of an apostle as the rest of them."

Our Lord Jesus Christ, who had trodden that very path, said to him:

"You're quite right, Andrew, this'll have to be sorted out. I shall decree that from now on, nobody can enter the Pearly Gates without passing through Teixido first."

"Thank you very much."

No sooner said than done. Our Lord Jesus Christ ordered that all Christians wishing to save their souls had to have traveled at least once to the sanctuary, whether in life, in death, or even when changed into unthinking animals, that's why the saying goes that whoever didn't go to St. Andrew of Teixido in his lifetime makes the pilgrimage in death. Around the area of St. Andrew of Teixido, at the very ends of the earth, facing a sea that no one sails for the waves heap mountains high, you can see hordes of scorpions, lizards, toads, all sorts of weird and wonderful beasts, vipers, and hairy tarantulas among them, bearing within them the souls of those who were not pilgrims in their lifetime, thus may the wise be saved by Our Lord God.

"What a stroke of luck, don't you think?"

Half-wits can brush up against death without even scenting or glimpsing it, the blind see death when they feel it escaping through the backbone and dogs scent it, even though half-wits can't, half-wits can't tell the difference between life and death. Roquiño Borrén spent five years shut up in a trunk, not even knowing that he was in a bad way, when they brought him out into the air he was even smiling. Roquiño Borrén bites his nails and nibbles whitewash from the wall, which keeps him amused. Nor can Catuxa Bainte, the half-wit from Martiñá, draw the line between life and death, the half-wit from Martiñá has no idea that death dims the sight so she bares her breasts to dead vixens and weasels, the sacristan sends her packing with a stick and a shower of stones.

"Clear off, you filthy beast! Beat it before I give you a good hiding!"

Benigno Álvarez went into hiding in the Maceda hills, between the Meda and the San Mamede mountains (Father Merexildo, the priest from San Miguel de Buciños, is like a hornet's nest of flies, an ant hill of flies, a maggots' nest of flies, you never see him but he's encrusted with flies), he went with Leandro Carro and Enriqueta Iglesias, the Comrade (the housekeeper to the priest in San Miguel de Buciños is called Dolores and she's old and has only one arm, Dolores reeks of mothballs and tipples coffee liqueur aplenty), Benigno Álvarez fell ill and died, they shot him twice after he died, apparently they were taking no chances, his brother Demetrio died too and his other two brothers, José and Antonio, escaped to Portugal. The guards handed them back over the border at Túy, where they were taken out to be shot in Volta de Moura, as was the way, at least half a league from the city, along the Vigo highway. (Women run after the priest in San Miguel de Buciños like rutting nanny goats, they won't give him a moment's peace, women are like lionesses that scent a man a mile off); the fellow they released was Eulogio Gómez Franqueira—thanks to the good offices of his uncle, Don Manuel, a civil servant for the Cenlle local council.

"Are you alright?"

"Yes, fine; so long as I keep talking they won't kill me, at least that's one thing certain."

Aunt Jesusa and Aunt Emilita can make neither head nor tail of what's going on. Aunt Jesusa and Aunt Emilita add an Our Father to the Rosary to entreat for the triumph of the Angel of Good over the Beast of Evil, their intentions are somewhat ambiguous but maybe it'll do, night after night scorpions and crows fall upon the ditches of the San Francisco cemetery.

"Is Damián in?"

"He's on his way to Santiago."

"On horseback?"

"No."

"By bicycle?"

"Yes."

Telma told Concha the Clam:

"Run down to the highway and don't stop till you find him, tell him not to come back here for they're out to get him!"

The Torcelo sacristan began telling tales of will-o'-the wisps, souls in purgatory and corpses resurrected that had been dead for over a century; the corporal in the Civil Guard didn't believe a word of it.

"That's not possible; they cannot resurrect anybody after a month, and even within the month they are few and far between, say what they like!"

The Torcela sacristan gave Concha the Clam three feelers from a stag beetle and a little soda-water bottle full of sanctuary lamp oil.

"Give this to Damián and tell him to head up Testeiro way, these carryings-on won't last long."

"Alright."

"And tell him not to forget to pray to St. Jude!"

"Not to worry."

St. Jude Thaddeus, glorious Apostle, see to it that all my scourges tumble down a well! Concha the Clam is an attractive, headstrong woman who plays the castanets well, indeed almost like a gypsy. St. Jude Thaddeus, up in heaven, free me from evil, hatred and malice! Things will have to return to an even keel, they can't continue at sixes and sevens like this.

"Indeed, but what if they do?"

"You'll soon see they won't."

Policarpo la Bagañeira's house caved in on him at the time of his father, Don Benigno Portomourisco Turbisquedo's death. So many folks were gathered in the house that it split open like a watermelon and Policarpo's trained weasels ran away on him, there were three of them, now he has two, Daoiz and Velarde, scuttling about the house. Robín Lebozán was the one who named them, trained weasels don't run away so long as nothing startles them. Luisiño Coot is blind now but not yet smitten with that dose of pneumonia, when Dorotea Expósito—Policarpo's mother—died, Ferret the priest had to intervene because her husband wouldn't have her buried on consecrated ground.

"Burn that bitch upon a heap of sawdust and then bury her outside the cemetery, it's no more than she deserves."

Ceferino Ferret the priest paid not a blind bit of heed, Ceferino Ferret the priest has always had a heart of gold, he would give away the shirt off his back and always looks out for those who are down on their luck, avarice is a mortal sin. My uncle Claudio Montenegro, a relation of the Virgin Mary, wanted to make up his full complement of domestic servants so he advertised the two positions vacant: chaplain and concubine, references accepted, when my uncle was told that Piggy had gone off to Orense to catch a dose of crab lice, he found it the most reasonable thing of all: the crab-infested whore, doesn't matter who, that's the very least of it for all crab lice are alike, gives a dose to Santos Cófora, Piggy, who then passes it on to his wife, Marica Rubeiras, who in turn passes it on to the bell-ringer—the spot is neither snug nor scorching hot, but at least it's quiet and secluded—until eventually Celestino Sprig is up to his eyes in crab lice, it's like a game of *correlativa*, with a little luck and the passage of time, the whole country winds up scratching themselves: then, as will happen, wars and calamities descend upon us. My uncle Claudio wants to spend the latter years of his life in peace and quiet, he has already lived through as much upheaval and vicissitude as a body can stand.

"God provided me with almost everything I need and anything that is lacking I'm happy to seek out for myself: I enjoy good health and money enough, I've seen ample years pass by, I have my own house, children aplenty, a horse, a dog, a gun, a cook, two maids, and the works of Quevedo bound in eleven volumes. Now if I could only lay my hands

upon a chaplain and a concubine that are worth their salt, each
one to their own, I'd settle down in the parlor to read all that I
still have left to read while awaiting death, with my dog at my
side, a glass of wine at my elbow, and the bell within reach.
Should I feel like a cup of coffee or a glass of *aguardiente?* A
tinkle of the bell and up comes Virtudes, the cook. Should I
want another log on the fire or them to saddle up my horse?
Two tinkles of the bell and up comes Andrew, my old manservant. Should I want them to wipe a stain from my jacket or
polish my spectacles? Three tinkles of the bell and up comes
Avelino, the young manservant who's a bit of a pansy. Should I
fancy a bit of the nookie? I tap a glass of anisette with the bell
and up comes the concubine, isn't that what's she's paid for?
Should I wish to save my soul? I drum my fingers on the table
and up comes the chaplain and grants me absolution, and
good money I pay him for it, too. And when each and every
one has done his duty, let them clear off and not annoy me, for
what goes on below stairs is no concern of mine, let them kill
one another if they want!"

"Listen, Don Claudio, would a Portuguese girl do as a concubine?"

"Why not, son, why ever not? Or a Chinese girl, it's all the
same to me, all I ask is that she be shapely, clean, and biddable
and speak both the Galician and Spanish tongues, the rest is
merely icing on the cake."

Nowadays chaste, wholesome ways have fallen into disuse,
these days folks have become foul-tongued layabouts, maybe
there's no sorting things out these days.

"Have you heard that the Moors have crossed the Straits of
Gibraltar?"

"That news is old hat, my friend, you're behind the times."

Father Merexildo's housekeeper, Dolores, had an arm amputated at the hospital because of a boil of a malignant nature.

"Don't you heed a word of it! A body can manage fine with just one arm, it's just because she's not used to it that things turn out as they do. It's the end of the world you say? Well, let it be the end, for all I care!"

Moncho Lazybones left a leg behind in Africa when he went off to serve his king and country. His cousins Adela and Georgina are always messing about with herbs, one of these days they're going to land in a scrape.

"I haven't been to the North Pole but I'm thinking of going there, not that I've been to the South Pole either, I've still a lot to see. At the North Pole there are seals and at the South Pole penguins, the penguins are friendly, trusting creatures. Guayaquil is where I like best. I had a whale of a time there, it's full of crickets but that didn't matter a fig to me."

My uncle Claudio Montenegro claims that he rode in the Liverpool Grand National in 1909 and he might have, my uncle spins a lot of yarns but then again he tells true stories that not a soul will heed, he rode a dapple-grey horse, the only one in the race, Peaty Sandy number 21, my uncle fell at the sixth fence and fractured his collarbone, indeed it might even be true. St. Macario brings luck to playing cards and raffle tickets but he's not much use when it comes to horses, Lázaro Codesal was blue-eyed and my uncle Claudio too, half-wit girls are more responsive to a bit of canoodling than half-wit boys, when you slip your hand down their bodice, they lie as still as serpents.

"Are you going to Lalín?"

"No, I'm heading for Maceiras, but if you want I'll go on to Lalín, makes no difference to me."

It hasn't rained for over a week and the turtle doves are

happily bathing in the streams, the shotguns were taken away by the Civil Guard. The Casandulfe Raimundo is talking to our cousin Ramona:

"I've no intention of signing up, the whole thing's absurd, I was just talking to Robín and he thinks the very same. People have lost their cool and it's turning into a very dicey state of affairs. I'm concerned about Baldomero Lionheart for Fabián—even though you'll have none of it—is a proper bastard, if you'll pardon me, you're looking very pretty, Mona, will you pour me a coffee? What's needed here is for some halfway decent sensible person to take over, people have lost respect for the old ways. Poor Spain! What a great country it might have been! Do you remember Blind Gaudencio, Ádega's brother?"

"The one who lived you-know-where in Orense?"

"Yes."

"Of course I remember him, he played the accordion really well."

"Well, a couple of nights ago they gave him a good thrashing because he wouldn't play what they requested. And Moucho is stalking about Orense in triumph, it's no fault of his, of course."

"Shall I bring you a drop of brandy with your coffee?"

"Please do."

"Shall I put on a little music?"

"No, don't bother."

Marcos Albite is delighted now that he has finished the St. Camilo.

"Do you want to see your St. Camilo? I've finished it, and even though I say so myself, it's the best St. Camilo in the world, they say it has the face of a dolt, well, you know the sort of face that saints put on when they're about to burst forth and perform a miracle. Shall I call in Ceferino Ferret to bless it?"

"Alright, it might be just as well."

The wooden St. Camilo that Marcos Albite made me is topnotch, it has the face of a fool but maybe that's just how it is, chances are it'll do to perform miracles.

"Thanks very much, Marcos, it's lovely."

"Do you really like it?"

"I do, I like it a great deal."

In Orense it's very hot in summer, even hotter than in Guayaquil.

"Aren't there too many strangers knocking about this year?"

"Too much of everything if you ask me."

Gaudencio took to his bed because of the thrashing he got, Anunciación Sabadelle looked after him, Nuncie, also known as Anuncia, who ran away from her home in Lalín to see the world but never got beyond Orense.

"Are you sore?"

"No, I'm alright now, I'll be back in the parlor this evening."

"Wait until tomorrow. You'd better rest a while longer."

The pigskin pockmark that Fabián Minguela has on his forehead looks as though it had been polished; Fabián Minguela is just as pallid as ever and as short as before, but he looks smarter and shinier now.

"Do you think we might bump into that unsavory fellow up in heaven?"

"Not at all, woman. What a thing to say! His sort can't get into heaven just like that, certainly not with that pigskin pockmark on his forehead, you may rest assured the angels wouldn't let him in with a mark like that on him."

Roque Marvís' Portuguese concubine—he's Tripe-Butcher's

younger brother and thus Lionheart's uncle—brewed a potion of figwort so that no mishap should befall Lionheart, but it had no effect for apparently there was something missing, the swallows bring figwort from the Holy Land and when some infidel or other boils their eggs in fresh water to scald and kill them, they place figwort in their nest and the eggs are resuscitated, if you toss a handful of figwort into the river, it will glide upstream and order the *encantos** to disclose where the treasure is hidden, *encantos* are daring but obedient creatures that always comply with God's commands, the *encantos* guard three treasures: the Moors', the Goths', and the monks' but they hand it over as meek as lambs when you recite a prayer; *encantos* can turn themselves from dragons or huge serpents into ghosts and flit through the air with a whistling sound.

Don Jesús Manzanedo gave a hollow laugh as he recounted the death of Inocencio Solleiros Nande, the bank clerk.

"Scared stiff he was! When I asked him whether he wanted absolution, he burst into tears, I kept him on his knees for a while to teach him a lesson."

Don Jesús Manzanedo's version of the story isn't true, Inocencio acquitted himself like a man and died with great dignity, when Don Jesús pointed his pistol at him and had him on his knees with his hands tied behind his back and was raining kicks at his kidneys and his balls, Inocencio called him a son of a bitch and spat in his face.

"Kill me, son of a bitch that you are!" he said. "You're nothing but a bloody butcher, that's for sure!"

The frogs in the county of Tipperary in Ireland are every whit as noble as the ones in the Antela lagoon and they, too, have surely seen much blood spilt, when channels of blood are

---

*Fabulous beings which guard hidden treasure.—C.J.C.

burst open, everything is swamped in blood and it takes a long time to staunch the flow, many a man bears a bat dangling from his heart.

Inocencio did not receive absolution, nor did anyone bring him a priest to hear his confession or give him the last rites, what Don Jesús noted down in his little book isn't true, no, Inocencio did not receive absolution, Don Jesús is a liar, he's very meticulous, too, but that's the least of it. Don Jesús had a daughter Clarita, whose sweetheart left her in the lurch because an uneasy foreboding had settled upon him, some folks are very chary, some folks would put up with any shame even when others would have long since settled the score.

"I'm off to fight for the fatherland, Clarita, so don't bother to write to me for chances are I'll be killed the minute I arrive."

When her father was killed, Rosicler set off for her family village but did not wear mourning, the authorities don't like to see mourning worn for certain deaths.

Benicia fries great blood puddings and pours wine without a stitch on with ancient pagan cunning, the sands of time run out for each and everyone, and I'm referring to later on, if you get my drift.

"It tastes better this way. Shall I pour wine over my tits?"

"Yes do. I'd enjoy that for I'm feeling down in the dumps."

The newspapers are very meticulous about detail: So-and-so refused extreme unction and died in deep despair while What's-his-name confessed and received communion with great fervor, dying in blissful resignation. This resignation and that despair customarily take place in the San Francisco cemetery, death summons death. We Guxindes have always enjoyed squabbling at *romerías* but now we're half crazy.

"I've had it up to my back teeth, Robín, there's no stopping this, it's like rampant cholera. Who would be capable of clamping down on folks and establishing a bit of order in the midst of this hullabaloo?"

"How would I know!"

They caught ex-Minister Gómez Paradela in Verín, sprinkled him with gasoline and set fire to him; according to Antonio, though nobody knows who this Antonio is, he danced a macabre jig to meet his maker.

"And what became of Antonio?"

"As I say, nobody knows who this Antonio is, nor the end that he met with, he may have been beaten to death, that's the most likely, they always end up beating that sort to death."

Fabián Minguela made overtures to Rosalía Trasulfe in the village.

"And what's more, you'll hold your tongue! You're here to please me and button your lip, do you understand?"

Rosalía murmured Amen to everything, Crazy Goat wasn't one bit crazy.

"I'm alive and kicking while Moucho wound up as he did: for my part, I hold that each and every one meets his end, depending upon how he behaved in this life, sometimes things don't work out like that but, more often than not, they do."

Robín Lebozán invites home for dinner his cousin, Andrés Bugalleira, who has just arrived from Corunna.

"In the Craftsman's Club they burnt books by Baroja, Unamuno, Ortega y Gasset, Marañón, and Blasco Ibañez, of course, while they left books by Voltaire and Rousseau, for apparently those names didn't ring a bell."

It says in the newspaper: On the seashore, so that the waters may wash away all that corruption and wretchedness, piles of books and pamphlets of criminal anti-Spanish propaganda and repugnant pornographic literature are being burned.

"Did you see Esperanza after her husband was killed?"

"No, she sent word not to go to her house."

Andrés wanted to go over into Portugal.

"If you have money enough on you and can get well away from the border, then fair enough, from Lisbon you can get to any corner of Europe, but if you don't have a few *pesetas* then watch your step for the Guards hand everybody back, they hand them over in Túy, a dicey spot to be in."

Chelo Domínguez from los Avelaiños—that's Roque Gamuzo's wife—is the envy of womenfolk the length and breadth of the country.

"May God find us all confessed, Amen! they say that Roque has a member the size of a six or seven month old youngster."

"But what are you saying, woman! All pricks are the same size."

"Well, maybe they are and maybe they aren't, some are a delight to behold while others are puny, paltry things."

"That depends, woman, that all depends."

"Depends on what?"

"What would it depend upon? You're like a half-wit!"

Moncho Lazybones speaks with wistful nostalgia of his aunt Micaela.

"I have golden memories of my childhood, of coffee lozenges, baked apples for dessert, of rose bushes laden down with red roses, of the times my aunt Micaela jerked me off . . . The poor thing was so affectionate and anxious to please, she used to jerk me off in order to kindle within my spirit the desire to live and curiosity about the world surrounding me."

"Don't talk nonsense! She used to jerk you off because she liked fondling your privates, all women enjoy that!"

Moncho's cousins, Ádela and Georgina, dance tangos with Miss Ramona and Rosicler.

"Shall I take off my blouse?"

"Alright."

Aunt Salvadora, the Casandulfe Raimundo's mother, is in Madrid, nothing is known about her for communications are cut off, maybe we could get news through the Red Cross. Uncle Cleto still plays his jazz band as usual and Aunt Jesusa and Aunt Emilita seem almost anesthetized, indeed maybe they are anesthetized.

"What a dreadful din! Cleto spends the entire day thumping that drum just to give us headaches, we don't know why he doesn't enlist in the Orense Crusaders and leave us in peace."

Aunt Jesusa and Aunt Emilita receive a propaganda pamphlet: Galician woman: consider how apt, now as never before, are the words of Quevedo: Women are the means by which kingdoms are lost (Lord, how common!), where the power of your influence in the world is concentrated.

"Can you make head or tail of this?"

"Not really, anyway for my taste they might have said Ladies instead of Women, it would have been no trouble at all to do so. I think what they're after is for us to knit sweaters, just you wait and see."

Uncle Cleto's dog, Hornet, spends whole nights howling, apparently she scents death in the air. Inundated with such wary premonitions, Aunt Jesusa and Aunt Emilita tittle-tattle, pray more than ever, and piddle more copiously than ever before, truth to tell the whole place is destroyed with them piddling to beat the band until the whole house stinks like a public urinal.

"It stinks of cat."

"Yes, of cats alright. What it smells of is piddling old women."

"Lord!"

The dead varmints hanging from the sacristan's vines bit by bit have tumbled to the ground, it's not even funny.

"Vying with one another?"

"Of course."

Dolores, maid to the priest in San Miguel de Buciños, hid Alifonso Martínez, a telegraph attendant, and when they went after him he was nowhere to be found.

"He didn't pass by here?"

"Not on my life, he didn't!"

Father Merexildo told Alifonso:

"Stay put and ride out the storm, just don't show your nose outside the door, this won't last forever."

"Yes, Father, and thank you, sir; it's Moucho Carroupo I'm frightened of, they say he's roaming about here all done up in straps and military belts."

"Not to worry, he won't come through the village, just you wait and see! He wouldn't dare try anything on with me!"

"May God be good!"

Mariquiña is from the village of Toxediño, in the parish of Parada de Outeiro, in the jurisdiction of Vilar de Santos, in la Limia, but that was years back, at the time of the Moors. The crow belonging to the convict Manueliño Remeseiro Domínguez is called Moncho, like the cousin that died of whooping cough, and it's a delight to watch it fly. Mariquiña is a pretty, penniless young cowgirl who every morning leads one cow, two sheep, and three goats out to pasture at the spot known as Cantariñas hill. Moncho the crow is learning to whistle, he already knows a few bars of the mazurka that Blind Gaudencio plays only when the mood takes him. Mariquiña's mother is a widow and in that house they know only too well the true colors of destitution and calamity. Don Claudio Dopico Labuñeiro is a schoolmaster, they're hard times these days for schoolmasters, and he's having an affair with Doña Elvira, the landlady of the inn where he lodges, and it seems that he's also bedding Castora, the servant girl. Up the mountain there's a crag shaped like a confessional, with a little seat and grille where the Moorish queen sits while they brush her tresses and air the treasure; Christians could watch the scene from afar but if they approached, it all simply vanished into thin air. Doroteo, the corporal in the Civil Guard who wears a corset, has been confined to barracks for several weeks. Doroteo knows off by heart large chunks of *The Sun Has Set in Flanders* by Eduardo Marquina.* One morning Mariquiña spied an ancient, noble-looking Moorish woman who called out to her by name.

"Mariquiña."

"Yes, ma'am?"

"Will you search my head for nits?"

And Mariquiña, being very respectful, replied:

"Certainly, ma'am."

The old woman, who was the Moorish queen from the Cantariñas hills herself, turned to the girl again:

"Will you give me a porringer of milk?"

And, just as before, Mariquiña replied:

"Certainly, ma'am."

Without telling her what was in it, the old woman filled her kerchief and ordered her not to breathe a word to a soul nor even to take a peek at it until she reached home and was sitting in front of the hearth with the doors and windows barred. Don Claudio and Doña Elvira are on first name terms only in bed,

* Poet and dramatist born in Barcelona 1879 and died in New York 1946. *En Flandes se ha puesto el Sol* was awarded the Real Academia Española's prize for historical drama. —Trans.

they don't even use first names when they're all alone and playing backgammon. Mariquiña kept her promise to the Moorish queen and when she untied her kerchief she saw it was full of gold coins, there were at least a dozen and a half gold coins in it. Mariquiña's mother was as pleased as Punch but, however much she questioned, she never discovered where the riches had come from. Adrián Estévez, the Shark, can outswim fishes and frogs, you wouldn't believe how well he can swim and hold out under the water. The following day Mariquiña went up the mountain and the same thing happened again but, as she was picking the nits from the Moorish queen's head, she started coughing for it was very cold.

"Don't splutter over me!" cried the old woman. "Turn the other way for I don't want to be baptised in your spittle."

In Ferreiravella, the Shark's village, they are all baptised and can spit at one another without a care in the world for over there they've all been Christians for donkey's years, at least a century or more. Once again Mariquiña returned home with her kerchief full of coins and her mother's enquiries met with a wall of silence, but one night she couldn't help it and her tongue wagged and both her fortune and life were cut off, for the gold turned into the pebbles of the road and of her body and soul there was neither sight nor sound again. When the inhabitants of Toxediño turned out to search for her up the mountain a voice from beyond the grave was heard calling: "For her pains, Mariquiña the prattler is now inside my belly fried in butter and garlic!"

"Poor Mariquiña! It was even worse than what befell Basilio Ribadelo, the muleteer from Sobrado do Bispo."

"Indeed, for although he wound up penniless at least he didn't lose his life!"

Rosicler's Argentinian relations who called the phonograph

a gramophone went off to Buenos Aires at the time when Don Jesús Manzanedo noted in his private obituary the death of Inocencio Solleiros Nande, number 37, 21 Oct. '36, bank clerk, from Alto del Furriolo, absolution granted (that's not true), they said they were going and off they went, to my mind they did right.

"There's going to be a real bloodbath here, nobody knows who will save their skin and who won't, all hell will be let loose, we wouldn't stay here for love nor money, when Spaniards are at daggers drawn with fellow Spaniards."

Alto del Furriolo lies between Ginzo de Limia and Celanova, folks were slithering about in blood and more than one body cracked a bone of the skeleton of his soul.

"Is it true that the grass shot up very fast?"

"It is, apparently to wipe out the traces of so much grief."

All of a sudden Aunt Jesusa fell ill, seriously ill.

"Did you call the doctor?"

"We did."

"And what did he say?"

"Well, that the poor thing is well on in years, she's worn out, there's nothing in particular wrong with her apart from old age and bit by bit her ticker is grinding to a halt."

"For goodness sake!"

When I went to visit her I found it all very mysterious. Hornet, the dog, couldn't cope with so many omens of death and Uncle Cleto only played the jazz tune *No me mates con tomate* time after time, over a hundred, maybe five hundred times a day, after a while you don't hear it any longer, it's like the wind soughing in the oak trees. Aunt Emilita and Uncle Cleto squabble about the site that Aunt Jesusa's body is to occupy in the graveyard, not that Aunt Jesusa is dead yet but she's got one foot in the grave already.

"The family graves are full up and we can't afford to fork out at the moment, just hold your horses!"

"No, but you wouldn't have our parents' remains cast into the river either."

"I wouldn't do anything, but you tell me what is to be done."

Aunt Emilita is a firm believer in prebends beyond the grave and the respect due to virtues that have stood the test of time.

"You should always bear in mind, Cleto, that both Jesusa and I are spinsters. It's just as well you left Lourdes behind in Paris!"

Uncle Cleto stared at Aunt Emilita as if to hypnotize her.

"What a beast you are, sister dear, you're just like a mule!"

Aunt Emilita burst into tears and Uncle Cleto stalked out of the room whistling after letting out a fart, as he always did.

"Let me know if there's anything you want."

The news coming in from all over is not very reassuring, maybe when Egypt was afflicted with the plagues, consciences clouded over, too, and began stuttering and stumbling.

"We nationalists have taken Badajoz."

"Why do you say we Nationalists?"

"I don't know. What would you have me say?"

Kitty-cat is a Zamora man who breezed into Orense and set about giving orders to all and sundry, apparently he had leadership qualities.

"Did he not have a bit of a squint?"

"Maybe, but who would dare look him straight in the eye!"

He got the name Kitty-cat because of his whiskers, he was called Bienvenido González Rosinos and was a chartered accountant. Kitty-cat was short of stature but very spruce and dapper, if there was nobody standing next to him he even looked tall. Don Brégimo couldn't abide short men and classified them in two large but very precise groups: the ones whose asses hens can peck, and the ones who have to sing as they go about their business for fear someone might tread on them.

"And neither sort is any good. Short men should be outlawed!"

"Yes, sir."

Kitty-cat was the organiser, instigator, and top brass of the Daybreak Squadron, which adhered to a very strict ritual, just like Italians. Kitty-cat was pummeled to death in Sprat's doorway. Gaudencio knows who did it but he won't tell and since he's blind he can get away with it.

"My job is to play the accordion. How would I know what happened when I'm blind? Can't you see I'm blind?"

"Of course, I can, pardon me; play on!"

Kitty-cat got just two punches: one on the throat and another on the chest, his attacker took it easy. Pura Garrote, Sprat, didn't like the incident one iota.

"Either folks calm down or I'll close the front door for the night and turf you out on to the street for this is a respectable house and I won't have folks kicking up a rumpus! Let that be an end to it!"

They left Kitty-cat's body a little farther down the street and sluiced down the stone slabs at the entrance to wash away the blood. Pura Garrote addressed the sorrowful clientele:

"And now you'll all sing dumb, do you follow me? You'd better simply forget this whole business as soon as possible."

"Yes, of course."

Anunciación told Gaudencio:

"May God forgive me but I'm delighted they killed Kitty-cat."

"Me too, Nuncie, me too."

"And what's more, I know who did it."

"Wipe the name from your memory, don't even let it cross your mind."

The memory of Kitty-cat did not last long however because events were tumbling over one another to squeeze into the memory.

"Will you pour me a coffee, Nuncie?"

"Yes, I'll fetch you one now."

Miss Ramona ordered her horse to be saddled up and rode off towards the mountains. In Arenteiro she came across a couple of Civil Guards.

"Good morning, Miss, where are you off to?"

"What do you mean, where am I off to? I'm off to wherever takes my fancy! May I not ride out whenever I please?"

"Indeed I meant no harm, Miss, you may go wherever you please, that's for sure, but it's just that everything is so messed up these days."

"And who messed things up then?"

"I really couldn't say, Miss. Maybe they just got all messed up of their own accord."

When Miss Ramona returned home, the Casandulfe Raimundo and Robín Lebozán were waiting for her. Raimundo smiled as he spoke.

"I've been summoned by the civil administration."

"What for?"

"I've no idea; Lieutenant Colonel Quiroga, the new governor, has summoned me."

"Are you going to turn up?"

"That I can't say, in fact that's just what I wanted to ask you: what do you think?"

"I don't know what to say, we'll have to think it over."

At times like that making the right choice is never easy.

Raimundo was in favor of turning up but Robín wasn't. Robín tried to put that idea out of his head.

"Heading for Portugal would be a mistake because of the Civil Guards, as you know, but getting away from here would be easy enough: you could join Barja de Quiroga's Galician Legionary Banners, I think war would be better than this."

Lieutenant Colonel Manuel Quiroga Maciá, civil governor of the province with responsibility for public order, summoned Raimundo to appoint him mayor of Piñor de Cea.

"I'm greatly honored, Lieutenant Colonel, sir, but I had been thinking of enlisting in the Galician Banners, in fact I was about to leave for Corunna."

"Your conduct is praiseworthy indeed. Could you recommend a trustworthy person for this office?"

"No, sir, I can't think of anyone just at the moment."

The radio announces that the triumph of the insurgents is complete. There's no government in Madrid now, the last crowd of blackguards, and frauds to betray us fled by plane to Toulouse. They have wholly ceded their powers to the Communists and their last achievement was the burning and destruction of the Prado museum.

"Gracious, if things are really that bad there won't be a sinner left to bless himself!"

María Auxiliadora Porrás, the sweetheart or sort of sweetheart who left Adolfito Choqueiro—Georgina's first husband—in the lurch spent a whole week in bed with Kitty-cat.

"Were you not ashamed?"

"Me? Why should I be? Bienvenido was a very manly sort, not overly tall but manly indeed, nothing can take away the good times, the stories that run about these parts are only idle gossip, folks are great begrudgers and say more than their prayers."

Aunt Emilita refuses to speak to Uncle Cleto.

"I'm a genteel person and see no reason to break breath to an unprincipled swine, may God forgive me, but my principles won't allow me do so! Poor Jesusa, she deserved a more respectful end!"

With Aunt Jesusa still present in body, accompanied by his jazz instruments, Uncle Cleto was delivering speeches: Citizens of Galicia, the new dawn of salvation and Spanish independence has broken!

"I never knew that your Uncle Cleto was so patriotic."

"No, he wasn't. It just depended on how the mood took him."

On our return journey from the cemetery, with Miss Ramona and me in front, Uncle Cleto said to Aunt Emilita:

"I'd like to talk to you, Emilita, and ask your forgiveness for any offense I may have caused you. Will you forgive me?"

"Of course I forgive you, Cleto, my dear! Did our Lord not forgive the very Jews that crucified Him?"

"Thank you, Emilita, and now just listen to me. There is no need to overdo it, do you get me?"

"No."

"Well, that makes no difference, but there's no need to lay it on with a trowel, within families it's better to admit defeat than to keep on fighting. Now will you admit defeat and give up?"

First Aunt Emilita blushed then she blanched and fell to the ground in a fainting fit, giving herself an almighty crack on the ribs in the process. While my cousin Ramona and I attended to her, Uncle Cleto went up home and started playing his jazz band: after he had, as usual, drily and savagely broken prolonged wind.

The Casandulfe Raimundo enlisted in the Galician Banners, national fervor was running high in Corunna: a boy J. T., a suckling kid and five cans of squid in their ink, the Civil Governor Don Francisco Pérez Carballo shot; Mrs. T., mother of the aforementioned and admirer of the glorious Spanish army, a salami, a frying sausage, and a dozen *chorizos*, the Commander of the Assault Troops, Don Manuel Quesada, shot; J. T. Esq., husband of the aforesaid lady and father of the aforementioned lad, four hens, six dozen eggs and four slabs of salt cod, the Captain of the Assault Troops, Don Gonzálo Tejero shot; I. A., a packet of quince jelly, the mayor of Corunna, Don Alfredo Suárez Ferrín, shot; a peace-loving lady, five bottles of Rioja wine (red) and five cans of olive oil, the Admiral, Don Antonio Azarola Grosillón shot; A. S., three rabbits and three chickens, General Don Rogelio Caridad Pita shot; a patriot, a box of Astorga cookies, General Don Enrique Salcedo Molinuevo shot. The Casandulfe Raimundo is downcast.

"There'll be a lot of crimes committed here, they're happening at this very minute, and a lot of idiotic goings-on, but the worst of it will be the step backwards for everybody, for the whole country. Poor Spain! The worst about these outbreaks is the triumph of vulgarity, there are times when mankind even takes pride in its vulgarity, strutting, proud as peacocks, those are the worst of times, the most dramatic and bloodiest of times as well, mediocrities show no forgiveness and disguise God in their own image and likeness, dressing up as clowns and yesmen, we may be set back a hundred years but you have to hold your tongue, there's no use trying to swim against the tide, nobody can fight against an undertow. Let it be as God designs!"

The weather picks up and the whole country is in a daze, the sun stirs the air we breathe and spreads the atmosphere with a strange unwholesome dripping. Miss Ramona is worried about Raimundo's departure but even more so about the rest of us men staying behind.

"Do you want to be taken out and shot? This place is going to be unliveable for men. Do you remember something that somebody or other said about man being a wolf unto his fellow man? It's like the opening of the hunting season as far as men are concerned, we women fare better, why don't you go too?"

"No, Mona, I'm staying put for the time being. I'll see if I can stick it out, that Moucho is a bastard, as you know as well as I do, but he wouldn't dare try anything on with me."

"Don't be so sure of that! Those types thrive on turmoil, they're all the same and they back one another up."

"Well, I can look out for myself."

In Rauco's inn people sip their wine in silence, it's very bitter to see that nobody trusts anybody else.

"Do you think Crazy Goat is happy with Fabián?"

"I don't think anything; that's their business, after all."

Miss Ramona is prettier than ever, with her deep dark eyes and hair drawn back, sadness seems to lend her a certain charm, she also wears a suit cinched at the waist.

"What's Robín going to do?"

"He's not sure, I'm not the only ditherer, we're all dithering and wondering what to do. This state of affairs has started to drag on too long."

Miss Ramona took a bottle of port wine and a deep tin of biscuits from the sideboard.

"Will you have a drink?"

"Yes, please."

"Pardon me for not putting out a plate for the biscuits, take them straight from the tin, there are some delicious coconut ones."

Miss Ramona sat down at the piano.

"What shall I play?"

"Whatever you want. Watching you is what I like."

Miss Ramona gave a pleasingly flirtatious smile, seldom had she seemed so pretty, and I know her well!

"Are you going to ask me to marry you?"

"Not at all, Mona. The very idea! I have no wish to drag any poor woman into dishonor, least of all you, Mona. I'm not cut out to be a married man, nor even a sweetheart, chances are I'm pretty useless at anything."

"Don't be so stupid! What makes you so sure you would be dragging me into dishonor?"

Miss Ramona played the *Waltz of the Waves*.

"It's a bit affected but nice all the same, isn't it?"

"Yes, very nice."

Behind her eyes, inside her head rather, she slipped away on me like a sad, restive gust of wind.

"Mona."

"What?"

"Do you think they'll shoot me?"

Aunt Emilita's already distant sweetheart, Celso Varela's Ponferrada woman. Marujita Bodelón has let herself go, she let down her cuffs and allowed her hair grow its natural color.

"There's no reason to go about giving rise to provocation. The authorities are right, we Spaniards should distinguish ourselves in some manner or other from the French or the English, in decency if in nothing else."

Celso Varela didn't follow a word of it but he held his tongue. Storms in the hearts of men are sometimes clothed in pretty uninspiring guise.

"The best thing is simply to sing dumb, things will settle down in due course."

"Yes, but if they don't?"

"I don't know, in that case then we'll have to start thinking about emigration or finishing it all off. What a terrible pity to see the best country in the world, well, one of the best, with blood flowing in the gutters."

Fina from Pontevedra is known as the Sea Cow, these nicknames spring from most unlikely sources, nicknames create themselves, sprouting overnight like field mushrooms; the Sea Cow is very funny and always in good humor.

"Is it true that you like priests better than anything else?"

"Oh, yes, sir, they're very very good, it's sheer delight to do it with them! You'll pardon me for being so outspoken!"

The Sea Cow goes to bed with Celestino Sprig, she also prepares rabbit stew, rabbit with onions and rabbit *à la chasseur* for him.

"You have to feed a man well in order to give him strength and keep him well pumped up."

Fina the Sea Cow's late husband, Antón Guntimil, never could get it up. He was born with very little breath in him and slipped away like a sigh at the end.

"The poor fellow was pretty useless, indeed he wasn't long for this world, anybody else would have lasted a while longer."

Resurrección Penido is called the Lark because she's just like a little bird. The Lark is a sorry sort of tart, her saving grace is that's she's young and obliging.

"And has she firm tits?"

"So they say."

Kitty-cat's death made a deep impression upon the Lark, she was the one who discovered the corpse.

"Didn't you hear any shouting?"

"No, sir, I heard nothing. As far as I can see he died without even opening his mouth, poor thing."

The Lark came from the village of Reporicelo, in the parish of Santa Marina de Rubiana, over in the Barco district, when she arrived she was barefoot, cold, and spoke not a word of Castilian. Portuguese Marta, who's a decent lass with a heart of gold, looks after the Lark.

"Do you think that any woman wants to become a tart? Don't you know it's because she has nowhere else to turn to having been run out of everywhere like a leper? Do you think money grows on trees or what, and is there just for the taking?"

Mercedes and Beatriz, the Méndez Cotabad twins, were very poorly with the whooping cough. They caught it when they were older and they had to be sent up to the mountains to breathe in the pure air. They were also fed on owl broth and taken by train, until they were nearly suffocated from the smoke, as far as Carril.

"Beatriz has broken her glasses again."

"What about Mercedes?"

"Mercedes, as well."

"Well, let there be no more mishaps! Send to Pontevedra for some more!"

Don Jesús Manzanedo and Kitty-cat snipped the threads of life—that mysterious little strand controlling the blood—of many a poor unfortunate upon whom God had turned his back. God takes no part in the quarrels of this world, that's for sure, that's why they talk of man being abandoned by the hand of God; around here in Orense, and in Pontevedra and maybe in other parts, too, people murdered without rhyme or reason—the ones taken out to be shot—are known as "green-gages."

"Greengages?"

"Yes."

"Like greengage plums?"

"I really couldn't say."

Maximino Segán from Amoeiro butted into the conversation:

"I know why it is. It's because the wan-faced folks would say to one another: Shall we go greengaging tonight? and that meant that night they would go out looking for folks to kill."

People sentenced to death by military tribunal were shot in the Campo de Aragón, right next to the San Francisco Cemetery. The Lark is like a little sigh. The Lark prefers soldiers because she reckons they harbor less spite.

"Are you coming back tomorrow?"

"No, tomorrow I'm on night duty."

The greengages holed up wherever they could, not all of them got to Alto del Furriolo in Orense, I won't list off all the place names for it's not my intention to scatter the country with crosses. Raimundo didn't know many people in Corunna but he soon made friends. The Galician Banners left on the Feast of St. Augustín and returned, virtually decimated, shortly after the Feast of the Faithful Departed, the least fortunate were those who fell by the wayside, the worst about wars is that lives are cut off before their prime, and that's against the law of God. In certain corners of Galicia kites are called windguzzlers, to guzzle meaning to gulp, gobble, bolt, in Portugal windguzzlers are called parrots. For two centuries or more then have children in Corunna flown kites in Parrot Street? The Casandulfe Raimundo is somehow related to Don Juan Naya, one of the men who knows the history of Corunna better than anyone, he could have enquired of him, in Galicia we're all related, one way or another, or relatives of relatives, at least. It could also be that, in times long past, the amaranth flower bloomed there, which in Portuguese and old Galician is also known as the parrot-flower. Today Parrot Street is in the excellent, welcoming red-light district of the city. Raimundo generally takes a stroll there in the evening, he goes in search of a little conversation. A cousin of Raimundo's who was second gunner in the 16th Light Regiment, their barracks is just around the corner, was once thrown out of the Half-tit's place because he hurled a piano from the balcony. Five or six gunner friends got together, one of them was a corporal, and agreed to chuck the piano off the balcony, proper animals they were! Just as well nobody was walking past down below! General Cebrián cancelled their leave and ordered them back to the front. If Half-tit were to discover that Raimundo is a cousin of Camilo the gunner—those folks from Padrón are half-crazed—she'd kick him out too, as quick as a wink. Dolores Montecelo Trasmil, at twenty-one years of age the youngest of the seven Alontras girls, is serving her time in Apacha's place, she's still convalescing after an operation for appendicitis but she's nearly over it by now. There are seven Alontras sisters: Inés—against pride and humility—has a line of little hairs, like a swarm of ants, running up to her navel; Rosie—against avarice and generosity—has a big ass and a fine pair of tits, better a feast than a famine; Mariquiña—against lust and chastity—squints a bit, it makes her look quite funny; Carmiña—against anger and patience—never says no to anybody, not that she's a slut but because she's so respectful; Rita—against greed and moderation—is always killing herself laughing and she thrashes about when they hold her down for she's ticklish; Amparo— against envy and charity—is as shy as a wallflower, but once she gets going she's the devil to hold back; and Dolores— against sloth and diligence—can read and write and say her five times tables: two of them live in Betanzos, two in Cambre, three in Corunna and all seven of them alive and kicking. In Parrot Street the whores and harlots of Ferreña's brothel also ply their comforting trade, just ask for Fatima the Moor; in Campanelas', ask for Pilar from Aragon, and in la Tonaleira's just ask for Basilisa the half-wit, who is the greatest slut of a tart in the whole wide world: all the nostalgic whorehouses, all the gymnastic, lovelorn brothels mentioned are of gentle, propitious nostalgia and merriment, vigilance committees screw free, gratis and for nothing for a bit of order never goes amiss. The Casandulfe Raimundo struck up a friendship with Dolores Alontra and since he's well-mannered and a gentleman, the madam allowed him into the kitchen. Miss Ramona sent for Robín Lebozán.

"I got a letter from Raimundo. He says they're going to give him leave."

"I'm delighted."

Robín looked worried.

"Mona."

"What?"

"I'm not going to join up. I'll be called up any day now. What's more, I'm going to let you in on a secret."

"Me?"

"Yes, you and nobody else. If Fabián Minguela as much as sets foot in this town I'll kill him! What they say about him is true enough."

For a few minutes Miss Ramona did not speak.

"Take it easy, Robín. Let's see what Raimundo has to say when he arrives. Have you talked to Cidrán Segade?"

"I have."

"And to Baldomero Lionheart?"

"Him, too."

"What do they think?"

"That Moucho is a good-for-nothing, but that it could be dodgy enough for he's a traitor and goes about with a whole gang."

"Who with?"

"I've no idea. I don't know them. They're not from hereabouts. I'd never seen them before."

"Do the Civil Guards know?"

"They say they want to know nothing about it, that it's none of their business."

"It's not? So whose business is it, then?"

"How would I know?!"

Bread is sacred, there are certain sacred things which are not respected when the world is turned upside down: sleep, bread, solitude, life: bread should neither be cast into the fire nor thrown out, bread should be eaten, if it grows stale, you soak it in water and the hens will eat it, if it falls to the ground, pick it up, kiss it, and place it where it will not be trodden upon, if you give it away to beggars, you should also kiss it, bread is sacred, it's like God above, whereas mankind is a ridiculous, bedraggled, miracle-seeking fowl, all puffed up with pretensions.

"Even worse than that."

"Yes, you're right: even worse than that."

Miss Ramona closed the shutters.

"It's all very strange. I can make neither head nor tail of what is going on, maybe many of us Spaniards don't understand what is happening But why so much bloodshed?"

From time to time Miss Ramona fell silent.

"War may be a noble thing when waged against foreigners that encroach upon your territory, like against the French in the last century, for instance. I don't know, for I'm not a man, we womenfolk always think along different lines. It may be a noble thing to fight against foreigners over territory, but over ideas that may not even be true and Spaniards against Spaniards! That's crazy!"

"Indeed, I think the same but I wouldn't say so, nor should you."

"No, then what am I to say? I won't sing dumb, all I want is for this to be over as soon as possible. People who hold blind beliefs can be very dangerous, and those who don't believe but pretend to are even worse. Faith is the corkscrew of conscience, the can opener which lifts the lid off conscience . . . , all I ask is to see an end to all this madness and soon."

"It'll last a while longer."

"Do you think so?"

"Indeed I do! Feelings are running high and nobody will listen to reason."

Miss Ramona pushed an ashtray towards Robín Lebozán. "Don't drop ash on my floor."

"Sorry."

Miss Ramona could not conceal her anxiety.

"Yes, the truth of the matter is that these blind struggles are treacherous, pig-headed, and soon turn sour, they're all mixed up too. Can you understand anything of what is going on? It sets people on edge and puts them in bad form, a man on edge and in bad form is worse than a scorpion."

"Well, may God preserve us!"

Nowadays it's like in ancient times, when folks walked to the Holy Land and men were guided by the color of women's eyes, the clouds, the taste of fruit along the way, and the flowers and the bees within them, guided by the scent of wilderness and meadow, head north, head south, we're heading alright, we're heading all wrong, we're lost and we'll never see our homes again etc. Martiño Fruime's gang was overtaken unawares by events when they went to reap in Belinchón, over Cuenca way. Do you remember those verses *Castilians in Castile* by Rosalía de Castro? Martiño's gang was made up of nine men and six women, one of whom gave birth upon the threshing floor, and there were also three children of six or seven years of age. When the ball started rolling Martiño Fruime spoke to his people:

"Now, you all know what's going on, I think we'd better head back home, they're about to slaughter one another here and there won't be a soul left."

"But they say the Fascists are in command in Galicia."

"What difference does that make to us? Your home is your home, no matter who's in command."

"True enough."

Guided by the polestar, walking by the light of the moon at night and sleeping by day, as well as crossing two front lines, Martiño Fruime's gang went from beyond the Tagus to the village of Nesprereira, in the parish of Carballeira, in Nogueira de Ramuín, a town of knife grinders and their home. The reapers who left as white as lilies returned home as brown as berries. Praise be!

"Did you always think we'd get here safe and sound?"

"I did."

The first client to have dealings with Dolores after they operated on her for appendicitis was Don Lesmes Cabezón Ortigueira, a medical and surgical practitioner and one of the heads of the civic militia the Corunna Cavalry, which is a sort of patriotic political militia.

"Do you hurt?"

"Yes, sir."

"Well, just grin and bear it then, isn't that what I'm paying you for?"

"Yes, sir."

Rumor had it that Don Lesmes was involved in the Campo de la Rata shootings and assaults upon the Masonic Renaissance Lodge and the Thought and Action Lodge, you are swept away by the deaths of your fellow men until all of a sudden you find yourself surrounded by dead bodies and it dawns upon you that you, too, are killing and ravaging.

"Do you know anything about it?"

"What would I know?"

Don Lesmes goes to Apacha's place in secret for a man in his position has to keep up appearances. He told Dolores that he was a priest called Father Vicente.

"Don't breathe a word to a soul, my dear, the flesh is weak and sinful, but you mind your own business."

"Yes, sir."

One night Don Lesmes raised a rumpus because a pipe burst while he was up to what he was at, and well, of course, it gave him a terrible fright.

"Sabotage! Sabotage!" roared Don Lesmes, buttoning up his fly. "An attempted coup! There'll be examples made of some about here! This is nothing but a den of Reds!"

Apacha soon took him down a peg or two.

"Look here, Don Lesmes, with all due respect, there's not a Red in the house, is that quite clear? We're all as staunch nationalists here as the best of them, and myself first among them! I want to make that abundantly clear, do you understand? Let there be no mistake about it! And if you don't button your lip, I'll call Don Oscar, who is a good friend of mine, and he'll soon sort you out. Here in my place folks may let their hair down but there is no question of conspiracies, do you understand?"

Don Lesmes ate humble pie.

"Pardon me! It's just that I thought it was a bomb, you understand."

The Casandulfe Raimundo had no idea who Don Oscar was, nor did he enquire, why should he? What difference does it make what goes on in brothels? We Nationalists have taken Toledo. Why do you say "we"? And we have freed the Alcázar. The Casandulfe Raimundo notices that his temples are throbbing, maybe he has a temperature. Franco is appointed *Generalísimo* of the Army, Air Force, and Navy, and Robín Lebozán declares that he's not joining up, he'll soon be drafted, each and everyone goes his own way and at his own pace. Miss Ramona rides her horse, nibbles biscuits and ponders, she's always pondering events. We Nationalists are at the gates of Madrid. Why do you say "we Nationalists"? When the Casandulfe Raimundo came back to the village he found Miss Ramona rather peculiar.

"What's the matter with you?"

"Nothing, why?"

"No, I just thought there was something wrong."

Puriña Córrego, the eldest of Miss Ramona's maids, was found dead one morning with a little pencil-like snake crawling on her forehead.

"What happened?"

"She died of old age. The bell tolls for all of us sooner or later, some folks don't even reach old age."

Apart from Antonio Vegadecabo and Sabela Soulecín, Miss Ramona has no mementoes left of her father's days.

"There's the parakeet."

"Yes, the parakeet, of course."

Fabián Minguela, Moucho, will lure neither Cidrán Segade nor Baldomero Lionheart out of their homes, he wouldn't dare. Fabián Minguela kept a stone's throw away, first from

Cidrán's house then from Baldomero Lionheart's, when he saw them coming, he sent ten men to capture them and bring them bound hand and foot. When they reached Cidrán Segade's place they were met with a volley of bullets. He handed himself over when his house was burned down. Nobody ventured forth as the shots rang out nor as the flames of the fire lit up the sky. Miss Ramona held the Casandulfe Raimundo and Robín Lebozán back, both of whom were at her house. They struck Ádega across the face with the butt of a gun then left her unconscious and tied to a tree. Baldomero Lionheart also met them with gunshots, his aim was unswerving and he shot one of them dead. Baldomero Lionheart handed himself over when they caught hold of Loliña, his wife, and five children who had to be gagged with a sack for they kicked and bit.

"Good Lord, what sort of folks were they at all!"

Fabián Minguela, the dead man who killed Lionheart, who was to kill Lionheart, smirked like a rodent at his prisoners, whose hands were tied behind their backs, their eyeballs crisscrossed with blood vessels and both standing in stony silence.

"Get moving!"

Fabián Minguela's patch of pockmarked skin shone on his forehead. Miss Ramona's macaw is a creature used to other climates and a different sort of scenery, here it looks bored and miserable. Fabián Minguela has thin hair: by the light of the moon the dead man who killed Lionheart looks like a corpse.

"Bet you never thought you would be in a jam like this?"

Neither Cidrán Segade nor Baldomero Lionheart as much as opened their mouths in reply. What difference does it make whether the Bidueiros half-wit was killed by mistake? Fabián Minguela has a forehead like a terrapin's, maybe worse, since this whole business started you can no longer hear the creaking axles of the carts the moment the sun sets.

"Do you realize that my big moment has come? And about time, too!"

The little star that lit up Lionheart's forehead had gone out—at times it was as red as ruby, then blue as sapphire, purple like amethyst, or white like diamonds—and the Devil seized his chance to kill him by treachery, he had only a couple of hundred steps left to take. Fina from Pontevedra is like a coffee mill, what Fina from Pontevedra likes is jigging about and dancing to the Cuban Son tune *Get Moving, Irene,* her husband died for want of aptitude, he was crushed by the train for want of aptitude. After removing his wallet and identification papers, Fabián Minguela's men left their dead comrade in the gutter, the night has a thousand sounds and a thousand silences that press upon the souls of travelers and resound like an echo in their hearts. Fabián Minguela is looking pallid, well, no paler than usual, that's just the way he is.

"Are you afraid?"

Every morning Pepiño Pousada Coires. Plastered Pepiño, goes to Mass to entreat for mercy.

"It's true, isn't it, that one of the deeds of compassion is burying the dead?"

"Yes, son."

Plastered Pepiño was terribly frightened and could only dimly make out a faint little light glowing in answer to his entreaties. Fabián Minguela has a beard like a gooseberry: a few hairs here, a few hairs there.

"I don't think you'll have time to cheat me at dominoes. Won't you talk?"

Maybe Ricardo Vázquez Vilariño, Aunt Jesusa's sweetheart, is at the front firing shots, or keeping accounts in the company office, he wouldn't have been bumped off yet. Fabián Minguela's hands look slimy, not even sick people looking like death warmed over would have such cold, clammy, soft hands.

"Do you want to say a prayer to Christ Our Lord?"

Fabián Minguela always looks the other way, like the San Modesto toads, there are three of them but there might as well be a hundred.

"Are you shitting yourself?"

Fabián Minguela speaks in a falsetto voice like the seven handmaidens of the Holy Scriptures.

"Ask my forgiveness."

"Untie my hands!"

"No."

Fabián Minguela, the dead man who killed Lionheart, strokes his balls, sometimes he spends longer than others fondling them.

"I told you to ask for my forgiveness."

"Untie my hands!"

"No."

Eleuterio the Britches, Tanis the Demon's father-in-law, has been as meek as a lamb since this brouhaha began, some folks lose their grip whereas others keep their cool. Fabián Minguela, the dead man who also killed Cidrán Segade and maybe another ten or twelve to boot, wouldn't wear out good shoe leather, he lagged a couple of paces behind and fired a shot at Baldomero Lionheart's back: when Baldomero fell to the ground, Fabián fired another shot, this time at his head. Baldomero Marvís Ventela, or Fernández, alias Lioneart, rose to the occasion and died without a single whimper, he took a while to die but he died a dignified death without giving respite, comfort, or a moment of joy to the man who killed him. Fabián Minguela told Cidrán Segade:

"You keep on walking, you've still half an hour to go."

Baldomero Lionheart's dead body lay at the bend in the road at Canices, the first to spot it, in the uncertain light of dawn, was a blackbird on the bough of an oak tree, when day breaks, birds twitter like crazy for a few minutes and then a hush falls upon them, apparently as they go about their own business. Baldomero was lying face downwards, with blood on his back and on his head, blood in his mouth, too, blood and earth, and his tatoo covered up, soon the maggots will start to devour the woman and the serpent, the weasel sipping the dead man's blood scuttled off all of a sudden as if someone had startled it on purpose. The news spread like greased lightning.

"Like wildfire?"

"Well, yes, or maybe even faster."

In the evening, when the news reached Sprat's brothel, Blind Gaudencio was playing the mazurka *Ma Petite Marianne* on the accordion. Gaudencio didn't as much as open his mouth but played the same piece over and over again until the early hours of the morning.

"Why don't you play something else for a change?"

"Because I won't. I'm dedicating this mazurka to a dead man whose blood is not yet cold."

Life goes on, but not quite the same as before. Life never goes on the same as before, much less so in the midst of grief.

"Is it eight o'clock yet?"

"Not yet. Today is creeping past slower than ever."

The mazurka *Ma Petite Marianne* has some very lovely, very catchy bars, you never tire of listening to it.

"Why don't you play something else for a change?"

"Because I don't want to. Can't you see this is a mazurka of mourning?"

What Jules Wideawake enjoys better than anything is nuzzling the breasts of Pilar, his wife, some married couples are on very good terms, which is just as it should be.

"Will you really let me kiss your breasts, my love?"

"You know that I'm all yours. Why do you ask since you know already?"

"Because I like to hear you talk dirty, my love, it suits you widows very well."

Pilar tried a flirtatious gesture.

"Lord, what a fool of a man!"

Throughout the area there are lots of sawmills churning out coffins, if things go on like this soon all these pine forests will wind up boxing in dead bodies.

"Do they offer a discount on bulk orders?"

"Yes, ma'am, a hefty discount, indeed heftier and heftier until eventually they're giving them away."

When Uncle Rodolfo heard that his cousin Camilo had married an Englishwoman, he ordered notepaper embossed with a letterhead in English, nobody could get the better of him.

"That Camilo fellow was always very pie-in-the-sky. Imagine going and marrying a foreigner when there are plenty of girls at home!"

Uncle Cleto spends his day vomiting, next to his rocking chair he keeps a pail to vomit in for greater convenience and cleanliness.

"Do you know anything about Salvadora?"

"No, we haven't heard a thing, the poor creature is still in a Red zone. May God preserve her from harm in the midst of so much crime!"

Uncle Cleto manages a great array of vomit, sometimes one color and consistency, other days different.

"Variety is the spice of life, don't you think?"

"Don't you believe a word of it! The other evening Blind Gaudencio got stuck in a mazurka and not a soul could make him change, apparently he just got a taste for it."

"Maybe."

The remains of the Saintly Fernández and his martyred companions are kept in Damascus in the Spanish convent of Bab Tuma, now it's known as the Église Latin, rue Bab Touma, in a glass urn where you can see the skulls, tibias, and fibulas all beautifully and tastefully laid out, the Franciscans were always very tasteful in their presentation of relics, in the convent they sell some very seemly French postcards.

"Do you know that Concha the Clam can sing like the very angels?"

"Yes, I heard something to that effect.'

Now they've banned advertisements for Oriental Pills, for the development, firming, and building up of breasts, to my mind they did right for Spanish women would do well to content themselves with the tits that God gave them, and make no bones about it. Jules Wideawake likes big breasts but that's what Pilar has already.

"Slip your breasts out of your bodice."

"No, little Urbanito isn't asleep yet!"

Cidrán Segade's body was found on the outskirts of the village of Derramada, about half an hour's walk from the bend in the road at Canices. His eyes were open and he had been shot in the back and again in the head, as was usual, of course, and the body was scarcely cold. Ádega was still bleeding from her nose, brow, and mouth from the whack they gave her with the butt of a gun. Ádega closed her late husband's eyes and washed his face with her saliva and tears, loaded him on to the oxcart and took him to the graveyard. Between them, Benicia and she dug a grave and buried him deep down shrouded in a brand-new linen counterpane, the best she had and had been keeping aside, God knows what for, since Adam was a youngster. Kneeling upon the bare earth, as air bubbles gurgled from the folds in the shroud, Benicia and Ádega prayed an Our Father.

"That's your own father lying dead down there, Benicia, and I swear, may God grant me strength to live long enough to see the man who killed him lying six foot under! Do you hear me, Benicia?"

The distant creaking of the axle of the oxcart was like the voice of God answering that he would indeed grant her the strength to see the man who had killed Cidrán dead and buried. She wouldn't utter his name, she just wanted to see him dead and his remains sullied.

"Are you listening, Benicia?"

"I am, mother."

Ceferino Ferret, one of the two brothers of Baldomero Lionheart's who were priests, said a Mass for Cidrán Segade's soul.

"But I can't say who it is for, Ádega, it's not allowed in Orense."

"That makes no difference. God is no stickler for detail."

The Casandulfe Raimundo thinks that we Spaniards have lost our marbles.

"All of a sudden?"

"That I really couldn't say, maybe we were always like that."

The Casandulfe Raimundo is dying for his leave to be up, he hasn't long left now.

"The front is more civilized, it doesn't do to say so, but at least they're not murdering one another there, there's less malice, there is still malice, of course, but it's not so blatant. This catastrophe has sprung from the ideas and evil ways of the cities whipping across the countryside, so long as people run about the streets the whole world will continue out of kilter, that's God's punishment upon us."

Father Santisteban, S.J., delivers some heroic, solemn, disjointed sermons which are well received by the ladies, a risky business; Father Santisteban, S.J., believes in the effectiveness of purifying flames, another risky business. Fortunato Ramón María Rey, the son that the Saintly Fernández left in the foundling hospital, became known as Ramón Iglesias and lost the thousand *reales* his father left him as an inheritance, you need your wits about you in that sort of business.

"And where did all the loot wind up?"

"Where would it wind up?! Chances are whoever could lay their hands upon it shared it out amongst themselves, everybody has to live, they have to eke out a few *pesetas* wherever they can."

This whole business is getting on Uncle Cleto's nerves, shattered nerves are a symptom of lack of breeding, with Father Santisteban at the head, forgive me, sisters, I'm sorry but that's how it is. Father Santisteban is a vulgar lout, Father Santisteban is nothing but a scoundrel dressed in a cassock with a headful of dandruff and hot air. If he could, Father Santisteban would hear our confession, grant us absolution, and when we were all in the prime of life he would pack us off to the other world to sit on a cloud strumming the harp. Father Santisteban is nothing but a scoundrel coming here to sip your cascarilla tea.

"If you don't want to hear me out, then cover your heads with a pillow."

Miss Ramona runs her fingers lightly over the nape of Robín Lebozán's neck; the two of them are sitting on a stone bench, as evening falls and the stag beetle with its patent leather shell flits about, the goldfinch twitters in the hydrangeas, and the centipede scuttles up the stems of the rambling rose, this is peace in the midst of war.

"I'm out of sorts, Robín, and very depressed, I'm longing for you to ask me something so as not to reply."

Robín smiled wryly.

"Shall I kiss you?"

Miss Ramona smiled too. She made no reply but allowed him to kiss her.

"I'm just as down as you are Mona, and scared, too. This state of affairs is awful but if the Nationalists get the upper hand it could be even worse, don't ask me why, I wouldn't know what to say, well, I mean, I wouldn't want to tell you."

Robín Lebozán and Miss Ramona kissed slowly but without any great outburst of passion. Coolly and with gentle, coy acquiescence, they caressed one another.

"Go now, I don't want you to stay here tonight."

"As you wish."

From this moment onwards nobody shall call him by his real name ever again. That Moucho Carroupo laughs and laughs but it's not true, Moucho Carroupo's conscience doesn't trouble him, maybe his conscience does indeed bother him and he just doesn't realize, he's afraid, afraid of three things: sin, solitude, and darkness, that's why he always carries a gun. Rosalía Trasulfe, the Crazy Goat, sponges his privates down with a potion of sea poppies and she's fed up with two things, or maybe even more: sleeping with the light on and him coming to bed all done up in his military belts and buckles.

"Yes, with all his gear on, a pistol in his belt and sometimes, even with his boots on."

Moucho is smiling at someone, not even he really knows for sure at whom, and he's envious of almost everything, that's no way to live, when a body is scared and shamelessly softsoaping and turns as green as a lizard with envy, it leads to no good, first a body holds their tongue, then resentment spreads like verdigris on a copper cauldron until finally a body takes folks from their homes and scatters the night with dead men, with bullets in the back and in their head, apparently that's the way. When a whore composes verses to the Virgin Mary, it's because she would like to have been the Virgin Mary, hardly anyone is who they would like to have been.

"Sprat, will you give me a night on credit?"

"I will, son, come on in! But don't be talking about Baldomero Lionheart, I've heard all about it already."

Baldomero Marvís, Lionheart, was as brave as the Singapore tiger or the Zacumeiro wolf, they had to shoot him in the back when his hands were tied for face on and with his hands free they wouldn't have dared; his second brother, Tanis the Demon, is as strong as the bull on the island of San Balandrán, whose balls rumbled in the violent north-westerly wind, and as smart as Queen Lupa's lizard, which knew the multiplication tables as well as the capital cities of Europe. If he doesn't screw things up, Tanis the Demon could floor the blessed ox at the Bethlehem gate—and the mule too if he caught it right—with one single blow between the eyes. Tanis the Demon also breeds wolf-hunting mastiffs, Kaiser had to be destroyed for he was left badly injured after a scuffle with a wolf. Tanis Gamuzo is a foot soldier in the 2nd Battalion of the Number 12 Saragossa Infantry Regiment, he has been detailed to the recruiting office.

"Do you remember Don Jenaro and Don Antonio, those two fellows from Valencia who hung about with Manuel Blanco Romasanta?"

"No, sir, I can't say I do."

They "greengaged" Leoncio Coutelo—the Allariz republican who taught a crow to whistle the *Marseillaise*—in order to make an example of him. Blind Eulalio, too—that's Leoncio's brother—for being such a groper and so lacking in respect. Etelvino is at the recruiting office with Tanis the Demon as batman to Lieutenant Colonel Soto Rodriguez.

"The main thing is to ride out the storm and we'll see what happens then."

Policarpo la Bagañeira, who's no good for anything else but a good hand with animals, looks after Tanis the Demon's dogs. He also takes Caruso the horse out to stretch his legs now that the war has whisked Etelvino away.

The list of lads wholly exempted from military service is as follows: Ramón Requeixo Casbolado (Moncho Lazybones)—right leg amputated; José Pousada Coires (Plastered Pepiño)—severe cerebral disorder; Gaudencio Beira Bouzoso—blind; Julián Moisteirón Valmigallo (Hopalong from Marañis)—lame; Roque Borrén Pontellas—mentally deficient; Mamerto Paixón Verducedo—paraplegic resulting from fracture of the spinal vertebrae; Marcos Albite Muradás—both legs amputated; Benito Marvís Ventela, or Fernández (Benito Scorpion)—deaf-mute; Salustio Marvís Ventela or Fernández (Shrill)—mentally deficient; Luis Bocelo Cepamondín (Luis the Coot)—castrated and blind, those are the ones that spring to mind for the time being, though there may be one or two others besides. Robín Lebozán Castro de Cela was declared fit for auxiliary service but was not called up.

"All the better for him, don't you think?"

It's like God's punishment upon us, more than likely we have offended God with our sins, the country hereabouts was the seventh heaven and now, with all this savage, grievous, blind bedlam, they're turning it into a state of limbo.

"You mean the depths of hell?"

"Maybe. You're on the right track, the truth of the matter is that it can lead only to the destruction of the flesh."

Ricardo Vázquez Vilariño, Aunt Jesusa's sweetheart—this is just guesswork—got a bullet in his heart (that's just a manner of speaking), how many deaths will there be now if you take Nationalists and Reds together? Eleuterio the Britches, Tanis Gamuzo's father-in-law, is a shit not even worthy of being spoken to.

"Eleuterio."

"Yes, sir?"

"Go to hell!"

"Yes, sir."

Eleuterio has the wind up and he has it coming to him from the prostitutes in Sprat's place, you see they simply won't let him.

"Let's see you spit in the face of your son-in-law, you bastard!"

Portuguese Marta cannot stand the sight of Eleuterio, she loathes his guts.

"It's easy enough to spit in the face of a blind man, isn't it? Why don't you square up to a man that could defend himself? Are you afraid of getting a sock on the jaw or what?"

In spite of what Miss Ramona had said, Robín Lebozán spent the night with her.

"I promise not to bother you, Mona, but every passing day I get more scared of being alone."

"For my part, I find this house too big for a woman on her own."

Miss Ramona may be just a touch thinner.

"That's the law of the land, Robín, and some wretch or other—you know who I mean—is trying to go against it but you cannot go about wantonly killing in these mountains, hereabouts he who kills will surely die, it may take some time, but die he will, mark my words! There are still men about here who will see to it that the law is upheld. In our families, Robín, both law and custom are respected, but even if all the men were to die then there's still Loliña Moscoso and Ádega Beira to avenge their dead, and both of them are decent, courageous women. And if they, too, were to die, then there's me, I swear, may God forgive me, I'm not just saying that to impress you."

Rosa Roucón, Tanis the Demon's wife, is fond of anisette, but there are worse things in this life.

"They say that a body I don't want to name made blood puddings with blood from one of God's children, and we're God's children all of us, but he is cooking his own goose, may the food stick in his gullet and choke him to death, Amen, Lord. That person I don't want to name takes a measure of blood from one of God's creatures, so I was told by somebody who saw it, laughing hollowly as he does so, two quarts of milk, four heaped tablespoons of flour, a few spoonfuls of sugar, salt, cinnamon, and three beaten eggs, smears the pan with pork lard, and fries the batter in thin rounds and serves it sprinkled with orchid blossom honey, may God strike him dead!

Catuxa Bainte can't swim, somehow or other she manages to stay afloat when she bathes in her birthday suit, shrieking with laughter, in Lucio Mouro's millpond.

"The leeches will go up your arse and somewhere else, too, you wretch!"

"No they won't. I'm keeping my buttocks clenched."

"Well, you might."

Lucio Mouro the miller, that wildflower of *romerías*, was found dead on the road to Casmoniño on the morning of the Feast of St. Martín. He had a gunshot wound in his back, another in the head, apparently that's their way, and a sprig of gorse flower on the peak of his cap. Catuxa Bainte buried him without any to-do.

"Was he anything to you?"

"Yes, he owned the water."

There is blood spilled on every square inch of this mountain, sometimes it serves to nourish a flower, and tears spilled too, but folks don't notice them for they are just like the morning dew. Earthworms scent below the ground, moles too, and the glowworms have already doused their lamps until next year, it's going to be a very bleak Christmas this year.

"When will next year come?"

"I don't know, in due course, as usual, I dare say."

Lucio Mouro had already been healed of the supurating boil which he had on his foot. Catuxa Bainte cured him by anointing it with ashes then saying the customary words: boil, spoil, skid off, skiddoo, the Holy Bishop has just passed through and the ash from the hearth is after you. It was a terrible pity they killed Lucio Mouro, just when the boil on his foot had healed up. Moncho Lazybones has his doubts about the sense folks have.

"Let them say what they like but, with such a commotion going on, we may end up worse off than we were before. Folks are very proud and that's doing the country no good, but I'll hold my tongue for I don't want to land myself in a jam."

Camilo José Cela

"You're right; the minute you slip up at all they find fault with everything and haul you up on a charge, all this summonsing bothers me, but there's nothing to be done but put up with it."

Moncho Lazybones has a touch of the nostalgic poet, the elegaic bard, within him.

"What a hoot my cousin Georgina is! When her husband went and hanged himself and the judge ordered the removal of the corpse, Carmelo Méndez slipped his hand up—no, not up to the judge, why the very thought!—up the widow. Do you remember Carmelo Méndez, the great hand he was at snooker and the smoke rings he used to blow when he smoked cigars? Well, he was killed in the siege of Oviedo, I only heard the other day, he was shot right in the temple."

Last summer there were frogs in the Miangueiro spring, nobody knows where they could have come from, it's an odd thing for there to be frogs in the springs of graveyards, mosquitoes certainly, mosquitoes are all over the place. Don Brégimo, that's Miss Ramona's father, God rest his soul! used to play foxtrots and charlestons sitting up on the graveyard wall, what blatant disrespect! Don Brégimo was a past master on the banjo.

"Folks seem to want the dead to be bored stiff, but what I say is: why should they be bored stiff? Have they not enough on their plates with being dead already? The dead fall into two types: the ones that are bored stiff and the ones that have a whale of a time, and you shouldn't mix them up, isn't that so?"

"Yes, sir, why wouldn't it be so?"

Don Brégimo was a great one for philosophising and other conversational delights.

"When life dies, death is born and begins to live, it's like a game of *correlativa*, in Orense there was a land registrar who

212

was a great *correlativa* player, he died of a blocked bowel, he went for at least a month without shitting, the life of death lasts until the last maggots die of hunger and old age, isn't that right?"

"Yes, sir, of course it's right. It's as plain as day."

Don Brégimo expressly ordered in his will that a single Mass should be said—not sung—for him, and that a whole twenty *pesos* be splurged on fireworks for the night he was laid out. Folks had a whale of a time while he slept the first moments of his eternal rest with four wax tapers around him.

"What a lovely corpse he makes in his uniform!"

"Yes, indeed, all corpses should be laid out in uniform."

"I'm not so sure, I think that could lead to confusion, they also look great dressed in a monk's habit, in mufti even, in Galician costume they look ridiculous, anyhow it's forbidden, well, chances are it's forbidden now, there are corpses which look good no matter how they are laid out just as there are corpses which are a calamity, that look like a heap of shit, not to put too fine a point on it."

"Soutollo, control yourself!"

Florián Soutollo Dureixas was a Civil Guard at the Barco de Valdeorras post, he was a skilled piper and highly knowledge-able about the plague, consumptives, lepers, the dead and the dying, apparitions, he was also well versed in healing powers and magic and he could reproduce the strangest sounds with his mouth: a dove cooing, a cat mewing, an ass braying, a lady farting, a sheep bleating, etc. Florián Soutollo was killed on the Teruel front, it was foreseen and yet not foreseen, a bullet struck him between the eyes and he died immediately, maybe his soul was damned for he didn't even have the time to make an act of contrition, he had half a packet of cigarettes left and the priest polished them off, a little Palatine priest who had developed a taste for smoking the cigarettes of the dead. Policarpo la Bagañeira is always over at Miss Ramona's house these days. He takes Caruso the horse out to stretch his legs and also runs errands for her.

"Are you going to Orense?"

"If you send me there."

"No, I don't want to send you there especially, but if you should be going for one reason or another, let me know, and maybe I'll ask you to do something for me."

"Fair enough."

Father Mariano Vilobal, the priest famed for farting, fell from the belfry and struck himself a blow to the nape of the neck, there are bitter times in history: the Punic Wars, the 1918 flu epidemic, the Riffian campaign, there are times of grief that seem singled out by the hand of death, while he was hurtling through the air Father Mariano let off the last fart of his life.

"There's one for the Protestants! Death to Luther!"

The last living moments of someone who knows he is about to die stretch out like a rubber band and allow for many more memories than you'd credit.

"But what if the dying person doesn't realize they're dying?"

"Then it's just the same as ever. Time doesn't play tricks."

Once, in Sprat's brothel, Nuncie Sabadelle went to bed with the dead man Bienvenido González Rosinos, Kitty-cat, and when they had finished she asked him a very bitchy question.

"Did you come?"

"Did you not notice?"

"Sorry, my mind must have been elsewhere."

Kitty-cat was a haughty half-gypsy and didn't go down well with the girls in Sprat's brothel, when he was found dead not one of them shed a tear. Citizens of Galicia, the new day of unity and Spanish grandeur has dawned!

"What's that?"

"Nothing, I was just remembering Uncle Cleto playing his jazz band."

When the Casandulfe Raimundo's leave was up, they sent him to the Huesca front. With great care Miss Ramona got all his clothes ready.

"Are you going to put in a request to be made provisional subaltern?"

"No, why should I? If your number's up, you're a goner, whether you're an officer or a private. At the front they say that every bullet bears a name, if there's one with yours on it, it'll get you even though you hide beneath the very rocks."

"Indeed that's true."

Don Jesús Manzanedo died with his flesh rotting and, what's even worse, stinking to high heaven: he was also scared stiff of what lay ahead for him in the next world.

"He had it coming to him, murderous wretch that he was."

"Well, that's another matter."

Facundo Seara Riba, a sergeant in the Service Corps, has a heart of gold, and when it comes to doing a body a good turn, he'd give you the shirt off his back.

"What do you think of the Moors?"

"Bastards, if you ask me! Just imagine that Vali, Monforte, Abd Alá el-Azziz ben Meruán, the wizard, scratching his leprous sores in the midst of all those starving, flea-ridden creatures and him stoning them with gold coins to the point of crippling them. Well, I'll say no more, for it's best to hold your tongue."

The Casandulfe Raimundo was hit by a bullet on the Feast

215

of St. Andrew, his luck was in in that it struck him on the leg and not on the front of the femur, there weren't many shots fired that day, very few indeed, but all it takes is one bullet with your name on it to shoot from the barrel of a gun fired by the bastard on the other side, if it hits you on the head, you've had it, danger lurks for the unsuspecting and since there had been nothing doing that day, the Casandulfe Raimundo had grown cocky and they hit him, well, all the others had grown cocky, too, but he was the one they hit that day.

"Might he have been killed?"

"Of course he might have, if they'd just struck him a bit higher up."

Blind Gaudencio only plays his mazurka on special occasions, here at the front there's less bitterness and good luck can always open doors. Don Clemente Fat-of-the-land, well, Don Clemente Bariz Carballo, from the store, could not bear the horns of adultery that Doña Rita, his wife, adorned him with—she was having an affair with her spiritual director, that's Father Rosendo the priest—so he put a gun in his mouth and shot himself, and to think that it was still peacetime and he went and did himself in.

"Is it true what they say about his brains sticking to the lamp?"

"So it seems."

The Casandulfe Raimundo did the rounds of two or three field hospitals, they were small and ill-equipped, with nothing but bandages and tincture of iodine, until finally he was sent off to Mirando de Ebro, where the bullet was extracted from his leg, it was chock-full of Italians there, then they sent him on to Logroño, to the School of Skills and Trades, he was treated well and made several friends there, the sheets were

spattered with blood stains but that hardly mattered, there's no
need to be too fussy.

"Where are you from?"

"From Eliorriaga, just outside Vitoria, my father is in the
Post and Telegraphs."

They lopped a leg off Moncho Lazybones in the land of
the Moors, truth to tell, it's the same story the whole world
over.

"What do you make of the Moors?"

"What can I say? They didn't treat me particularly well but,
on the other hand, they seem no worse than the Christians."

Moncho Lazybones was always very level-headed, somewhat fanciful but level-headed all the same.

"Where did you leave your leg of flesh and bone, you
wretch?"

"In Melilla, you know that as well as I do haven't I told you
umpteen times, but what matters for me is coming back, hereabouts things are starting to turn very sour, yet the ones going
about scattering death in this area are not Moors."

The Casandulfe Raimundo was in ward 5a, there were
twenty-four beds in it and an oil heater that burned night and
day, just as well, too, for in Logroño it's bitterly cold in winter.
Under the charge of Sister Catalina, a redoubtable, enterpris-
ing woman from the Rioja area, two nuns and two nurses, all
four of them very young, tended the wounded in ward 5a.

"When I order the Rosary to be said, the Rosary is to be said,
is that clear?"

"Yes, Sister."

Adrián Estévez Cortobe, the Shark, the diver who wanted to
steal the bells of Antioch from the Antela lagoon, was killed on
the Madrid front, his body was riddled with machine-gun fire.

"Was it just a stroke of bad luck?"

"What can I say?! What do you think?"

Mamerto Paixón did not go off to the war but invented a flying machine and smashed himself to smithereens in no time at all.

"To my mind, it was a fault in the transmission. I'm just dying to get better to have another bash at it."

Within a few days the Casandulfe Raimundo unexpectedly found himself in the company of his cousin Camilo, the gunner.

"What's up with you?"

"Well, they got me, as you can see."

"Where?"

"In the chest."

"For goodness sake!"

With the sum of ten *pesetas*, Doña María Auxiliadora Mourence, Porrás' widow, headed a subscription to buy arms abroad.

"If all us Spaniards donate ten *pesetas*, each and every one, it'll amount to a tidy sum."

Basilisa the half-wit, from la Tonaleira, is "war mother" to poor little Pascual Antemil Cachizo, a corporal in the Zamora 8th Infantry Regiment, she writes to him every week and sends him chocolate and tobacco, Corporal Antemil was killed but, since Basilisa the half-wit has no idea, she continues to send him chocolate and tobacco, the odd week she sends him a *chorizo*, too, which somebody or other surely enjoys for nothing is allowed go to waste here. The Casandulfe Raimundo and his cousin are the only ones in ward 5a to have their own toothbrushes.

"What about toothpaste?"

"Yes, they have a tube of Colgate between them."

One morning Sister Catalina hove in sight wielding a tooth-brush in her hand and laid into the whole gang of them.

"Now let's get one thing straight, you're a crowd of filthy beasts, God give me patience! This hygiene business is terribly important, you have to keep yourselves nice and clean so as to kill the germs, d'you understand? and since those two Gali-cians are the only ones to have their own toothbrushes—two Galicians with their own toothbrushes, for goodness sake!—the rest of you should be downright ashamed of yourselves! I requested a toothbrush for this ward from the Colonel and it has been granted, so here you are!"

Sister Catalina held up a caramel-colored toothbrush for all to see.

"Can everyone see?"

"Yes, Sister."

"Well then, from this evening onwards while we are saying the Rosary I'm going to brush everybody's teeth, starting down at this end and finishing at the other."

Hornet the bitch died of a stomach upset, apparently the previous night Uncle Cleto had vomited up some highly indi-gestible alcohol-soaked foods and the poor creature wasn't up to it. In contrast, Miss Ramona's borzoi, Tsarevitch, is sleek, elegant, and a delight to behold.

"Are you sure I shouldn't change his name?"

"I really couldn't say . . . , just don't call him anything."

Alifonso Martínez saved his skin by hiding with the priest in San Miguel de Bucifios, not a soul knew where he was, except, of course, for Dolores, Father Merexildo's housekeeper, not that Moucho would have dared tackle a priest.

"Has he shown his face hereabouts?"

"No; it's ages since I've seen him."

The Casandulfe Raimundo and his cousin Camilo the gunner had their beds side by side with only a little bedside table between them, the one chamber pot did for both of them. A fellow called Aguirre died, he took a fit of vomiting blood and died so they seized their chance to ask Sister Catalina for permission to change beds.

"Who stole Aguirre's lighter?"

"Not me, Sister, I swear."

It was Isidro Suárez Méndez, who always stole everything from the dead: a few *pesetas*, lighters, hip flasks, watches, photos but I couldn't bring myself to accuse him, I wouldn't have put it past sister Catalina to turf him out into the street.

"I believe you, though thousands wouldn't."

Sister Catalina was more of a woman than that poor Angustias Zoñán Corvacín, the newlywed whose husband ran off an hour and a half after marrying her so, of course, she took the veil.

"And what ever became of her?"

"I don't know, nothing more was heard of her, maybe she died of anemia."

"More than likely."

"Or maybe she got stung by a gadfly and went lame."

"Maybe."

The young ladies from the Fronts and Hospitals Board go round the hospital to boost our spirits, they're known as *Margaritas* after the wife of King Charles VII, the Marquis of Bradomin waited on the royal couple at the Estella court, Valle-Inclán tells the story in *Winter Sonata*; the *Margaritas* distributed scapulars and packets of cigarettes amongst the wounded troops, as well as woollen stockings, warm shirts, jerseys, and other articles of clothing, little bottles of various types of brandy, which sting your throat like turpentine, truth to tell, they treat us as though we were paupers at a St. Vincent

de Pau soup kitchen. The *Margaritas* wear khaki shirts
and red berets for they're Carlists, of course, more often than
not they're known as *Requetés*, and their chief, Doña María
Rosa Urraca Pastor, or maybe she's Rosa María, I don't know,
is a bit lanky but Camilo the gunner fancies her all the
same.

"She's a fine figure of a woman, indeed there's something
about her that reminds me of General Silvestre, Don Manuel
Fernández Silvestre, general in the disastrous defeat at Annual."*

"Is it her moustache?"

"No, it's her walk—the strides she takes."

Casiano Areal, the manager of the Spanish Biscuit Factory,
formerly the English Biscuit Factory, was the only one who
could hold Doña Rita back once she got going.

"Look here, Casiano, may God forgive me but if my husband ever again goes and shoots himself after all the money he
has cost me, I swear to you, as sure as there's a God in heaven,
I'll kill him."

"Take it easy, ma'am! Just calm down and make sure to feed
Don Rosendo up, the main thing is to get him on his feet again
so that he can play ball, make him some eggnog with sherry
wine."

Three *Margaritas* visited ward 5, carrying presents in a basket.

"Soldier, I'm going to present you with a scapular of the
Sacred Heart to preserve you from all evil. Just look what it
says: Bullet, halt, for the Sacred Heart of Jesus is with me."

* Under the command of General Fernández Silvestre, the Spanish army
suffered a humiliating defeat when they were overwhelmed by Riffian
tribes led by Abd-el-Krim at Annual, Morocco in 1921. For the Spanish
public the defeat was as shocking as it was unexpected. —Trans.

Camilo the gunner blanched, every drop of color drained from his face.

"No, no, thank you very much all the same, but give that to someone else, please, I beg you, I was wearing one fastened to my battle dress with a safety pin and barely a month ago they had to remove it from my shoulder, with all due respect, miss, the Sacred Heart is bad luck for me."

The *Margarita* blew her top, it was just like a red rag to a bull.

"Blasphemer! You dare to scorn the Sacred Heart of Jesus! You filthy Red!"

Sister Catalina put her spoke in and defended Camilo the gunner. Nobody was going to lay a finger on her troops.

"Get out of here, you cheeky minx! Out! Nobody interferes with my boys, is that clear? Get out of here this minute! And don't ever set foot in this ward again without my permission!"

Sister Catalina was a brave, courageous woman, and not easy to handle, but for her we wounded soldiers were both sacred and her property. This applied only to Spaniards for Sister Catalina would have nothing to do with either Italians or Moors.

"Nope! Let their own nuns take care of them, if they have any, I'm having no mixum gatherum here."

Casimiro Bocamaos, the sacristan in Santiago de Torcela, was scared out of his wits.

"Do you think we'll ever get out of this pickle?"

"I really couldn't say, mankind can withstand a lot, let's hope for the best."

When their health began to improve and they could move about a bit, the Casandulfe Raimundo and his cousin used to go to the Two Lions Café in General Mola Street in the afternoons. Sister Catalina would give them each a pass for a cup of coffee, a drink, and a cigarette apiece, sometimes they took Chomín Galbarra Larraona with them, a *Requeté* from the Lácar division, missing both hands and eyes, a Laffitte bomb blew up on him at the wrong moment, mowing off his hands, and scooping out his eyeballs so you had to help him both to drink and to smoke. A Cuban legionnaire, blind and part mulatto, also used to frequent the café, and he would while away the dead hours of the day humming a Son tune, of which the chorus went like this: I come from Vuelta Abajo, so I work like a jerk. Chomín was a good soul and it would break your heart to see him. The Casandulfe Raimundo used to read the *New Rioja* newspaper aloud to him, but the worst was the afternoon he wanted to go with whores, he used to get randy just thinking about it, the whorehouse is on the other side of the river, between the abattoir and the electricity plant. In Leonor's whorehouse there are only two tarts: Urbana and Modesta, her daughters, wretched and thin as whippets, their father was shot for belonging to the UGT.* in Leonor's place you go straight into the kitchen and there's only one bedroom crammed with religious prints, it would give you the willies, there's Our Lady of Perpetual Succor, St. Rita of Cascia, the Immaculate Conception, the Sacred Heart of Jesus, the Virgin of Pilar, St. Joseph with his budding staff, the Infant of Prague, as well as an iron bedstead, two bedside tables, a chair, a bench, an alarm clock, a chamberpot, a washstand, a portable bidet, they kept the permanganate tablets in a soup tureen. Urbana and Modesta burst into tears and would have nothing to do with Chomin.

"I can't, it just makes me feel I don't know what . . . The poor thing has no means of holding on."

---

* Unión General de Trabajadores, a powerful socialist trade union. — Trans.

Then Leonor herself said to the Casandulfe Raimundo:

"They're still young and haven't learnt to put up with things yet, but don't you worry, we won't send the poor creature away like that, I'll take care of him myself, he's blind so he won't make any sort of a fuss, just give me a minute or two to wash down and sprinkle a drop of scent on myself."

Celso Masilde, Chapón, is in Logroño, he's a soldier in the Bailén 24th Infantry Regiment. Later Chapón was involved in the guerrilla skirmishes, he was involved with Bailarín's party and later on with Benigno García Andrade, Foucellas, there's many a one believes he was killed around 1950 or '51 up the mountain in an ambush laid by the Civil Guard, but there's not a word of truth in it, for I was with him in Tucupita, the capital city of the Amacuro Delta region, Venezuela in 1953. Chapón had married a very rich, very fat lady called Pearl Blossom Araguapiche, and whiled away his time classifying the fish of the Orinoco river. The Casandulfe Raimundo and his cousin got caught up in the hullaballoo that blew up over the army stores in the hospital when over forty cheeses vanished, the Colonel was fit to be tied.

"Those blackguards will have to be made an example of, discharge all the ones that can walk, walking will set them on their feet, so let them bugger off!"

The Casandulfe Raimundo and his cousin found themselves in the street through no fault of their own.

"This isn't fair," they told Sister Catalina. "We had nothing to do with the theft of the blasted cheeses and now they kick us out like thieves before we're back on our feet again, the worst of it is that the Colonel won't even listen to us."

"Be patient, lads, in the army you've got to be patient and learn to put up with things."

Don Jesús Manzanedo's daughter, Clarita, had a sweetheart

called Ignacio Araujo Cid who was a clerk in the Pastor Bank, personal credit section, when Don Jesús began making entries in his notebook, it gave Ignacio the creeps and he joined up, shortly after reaching the front he was killed. The Casandulfe Raimundo and his cousin went into the Two Lions Café.

"We'd better find an inn for the time being, what happens later on is anyone's guess, I've still a little money on me and we can tell Mona to transfer the ready cash, let s see if it reaches us or not."

The Casandulfe Raimundo and his cousin were on the mend, but they weren't quite themselves yet, that's for sure, but it might have been worse. Within two or three hours, they were settling into the Estellesa Inn, owned by Doña Paula Ramírez, right next to the Pastrana Funeral Home in Herrerías Street: full board, including laundry, 2.75 *pesetas*.

"We'll be as right as rain here, just you wait and see."

Robín Lebozán spends the evenings at Miss Ramona's house, both of them feel guilty for something which is not their fault, that sometimes happens and only the passing of time can remedy it.

"I think I was utterly in the wrong, Mona, maybe I spend too much time passing judgement and heaping scorn upon others, and that's no way to live, life follows other paths, I'm greatly alarmed, Mona, even more alarmed than you are. I think that within fifty years people will still be pondering this madness, for this is complete and utter madness and with all those heroic, religious and political frauds you need to watch your step for they don't give a hoot . . . Tonight I really would like you to play a Chopin polonaise on the phonograph, or better still, on the piano . . . , it's days since we've heard from Raimundo, I wonder how he is? He won't even imagine that we miss him . . . , this evening I really would like to pour me a drink . . . How odd it all is, Mona! Suddenly I feel on top of the world, let's see how long that lasts . . . , why don't you hitch up your skirt a little?"

Miss Ramona was sitting in the rocking chair and she smiled silently as, little by little, her skirts slipped up her legs.

"Say when."

Doña Paula Ramírez's husband is called Don Cosme and he is a clerk in the local Treasury office; Don Cosme is a short but dapper little sissy who does his hair with Brylcream and every Sunday, for a bit of entertainment as well as to earn an honest crust, plays the tuba in the municipal band: *The Legend of the Kiss, Luis Alonso's Wedding, The Bolero,* and the dance tune *Dolores.* Doña Paula is a brawny, buxom woman who keeps Don Cosme to run errands for her and then calls him Beethoven with infinite scorn.

"Run and fetch me some spinach, Beethoven, and don't take all day about it! Fetch me some charcoal, too, then nip into the funeral home to see who that fancy coffin they took out this morning was for!"

"I'll go in a minute, Paulita, just let me finish the paper."

"You'll finish no paper! Duty before pleasure!"

"Alright, alright."

There are five of us boarders at Doña Paula's: the bronchitic priest, Father Senén Ubis Tejada; a retired asthmatic Infantry Sergeant-Major, Don Domingo Bargasa Arnedillo; the prosthodontist, Don Martín Bezares León, suffering from inflammation of the testicles and us two war wounded.

"It would be even worse if we were old and decrepit, don't you think?"

"Of course, man!"

Article number 2 of the 1852 public welfare regulations establishes that those who are in most need are the insane, deaf-mutes, the blind, the handicapped, the infirm, and maybe they're not far wrong. The couple at the inn have an only daughter, Paulita, who is repulsive, the poor thing is just like a sewer rat, with whiskers and sideburns into the bargain, she wears specs, she's really what you would call revolting, utterly revolting.

"Why don't you set your sights on her? I think if you buttered her up a bit they might feed us better. You have a brass neck, so why don't you have a go?"

"But why don't you try?"

The Casandulfe Raimundo and his cousin Camilo the gunner went to do the rounds and give jabs at the hospital, walking sets you on your feet, as we already know, Sister Catalina still gives them coupons. A few days later they were sitting in the café when the following conversation arose:

"What were you saying about this business of Lionheart and Cidrán Segade?"

The Casandulfe Raimundo's expression grew grave and he lowered his voice.

"Nothing. What can I say?"

His cousin Camilo the gunner took a sip of brandy and stared at the floor as he spoke:

"What do you think we should do?"

"I don't know. Be patient for the time being and don't breathe a word to a soul, we'll have to wait until all this blows over and the whole family can get together to make a decision. There are a lot of us Moranes and even more of the Guxindes. All those who are alive should be able to have their say. You-and-I-know-who will have to pay the price for his deed, he won't get away scot-free, don't you worry, for that's the law that governs us. Let's talk about something else, for what will be, will be."

Camilo the gunner ordered two more drinks.

"Have you more coupons left?"

"No, but just this once."

When the brandy was poured, the Casandulfe Raimundo fell silent.

"Can't you drink to our good health, at least?"

Home is four days' train journey away, which is a killer.

"If only I could, I'd go home right now."

"Me, too, for Chrissake! I'd give my gun to the first person I met in the street."

The Casandulfe Raimundo and his cousin Camilo the gunner were on the mend but they were bored stiff and stone broke as well. From the poker games in the Iberia Bar they won just enough to cover their expenses at the inn, nor could they afford to venture too much either upon Paulita, a creature as ugly as sin who turned out to be above temptation, which is not playing above board, and although he spared no effort but screwed his courage to the sticking point, Camilo the gunner failed in his attempt to seduce her in order to prosper.

"Or even to subsist?"

"Yes, or even to subsist, you're not too far off the mark there."

The wife of Don Atanasio Higueruela Martín, a Segovian from Tabanera la Luenga, conjurer, fortuneteller, hypnotist, he could also read people's thoughts and predict the future. Are you sure he's not some sort of a Mason? ran off with a Moor, Don Atanasio was foaming at the mouth.

"What sort of a trollop is she anyway to run off with a Mohammedan?"

"Do you know where she is?"

"I don't, nor could I care less, I've already cut her out of my life."

"Goodness!"

Conversations about women bring great consolation to the souls of men.

Camilo the gunner tried to pour oil on troubled waters.

"Look, Señor Higueruela, as we all know, there are women that are bitches, others that are lame, others deaf, ones with conjunctivitis, some are governed by their wombs, while others have bad breath, bad backs, some run off with Moors, or Christians—it makes no difference to them—while others want to lead you along the path of righteousness and make an honest man of you, to hell with that! then they preach at you morning, noon, and night, handing out advice and keeping tabs on you as if you couldn't give them the run around, like exemplary mothers they are, and there's not a body could stick them, why can't they just leave well enough alone? maybe they just can't. Women are good, I know, but not all of them, of course. That Paulita, for one, is a fiasco, an utter mess, but by and large they're good, so we can't complain, the worst of it is that they're a pain in the neck and spend their lives organizing everything . . . Listen, do you know anybody in the Nancleres de Oca Hospital?"

"No, why?"

Robín Lebozán sat up all night writing. He feels almost out of sorts and makes himself a cup of coffee over a spirit lamp, he has only to light the wick, at least the coffee will be hot, between sips Robín reads what he has written and half-closes his eyes to think.

"Indeed, there's no doubt I've earned myself a cup of coffee. Some things are very far away and others close at hand. Memory churns up the order of events and names of people, memory doesn't give a damn, the truth of the matter is it's all very faraway. At that time Benicia was only a little girl and Ádega—recently widowed—still a fine figure of a woman, Mona was always very elegant, stories jostle inside your head though in our family there was never a plausible account, this is no scrutiny of conscience even though it may appear so, Raimundo always liked to venture up the mountain, I never had overly good health, I remember one day he said to me: I go out hunting wolves and wild boars but not rabbits, I leave that to Castilians, who set out in the morning for the country with a gun on their shoulder and shoot at everything that moves just in case it is alive: a pigeon, a rabbit, a child, they don't give a hoot. Raimundo was over on the Spanish-speaking islands of the Mississippi Delta . . . , one gentleman said to another, without any apparent point: mark my words, sir, the wise man is the bugger that will die young . . .

Robín Lebozán's head fell on his chest, when he began to turn ideas over in his mind, he dozed off—a sure sign that sleep had overtaken him, something that happens to all of us.

"Why didn't you go to bed?"

"Well, you see, I was up all night writing, I'm going to snatch forty winks now for if I don't I'll be exhausted for the rest of the day."

Tanis Gamuzo uproots nettles with his left hand and doesn't even stop for breath, nettles only sting those who let them, it's not hard to pick them without getting stung, dogs howl from boredom, also when there's a full moon in the sky or someone is about to die, and the swans in Miss Ramona's garden, they must be ancient by now, Romulus and Remus, ancient for swans that is, of course, indifferently glide up and down their pond, for that's their thing. Tanis Gamuzo chuckles softly when he hears that bit about uprooting weeds.

"I may be a whore but you are a bastard, which is even worse. And if you like, I'll say so in front of everybody, the owner too, if you don't get out now, keeping your eyes on the ground, mind you, I'll say so in front of the whole bar. Do you understand?"

Portuguese Marta loathes Eleuterio the Britches. She can't bear to lay eyes upon him since the day he spat in Blind Gaudencio's face.

"Let's see you spit at me! I wear skirts and you britches but you wouldn't dare try it on with me for you are nothing but a wretch and a shit, if you as much as try, I swear I'll kill you."

Sprat threw Eleuterio the Britches out into the street and ordered Portuguese Marta into the kitchen.

"Don't show your face about here, don't even let it cross your mind! And you pour yourself a coffee and keep your shirt on, there'll be a lot of work today for an Italian regiment has arrived."

Don Venancio León Martínez, a commercial actuary, genealogist, and collector of coins, is somewhat sickly and something of a swine. In addition, he spends his life sucking coffee lozenges and has evil thoughts, Don Venancio committed suicide in Our Lady of Carmen's municipal cemetery, that's what the cemetery in Logroño is called, though hardly anyone knows, the cemetery lies on the road to Mendavia, heading towards the Piedra bridge, you don't have to cross the Ebro Chiquito, beyond the abattoir, the power station, and Leonor's place, Don Venancio dropped by Leonor's place beforehand and screwed Modesta for all he was worth, a sharp bouncing screw, with no great finesse, Modesta thought him a bit absent-minded.

"Don Venancio was a bit odd. He wouldn't let me rinse his privates down with permanganate and he started praying to Christ Our Lord. He was also retching and squinting a bit, maybe something was paining him, his head or a tooth, who knows?"

Don Venancio was devoted to music and played the harp with a steady hand, only he used to write arp without an aitch.

"Wouldn't he remind you of King David?"

"Not really. Who he reminds me of is Mary Pickford."

Don Venancio did not kill folks but he used to abduct women, all of them Reds, it was a hoot, he used to abduct women and afterwards he would jerk off.

"It takes all sorts! And what did he get out of it?"

"I really couldn't say, and the worst of it is that now we can't even ask him."

Don Venancio began to go off the rails a bit when Monsignor Múgica, the Bishop of Vitoria, left the Nationalist zone, that must have been about halfway through October, Don Venancio was a very sensitive soul and a devout Catholic and ever after that incident he never fully recovered.

"Look here, Modesta, give this gold sovereign to your mother at sundown, not beforehand, and tell her that it's a present from me and to keep it well hidden away and not to show it to anybody."

Don Venancio reached the cemetery about six o'clock in the evening, kneeled down before the tombstone on his parents' grave, Don Miguel and Doña Adoración, and calmly said a Rosary for them, the sorrowful mysteries, nothing about the joyful or glorious mysteries; when dusk began to fall, he got into a niche, took off his trousers and his drawers, fondled his sticky, drooping privates and drank the poison along with a bottle of Franco Española red wine—the vineyard is not far off—after that Don Venancio never opened his eyes again but apparently he did something odd for his false teeth fell out.

"Why that's just fancy!"

"Indeed, but Don Venancio was always a bit touched, that's the truth."

Robín Lebozán woke up feeling sick, his bones aching.

"Shall I bring you an aspirin or a bowl of soup?"

"No, coffee would be better, bring me a coffee with milk."

Robín Lebozán's whole body started to shiver and shake. Miss Ramona placed two more blankets on the bed and made up a hot-water bottle for his feet.

"That's because the fever is rising in you, just lie still, when you break out in a sweat you'll feel better . . . This is all we needed to set tongues wagging!"

It took Robín Lebozán three days to get well. He ran a very high temperature and was even delirious.

"Did I talk a lot of baloney?"

"No more than your usual, you threw a fit of jealousy and called me an unfaithful spouse . . ."

Miss Ramona gave a cool, knowing smile.

"I've never thought of marrying you, Robín. I hardly ever think idle thoughts."

Robín Lebozán replied with a gallant smile:

"Pardon me, Mona, apparently I did indeed think of it, what do you expect! I spend my life daydreaming about everything."

As a result of the bullet wound he got in the chest, Camilo the gunner was given an honourable discharge and sent home, every cloud has a silver lining and endurance brings its own reward. My God, that was some punishment he took in the neck! But that was when they removed the Sacred Heart from his shoulder! The doctors were none too skilful with the anesthesia, nor swift with the scalpel, nor when it came to the red tape either, there's no hurrying folks in high places, naturally, apparently they were snowed under, the Military Government gave him a form with two or three mauve stamps on it: By order of the Rt. Hon. Gen. Commanding Officer VI Army Corps, permission to travel is hereby granted to Camilo N. N., Private in the 16th Reg. Light Art. to travel hence to Negreira (Corunna) for the purposes of establishing residence there, having been declared unfit for armed service by the Military Medical Board. The said journey shall be undertaken by rail and the expenses thereof shall be borne by the State. Authorities along the route are hereby requested to allow him travel without let or hindrance and shall undertake to afford assistance and supply whatever rations be necessitated in the circumstances. Logroño, June 21, 1937, 1st Year of Triumph, Military Governor, signature illegible.

"But why didn't they pack him off to Padrón?"

"I don't know. Maybe he was on the run from some sweetheart or other that he didn't want to marry, how would I know?"

The sergeant major who handed over the document gave him a nasty smirk and said:

"To hell with it! All this is over for you now and you still fresh as a lily! Well, much good may it do you! You young scoundrels have all the luck."

"Yes, sir."

Suddenly it was as if we had been talking about the conquest of Mesopotamia. Miss Ramona's father, Don Brégimo, didn't want a dreary funeral with wailing and gnashing of teeth. Don Brégimo had a healthy respect for life, he used to play foxtrots and charlestons on the banjo and he ordered fireworks for his funeral. Robín Lebozán told Miss Ramona:

"You were saved by your father, but well you know that nobody could save me from weariness, and that's very harrowing, Mona very harrowing indeed, believe me."

My uncle Claudio is getting long in the tooth but nothing ever makes him turn a hair. Nothing that may happen in this base world can throw him off his stride.

"They're adventurers each and every one of them, son, adventure may justify the life a man leads, that's for sure, just take Cecil Rhodes, for instance, or Amundsen, the conqueror of the South Pole who died at the North Pole, but that's another matter, the worst thing in this life is to go about scattering death. Spain is not a slaughterhouse, those bloody false heroes have no wish to work but would rather run about in search of adventure, appeasing miracles and defying God and His very plans. For you the most that can happen is that you lose your life, all of us will lose our lives sooner or later, but first they will lose their dignity, you get what I'm driving at, then their decorum, for in the wake of adventure will come starvation, that's always the way, and then the destitution of souls, the auctioning off of conscience."

The Casandulfe Raimundo took a turn for the worse, his leg swelled up and his temperature rose to 38.5C. They had to readmit him to hospital, this time in Nanclares de Oca.

"Do you know anybody in the Nanclares de Oca Hospital?"

"I do, why?, I know somebody nearly everywhere."

"For goodness sake! Some people have all the luck!"

In the Nanclares de Oca Hospital, the Casandulfe Raimundo made friends with the *Requeté* Corporal Ignacio Aranarache Eulate, Pichichi, for whom he had a letter of introduction from Don Cosme, the tuba-playing innkeeper.

"How is Doña Paula keeping?"

"Fine, ruling the roost as usual."

"What about Paulita? Christ, but she's a sight for sore eyes!"

"She's fine, too, last month she had the colic."

"For goodness sake!"

Over Orense, many leagues away, the storm is lashing down. Sprat wraps herself in her Manila shawl covered with little Chinamen with ivory faces, three hundred Chinamen at least, maybe even more, and she prays the Litany of Our Lady: turris davidica, ora pro nobis, turris eburnea, ora pro nobis, domus aurea, ora pro nobis. Sprat's may even be the finest Manila shawl in the entire province, perhaps even in the whole of Nationalist Spain, not even Pepita from Saragossa, nor Lola from Burgos, nor Apacha from Corunna, nor Petra from Salamanca, nor the Chiclana woman from Seville, nor the Turkish woman from Pamplona, nor the Madrilenian woman from Badajoz, nor the Fairy Cake from Granada have anything that could even hold a candle to it, Sprat's is quite some shawl.

"How much do you want for it, Doña Pura?"

"It's not for sale, sir. However much you offer, sir, the shawl will not leave this house."

The wooden St. Camilo that Marcos Albite made for me is the best in the world, it has a stupid looking face but it's fine, it's a delight to behold.

"Don't take it off to the war with you. You don't want to lose it or get it all smashed up."

"No, I'll give it to Miss Ramona for safekeeping."

"She won't laugh at us?"

"I don't think so, Miss Ramona is a charitable soul and very well-mannered."

"That's for sure."

The authorities never found out but the Segovian Don Atanasio Higueruela, a sort of wizard whose wife ran off with a Moor, was a Rosicrucian, he had a heraldic shield and the four roses tattooed on his arm, it's just that he never used to roll his sleeves up. Don Atanasio believed in the transmigration of souls, in the brotherhood of mankind, and universal gravitation.

"Look here, Señor Higueruela, the sensible thing is not to shout your opinions from the rooftops; you might get away with universal gravitation, but keep the others under your hat for people have wicked minds and you might be letting yourself in for a nasty shock."

"You think so?"

"Look, if I didn't think so I wouldn't be saying this!"

Blind Gaudencio is his own master.

"Gaudencio, a *peseta* for a mazurka!"

"Depends which one."

Rosalía Trasulfe, the Crazy Goat, never breathes a word of complaint.

"I was patient and God rewarded me with the sight of him dead like a cat flattened by a truck, what you have to do is wait, just bide your time, the Good Lord will eventually strike down the best of them, and that bugger is dead now, not that he was the best of them, of course, but there's no need to tell you that for it's something you know only too well."

Ignacio Aranarache Eulate, Pichichi, studied for the priesthood at the Tudela seminary but he never got to say Mass, he got out in the nick of time and now he's studying law in Valladolid, he's in third year already, the lad is a good sort, a bit on the short side, but he has a heart of gold, a bullet went through both his legs but he's nearly over it by now.

"That bloody Don Cosme, is he still tootling on the tuba?"

"Indeed he is, and very well, too, I believe."

"How are things working out for him at the Treasury office?"

"I don't know. Swimmingly, I suppose."

Pichichi speaks admiringly of a relative of his, a distant uncle, Don José María Iribarren, the author of the book *With General Mola: New Scenes and Aspects of the Civil War.*

"Those pages brought my uncle nothing but vexation for the undercover soldiers in Salamanca wanted to rub him up the wrong way and they very nearly succeeded."

Nuncie Sabadelle continues to bestow her charitable favors upon Blind Gaudencio.

"What harm is there in a man and a woman going to bed to mess about? Do you think blind people have no feelings or what?"

Gaudencio is deeply grateful to Nuncie Sabadelle.

"Shall I play the *Blue Danube?*"

"Do."

"Or what about the *Yira, yira* tango?"

"Play that too."

Gaudencio likes to hear Nuncie's sweet, melodious voice and to gently fondle her ass.

Pichichi's relative had been secretary to General Mola, the latter quite capable of intervening in no uncertain terms, if he doesn't watch out he'll miss the boat and find his biographer dead, buried, and already kicking up the daisies. According to Pichichi, his uncle's persecutor was a certain fellow who used to write articles in the newspaper outlining what you should do so as not to be cheated when buying a used car.

"So how come he has such influence then?"

"How would I know?!"

The Casandulfe Raimundo is terrified of undercover soldiers, those ministries in Burgos and Salamanca, well, in other places, too, are even more dangerous than the front line, undercover soldiers are cowardly sons of bitches, what they're after is to prosper furtively even though it means selling their own grandmother to do so. What do they care whether they go about spreading calumny, grief, or even death, you offer the dead confession and that's it over and done with, brimming over with zeal, do you see what I'm saying, what you need is for the boss to notice your patriotism. Long live Spain! there's no call for things to be all hunky-dory, it's good enough for things to take their own course, to go their own sweet way without interference, the perilous truth is not as handy and convenient as safe mediocrity, many's the one doesn't grasp that but only too well I know what I'm saying. up there in the ministries anything goes: informing, traps, tip-offs, undercover soldiers shitting their britches with fear, a few days back, while he was still in Logroño, the Casandulfe Raimundo said to Camilo the gunner:

"When all this is over and done with it'll be the pen pushers that will call the shots, mark my words, the judiciary and the press and propaganda people, the undercover soldiers are well organised and instead of frequenting whorehouses they spend their time mulling over whatever they feel like, they're forever praying in order to butter up the wives of military personnel and win their backing—from the Colonel upwards—the one thing they have no wish to hear are gunshots, they earn a living and save their skins, while we'll always be on our uppers and we risk—even lose—our lives at times but that hardly matters."

Pichichi also sees a dicey, uncertain future ahead.

"Even the fiercest fighting bull can be led by the nose, that's as clear as crystal, nor do I see any way around it. It's unfair, don't you think? and God shouldn't allow such things to happen, but God isn't even aware of such goings-on, maybe he doesn't care either. When that bullet hit me I cursed God and I didn't kick the bucket, nor did God punish me, I haven't kicked the bucket yet—that's a sure sign that God doesn't give a fig about us, and it's not everybody you can say such things to. Have you ever thought of committing suicide? I haven't, I don't think you should ever commit suicide, just in case."

The sands of time run out for each and every one and Rosicler grew up, as all women do, alluringly.

"Today I'm going to be unfaithful to you with you-know-who, Mona."

"What a slut you are, Rosicler!"

The sands of time run out for each and every one, the dead included.

"But how do they manage to tell the time if they can't see a clock?"

"That I really don't know, I really know hardly anything of what goes on but I'm making the best of a bad job."

Robín Lebozán doesn't suppose he was ever lucky in his whole life.

"Maybe things would have gone better but I couldn't get used to the family, Mona, I mean my family, they're all idiots. I never learnt to live in the city and that, too, has it's price to pay, my family are boring, cheerless, unaffectionate disciplinarians, my family is united only on the surface and they kill time numbing themselves with the sermons of priests and nuns and creating bad humor, bad blood. My family are like Venice, just like the city of Venice, Mona, living on memories yet slowly but relentlessly sinking unawares. For years now my family haven't had a clue about what's going on around them, but maybe that's all for the best."

When he finished his speech, Robín Lebozán fell asleep and Miss Ramona tiptoed out of the room so as not to disturb him.

"The truth of the matter is that neither of us is having too much luck.'

Ádela and Georgina, Moncho Lazybones' cousins, dance cheek to cheek with Miss Ramona and Rosicler.

"Shall I slip a breast out of my bodice?"

"No, better take your blouse off."

The Red Cross sent a communique stating that Aunt Salvadora, the Casandulfe Raimundo's mother, died in Madrid of natural causes, Uncle Cleto feels very self-important and bashes his jazz band with an almost joyous touch, a New Orleans black couldn't have done better.

The Casandulfe Raimundo imagines that a younger and perhaps slightly more cultured character than Don Atanasio Higueruela from Segovia might have been able to reel off the following paragraph:

"The Official Bulletin is even worse than the war itself, it doesn't do to say so but it's the patent truth, believe me, the Official Bulletin is a weapon in the hands of the Holy Joes, they're the ones that are going to win out in the end, conquerors for fifty years or more, first things first, the congregations know how to earn the dough and share cut the profits and jubilations but, above all, they know how to handle their tools: warrants for the seizure and destruction of pornographic, Marxist, atheistic, and, by and large, corrupting books (scourges of the soul stem from reading), suppression of coeducation in schools (promiscuity), appointment of city councils by civil governors (for the sake of unity), purge in civil service (the common weal should not be administered by traitors), the cult of the Virgin to be made compulsory in schools (together with the Roman greeting Ave Maria), the establishment of censorship for the press, books, theater, cinema, broadcasting (liberty should not be confused with libertinism), freedom of meeting and association to be abolished (dissemination of false truths), abolition of civil marriage (concubinage) and divorce (debauched contractual sophistry), prohibition of the use of names not appearing in the Sanctoral calendar (crusade against paganism), the worst of it is the setback it will be to Spanish history."

Poor Higueruela would never have thought of the foregoing nor would anything of this nature ever have occurred to him. Higueruela tried not to think too much and kept his thoughts under his hat but the Casandulfe Raimundo had to attribute this to somebody or other.

"Do you mind?"

"Me? Not at all."

Tanis Gamuzo's dogs are fearless but quiet, they never lash out at anybody in vain, Kaiser was left badly injured by a wolf and Tanis had to use his knife to destroy him, it was a terrible pity but there was nothing else to be done. Tanis Gamuzo also has four mastiff breeding bitches: Butterfly, Pearl, Witch, and Blossom, though he doesn't often take them up the mountain for they're worth a pretty penny and might meet with some mishap or other, it could get them all worked up and upset the mother dog. Tanis is known as Demon for he's a very demon in his thoughts, he thinks better and faster then anyone hereabouts. Tanis' wife is called Rosa, she's the daughter of Eleuterio Roucón, Britches, the client they threw out of Sprat's place for spitting in the face of Blind Gaudencio. Britches is scared of his son-in-law for he knows that one day he will smash his face in.

"Let's see you tackle Tanis, you bloody swine! Bet you wouldn't dare square up to a man who can look you in the eye, you wretch!"

Demon loves to skinny dip in Lucio Mouro's millpond, sometimes the half-wit from Martiñá ducks about with him.

"Watch out, girl, or you'll drown!"

Lucio Mouro was found dead one black morning on the road to Casmoniño, it's a generous hand that metes out sorrow, apparently grief abounds in this world. Catuxa Bainte, the half-wit from Martiñá, buried the miller with tears streaming down her face.

"He was a good sort, one that would never throw stones at anybody. He owned the water and the flowers, the reeds on the banks as well, and was great at weaving fine, sturdy baskets. I know who killed him and I'll live to see him die one day."

Rosa is bone lazy and lets her children run about scruffy and dripping snot, but neither Tanis nor the children could care less, running about filthy is what they're used to.

"With these dogs of mine you could tackle anybody, a lion, a bear, a panther, even, it's all the same to them, my dogs fear no one because they're well able for anything, strength courses through their veins."

Tanis Gamuzo is the strongest man in the whole district, he can hold a horse with one hand or kill it with one thump of his fist on the neck or on the chest, cutting off the blood flow, he gets a laugh out of his own strength. Neither Portuguese Marta nor Anunciación Sabadelle, nor any other girl from Sprat's brothel will have anything to do with Eleuterio the Britches.

"He could starve to death or die of leprosy, for all I care. I wouldn't lift a finger to help him nor even look him in the eye!"

Tanis also keeps cattle dogs, as shrewd as rats and smart as centipedes, but they're a dime a dozen and don't even have names, for there's no point giving them names when they're not worth anything, they're whelped, wander about and die, with no bother at all, they're very smart at herding beasts, which the mastiffs will worry given half a chance. Rosa has a taste for anisette, we all have our little failings, we all nurture our weak points and nurse them along to keep them alive. Neither nettles, vipers, nor scorpions will sting Tanis Gamuzo.

"Does he have a tough skin or what?"

"No, it's just that he won't let them, your uncle Claudio Montenegro refused to be stung or get bothered, it's something you either have or don't have, when he thought they were out to get him he surrounded his house with wolf traps, he laid at least seven of them, and bided his time, that bloody Wencelas Caldraga got caught in one and your uncle Claudio waited three days before releasing him, his ankle was raw flesh and you could see the bone, the rest of them fled like hares and told no tales either."

"Like dead men?"

"Indeed, just like dead men."

The Casandulfe Raimundo was discharged from the Nanclares de Oca Hospital, they couldn't keep him there forever, Ignacio Aranarache Eulate, Pichichi, was sent home too, still limping slightly but alive and well, the same cannot be said of poor Chomín Galbarra Larraona for he was still alive, indeed, but blind and missing both hands.

Time goes by, commemorations and pretences, too; each time we Nationalists take a city the people in the rear-guard take to the streets in celebration, there are fewer cities left now, chances are this whole business is reaching its conclusion, in the battle of Alfambra the soldiers fell like flies, Adrián Estévez Cortove, the Shark, died on the Madrid front, so riddled with shrapnel his body was like a sieve, we war veterans—the Punic Wars, the Boer War, the Great War, the Melilla War, the

Civil War, this is a civil war—bear an obituary engraved upon our hearts and shudder remorsefully as we recall it each morning, all we Spaniards study one another in Ferdinand and Isabella's burnished looking glass, Dolores Montecelo Trasmil, the youngest of the seven Alontras girls, has fully recovered now from her appendicitis, it would gladden your heart to see her as fit as a fiddle, youth has been decimated, provisional second-lieutenant reduced to a corpse, and the survivors console themselves with the thought that they'll have four girls and a cripple apiece, reconquest of Teruel, Aguirre, I don't know what his first name was, died in the next bed in the Logroño Hospital, he was hit in the retreat from Teruel, Fátima the Moor, in Ferreña's place, recalls her friend Salem bem Farache, a mulatto Moor with a moustache who refused to let them cut off his leg because he'd rather death than mutilation, maybe he did right, Ignacio Araujo Cid, Clarita Manzanedo's sweetheart, had hardly set foot in Belchite when he was killed, he died with no wish to escape the clutches of death, fugitives from the Red zone who can find no lodgings in the city, you'll find cheap apartments in Galicia, they've sunk the cruiser *Baleares* on us, Carmelo Méndez, Georgina's second husband, died on the Oviedo front, he was hit on the temple, that's no different from the *coup de grace*, one night when it was bitterly cold Basilisa the half-wit, the greatest slut of a whore in the whole of Galicia, said to Javierito Pértega, who was a bit of a pansy: Us women are better made than you men, are you not ashamed to run about with your balls hanging down like that? and Javierito Pértega replied: It's no fault of mine, anyway you're nothing but a brazen hussy, lead a chaste life and don decent Christian dress to forge the fatherland! put your mind to it, woman! reconquest of Belchite, Perpetuo Carnero Tascón, the son of Don Perpetuo Carnero

Llamazares, the well-heeled storekeeper from León who stipu-
lated in his last will and testament that his collections of fans,
stamps, and gold coins should pass to Sprat, died in the Al-
cubierre mountains, he was hit on the leg, the wound itself
wasn't so serious but they took their time about removing the
bullet so he bled to death. Pilar from Aragon is covered in
pockmarks, it even makes her randy, no, it's the other way
around, when she's turned on she makes everyone feel randy,
boys and girls must wear full bathing costumes from the age of
two upwards, morality should spring from the individual,
we've crossed the Ebro, Florián Soutullo Dureixas, Civil
Guard and piper, died in the reconquest of Teruel, he got a
bullet between the eyes, Marujita Méndez is a big sweaty red-
head from Zamora, she's also fond of playing solitaire and
drinking soda water, from time to time she slips into the Betanzos bar and orders a soda water, Monsignor Olaechea, the
Bishop of Pamplona, grew tired of calling for the bloodshed to
cease, Lérida, Balaguer, Tremp, Tortosa, and the Arán valley
all taken, Isidro Suárez Méndez, the fellow who stole from the
dead in the Logroño Hospital, died on the Burriana front, he
was bathing in the sea and, since every time he stuck his head
above water they fired a pot shot at him, he drowned, do you
see that gentleman with the dickie bow and spectacles? you do?
well, that's my uncle Lorenzo, a man who can fart at will, two,
three, fives times even, as often as he feels like, women of
Spain, your adornments and your dress must not ape the foul
fashions of treacherous Jewish France, measures are passed
against the abuse of banquets, stupid tarts will never leave
poverty behind, it serves them right, Joaquina is a stupid tart,
you have only to look at her, all the clothes she wears are
darned, what good does it do her to have breasts like big, sweet
melons, stupid tarts are hopeless, to hell with them! never

forget this, Spaniard: the one-course meal is not a German novelty but an ancient Hispanic tradition, Castellón and Burriana both taken, Infantry Corporal Pascualiño Antemil Cachizo died in Peguerinos, Basilisa the half-wit, his "war mother," still sends him chocolate and tobacco, to be eaten and smoked by somebody or other, have no fear! it certainly doesn't go to waste, Inés Alontro caught a bad dose of the clap from a Moor. but that wouldn't kill anybody, that's true, although she had a terrible time of it, young lady postulants in patriotic matters wear the Spanish mantilla, the Extremadura offensive and capture of Don Benito, Villanueva de la Serena y Castuera, Urbano Randín Fernández, a squinting smuggler and bug-hunter, then a soldier in the Service Corps, was killed in Jarama, he was setting rabbit snares, that was his job was after all, but then he blew his cover and they nabbed him, why don't we smoke a hash pipe? for I'm fed up with bores and with taking orders, women trafficking in fleshly pursuits may not flaunt themselves in public nor walk the streets, the Reds have crossed the Ebro, there's going to be a hell of a hullaballoo here, Ricardo Vázquez Vilariño, Aunt Jesusa's sweetheart, well, in a manner of speaking, was killed in the capture of Santander, no, it wasn't in the capture of Santander, it was in Teruel, on January 1st 1938, that very day Commander Juan Barja de Quiroga, head of the Galician Banners was killed too, Ricardo Vázquez was shot in the heart, well, so they say, Portuguese Marta keeps three diamonds and another three rubies in a little tin box which she never lets out of her sight, not that anybody knows, the civil governor of Valladolid advises against attending public executions by firing squads: at present the military courts are engaged in the sorry task of carrying out sentences, in the place where these events are carried out an unaccustomed crowd has been observed to as-

semble, among them children of tender years, young girls and
even ladies . . . , the presence of such persons says very little
in their favor, etc., capture of Tarragona, Barcelona, and Ger-
ona, Filemón Toucido Rozabales, the unauthorized attorney
who was able to give Teresita del Niño Jesús Minguez (the
runaway wife of Medardo Congos the vet) such delight, was
relieving himself when someone, maybe for a bit of a lark, but
meaning no harm let's say, fired a bullet into his head, Sebas-
tiana!, Yes, Don Romulus, sir? Get out on the balcony in your
petticoats until you catch cold! Women of Spain, each stitch of
your industrious needles is certain victory against the cold that
tortures the soldiers sacrificing themselves in order to build the
fatherland, capture of Madrid, April 1st 1939, the Year of
Victory: upon this day, capture and disarming of the Red army
etc. The war is over.

It rains as it has always rained, I can remember no other
rain, no other color, no other silence, it rains slowly, gently,
monotonously, it rains with neither beginning nor end, they
say that water always returns to its source but that's not true,
again I can hear the blackbird sing but its song is different now,
not entirely harmonious and in tune, it's sadder and clouded
and seems to come from the throat of a phantom bird, from a
bird that is sick in both memory and soul, it may be that the
blackbird is older and disillusioned, there's something different
in the air, some men have stopped breathing, heads have
rolled and base deeds been done on this mountain, but tears
have also flowed, floods of tears been wept, the earth is the
same color as the sky, and the same noble, nostalgic substance,
and the line of the mountain was blotted out behind the silent
rain, the soft green and the soft ashen grey provide cover for the
fox and wolf, the war did not strangle the wolf, did not finish
off the wolf, did not kill the wolf, the war was man against

fellow man and his cheerful form, now man's silhouette is sad and as though he were ashamed, I'm not entirely clear about it but to my mind the war was lost by mankind, that grievous creature in misadventure, that bitter creature that never learns his lesson. If someone were to ask for peace, piety, and pardon, nobody would pay any attention, victory is heady but venomous too, victory eventually confounds the victor and lulls him to sleep. The Casandulfe Raimundo has worsened, Miss Ramona told him:

"Soon you'll be as right as rain once more, have no fear, the main thing is to have lived through to the end."

When a silence falls Spaniards say that an angel has just passed over and the English say that a pauper has been born. The Casandulfe Raimundo took a few minutes to reply.

"You're very good to me, Mona, do you think I'm alive and well just like before?"

"Yes, Raimundo, alive and well indeed, you'll soon see in a few days' time."

Robín Lebozán presented the Casandulfe Raimundo with a bottle of whisky.

"It may even be the only one in the whole of Galicia, the oldest of the Venceáses has just brought it to me from Portugal, so keep it safe."

It was a mistake to leave the settling of accounts to the judiciary, the infantry would have done a far better job, quicker and more lenient, the odd blunder is neither here nor there, it says in the *Aeneid* that the gods missed the mark too, so the odd slip-up can't have mattered then either, what matters is not the jumbled violence of the bold, whoring hard-drinking fellow, who smartly even scornfully stakes his life but rather the jumbled violence of the administrative coward, a rank-respecting coward who earns his living only with cautious avarice, a repulsive dim-witted fellow, no indeed, the worst is the cold, sustained violence of mediocrity hauling up on a charge the gushing torrent of life, that's not justice but rather a carnival sideshow, the moth from the ministries is much worse than the wild beasts of the mountain, meaner and more vindictive, then mankind loses his bearings, becomes unhinged and falls down, he does not weary, flee and kill himself, no, rather he takes fright, shrinks, and pines away, becoming sluggish and deeply embittered, encouraging foolishness and rules and regulations, you have only to read the paper to see it, there's nothing either fair or even brave about it, justice is still a pipe dream and bravery but a sorry flower crushed by red tape: at six o'clock yesterday morning, in fulfilment of the seventy-three death sentences passed by the court-martial which was held last Thursday, etc.

"It was an awful jolt to me, Mona, I can still see only hazily, it may take a while for my sight to clear."

"Don't even think about it. Don't open that bottle of whisky, keep it and enjoy it on your own. I'm going to make you a sort of cocktail, and one for you too, Robín, of course."

The Casandulfe Raimundo was partial to a cocktail: equal parts of red vermouth and gin, a few drops of bitters, a sprig of mint and a morello cherry.

"I'm out of ice."

"Never mind, we've goodwill enough to chill it."

As he sipped his cocktail, the Casandulfe Raimundo forgot his black despair.

"In the Café America and the Yacht Club in Corunna, drinking cocktails was all the rage, the Café America was in Real Street, approaching from the left-hand side, but you had to watch out for Don Oscar, I used to go there with my cousins and sometimes with Amparo, what a great girl Amparo was! I should go back to Corunna one of these days to see her, maybe she has a sweetheart now, indeed chances are she has a sweetheart."

Benicia can neither read nor write, nor does she need to, I'm not so sure that this business of reading and writing is any use at all. Benicia has nipples like chestnuts and, all in due course, the smile returned to her face.

"Benicia.'

"Yes, Don Raimundo?"

"Run down to the store and fetch me some matches and writing paper."

"What about stamps?"

"Yes, bring me two or three stamps as well."

"Do you want the ones with Queen Isabella or with the *Caudillo?*"

The Casandulfe Raimundo smiled.

"Whatever they have'll do, just bring whatever the hell they have."

This year not many people are going to the *romerías* of Our Lady of Corpiño in Santa Baia, over beyond Lalín, this is a year of the ignorant deceased, astonished prisoners, and nomads with the compass of their heart split in two, this year fewer folks possessed of the Devil are going and more Civil Guards, apparently the old ways are changing, fewer showmen and pipers are going too.

"Is it alright to play the pipes?"

"So long as it's daylight."

Beneath a spreading oak tree a rosary seller is thumping an innocent lad with a rosary to make him spew up the Devil.

"You swine, to want to keep that Devil within you! Spew it up! Satan, you fiendish bugger, come out of the body of that young man!"

The Casandulfe Raimundo grows bored, he sees everything in a strange almost artificial light, so, of course, he grows bored.

"Shall we go, Mona? For my part, even witchcraft in Galicia has gone off the rails. Why were we not born a hundred years later?"

On the homeward journey the Casandulfe Raimundo was gloomy and silent most of the way. They drove in an old Essex which Miss Ramona had bought from a Portuguese, the solemn black Packard and the smart white Isotta-Fraschini had been requisitioned at the outbreak of war never to be seen again, someone must have made good use of them.

"A penny for your thoughts."

"Nothing, I was just turning an idea that I don't like over in my mind."

It rains with courtesy, love, and serenity upon the empty green fields, upon the rye and the maize, maybe it rains without gallant courtesy, devoted love, nor gentle, benevolent serenity, maybe it's lashing down in sudden outbursts for the rain too has been robbed of its refinement, seated beside Miss Ramona, the Casandulfe Raimundo, somewhat reluctantly, spoke once more.

"Spain is a corpse, Mona. I don't even want to think about it but it scares me that it should be a corpse, what I don't know is how long it will take to bury it. Please God let me be mistaken! Please God it isn't dead but only fainted and may yet awake! Spain is a beautiful country, Mona, that has turned out all wrong. I know it's frowned upon to say such things, but, say it I will, Spaniards have hardly the spirit left to live, we Spaniards have to make a tremendous effort and go to great lengths to prevent other Spaniards from killing us."

Miss Ramona and the Casandulfe Raimundo reached the village before sunset.

"Just leave me home, Mona, I'm tired and I'm going to go straight to bed without any supper."

"As you wish."

Life trots along at the side of death, apparently that's God's law, some call it inertia while others don't even notice either life or death.

"You're looking pale, Nuncie, you're a bad color."

"I haven't been sleeping well for three or four days now. I don't know what's wrong with me, maybe it's the monthlies that have me all screwed up."

Gaudencio plays the accordion listlessly, the voices of outsiders cannot rouse enthusiasm in the heart, Portuguese Marta is a respectful, obliging girl, she knows her trade inside out.

"I do what I know with the best will in the world. I'm paid to give pleasure and I ask no questions."

Gaudencio plays the waltz *Tales from the Vienna Woods* by Strauss, it's delicate, romantic, and very elegant, Sergeant Clemente Palomares, a sergeant in the Service Corps, likes to give the girls a hard time, he enjoys tanning their hides, the truth of the matter is it's something we all enjoy, it's just a matter of paying over the odds or finding a girl who'll let you.

"I'm paid to give pleasure, so long as you're paying, anything goes, alright? but if you draw blood, god damn you! and if you make me cry I'll kill you, I swear to God I'll kill you!"

"I'm going to give you a ruby and a pearl, Marta, the ruby is like a drop of blood and the pearl is a tear, just like a tear."

"Fair enough."

Pura Sprat reeks of garlic, not because she likes it but from necessity, she has high blood pressure and she takes garlic and olive oil for breakfast to see if it'll lower it, garlic is good against the plague as well as for warding off vampires and expelling worms, the worst about garlic is the stench it leaves on your breath. Don Ángel Alegría, orthopedics, prosthetics, collects welfare service emblems, Miguel de Cervantes Saavedra, prince of Spanish genius, Spanish Infantry, eighteenth-century fusilier, Majorca, luminous pearl of the bright archipelago. Don Ángel suffers from inflammation of the testicles so that his works are puffed up like a cauliflower and the girls in Sprat's place avoid him like the plague.

"No, no, let him go to bed with his wife, and if he doesn't like that, then let him bugger off and make the best of it, in this life we all have to bugger off and grin and bear it, Don Ángel has putrid privates, and I won't have him tainting me forever, after all, I live on my health."

Mamede Pedreira was sentenced to death because he was caught with arms up the mountain, a serious crime, his mother stationed herself at a bend in the road where Franco was to pass by and tossed him a note pleading for clemency, his bodyguards, thinking it was a bomb, shot and killed her, then when he read the note, Franco reprieved Mamede and commuted the sentence of death by garrotting to thirty years' hard labor, Mamede Pedreira escaped while he was being transported to another prison and now he's holed up in Xurxo Lameiro's house, although nobody knows, well, his wife knows, of course, but his wife is aboveboard and a trustworthy sort, Mamede Pedreira lives down at the bottom of a dried-up well, he has a mattress and a blanket, they lower food to him on a rope running over a pulley, every couple of days he comes up at night to stretch his legs and have a wash-down.

"As far as I'm concerned, you can stay down there as long as you wish, and the same goes for Carmen too, this state of affairs can hardly last forever."

"I really don't know what to say, it may go on longer than any of us would credit."

Up and down these mountains, many years back, roamed Lázaro Codesal, the lad with a shock of fiery hair and eyes as clear as water from a spring, Lázaro Codesal was killed by the Riffian Moors and there's not a soul remembers him now.

"Not even the odd lass he left in the family way?"

"Not even that."

Folks keep quiet about it but nothing is ever the same as before, much less so now, nothing ever follows the same course twice, there are clients in Sprat's place who no longer pant for pleasure for they have breathed their last and are dead and buried, Don Teodosio, Doña Gemma's husband, died of his heart, Visi was the tart that Don Teodosio liked better than any of them, she was always so affectionate and obliging, that lout Don Jesús Manzanedo died stinking to high heaven, the girls in Sprat's place always gave him the slip, even though he would give them a tip of eight or ten *reales*, Bienvenido González, Kitty-cat, was a shit, too, but he got two good blows of a fist in the doorway, one on the throat and the other in the chest, Resurrección Penido is known as the Lark because she looks as though she is about to flap her wings and take off, the Lark got a terrible fright when she came across the body, the Lark was the first to see Kitty-cat's body, nobody in Sprat's place shed any tears over that death, that man was a bad lot, you could see it on his face, Portuguese Marta can read the souls of men, Portuguese Marta is justly renowned for being a good lay, randy and ripe for the picking, according to those in the know her ass creaks like a watermelon, I was just remarking that she's not the only one that happens to, it's said of other girls too, Gaudencio played a merry bullfighter's *paso doble*, *Marcial, You're the Greatest*, Ricardo Vázquez Vilariño, Aunt Jesusa's sweetheart—that's what we all say although there's no truth in it—also used to frequent Sprat's place, though not often, it was mere therapy to cool the hots, sometimes they get so bad a body can't even walk with them, any woman would do Ricardo Vázquez Vilariño, he was a tough nut and all he asked was to be let, on the few occasions he went to Orense, Lucio Mouro would drop in at Sprat's place, Lucio Mouro had a taste for buxom women, sweet anisette, and tangos.

"That bugger Gaudencio plays the accordion very well, indeed he plays it better than anyone in the whole wide world!"

Clarita was left fatherless, that bastard Don Jesús, but without a sweetheart, too, the unfortunate Ignacio Araujo Cid, who couldn't stomach it and let himself be killed in the war, chances are he let himself be killed, bastards call the shots in the lives of their fellow man and kill him with spiteful joy and the luckless die and dejectedly let themselves be killed with cautious, humbled despondency, at times Don Jesús and his son-in-law that might have been would also go to Sprat's place, folks need relief and seek it out, that's for sure, a fellow I don't think ever went to Sprat's place was Camilo the gunner, I don't know why I say this for he's not dead either, he's from faraway and hardly ever sets foot in Orense.

"Does he head more for Pontevedra?"

"Yes, and for Santiago, especially for Santiago, folks from Padrón might as well be from Santiago."

The others mentioned are dead and buried now, God rest their souls! And others who shall remain nameless because everything has its end, anyway, not all the dead have been Sprat's clients, some weren't, there are other brothels in Orense, in his hellfire sermons Father Santisteban, S.J., calls them bordellos, bawdyhouses, and houses of ill repute.

"They have umpteen other names as well, not that that old windbag would know."

Most folks harbor a traitor within them, not that it's of such importance for it's merely one of the characteristics of mankind, a recognized trait, just so long as you're aware of it, when Don Casto Borrego Sánchez-Puente's level of uric acid was lowered, he became less aggressive, before there wasn't a sinner could stick him, the girls in Sprat's place were panic-stricken when they saw him coming and even Sprat herself, who would bend over backwards to help, never dared take him on, better to let him leave without paying, one night Don Casto was hit by a motorcar, he wasn't killed but both his legs were fractured nor did the driver stop to offer assistance, Don Casto says the driver was an Italian, that all the passengers in the car were Italian, goodness knows! the night watchman picked him up and half-dragged him along the street to the first aid post; apparently Don Casto shit in his britches from the shock.

"Listen, Doña Pura, do you remember that little lieutenant with the moustache from Malaga by the name of Fermín Pendón Paz? Of course you do, the fellow that jacked off in the parlor to save a few *pesetas?*"

"Of course I remember! What happened to him?"

"Nothing, except that he was killed last night by a bottle, he was hit by one of those big soda-water bottles, and the bottle was well and truly drained dry."

"Poor soul! Where did that happen?"

"Right in the middle of the street, just when he was coming out of One-eyed Mackerel's place, there was a whole commotion and the military authorities intervened."

"Did you ever hear the likes of it!"

The Casandulfe Raimundo told Robín Lebozán Castro de Cela:

"It's up to you to summon all the relations in the name of Uncle Camilo, I think the time has come to summon the Moranes, of course, and the Guxindes, too, it makes no difference that we're such a huge gathering for we have important matters to discuss, everyone should have their say, and until we're all gathered together, we should hold our counsel, Mona will let us have her house, it's the most suitable venue."

Don Brégimo, Miss Ramona's father, had been a friend of the famous acrobatic airmen Vedrines, Garnier, Leforestier, and Lacombe, who would turn pirouettes up there in the void and by night silhouetted their planes with colored lights, seats cost 25 or 50 *centimos*, depending on where they were, and the ladies used to dress up to the nines in big broad-brimmed hats with veils, but that was years ago, before Miss Ramona was even born.

All us Moranes are horse-faced with gaps between our teeth, sometimes quite big gaps, as Camilo the gunner once recounted, it is also said that we stink of steers and that we enjoy squabbling at *romerías* and weddings but that's not true, it's less pronounced in the Guxindes because they're more mixed blood, or maybe that's just the way they are, I won't deny it, a race has nothing to lose from crossbreeding, indeed it gains, though at the same time the traits may be lost, the same goes for a blood line, but bear in mind what they say: the first generation makes, the second one takes, and the third one breaks, if you see what I'm driving at. Not all of us Moranes are descended from Marshal Pardo de Cela, although most of us are, at that time marshal didn't mean captain of troops but stableman. Uncle Evelio is a good-looking Móran, Uncle Evelio is known as Wild Boar because he's wild and stocky, Wild Boar scarcely ever ventures down from the mountains and wouldn't even bid an outsider the time of day, during the war Wild Boar had his own problems to contend with but luckily he was well able to ride out the storm.

"This is a feud among starvelings, real men don't go about killing one another at the drop of a hat, those fellows are like the French, and what they're up to is just like teaching goats tricks, it wouldn't even occur to anyone who wasn't a gypsy to teach goats tricks."

Wild Boar enjoys eating, drinking, smoking, screwing, and going for a stroll, Wild Boar is a gentleman of honorable, traditional ways, in that respect he's just like your uncle Don Claudio Montenegro.

"So you want to defend your fads with the gun? Fine, go right ahead, but you fire the shots yourself, don't order someone else to shoot on your behalf, you brave it up the mountain with a shotgun and we'll soon see, when it comes to the moment of truth folks get shit scared, folks soon get cold feet and start making excuses and asking what time it is."

Wild Boar has lived seventy long years and wears spectacles.

"It's a matter of age, when I was young I could see better and farther than anybody else but that wasn't to last all my life, as I know full well: wearing glasses when you're old is not the worst of it, even worse is wearing them while you're still young, young people with glasses are either seminary students or pansies."

"Gracious, Uncle Evelio!, surely not all of them?"

"Well, nearly all of them, I won't deny the odd exception."

Wild Boar's wife died many years back, over half a century ago, Wild Boar's wife was a fine looking, witty woman who always wore a pearl necklace and went about dressed to the nines. Wild Boar never remarried, although he had no shortage of opportunities and flitted from one woman to the next like a hummingbird all his life, I love her, I love her not, I'll give this one a son and pay for him to be trained as a priest, I'll give that one a daughter and set her up with an inn, and so on, for his late wife's tombstone Wild Boar ordered a slab of white marble upon which he had the following epitaph engraved: Since you were called María, the name of the Mother of God, I shall always regret not having your photograph taken.

"But that isn't even verse."

"I know, but Wild Boar was never much of a hand at verse."

Wild Boar graded the objects of his scorn and loathing in descending order, as follows: priests, soldiers, Italians, customs officials, gravediggers, short men, and people with stammers.

"What about the Portuguese?"

"No, he didn't include them."

As well as having a stammer, Sabiniano Sagramón Roidiz dribbled like an altar boy when he spoke, Sabiniano was a creep who went through this valley of tears spraying everyone with spittle, he would leave them drowning in saliva, his wife, Justinita Cereixal Roibós spent her life being unfaithful to him until one fine day, sick and tired of pretense and gossip, she reached the end of her tether, shut him up in the lunatic asylum and took off with a fellow from the town of Alcalá de Chivert in Castellón by the name of Felipe Albiol Forner who had a workshop where they produced sugared almonds.

"And sugared hazelnuts, pinenuts, and other types of nuts?"

"Yes, they produced those too, that fellow Albiol stopped at nothing and would sugar anything that came his way."

Justinita never played her lover false although she was even offered all the tea in China to do so, she was never unfaithful to Albiol, apparently all the urge left her with Sabiniano.

"He's so spick and span!"

Justinita was the niece of Wild Boar's late wife and so related to him through marriage, Justinita used to dress in city style and wore high heeled red shoes fastened at the ankle.

"Not that it matters, you have to keep your feet on the ground, it makes no difference whether you're a chink from Ciudad Real or whatever but you have to be something, this business of wearing tartish shoes is the least of it, you have to put your roots down somewhere or other, that's all that matters."

Wild Boar sent for the Casandulfe Raimundo.

"It seems that tempers are cooling off. What are you thinking of doing with that wretch? you know who I mean."

"You can well imagine, Uncle Evelio, everyone will have to have their say, I've already told Robín to summon everyone."

"Fair enough, there's no hurry for time is on our side."

Marujita Bodelón Alvarez, that's the Ponferrada woman who walked out with Celso Varela, kept Don Jesús' death notice: The illustrious Señor Don Jesús Manzanedo Muñiz, Veteran Nocturnal Worshipper, Order of Slave of Merit of Our Father Jesús, Lawyer and court attorney, passed on after receiving extreme unction and the blessing of His Holiness, R.I.P. This notice may be exchanged for a two pound loaf of bread to be collected seven days hence at the San Cosme bakery, distributed as an act of intercession for the soul of the deceased.

"Some death notices are delightful, don't you think?"

"Yes, dear, some death notices are delightful."

"Well, God rest his soul!"

"Yes, indeed, the greatest test of the existence of God would be for Don Jesús to manage to rest in peace."

Marujita Bodelón saw sense and married a Moor called Driss ben Gauzzafat from Franco's bodyguard.

"He's very good to me and a real Christian in bed, only that my Driss has a prick like the one on St. Facundo's ass and when it unsheathes, you'd think the world was about to drop out of it."

"Marujita!"

"Pardon me, but it just sort of slipped out on me."

It's going to be an uphill struggle for things to return to normal, folks have acquired the taste for doing nothing and roaming about, a country cannot rise from its knees like this and soon we'll all be feeling the pinch, that's if the English or the Germans don't cross the border on us.

Abd Alá el-Azziz ben Meruán, the Portuguese, was a Moor too, although he's been dead for several centuries now, there were always Moors hereabouts, some hoarding gold and precious stones while others went about spreading lice and scratching their leprous sores, there's many a Spaniard nowadays descended from the leprous Mohammecans, you can tell them a mile off. Don Clemente Bariz, Doña Rita's husband who went and did himself in, was known as Fat-of-the-land for he had plenty of dough and ill will and had been plentifully cuckolded into the bargain, he had plenty of everything, indeed, Doña Rita wanted Father Rosendo Vilar, the priest that she was having an affair with and with whom she wound up blessing her union, to administer extreme unction *in articulo mortis* to Don Clemente.

"I can't, my dear, the sacraments may not be administered

when the danger of death is not due to illness—it's not allowed."

"But what danger are you talking about if he's as dead as a doornail already?"

"For pity's sake, you're right!"

Then Doña Rita laid the table with a clean white cloth, a tray with little balls of cotton wool—she had to make them out of a sanitary towel for she was out of cotton wool—another with hunks of bread, wedges of lemon, holy water, etc. and Father Rosendo said a prayer:

"Bendicat te omnipotens Deus . . ."

"Amen."

Georgina and Adela are cousins of Moncho Requeixo Casbolado, Georgina popped off her first husband, Adolfito Penouta Augalevada, Buffoon, or maybe he hanged himself, opinions differ, by dosing him with a potion brewed from buttercups and she tamed the other fellow, Carmelo Méndez—later to be killed in the siege of Oviedo—by purging him weekly with *olivillas*. Adela munches magic herbs and wanders through life in a trance, Moncho is eternally grateful to his Aunt Micaela, the mother of his cousins, because she used to jerk him off when he was a lad. Some things are never forgotten.

"Nowadays families are scattered far and wide and everyone goes their own way."

It was a shame the Shark was killed before he could steal the bells of Antioch, it'll be no easy matter to find another diver as good as the Shark.

"Do you remember that night when you both went to Sprat's place to take the chill off your bones?"

"Of course I do! And why wouldn't I remember it? Some things are never forgotten."

Poor Aguirre died vomiting blood and Isidro Gómez Méndez, I mean Isidro Suárez Méndez, robbed his body, as he used to rob all the bodies of the dead without exception, afterwards Isidro was killed on the Burriana front while he was bathing. I don't know why I sometimes recall the hospital and war scenes, well, truth to tell I recall everything.

"Is that a good thing do you think?"

"I'm not so sure."

Miss Ramona also goes to visit Wild Boar, a sort of patriarch who doesn't always consent to be seen, Wild Boar has a mermaid tattooed just above his shoulder blade, he only shows it off on his Saint's Day which is May 11, for the saints Antimo, Evelio, Máximo, Basso, Fabio, Sisinio, Diocletio, Florencio, Anastasio, Gangulfo, Mamerto, Mayolo, Iluminado, and Francisco de Jerónimo, May 11 is Camilo the gunner's birthday, Wild Boar has a distinguished gait and a shock of curly hair.

"Look here, Mona, life is hard on each and every one of us, life rejects death just as death strangles life, death always wins out in the end since it's in less of a hurry and more brazen."

"Yes, Uncle Evelio."

"Yes, indeed it does! Listen, Mona, the war is over and many's the wretch was stranded up the mountain or left lying in a ditch with his belly or brains spewing out, but nearly all of us men in the family are still in our proper place, not having had to learn another language or other ways. This business of forcing change upon folks is a bad job and grievous for the soul."

"Yes, Uncle Evelio."

"Indeed it is! Look, Mona, I don't think much of the Italians, the Greeks, or the Turks, I prefer the English, the Dutch,

and the Norwegians, they're not so much fun but more trustworthy and they don't holler quite so much."

"Yes, Uncle Evelio."

"Indeed I do! Would you like a drink?"

"Yes, Uncle Evelio."

"Can't you say anything but 'Yes, Uncle Evelio'?"

Wild Boar poured two glasses of rum.

"This is good stuff, a drop of rum never did anyone any
harm. Sailors take it so as to hold their own against the sea, and
it's good for women, too. Do you know Don Ángel Alegría, the
orthopedics fellow?"

"No, I don't. Why do you ask?"

"No reason really, just out of curiosity."

The seven Alontra sisters are riding out the storm, one way
or another, events tend to shake up men with greater fury than
women, it's not a hard and fast rule but comes close enough to
do, the worst that can befall a man is not knowing how death
will catch him out, I don't mean the death of the soul and
eternal salvation or eternal fire, I mean the death of the flesh
and his way of snuffing the candle, the Moors wouldn't allow
as much as a finger to be amputated because they have to pass
through the gates of paradise whole in limb and body, a buried
corpse eaten up by maggots is not the same as a body sub-
merged in the sea and gobbled by sardines, or torn asunder and
devoured by dogs, or incinerated and scattered as food for the
sparrows, the bodies of men will always be devoured eventually, women are not beset by these scares, the seven Alontra
girls are still alive and kicking, hale and hardy, handsome and
hearty, into the bargain.

"And what about Dolores, did she get over her appendicitis?"

"Now you're talking! She's blooming like a rose, she's a delight to behold."

Robín Lebozán and the Casandulfe Raimundo linger over enjoyable, long-winded philosophizing, Miss Ramona invites them to tea, the most talkative one is Robín for Raimundo is rather tired, he's been feeling under the weather for several days:

"You can live or you can make a pretence of living, Raimundo, since I'm not overly robust, since I'm rather sickly in fact, I go through life making a pretense, the truth of the matter is that in comparison with you, for instance, I've seen very little of life. I would like to have lived life more to the full but I have to accept my lot, have patience! I don't think that anything at a remove from us either lives or exists, you know what I mean, the axis of the whole world is here within our very own hearts and Mona's house, what's faraway might not even exist: a Peruvian Indian blowing on a bamboo flute, an eskimo flaying seals, a Chinaman puffing opium—can you imagine it?—a black playing the saxophone, a Moor charming snakes, a Neapolitan eating spaghetti, the world is very cramped and life very short, Moncho Lazybones went around the entire globe, true enough, Moncho Lazybones had love affairs in Guayaquil, but the rest of you never left these mountains except to go to war, well, not all but most of you, and I didn't even get that far, nor can anybody be sure that this business of seeing so much of the world does you any good at all, but what does do you good is a young lass, sitting on a low stool before a blazing fire, playing the lute, those are the old ways, the ones that were lost in the upheaval, now everything will be so much the worse, one era dies and another is born, Raimundo, the rye shoots up and withers away each year but the oak tree outlives man, there's no need drown in shit, Raimundo, you know what I mean, better to blow your brains out first."

The Casanculfe Raimundo looks downcast.

"You mention the upheaval, Robín, true enough, there are things that will never be the same again, we will never see things set to rights however long we live, old ways swept aside by the upheaval . . . I don't know, do I seem very uprooted to you? Maybe the mistake I made was not dying young, well, younger than I am, that is . . . I beg both of you to forgive me, will you pour me a brandy, Mona?"

"I will, Raimundo, shall I play the piano?"

It rains upon the waters of the River Arnego, which flows past, turning mill wheels and scaring folks with goiter and folks who have caught a chill cast by the evil eye of the toad and the venomous salamander, it also lashes the dying too, while Catuxa Bainte the half-wit from Martiña, whistles stark naked up Esbarrado Hill, with her tits dripping wet, her hair trailing like a bough of weeping willow and a fledgling sparrow in her clenched fist.

"You'll catch your death, Catuxa."

"Not me sir, the cold slips off me like water off a duck's back."

It seems like yesterday that the gale that sowed the seeds of grief in the memory swept over here.

"What shall we do with the dead?"

"The same three things as always, my dear, the same three things as we've always done: wash their faces then bury them, say an Our Father, and avenge them, for death cannot be doled out scot free."

"True enough."

It rains down upon the waters of the River Bermún, the stream that shrieks like a drowning child, it rains down upon the waters of the five rivers: the Viñao trickling from the Valdo Verneiro plain, the Asneiros gushing forth from the Two Priests Crags, the Oseira refreshing the pelts of the Oseira monks, the Comezo hurtling northwards along the track of the Lame Vixen, and the Bural where the girls of Agrosantiño launder their kerchieves, it rains upon oaks and chestnuts, cherry trees and willows, upon men and women, upon gorse, bracken, and solemn ivy, upon the living and the dead, it rains upon the whole countryside.

"That's the only thing nobody has been able to tamper with."

"Thanks be to God."

At my uncle Claudio Montenegro's funeral we were all gathered together and there were some tense moments when the civil governor appeared, luckily tempers cooled right away, my uncle Don Claudio Montenegro never let anyone get on his wick, he caught the unfortunate Wenceslas Caldraga in a wolf trap and kept him howling for three days without a bite to eat nor a drop to drink, not even bread and water, when he released him he was as meek as a lamb.

"Did he come leaping out?"

"Yes, sir, limping but leaping."

The dead man who killed Lionheart and Cidrán Segade to boot is not dead yet, but he has one foot in the grave already, between the Feasts of St. Marta and St. Luis three years ago he left at least twelve or fifteen people dead, maybe even more, and now he reeks of death, folks hurry out of his way when they see him coming.

"Do you not get that whiff of the damned off him?"

One morning as he was returning from Mass, Blind Gaudencio fainted right in the middle of the street, it was as if he had taken a fit of the vapors.

"That's the accordion player from Sprat's place, maybe the poor fellow hasn't had a bite to eat."

Down at the municipal stores they gave Gaudencio a cup of coffee and he soon came to.

"Did you hurt yourself?"

"No, sir, I saw that I was going to faint so I just sat down."

When he got back to Sprat's place nobody was any the wiser for the girls were asleep. A guard with a hacking cough accompanied him.

"Here we are."

"God bless you!"

When he climbed into bed, Blind Gaudencio covered up his head and whole body so as to sweat it out.

"That'll do me good, I'm sure it was a draught that caught me just at a bad moment or when I was lying awkwardly."

That night Gaudencio played the accordion as if nothing had happened.

"Gaudencio."

"Yes, Don Samuel?"

"Play that lovely mazurka, you know the one I mean."

"Yes, sir, I do, but you'll have to excuse me for it's not appropriate this evening, indeed it is hardly ever appropriate."

Basilisa the half-wit is a prostitute in Toraleira's place in Corunna, they say that Basilisa the half-wit is the greatest slut of a tart in the whole wide world but that isn't true, that's something nobody can ever know, Basilisa the half-wit was sending chocolate and tobacco to the late Corporal Antimil until she grew fed up, Basilisa the half-wit never found out that Corporal Antimil had died, she thought he was fickle, like all men except for Javierito Pértega who is a pansy and good for running errands that are not too demanding he's also good for kicking in the ass.

"Are you not ashamed to have your privates hanging down like that?"

Don Lesmes Cabezón Ortigueira, medical practitioner, surgeon, and one of the chiefs of the Knights of Corunna, fell into the sea in the fishermen's wharf, in the very spot where a whale was once seen, and he drowned, he may have been pushed, Dolores Alontra started laughing when she heard the news.

"He was a dirty old man that gave the girls a hard time of it. It's a good job he drowned."

The ghost of Benitoña Cardoeiros, the spent old woman savaged by the ripper Manueliño Blanco Romasanta, still wafts on the air in the Alvar meadow oak grove which is full of nightingales.

"There are bullfinches and goldfinches, too."

"Yes, ma'am, as well as greenfinches, blackbirds, and dun-colored larks, there's everything over in the Alvar meadow oak grove."

All Souls' Day should be spent in peace and quiet, in the old days it was customary to go and play the bagpipes and eat cakes in the graveyard. The dead weigh heavy upon us and nobody should forget them.

"One day will all the dead be numbered?"

"Never ever. Some say that the dead breed more dead, that may be the case but I don't think so."

On All Souls' Day 1939 the Second World War had already begun, the Feast of St. Charles falls shortly after All Souls' Day, and upon the Feast of St. Charles in the year 1939, summoned by Robín Lebozán, twenty-two men—all of them blood relatives—assembled in Miss Ramona's house: the Casandulfe Raimundo, nobody ever uses his real surname because it carries the seeds of grief within it, but that is a tale that is long and painful in the telling, for some time the Casandulfe

Raimundo has been rather despondent and reluctant to talk; the four quick-witted Gamuzos: that's Tanis the Demon who can floor an ox with one hand—his wife fell down the stairs on him and broke her leg, chances are she had a drop too much anisette on board, Roquiño the Cleric of Comesaña with his colossal member that's famous throughout the country, it's a bit chafed at the moment but as fine-looking as ever, Matías the Joker, who hasn't danced for months, and Julián Wide-awake—pocket and wristwatches, alarm clocks, cuckoo clocks, both wall and free-standing—Celestino Sprig and Ceferino Ferret are not present since they are priests, Benito Scorpion and Shrill Salustio are exempted on account of their disabilities; the three Marvises from Briñidelo, Segundo, Evaristo, and Camilo, who are fearless by nature and ride the toughest of colts bareback with not a thing to grip on to, their father, that's Roque—he was not present since he's well on in years—stayed in Esperelo with his Portuguese woman; Don Camilo and Camilo the gunner, Don Camilo is suffering from earache, quite severe earache, but since he has a modicum of common sense, he says nothing; Don Balthasar and Don Eduardo, Don Camilo's brothers, one is a lawyer and the other an engineer; Lucio Segade and his three eldest sons: Lucio, Perfecto, and Camilo, it was quite a job to restrain them for they wanted to mete out justice by their own hand and wouldn't listen to anybody; Uncle Cleto, who won't shake hands for fear of germs; Marcos Albite, who arrived lurching along the cart tracks in his little cart pushed by the half-wit from Martiñá, silent beneath his umbrella Marcos Albite looked like a soul sentenced by Our Lord to a spell in purgatory; Gaudencio Beira was not required to attend on account of his blindness; Policarpo la Bagañeira, carrying a trained mouse in his pocket, as a mark of respect he didn't take it out; Moncho

Lazybones the discoverer of the *ombiel* tree, the tree with leaves like snail flesh; the venerable, even-tempered Uncle Evelio and, of course, Robín Lebozán. Some came from far afield, all of them wearing hats, peaked caps or berets, some of them on familiar terms and others more distant in their manner, Don Camilo was turned out in a derby and an overcoat with a wolfskin collar, they were waited on by Miss Ramona, Ádega, her daughter Benicia, the half-wit from Martiñá and Moncho's two cousins, Georgina and Adela. Miss Ramona's servants scarcely count for they have one foot in the grave already. The men dined off a choice of bacon broth or pork pie, with nipple-shaped Galician cheeses, quince jelly, and peaches in syrup for dessert. When twelve o'clock struck Don Camilo made a sign and everyone sat down in silence and lit their cigars, Don Camilo had brought cigars for everyone, while the women poured coffee and *aguardiente,* and then headed for the kitchen, not one of them lingered to eavesdrop at the keyhole because men are the ones who order the lives of men and women know and respect these ways, some feuds women may mention only in bed, with just one man and, even then, not always.

"Stand up! Our Father which art in Heaven . . ."

"Our daily bread . . ."

When they sat down again, well, not everybody for there weren't seats for all of them, when almost all of them had sat down again, Don Camilo looked to Robín Lebozán:

"Our relation Robín Lebozán Castro de Cela will fill us in, speaking only the truth with no attempt to conceal the facts."

In a clear voice Robín related in minute detail what all of us already knew and when he had finished he asked:

"Shall I tell you the name of the fellow who killed Baldomero and Cidrán?"

"Do."

Robín glanced down at the floor.

"May God forgive me! It was that fellow called Fabián Minguela Abragán, known as Moucho Carroupo and with a patch of pockmarked skin on his forehead, you all know who he is and none of you, from this moment hence, should utter his name."

The silence was broken by Evelio Wild Boar.

"It's up to you, Camilo."

Without uttering a word and with a solemn expression upon his face, Don Camilo also lowered his gaze to the floor. Although as anticipated, the decision sent a shiver down the spine of all present.

"Who is the order for?"

Still in silence, Don Camilo looked in the direction of Tanis the Demon who then stood up, took off his hat and crossed himself.

"May the Blessed Apostle St. James and our relation the Saintly Fernández assist me! Amen! When you hear a sky-rocket go off, you'll know that's it."

The meeting gradually broke up in an orderly fashion: the three Marvises from Briñidelo left on horseback without delay for they had a long way to go. Don Balthasar and Don Eduardo went off to sleep in Lalín in the house of their distant relative Freixido the priest, they went by car, it was a pig of a night—all the better for there's not all the bother of requesting safe-conduct from the Civil Guard. Don Camilo left with Uncle Evelio Wild Boar, Camilo the gunner slept at the Casandulfe Raimundo's house, and the other three Gamuzos from elsewhere were put up for the night at their brother Tanis' house, it all worked out well and nobody said more than they ought to have, the only ones to stay in Miss Ramona's house were

Moncho Lazybones, who is missing one leg, and Marcos Albite, who is missing both legs, it was a rough night for lame folks to be out on the mountain. Catuxa Bainte slept curled up on the porch, and suddenly a deep and silent peace fell upon Miss Ramona's house. Before departing, Don Camilo left an order for the priest Ceferino Gamuzo, Ferret the fisherman, St. Peter was a fisherman, too.

"He's to say a Mass for the soul of I-won't-say-who. Nor is he to ask any questions about what he should be able to guess, and let him sing dumb."

"Yes, Don Camilo."

Upon Miss Ramona's house as well as upon men and women there descended a mist which gradually blotted out, one by one, the words that were spoken and which still wafted upon the air. Memory is no match for the mist, and so much the better.

"Shall we talk tomorrow?"

"Well, better the day after, tomorrow I have to go to Carballiño."

"They say that St. Ramón Nonato is the patron saint of gamesters, gamblers, cardsharpers, and shady runs of luck."

"Why so?"

"How would I know!"

Crazy Goat cannot be accused of having gone to bed with whoever, you know full well who sucked Crazy Goat's tits but don't let his name pass your lips, for everybody goes as far as they're let, and that's nobody else's concern. This business of whether she went to bed with this one or that one makes no difference to anyone but herself. All women have the right to toss in the hay with whoever takes their fancy. You say he's a bastard? Well, maybe you're right, there's many a bastard about, but that doesn't matter.

"Do you think Crazy Goat would dare mess about with a wild boar?"

"What business is that of yours?"

"It has been raining without let up since the Feast of St. Ramón Nonato, who runs a gambling den in Carballiño, on the road to Ribadavia, the day when they least expected to be caught by the Civil Guard and all wind up behind bars."

"Pardon me but the fellow that runs the gambling den on the Ribadavia road is not St. Ramón Nonato but St. Macario, there's no call to mix them up."

"Well, sure it's all the same, they're saints anyhow."

A leisurely rain falls straight down upon the grass, the tiled roofs, and the windowpanes, it rains but it isn't cold, I mean not really cold. If I could play the fiddle, I'd spend the afternoons playing the fiddle, if I could play the harmonica, I'd spend the mornings and afternoons playing the harmonica, if I could play the accordion, I'd spend the mornings, the afternoons and the evenings, indeed I'd spend my whole life playing the accordion. Gaudencio plays the accordion better than anybody, since I can play neither the fiddle, nor the harmonica, nor the accordion, since I can play nothing at all, I might as well have died as a child and saved them all the trouble of grieving over me, I spend the afternoons messing about with whoever I can, in the mornings and in the evenings I'm kept more entertained, at times I can't mess about with anybody but that makes no difference, isn't that why I've got two hands, men just have to accept how fate has ordered their lives because all that has been settled even before we came into this world. Don Samuel Iglesias Moure is the proprietor of a chandler's in Father Feijoo Street, Don Samuel looks like he's made of wax and his wife the same, folks call him Celestial, some evenings Don Samuel drops by Sprat's place to let his hair down and listen to the accordion, only he's seldom in luck with the tunes, for he's very fond of a mazurka that Gaudencio seldom plays.

"Why don't you play it the odd time?"

"What difference does that make to you?"

Celestial likes to go to bed with Portuguese Marta. He likes to spin her yarns.

"Since she's big and buxom you get great relief and satisfaction out of her. Portuguese women are very considerate."

"Yes, sir, that's what everybody says. And very respectful, too."

"That's for sure."

Don Servando goes in ahead of Don Samuel, Don Servando does not have to wait in line since he is a provincial deputy, Don Samuel takes Portuguese Marta a spiral candle as a gift.

"Shall we light it?"

"No, I'd rather take it new to the Holy Christ of the Sacred Blood. Hold on a minute while I get undressed and wash my privates down a bit, there's time enough."

Don Servando always threw his weight about with Eleuterio the Britches, whereas to Don Samuel he was most affable.

"They're chalk and cheese, Don Samuel is a gentleman, a bit wheyfaced but a gentleman all the same, and his wife, Doña Dorita, is a real lady, Doña Dorita distributes clothes to the poor, they're very good people, clean living, upright, and trustworthy people.

Don Isaac is Don Samuel's brother, Don Isaac is a noodle seller, his Vesuvius brand macaroni is renowned throughout the whole of Galicia, Don Isaac turned out a pansy, but that's a matter of birth and could happen to anybody, to you or me even, but he carries it off in a dignified manner, you'll never catch him propositioning anybody, Don Isaac plays the harmonium in the church of St. Mary the Mother and other places too if he is called upon for some wedding or other, at home Don Isaac plays the lyre, an instrument from which he draws out beautiful, melodious arpeggios, presiding over Don Isaac's house is a plaster of Paris bust of Pope Pius X colored crimson, gold, blue, flesh color etc. The Pope rests just above the lyre upon a whatnot draped with the Spanish flag.

"My brother is a real artist, a full-bodied artist and musically very gifted, to my mind he wound up a pansy from indulging his feelings."

"Maybe, I don't deny it, that sometimes happens."

"Chances are Lucio Mouro the miller was killed by the same fellow as killed the other two."

"Who?"

"Hold your tongue, you dope! Don't you know who I mean?"

"Sorry, I wasn't thinking."

Lucio Mouro was shot in the back and again in the head, he was wearing a flower—a buttercup—stuck in the peak of his cap when he was killed.

"Catuxa, do you remember how good he was?"

"Why wouldn't I remember?"

Rosicler was ten years old, maybe not even that, when she jacked off Jeremiah the monkey for the first time.

"And what's the point of that then?"

"I don't know, but there's no harm in knowing things."

"Yes, indeed, that's true."

"Anyway they come into your head without warning."

When she discovered that monkeys had willies just like men only smaller, Rosicler was delighted.

"I must tell Mona, though she probably knows already."

Celestial the chandler, that's Don Samuel Iglesias Moure,

went into town one day on an errand and they came across him unawares rolling in the hay with the half-wit from Martiñá in the loft of Marcos Albite's house.

"How could you let yourself, Catuxa, you trollop?"

"Well you see, I just came to wash out Señor Marcos' pee can and Don Samuel gave me a *peseta* and took out his dick."

"Just like that?"

"Yes, sir, just like that. I said to him: here, everything is doomed in the end, oh glorious apostle St. Jude Thaddeus, who wert the first king of Babylon, turn my sorrows into joy in answer to this prayer, and then he tossed me down in the hay."

Tanis the Demon said to the Casandulfe Raimundo:

"Don Camilo's orders shall be carried out, as sure as there's a God in heaven, they'll be carried out! I've thought it all out, now what I have to do now is let it seep into my bones until my conscience begins to niggle me, after that it'll all be as easy as pie, it won't be hard for he struts about like cock of the walk, maybe he thinks that it's all over and done with now and that things will go on like this forever, but so much the better that he should believe that and go his way unperturbed."

Tanis the Demon whets his two hunting knives on the grindstone, one of them has a hilt made from antler and the other from Peruvian silver and both of them bear his initials, Tanis Gamuzo's knives have seen some years of service now but they've weathered well for they're top quality and well maintained.

"They see precious little flesh for I don't go out much now, and if a knife doesn't get flesh it loses its edge."

Policarpo la Bagañeira has lost the taste for watching the Santiago omnibus pass by, jolting along the road and spluttering like an asthmatic Portuguese, although he's missing three fingers from his right hand, Policarpo la Bagañeira can still roll a neat cigarette, packets of tobacco are full of threads nowadays, the best thing is to dump it out on a newspaper and remove the threads, if you burn them in an ashtray they scent the air, perfume it with their aroma, on the Santiago omnibus there are always two or three priests nibbling dried figs and apricots, sweet things are proper to priests, comics have a sweet tooth too, Policarpo la Bagañeira claims he can train frogs but I don't believe a word of it, frogs are difficult creatures to train for they're part sly and part stupid, which is as bad as they come, you can train women by giving them vinegar to drink, the problem is they won't let you, nowadays they're a brazen, rebellious lot Policarpo la Bagañeira chortles softly at his own jokes, he fancies Sweet Choniña, Méndez the confectioner's wife, but Sweet Choniña wouldn't give him a second look. Antón Guntimil, Fina Ramonde's late husband, was crushed to death by a freight train in Orense station, well, not really crushed, more sliced in two, Antón Guntimil had a stutter and was something of a simpleton. His wife always used to say to him:

"The monk at evening mass has a whopper of a willy, a proper willy twice the size of yours, you idiot, for an idiot is what you are, are you not ashamed of yourself?"

"Not at all woman, what can I do about it?"

When Aunt Lourdes was smitten by smallpox the French left her to die, say what you like, then to crown it all they tossed her body into a common grave along with Poles, gypsies, Moors, and chinks, as far as that's concerned the French look out for themselves, nor do they care whose corns they tread on. Moncho, the cousin of Manuel Remeseiro Domínguez who had the name of a crow, or maybe it's the other way round, died of whooping cough when he was about six or seven years of age.

"He didn't last long."

"No, indeed he didn't, apparently he wasn't up to much."

Moncho the crow can whistle a few bars of Blind Gaudencio's mazurka, although he doesn't know the whole tune yet.

"Is it a fact that Manueliño Remeseiro had his own little tiffs with María Auxiliadora Porrás, the sweetheart who ran out on Adolfito because he didn't look long for this world?"

"Stuff and nonsense! Who ever told you that?"

Miss Ramona had no luck with men, well, with future husbands that is, apparently she set her sights too high and, of course, missed her mark, in these matters, you have to eat humble pie for time and tide waits for no man. Miss Ramona always took it for granted that she could marry whoever took her fancy, that she could pick and choose, but she was wrong and now she's well on the way to dying an old maid.

"Well, an old maid but not a virgin, of course, what would bother me more than anything else would be not to have lost my virginity in due course, it'd be a terrible slap in the face to reach the age of twenty-five still a virgin, the fact of the matter is it wouldn't occur to anybody."

Robín Lebozán writes poems in Galician, but what he won't do is show them to anybody.

"No, as far as I'm concerned this business of reading your own poems aloud is an act of immodesty, anyway who could care less?"

The Casandulfe Raimundo hasn't fully recovered yet, he's still taciturn and surly, only his good manners save him.

"I'm longing to hear the skyrocket go off, tomorrow I'm to visit Uncle Evelio to perk my spirits up, isn't it a crying shame, an old man consoling a younger one! Uncle Evelio's orders must be carried out, I know, orders are orders, after all, but I'm dying to hear the skyrocket go off, a death is settled only by another one and it's not a matter of personal choice, we should all wear a buttercup or a gorse flower in our hats, Noriega Varela used to wear gorse blossom from the graveyard every Sunday and on days of obligation."

"In mourning for whom?"

"Nobody in particular, Don Antonio's gorse blossom was in remembrance of the dead, all the dead are God's own, the dead are very fond of flowers, notice that the most beautiful flowers always grow in graveyards, the souls of the dead escape through the flowers growing on the graves, if you place a stone on top of them the souls can't breathe."

Despondent and withdrawn, the Casandulfe Raimundo treads the paths of grief.

"The dead through whose veins coursed the very same blood as mine passed by here singing, they were just like me, indeed maybe it was me unbeknownst to myself, when their blood was spilled upon the ground, when their blood was shed, the wolves ran off howling and yowling, there are men who should never have been born, I'm just longing to hear the skyrocket go off, Tanis holds Uncle Camilo in high esteem, he calls the shots, well, all of us hold Uncle Camilo in high esteem, when Tanis lights the fuse of the skyrocket he'll heave a sigh of relief, may God preserve us all, peace should spread like lightning when the law is carried out, the same law has governed these mountains for years now and all the family dead demand that the law be fulfilled, some men spring from one blood line and others from another, it's not just a matter of chance."

The Casandulfe Raimundo plays chess with Robín Lebozán, he always beats him.

"Your mind is wandering."

"No, that's just the way I am, I'm no good at this sort of thing, you know."

Pepiño Pousada Coires, Plastered Pepiño, is an electrician, well, an electrician's assistant in the Repose Coffin Factory, there are a lot of coffin factories around here, they make them in black and white, for babes in arms, the luxury ones are made of oak and imitation mahogany, you don't see red, green, or yellow coffins, Plastered Pepiño wanders about with his mouth hanging open, Plastered Pepiño likes groping little boys or cherubs rather, Plastered Pepiño married Concha the Clam, folks do many a thing from habit, and he had two feeble-minded daughters that died shortly afterwards, Concha the Clam ran off on him, apparently she got fed up, Concha the Clam was a cheerful soul and skilled at playing the castanets, she spent all her time playing the castanets and singing music-hall tunes, one day they came across Plastered Pepiño with the deaf-mute Little Simon the Lamb, six or seven years of age and very thin and puny, you could see the fright on his face, you needed only a glimpse, it would even make you laugh, Plastered Pepiño was laying into him from behind and had him by the throat, he had nearly strangled him, Plastered Pepiño was sent first to jail and then to the nut-house.

"In the nut-house they give you an even worse hiding than in jail, clearly beating up nuts is more fun."

"More than likely."

Plastered Pepiño was released in return for allowing himself to be castrated, truth to tell, it didn't do him much good, when the war broke out Plastered Pepiño took to going to Mass every morning to intercede for his fellow man and entreat for mercy, charity, clemency as well as other favors that have fallen out of use, scorpions and toads have to be set free, you have to let them run away, it's the same with men and tame animals: mice, snails, crickets, and wild animals too: genets, lynxes, badgers, you stretch an alder bough across the river of the border of death and scare them off with holy water, not with gunshots.

"Why is mankind such a restless, unsettled creature? It must be the influence of the Devil."

Robín Lebozán was over the moon when he found the sea-shell his mother had given him, it was behind some books and hadn't been seen for over ten years, if you hold it to your ear you can hear the sound of the sea, you can also hear the skirl of Blind Gaudencio's mazurka, I mean the one he will hardly ever play, the forbidden mazurka, well, not quite forbidden but the closest thing to it.

"Shall we play another game of chess?"

"If you like."

Robín Lebozán takes a while to get to sleep, this has been going on for some time now, sometimes he wakens up at two or three in the morning, he lies awake and takes a long time to nod off, there are days when he sees dawn break.

"Why don't you take a cup of lime-blossom tea before going to bed?"

"Yes, I'll have to do something, this insomnia is a bad scene."

Nobody killed Hornet the bitch, there was no need to, the bitch Hornet died of a severe stomach upset, chances are Uncle Cleto vomited bile the last couple of times, dogs can't withstand a lot, less than you'd think, on the other hand Tsarevitch the dog is graceful and distinguished, but they don't call him Tsarevitch or anything at all now, dogs understand the tone of voice better than words.

"Do you know the stories about Pepa the She-Wolf and Xan Quinto?"

"Indeed I do, as well as the ones about Truco and Louzao and Ventoselle."

"What about the story about Mamed Casanova, who dressed up as a rich Indian that was dead and buried?"

"Yes, sir, I know them all. When I was a youngster my relative Don Marcelino Andrade made me learn them all off by heart when he took me in out of charity, so I can reel them all off, if you want me to begin I will."

"No, there's no need."

When he wakens up during the night Robín Lebozán lights an oil lamp, the electric light is like a feeble, sickly glowworm, it's no use at all, Robín Lebozán reads over what he has already written and corrects the occasional cacophony, repetition, or vague, imprecise word, he also changes the odd punctuation mark, here a comma would be better than a colon, parenthesis doesn't go here, etc., Robín Lebozán thinks that everything is on the wane, this business of novels is just like life itself, things grind to a halt, sometimes all of a sudden, your heart is in your mouth and life passes away, escapes through your eyes and mouth, also just through the mouth, stories always end with a full stop, as soon as the son of a bitch is killed off that's it, remember Poe's words again: Our thoughts were palsied and sere, our memories treacherous and sere, I would like to have neither thoughts nor memories but I can't, I would like to be like the rose and the honeysuckle, which only have feelings, maybe small, feeble animals—slugs, dragonflies—have hollow, disconsolate souls like roses and honeysuckle.

"Are you asleep?"

"No, I just snatched forty winks."

Don Claudio Blanco Respino sat down and ordered Doña Argentina Vidueira, widow of Somoza, to hold her tongue, after that he addressed himself to his brother-in-law Gerardo Vagamian, he didn't normally trouble to use the title Don, and said:

"Can you imagine a medieval king murdered by his own jester before the entire court during the glittering celebrations of a military victory? Well that's just what happened to Dino V, the Duke of Béttega, who wore a hairpiece and had a glass eye, an iron hand, and a wooden leg. After clubbing the jester to death, drawing and quartering him for the convenience of the vultures, his seven sons split their sides laughing and celebrating their blameless orphanhood by covering all the nuns in the convent, leaving each and every one of them with child, the event is recounted in minute detail in the *Chronicle of Aristides the Leper* with names and all, I couldn't recount all the adventures of that family from memory."

Miss Ramona always doubted Don Claudio Blanco's word.

"To my mind he's a blabbermouth. Half the stories he tells are downright lies."

Uncle Cleto goes to pay Miss Ramona a visit, he looks more dishevelled and crankier than ever and walks in zigzags so as not to step upon the cracks in the pavement. Uncle Cleto sings *La Madelón* and marks the end of each verse by breaking a volley of wind, Uncle Cleto laughs, screws up his nose and half-closes his eyes, he looks like a Chinaman, Uncle Cleto is dirtier yet cleaner than ever before, folks don't understand this but it's the truth, and he looks worried, Uncle Cleto is very hygienic and concerned, everyone knows that, very finnicky and protective of his health, he uses a great deal of alcohol for disinfecting himself but at the same time he goes about filthy, he never changes his underwear, he throws it out when finally it falls off old and dirty, Uncle Cleto vomits when he gets bored, he pukes in the chamber pot or behind the dresser, it's all the same to him to vomit on the wall, sometimes he vomits over himself because he is sitting in a comfortable position and doesn't want to budge, this visit Uncle Cleto paid to Miss

Ramona took place some time back, shortly after the outbreak of the war.

"Mona dear, these are terrible times we're in and immense problems that have to be tackled are being heaped upon us, where shall we bury Jesusa? All our family are in the tomb already, each one in their own grave, but there's hardly room to swing a cat in the vault, just as well I left poor Lourdes in Paris! Can you imagine the how-d'ye-do it would have been if I hadn't left poor Lourdes in Paris? Problem number two—as I say it's problems all the way—how are we to take Jesusa's body out? Emilita will want her to go out the front door, just wait and see, you know what Emilita's like, she never had anything but cotton wool between her two ears, in that case everything will have to be cleaned up for it's filthy, the very thought of it would make your flesh creep but for at least fifteen years now nobody has gone in through that door, nor cleaned the ceilings nor the walls, or anything, mice are nesting in the furniture and centipedes and earwigs are making themselves at home behind the paintings, on the mildew behind the paintings, it's very damp in Albarona."

"Can we not get someone in to do it?"

"Yes, of course we can, I'll take care of that, when I give the word a man will come and remove everything from the hallway—boxes, papers, all the heaviest stuff, everything—to light a bonfire, then you'll go in but nobody else."

"Fair enough."

Death is a habitual stupidity, a custom that's losing prestige, old races despise death, death is a habit, notice that women have a great time at funerals, dishing out orders and advice, women feel at home at funerals. Father Santisteban, S.J., speaks of death with great assurance, maybe he gets that from his calling, the Bible says that a living dog is better than a dead lion, and it's surely true, better a living earthworm than a beautiful dead woman, for what shall it profit a man if he gain the whole world but suffer the loss of his soul?, put like that you can't gainsay it, Uncle Cleto plays his jazz band, tapping the table, the glass, the bottle, the chamber pot, the window frame with a little rod, everything yields its own sound, the knack of it is in making each object ring out just at the right time, not too soon nor too late, Aunt Jesusa will never again hear Uncle Cleto's farts for beyond the pearly gates no ignoble sounds are heard, Aunt Emilita was left all on her own.

"Nobody ever got down to the very bottom of the Antela lagoon, whoever crosses the Antela lagoon loses their memory and is damned for the whole of eternity, folks with no memories cannot be saved because God and the saints hold memory in high esteem, both suffering and the soul nestle in the memory."

Don Claudio Blanco Respino has no time for Doña Argentina Vidueira, widow of Somoza, a woman who says more than her prayers, gossiping is a vice which gives rise to terrible evils within society, hell, what a sentence! gossiping can even cause wars, epidemics, and other catastrophes, Don Claudio, the brother-in-law of one-eyed Vagamian, is silently pensive, you could have heard a pin drop, or the buzzing of a fly, the Antela lagoon is full of flies, mosquitoes, frogs, and water snakes, and the dead of Antioch beg forgiveness by tolling the bells on St. John's Eve, the bells sound very odd with the water above them.

"What sort of thoughts are those! My conscience must be troubling me!"

Don Brégimo Faramiñás, Miss Ramona's father, played the banjo just as the fancy took him, the worst of it is that he died, Roquiño, the half-wit who was shut up for five years in a brightly colored tin trunk decorated with frets and zigzags, catches many a thrashing from Secundina, his mother, who smokes when nobody is looking, she washes the butts with vinegar and carefully prepares the tobacco, it wasn't a man who cleared out the hallway in Uncle Cleto's house, it was Secundina, on the recommendation of Remedios, the owner of Rauco's Inn.

"She's a dolt but a steady worker and the half-wit is no trouble for she puts him in a corner and he stays nice and quiet the whole time, at times he scarcely breathes."

Miss Ramona told Uncle Cleto:

"Remedios says there isn't a man but Secundina will make a good job of the cleaning, she can come first thing tomorrow morning."

"Alright then, tell her to come tomorrow morning at twelve on the dot but not before."

Miss Ramona's mother drowned in the River Asneiros, some folks would drown in a washstand, Miss Ramona's mother was a distinguished, witty woman, one of those women that are constantly wishing to die.

"I remember that she was very fond of Bécquer's poetry."

"It wouldn't surprise me."

In Uncle Cleto's house everything is shabby and threadbare, the pump for drawing water up from the well broke down, the windowpanes are smashed, nearly all the windowpanes that is, there are pieces of cardboard and old cans stuck in their place, as well as the seat of a cane chair, there's no light, the telephone was cut off, and every day the house is more encrusted with cobwebs, Hornet the bitch died howling, Hornet the bitch howled because she scented two deaths, Aunt Jesusa's and her own, Secundina heaped up boxes and papers, as well as jackets, slippers and a roll of oilcloth at least ten meters long and set fire to it when she was told to do so, but not a moment before, some folks are superstitious and others aren't, it's a matter of taste, some folks believe in miracle cures and taking the waters while others don't, it could also be a question of a person's upbringing, there are genteel, mannerly gods, bearded Sucellus and Germunno with his little horns and uncouth, loutish gods, it's bad luck to even utter their names, a tide of ignorance is sweeping over us but there's nothing we can do about it, nor is there any avoiding it, the other night Robín Lebozán warned Miss Ramona:

"This tide of ignorance will lead to deeply embittered reactions, Mona, I know of no antidote to this poison."

"Nor do I, Robín, let's hope it passes over without drawing us into the thick of it."

The Casandulfe Raimundo hums *Sacred Heart* when he is shaving, sacred heart, you shall reign, our icy you shall always be.

"Don't you know anything else?"

"What's that got to do with you?"

The Casandulfe Raimundo also lilts *Cara al sol** and *My Steed*, he whistles *El Oriamendi*** for he doesn't know the words, it's the same with the *Himno de Riego*,*** though you have to watch your step with it in case you tread on someone's corns. The Casandulfe Raimundo never forgets the white camellia for Miss Ramona, apparently his memory hasn't been affected by this bout of despondency.

"Here you are, Mona, this is a sort of pledge, so you can see that I never forget you."

* A Falangist hymn.
** A Basque anthem.
*** The Republican hymn which became the Spanish National Anthem during the Second Republic. —Trans.

"No, Mundo, I know this is a pledge, as you say, pledges don't even have to be remembered, they're just like breathing, for you I'm like the breath you draw, it's sad but it's true, indeed maybe it's not even sad."

Baldomero Marvís Casares, Tripe-Butcher, the father of the Gamuzos, always said that winning was every bit as hard as losing, you have to tread firmly in this life, indeed, but yet not causing a stir or throwing your weight about, throwing your weight about can lead to bad results for sometimes blows may rain, and not everybody's wounds heal easily, some don't, Nuncie Sabadelle wanted to see the world but she didn't get beyond las Burgas, a person thinks that they have to swallow everything that comes their way but then they see that it's not so, and will have none of it and then they have to bow to the inevitable so as to avoid a dressing down, it's hard to have to fail and swallow the consequences, the frogs in the county of Tipperary are not a whit worse off than those in the Antela lagoon.

"Did you get a letter from Doña Argentina?"

"I did, she was the one who told me about the aviators, look what she says here: This is the Vedrines school, named after a famous aviator engaged by the public entertainment board to watch him fly past in his airplane, executing thousands of acrobatic feats in midair, by night he gave a show with his plane silhouetted with colored lights, but I've already told you that. What a sight the festivities were! You paid 25 or 50 *céntimos* to sit upon a folding chair, depending upon the location and the rest of them, especially the youngsters, were gathered around about. Am I boring you?"

"Not at all. Read on!"

"Alright. The women got dressed to the nines in wide-brimmed hats trimmed with flowers and birds and dresses down to their ankles. The aviators were called . . . , well, I won't read on for you already know that."

History gallops onwards like a runaway horse, like a greyhound after a hare, like a centipede, the white and yellowed pages of the calendar were falling like the green and gold leaves of the fig tree, just like the withered leaves of the fig tree, though there's not one of them left now, and mankind invented this knack of coldly impregnating cows without the bull covering them, as was the way ever since God invented cows and bulls, history rushes past crashing into time, sometimes things happen outside their time through the fault of history, for instance, why did Hannibal's elephants not come out of Noah's ark? Noberto Somoza Donfréan, Doña Argentina's grandson, is an up-to-date vet.

"Yes, indeed, I know it's the last word in science, I won't deny it, but that Noberto is a swine to be involved with this business of artificial insemination. Say what you like, but when I see him assisting at Mass with that holier-than-thou look on his face, what good will it do him, I ask myself, if he earns his crust poking about in the innards of cows?"

There's still some time to go before that situation will come to pass, history is not always the witness of an age, the light of truth, the life of memory etc., there's a lot of nonsense talked about all that.

"I can do nothing, I'm longing to hear the skyrocket go off, I won't be able to do anything until I hear the skyrocket go off, not that I feel up to much. Will you pour me a brandy?"

"I will."

Aunt Jesusa and Aunt Emilita always wept buckets, they spent at least half their lives weeping, Uncle Cleto never took a blind bit of notice, nor was it worth the trouble, so they like weeping? well then, let them weep! when they're weeping they're not annoying anybody, well, sometimes they do, but it doesn't matter if they bother somebody, maybe Aunt Jesusa is still weeping in purgatory.

"Or up in heaven."

"No, there's no weeping up in heaven."

When they told Uncle Evelio Wild Boar that Vicente Chabro, the Xilmendreiros fellow, was in Orense Hospital he said: "Kill him off before he recovers!" and went on puffing his clay pipe with a picture of John Bull on it. The following day Vicente Chabro was smothered with a pillow, well, two of them held him down while another sat on top of him until he breathed his last and nobody as much as turned a hair, the truth of the matter is that Vicente Chabro was a poor wretch that wasn't even worth a tinker's damn.

"What do you think a wishy-washy dead man is worth, even though he's from hereabouts?"

"I don't know; he couldn't be worth much, they may even be dishing them out for free."

It rains upon the Arenteiriño crossroads and the Ricobelo stream, the very spot where the vixens plunge in to cool their fever, while the axle of Ugly Thumpity-thump's oxcart—the brightest bug-hunter in the whole parish—moans and groans up the track to Mosteirón.

"Do you remember the time of the five hanged children in Mosteirón?"

The rain lashes down upon saints and sinners, upon the wise, the simple and the run-of-the-mill, upon ourselves, upon the Leonese and the Portuguese, upon men and women, animals, trees, plants, stones, it rains upon pelts and hearts and souls, souls too, it rains upon the three faculties of the soul.

"Do you remember the time when lightning struck two little girls in Marañís, beyond the Formigueiros hill?"

Miss Ramona, the Casandulfe Raimundo, and Robín Lebozán, each with their umbrella, stroll slowly in the rain, maybe they enjoy getting soaked.

"Could you live in a country where it didn't rain?"

"Yes, why not? A person can get used to anything, just look at the English and the Dutch, in countries where it doesn't rain there's life and feeling too, it's an effort to imagine it but that's how it is, I'm sure that's how it is."

Vicente Chabro, the fellow from Xilmendreiros died an insignificant death, neither small fry nor fools are granted extreme unction, nor is an autopsy even carried out upon them, what would be the point? even though they are smothered to death and thrashing about, it's not customary, hold your horses there, nor does anyone have time to waste, tossing busybodies into a common grave with an Our Father for every two of them is good enough, Vicente Chabro was a bad egg, even though he didn't mean it, and that, too, has its price to pay.

"Were his family notified?"

"No, they weren't, not that they would miss him anyway."

Robín Lebozán speaks of solitude, Miss Ramona and the Casandulfe Raimundo listen to him, the three of them are soaking wet yet calm, unhurried, and maybe even happy, Robín Lebozán is like a little philosopher who takes his hat off and speaks from time to time.

"Solitude is no bad thing, God is alone and has no need of company, but mankind is not God, of course, the Holy Scriptures say that solitude is a bad thing but I don't believe it, solitude airs the soul and company sullies it, often sullies it, the devil makes his abode in the heart of the solitary man but it's no hard task to scare him off, to drive him out, there's more room for happiness in silence than in the midst of a spree and tranquility goes hand-in-hand with solitude, might it not be the case that solitude only exists in the face of unwanted company? Mankind escapes from solitude when he fears himself, when he grows bored with himself, the masturbator—if you'll pardon me, Mona—can have no qualms of conscience nor can he grow bored when he is alone, the masturbator must proudly proclaim his glorious, independent solitude, Machado says that a solitary heart is not a heart, that's lovely, well, clever, but no more than that, for it's not true, nowadays you can't talk about Machado, about Antonio Machado, the secret is to live with your back turned upon everything, it's a difficult state of affairs to achieve, it must be close to beatitude, there are only two possibilities: that solitude is both desired and sought after, or that solitude is feared and is encountered against our will, in the first case it's a prize, in the second it's a price to pay, that of independence, the most prized blessing the gods can bestow upon man is that of independence, but forgive me for being such a bore to you both!"

Along the road Tanis Gamuzo crosses with his four she-dogs: Blossom, Pearl, Witch, and Butterfly, he takes them out for a walk to stretch their muscles a bit, though he doesn't usually set them on wolves for they're worth a pretty penny, the males are hardier: Sultan, Moor, Lion, and Sailor, Tsar has a broken paw, well, they're not always hardier, they're cheaper but that's the least of it, you can't take the dogs out for a run for they snap at one another, all the males know is how to tackle an enemy, they're quiet, noble beasts but at times they grow bored, tussling and snapping at one another, depending on how the mood takes them, at such times they can turn dangerous because of their incredible strength, Tanis' males weigh upwards of eighty kilos, Sailor maybe even a hundred, he can't be far off it, the bitches don't weigh quite as much but the difference isn't that great.

"When will we hear the skyrocket?"

Tanis the Demon smiled.

"Not long to go now, ma'am, not long to go."

Tanis takes good care of his mastiffs and treats them with affection, he feeds them properly, grooms them and removes ticks from their coats, has them vaccinated at the right time, takes them out for a bit of exercise, Tanis' dogs are the admiration, as well as the envy and the pride of the whole area, for many leagues around about there's not a dog could hold a candle to Tanis'.

"How much are your dogs worth, Tanis?"

"What's that got to do with you since I'm not selling them?"

Ádega disinterred the dead man who killed her old man, helped by her daughter Benicia, who has nipples like chestnuts, her breasts are a delight to behold, for the time being the dead man is not yet dead though die he will, there's no rush, the skyrocket may sound when least expected—the more normal folks act, the better—Ádega tells the story to Don Camilo, not that he's the only one to know the tale.

"You, Don Camilo, sir, are a Guxinde and my old man was, too, well, you're a Morán, rather, there are not so many Moráns left these days, it seems they've been dying off. With my very own hands and an iron hoe, blessed so that it wouldn't be smitten with the plague, I dug up the body of the dead man who killed my old man, my daughter Benicia and nobody else helped me, I know full well that God will forgive me for robbing a grave, all the dead are God's own, I know, but this was a special dead man, this one was more mine than God's, on the Feast of the holy abbot St. Sabas I went to the Car-

Camilo José Cela

balliño graveyard by night and fetched him back in the cart
beneath some bundles of gorse that smelled great, it took me a
long time to get him out of the ground, over three hours it
took, maggots were dropping out of the dead man and the
stench was vile, the dead whose souls are in hell stink to high
heaven, I threw the decaying flesh to the pig that I later ate, it
tasted great, the bacon joints, then the *chorizos*, and the head,
the hams well-cured in the smoke from the hearth, the loin,
the lard, not a crumb went to waste, whenever I thought of the
dead man my gorge rose and I tried to think of something else,
of Our Lord upon the cross, or my brother Gaudencio dressed
as a seminary student or blind and playing the accordion,
anything at all, and I would take a swig of wine, I shared out
part of the pig among the relations so they all had a chance to
enjoy it, they licked their chops, Miss Ramona was the only
one I told what I had done, she didn't open her mouth but she
shed a tear, kissed me, and gave me a present of an ounce of
gold."

Miss Ramona smiled wistfully and then spoke a few words to
Ádega that contained no great mystery within them:

"Nobody can lay a finger upon our men, Ádega, you see
how folks wind up that try to dodge the law of the mountain."

Rauco from the inn explained to Fausto Belinchón
González, the Civil Guard, that Gaudencio only played the
mazurka *Ma Petite Marianne* twice: on the Feast of St. Joa-
quín in 1936 and the Feast of St. Andrew in 1939.

"I heard tell that it was on the Feast of St. Martin in 1936
and St. Hilario in 1940."

"Then you heard wrong, folks get the wrong end of the stick
on purpose, apparently they have their reasons."

Ugly Thumpity-thump, with his bushy moustache and that

air of a reserved old grandfather of a fox, comes singing down the slope from the Foxiño hill.

"Did you see anybody?"

"Who was there to see?"

"Whoever. Didn't you see anybody?"

"No, sir, nobody."

"Cross your heart."

"And hope to die!"

Ugly Thumpity-thump has a hunch that the Guxindes are on the warpath, tight-lipped and on the warpath, when the Guxindes sidle past in silence the sensible thing is to get out of their way, and if the Moráns are behind them then you'd best not set foot out of doors for all hell is let loose.

"How long is it now since you drank water from the Bouza do Gago spring?"

"At least a month, these days I've been over by Xirei and Santa Marina way, the last wolf I saw was in San Pedro de Dadín, he's lurking up in the das Cobas crags on the road to Valduide."

"Fair enough."

Blind Gaudencio was kicked out of the seminary when his sight started to fade, apparently they didn't want to be lumbered with burdens of charity nor millstones around their neck.

"Nobody is a priest until he has said Mass, did this fellow say Mass? No? Well then get lost! a seminary is not an almshouse and the church must be able to sail freely without any useless encumbrances."

"Yes, Father Jimeno."

Father Jimeno was the study prefect at the Conciliar Seminary of St. Ferdinand in Orense, Father Jimeno was renowned for his foul temper and lack of compassion, he also stank of garlic and used to mutter in Latin, Father Jimeno was a consummate Latinist, Father Jimeno was especially fond of the diaphanous doctrine of the Angelic Doctor Saint Thomas Aquinas, all the wisdom of the Middle Ages is encapsulated within the *Summa contra gentiles*, nowadays effeminate, demonic doctrines, currents of pansy Masonic thought, are in vogue, Blind Gaudencio was lucky, truth to tell he can't complain, and God would not forgive him if he did, since he can play the accordion and is by nature eager to please he managed to find somewhere to lay his head in Sprat's place. Doña Pura is a good soul, she has turned her back upon God's commandments but in her heart of hearts she's a good soul.

"At any rate you won't be left in the street, you say you can play the accordion? Well then, play the accordion, that'll always help liven things up."

Anunciación Sabadelle is sweeter than Portuguese Marta, both of them have a soft spot for Blind Gaudencio, being blind is a great boon in dealing with women, Bricepto Méndez, the owner of Méndez Studios, took nearly two dozen studio photographs of young Sprat, draped in her Manila shawl in her birthday suit, it's a crying shame that Gaudencio couldn't see them, the blind can't get turned on through their sight but indeed they can through their hearing, smell, taste, and touch, especially touch, women nowadays are hicks compared with Sprat in her Manila shawl with one breast foreshortened, taken half against the light, art is art and nowadays there's a great deal of misfortune about. Visi does more clients than Fermina, nearly twice as many, I can't make head or tail of it myself, but that's the way it is, folks are as odd as two left feet. Don Teodosio usually goes to Visi, she already knows his fibs and foibles, and Don Teodosio returns home contented and happy as Larry.

"Don't go overboard on the anisette, Gemma, I've told you before that it's bad for your anal itch."

"Hold your tongue!"

"As you wish, you're the one has to put up with it."

Florián Soutullo Dureixas, Civil Guard from the Barco de Valdeorras post, and a past master at scales on the bagpipes, as well as healing and the magic arts, was killed on the Teruel front. No sooner had he arrived than bang! he was bumped off by a bullet between the eyes, Florián Soutullo had spoon-shaped sideburns and a little trimmed moustache. The padre smoked the half packet of cigarettes that he couldn't take with him to the other world.

"Requiem aeternam dona eis, Domine; et lux perpetua luceat eis."

In this business of war and doling out death, it pays to be quick off the mark, long after his death, they were still sending cigarettes and chocolate to Corporal Pascual Antemil Cachizo, Basilisa the half-wit didn't know that Pascual had been killed and she believed herself spurned, there's always a chance that some better bird may come along, Basilisa the half-wit was footloose and fancy-free, often a body doesn't know the score and during a war how much more so. Some folks die sooner, some die later while others like to tell the tale. Somebody will get some good out of the tobacco and chocolate left by the dead for nothing goes to waste around here.

"Do you know what the time is?"

"No, indeed I've never known, that's not something that even matters to me."

Kitty-cat died an uneventful death, none of the girls in

Sprat's place shed a single tear for him. On the contrary, they were all delighted, but some more so than others.

"Was he as much of a swine as Don Jesús Manzanedo?"

"There were two of them in it! He was different in his own way but there wasn't much to choose between them."

Lázaro Codesal was killed before he had even finished growing, sometimes death swoops with a zealous swiftness, Lázaro Codesal was killed by a Moor in the Riffian campaign, lead bullets are neither Moorish nor Christian, lead bullets are cruel and draw no distinction, they're blind too, almost all the blind play the accordion well, the line of the mountain was blotted out when Lázaro Codesal was killed and nobody has ever seen it since, not even the wolves, the owls, nor the eagles, Lázaro Codesal had carrot-colored hair and blue eyes as mysterious as turquoise, it was a terrible pity that bugger of a Moor hit the mark, though nobody—maybe not even the man himself—knows who that Moor was.

"Will you have a cup of coffee?"

"No, I won't be able to sleep if I do."

Robín Lebozán goes over what he has written, he knows whole paragraphs off by heart and even remembers the bits he scored out. Lázaro Codesal was the first death in this true story, right at the very start it says: Robustiano Tarulle died in Morocco at the Beni Ulixek post, chances are he was killed by a Moor from the Beni Urriaguel tribe, Robustiano Tarulle knew a thing or two when it came to getting girls pregnant, he knew his stuff alright, and also had a taste for it, etc. The last death has not yet taken place, there's always a death hanging over this never-ending story, it's like an endless sequence of deaths moved by inertia, Lázaro Codesal Grovas may or may not have been Robustiano Tarulle Grovas, that war was a long time ago, there were the Christians on one side and the Moors on the other and that way there was no confusion, in those days the news took a while to filter through but folks didn't take fright or weren't so easily embittered, disease was rampant but not so much blood was mindlessly spilled, the blood shed is not an amount but a proportion, and I know what I'm talking about.

"Do you know who's roaming about these parts?"

"No."

"Shall I tell you where?"

"Alright then."

Policarpo la Bagañeira is missing three fingers from one hand, a horse snapped them off, Policarpo can train animals from the hills, wild and tame alike, the ones that take one look at you and snap as well as the ones that hide and scuttle away, Policarpo la Bagañeira lowers his voice.

"He's down in Veiga de Abaixo, in that fellow Mingos from Marrubio's house, tomorrow he's off to Silvaboa."

"How do you know?"

"Unxía, Mingos' daughter, told me, I think her father sent her."

"Maybe."

Tanis Gamuzo is as strong as an ox, with one hand he could floor a mule, Tanis Gamuzo's mastiffs are noble and placid, powerful, brave but easy-going, when they grow bored they snap at one another, everybody knows that, Sultan and Moor are enough to scare off the Zacumeira wolf or the wild boar in Val das Egoas, which crept up the oak trees to eat the acorns, Sultan and Moor scent the signs of the bastard at a distance, the nine signs of the bastard, of course some of them don't reek so much, in fact hardly any of them smell, well, two of them do: the sweating hands and the sad smegma, but smell is smell after all, Sultan and Moor are reliable and good-natured but can turn fierce when they want to, though they hardly ever need to for they are immensely strong.

"What are you going to do?"

"What's that got to do with you?"

Tanis Gamuzo seems like he's half cracked, Tanis Gamuzo always thinks very fast, apparently his thoughts are jostling, some in the head, others in the heart, and others in the throat, thoughts that are palsied and sere, as well as memories swarming like hornets, memories that are treacherous and sere.

"Is it true that your teeth hurt?"

"Who told you?"

"Is it true that your ears ache?"

"What does that matter to you?"

Tanis Gamuzo tries to marshal his thoughts and memories, as well as his desires, duties, and conduct. Fear is like a weevil gnawing at the falsehoods of the soul, maybe it has been gnawing for years at the fragile falsehoods of the soul unbeknownst to anyone. The steps that have to be taken are taken simply, if you are accurate even with your eyes closed and a person cannot even stop to doubt, above men is the law of God, the law that governs us, it's as if God were spying on us through a slit between two clouds, God always holds a thunderbolt in his hand.

"I've thought it all out, may God forgive me but I've thought it all out, now all I need is to feel it until my conscience begins to give me pangs of remorse, first a little, then gradually more and more until eventually it's like toothache or earache, from that moment onwards it's all as easy as pie. It doesn't bother me that my teeth and ears ache a bit, well, they ache a great deal but that makes no difference, the pain will soon go."

Still by night Tanis Gamuzo reaches the das Lamiñas mountains, between Silvaboa, Folgosa, and Mosteirón, with folks asleep and the dogs howling in the chill of the night, Tanis Gamuzo is out with just two dogs for more are difficult to handle when they're out after flesh, apparently their sight mists over and they go crazy, dogs lose respect for their master if there are more than three of them and they take the notion into their heads.

"I can give up if I want to, it's raining now, truth to tell it's always raining, my teeth and ears are very sore now but that surely doesn't matter, they told me to do what they told me to do, but they didn't tell me it had to be a Tuesday, a Wednesday, nor a Thursday, they didn't fix a time, I can give up if I want to, it's just that I don't want to."

It rains upon the earth of the hills, upon the waters of the streams and springs, it rains upon the gorse, the oak trees, the hydrangeas, the reeds by the mill, and the honeysuckle in the graveyard, it rains upon the living, upon the dead, and upon those who are about to die, it rains upon men, upon animals both wild and tame, upon women and woodland and garden plants, it rains upon the Sanguiño mountain and the Bouzas do Gago spring where both the wolf and the odd stray she-goat drink at the spring, though it is the she-goat that never returns, it rains as always through the whole of life and the whole of death, it rains as in war and in peacetime, it's great to see the rain falling without an end in sight, the rain lashes down like before the sun was invented, it rains monotonously but also compassionately, it rains without the heavens wearying of raining and raining.

Tanis Gamuzo and his dogs trudged through the rain shrouded in a silent, wary cloud, Fabián Minguela trod fearfully along the path to Silvaboa, crossed the River Oseira by Veiga de Riba, for some time he had been afraid and carried a gun.

"If some bugger steps across my path, I'll kill him, as sure as shooting, I'll kill him!"

Tanis Gamuzo sat down upon a rock with a dog on either side. Tanis Gamuzo rolled a cigarette and took a long, relaxing puff.

"Can bastards be killed without warning, just like foxes?"

Day had begun to break when Moucho Carroupo stopped to drink at the das Bouzas spring. Tanis Gamuzo closed in.

"I warn you that I'm about to kill you; although you don't deserve it, I'm serving you warning."

Moucho drew his pistol but with one blow Tanis disarmed him, Moucho fell to his knees, wept, and begged for mercy. Tanis said to him:

"It's not me who's killing you, it's the law of the mountain, I cannot stand in the way of the law of the mountain."

Tanis Gamuzo stepped aside and Sultan and Moor delivered the necessary bites, just the right number of bites, not a single one too many.

"That'll do!"

Sultan and Moor dropped the dead man wagging their tails happily, Fabián Minguela died quietly and quickly, within two hours or so, a skyrocket resounded high above.

Miss Ramona smiled.

"God be praised!"

That night Blind Gaudencio, the whorehouse accordionist with his soul as pure as the lilies of St. Joseph, played the mazurka *Ma Petite Marianne* with special delight. He kept on playing it into the early hours of the morning.

"Don't you know anything else?"

"No."

Don Cándido Velilla Sánchez, a commercial traveler, asked the blind accordionist:

"Tell me one thing, are you glad that fellow was killed?"

"Yes, I am, indeed I am!"

"And are you glad too that the Good Lord God sent him to burn in the flames of hell?"

"I am."

SOLE APPENDIX

FORENSIC REPORT

Place and date as previously indicated etc.
Name of deceased: Fabián Minguela Abragán.

EXTERNAL EXAMINATION OF BODY

The deceased is an adult male of some twenty-five years of age, 1.60 m. in height and approximately 55 kilos in weight. Typologically asthenic. Nutritional state satisfactory. Frontobiparietal seborrhea and incipient baldness, dark brown hair. Nevus hypertrichosis in frontal region.

The deceased, in prone decubitus with the upper limbs in flection, was dressed in worn brown corduroy trousers which revealed tears as well as being soaked and spattered with blood stains, particularly upon the upper part. Greenish corduroy jacket damaged and showing tears on the left sleeve and shoulder of the same. Lapel soaked and spattered from dripping blood. Tear on right pocket. Grey cotton shirt, worn and grubby at the collar, with one button missing. The shirt collar is soaked with stains from dripping blood, the said blood also soaking a blue woolen jersey which the deceased was wearing beneath his shirt. Grubby white serge drawers with sticky traces of defecation and damp urine stains. The undershirt is also white serge, short sleeved, and bloodstained in the area of the right shoulder and front. The deceased was wearing brown boots over black cotton socks, both in tatters and soaked with blood.

Examination of the body revealed the following external injuries:

Tears on the right side of the neck where the muscles in the area are seen to be almost severed. A flap of skin hanging loose with subcutaneous cell tissue and many cutaneous fibres of the neck situated at 2 cms. below the thyroid cartilage and one cm. from the sternum shaft. One section of the wound runs as far as the frontal curvature of the collarbone and is some 7 cms. in length, while the other section runs up to the area of insertion before the hyoid bone and is some 5 cms. in length. The lips of the wound are not clean-cut but jagged and about 1 cm. from the main area of the wound. Lesions caused by toothmarks are clearly visible along an acute notional injury line (made by nonhuman teeth); a dental imprint is also to be found on the right lateroposterior area of the neck, that is to say behind the sternocleidomastoid and in front of the descending edge of the trapezius muscle. There are large tears in the right sterno-cleidomastoid muscle and in the thyroid on the same side and the anatomical relationship has been destroyed within the vascular-nervous system, which is in a state of total attrition with tears in the jugular and carotid.

Likewise, there are injuries caused by toothmarks on the outer ear and the right orbital area with a large tear starting in the malar region and ending close to the right corner of the lips. The nose also reveals grazing and small tears which are not of the same aetiology as the other lesions, given that they do not reveal toothmarks and by their longitudinal configuration may have been caused by a fall and subsequent dragging. The head of the deceased is thickly strewn with fallen leaves from the site in which it was discovered. Traces of blood are to be found in the mouth and nose.

Similarly, the left forearm reveals lesions caused by tooth-marks although hematoma injuries in this area are slight as a result of the protective padding afforded by the clothing. On the left hand there are large tears from a bite along the inner edge and hypothenar area as well as on the ring and small fingers, the latter being severely damaged and with the tip hanging loose. The right carpal area also reveals tears although these are not very large owing to the protection afforded by the leather strap on the watch of which the face, it should be noted, has been smashed to pieces. The right hand shows the imprint of a single bite in the thenar area with multiple grazing on the metacarpal epiphysis. The aforesaid hand is drenched with blood and between the fingers and the nails we found some short, straight hairs of some 5 cms. in length, pointed at the tip and of a greyish white color. Under microscopic examination they proved not to be human hairs.

Upon the right forearm there is a clumsily executed black-colored tattoo of a heart pierced by an arrow with the letters R.T.

On both calves there are large tears caused by bites. Traces of congealed blood upon both legs.

The body was in an advanced state of rigor mortis; albuminoid membrane was present in both corneas and a green abdominal stain may be detected on the right iliac fossa. Judging by the length of stubble, the individual must have shaved for the last time some sixty hours earlier.

INTERNAL EXAMINATION OF THE BODY

Autopsic examination performed in accordance with the modified Mata Method.

Cranial cavity. —We have detected no type of fracture either in the cranial vault nor at the base of the cranium. The meninges are normal, with a slight edema in the thickness of the arachnoids. The encephalon is normal and dissection revealed signs of ischemia. The periencephalitic arteries are normal and within the Willis' polygon some small atheromas were found. Cerebellum, protuberance and bulb normal.

Thoracic cavity. —Lungs moderately congested with a large number of carbonic inclusions upon the surface and in cross section. Interpleural adhesions in the right hemothorax with signs of fibrosis on the right epical area, perhaps resulting from a former phymatic process. The heart in systole, exsanguine, with traces of frothy, blood-specked fluid in the right cavities. Both the cardiac valves and coronary arteries are normal.

Abdominal cavity. —The stomach contained traces of partly digested food (traces of leguminous foodstuffs were found mixed with meat fibers and traces of hard-boiled egg). The liver large, edematous, showing no signs of cyrrhotic deterioration but which may, nonetheless, be identified as the liver of a drinker. Gall bladder in tension. Kidneys pale. Bladder empty. The remaining viscera are normal and lacking in medico-legal interest.

Dissection of the neck. —After making an H-shaped incision the frontal area of the neck, the findings of the external examination were corroborated. Detailed dissection revealed fractures of the thyroid cartilage in its apophysis or right lateral cornu as well as crushing and rupturing of three tracheal rings giving rise to frothy haemorrhaging in the trachea, likewise pervading the larynx, pharynx and the mouth. This blood is light pink in color and mingled with bronchial secretions. The jugular has been completely though raggedly severed and the carotid has a tear 1.5 cms. in length with a hematoma in the middle layer and lesions indicative of Amusant's sign in close proximity to the glomus area.

On the basis of this autopsic study we hereby arrive at the following

MEDICO-LEGAL CONSIDERATIONS

1.) *The death was not natural but violent and preceded by a struggle and defense (viz. grazing upon the knuckles of the right hand and multiple tears in the clothing).*

2.) *The aggressor does not appear to have been a human being, given that no injuries normally incurred by man are to be found (incision wounds, contusion, perforations, grazes, percussion injuries, strangulation marks, etc.). Only lesions caused by bites have been found, of which the biggest and those which incurred the death of the individual, were in the area to the right of the neck.*

3.) *Given the shape, size, distribution, intensity of the injuries and the geographical location where the attack took place, in addition to traces of hairs found in the right hand and nails of the victim, the attacking animal may have been a wolf.*

4.) *From the simultaneity and intensity of the bites, it is to be deduced that the individual was attacked not by a solitary animal but by at least two.*

5.) *In order to reconstruct the attack and struggle, we may summarize it thus:*

a) *The individual was walking up the mountain and, seconds before the attack, observed a wolf leaping towards his throat. Instinctively, and without time to make use of the firearm which he was carrying which was discovered at some distance from the body, the individual raised his left arm, thus covering his face and neck with his forearm, where the first bite was inflicted. The wolf then bit some centimeters farther to the left where the hand was, thus causing the injuries already de-*

scribed. At that moment the individual was knocked to the ground and struggled with the animal in an attempt to grasp it with the right hand, striking it likewise with the left fist, later to grasp it by the neck or the head (*viz. grazes upon the hand and hairs in the aforementioned hand and nails*). At that moment, seeing the individual fall, another, or other wolves pounced upon him, attempting to catch hold of the parts of the body which were most mobile (*both legs*), following the tropism instinct for mobility of prey (*injuries to both calves with tears in the trousers*). In the ensuing struggle the clothing was torn, buttons lost, etc. Finally, another wolf, or the same one as first attacked, seized on two occasions upon the area to the right of the neck (*two dental imprints on the inframastoid area*) thus inflicting the injuries described. Injuries in the malar region would be due to a bite immediately preceding those in the neck and which the animal then repeated (*viz. two imprints*).

b) Now lying upon the ground and with considerable hemorrhaging, the individual struggled in a more or less conscious state, releasing the animal and touching the injured areas (*viz. both hands soaked with stains of blood*) until the moment of death.

6.) It is most curious to note that the body of the individual, which was ravaged by bites, was not, however, in any way devoured, thus rendering incomprehensible this violent attack by wolves. The only logical explanation is that once the wolves had pulled down their quarry, they fled, startled by noises, voices, shots or some other difficult-to-imagine circumstance.

On the basis of this autopsic examination we may hereby reach the following medico-legal conclusions:

1.) That the cause of death was due to profuse external hemorrhaging from the right carotid-jugular area.

2.) That in the said cause of death, it is highly plausible that *vagal inhibition mechanisms played a part through stimulus of the carotid glomus (Amusant's sign observed).*

3.) *That the wounds inflicted appear to have been incurred by wolves and to be bites.*

4.) *That the time of death is calculated to be about seven o'clock yesterday evening.*

5.) *That, in the absence of human intervention and in the absence of signs of a struggle or human aggression, the cause of death, from a medico-legal point of view, may be said to be accidental.*

Forensic surgeon: Marcial Méndez Santos (signature and stamp).

Palma de Mallorca, summer 1983

Camilo José Cela, winner of the 1989 Nobel Prize, was born in Galicia in 1916. His father was Spanish; his mother, English. He studied law, medicine, and philosophy in London and Madrid and in his younger years worked as a journalist and an actor. He has been a member of the Royal Spanish Academy since 1957 and has been awarded numerous literary prizes and honorary degrees. Initially on the side of Franco in the Spanish civil war, he later became a radical opponent. Cela has published fifty books including eighteen novels and novellas as well as collections of stories, essays, and a number of travel books. His novel *Mazurka for Two Dead Men* was first published in Spain in 1983 and next to his first novel, *The Family of Pascual Duarte* (1942), is his most widely translated work.